Three Tales
FROM AN
ENDLESS JOURNEY

SHILADITYA CHATTERJEE

PARTRIDGE

Print information available on the last page.

To order additional copies of this book, contact
Partridge India
000 800 10062 62
orders.india@partridgepublishing.com

www.partridgepublishing.com/india

This book is dedicated to

The eternal memory of my parents;
My children and their spouses, Ankana and Ankit, Uday and Liz;
And most of all to Gopa, my constant support in this and all my
life's endeavours.

CONTENTS

THANESWAR
Around 280 BCE

NILGHAT DISTRICT
Last few years of the 1970s

KOLKATA MEGALOPOLIS
Mid Twenty-First Century

Thaneswar
AROUND 280 BCE

1

MENACE OF THE NIGHT

$\mathcal{A}$s soon as the wheel of the leading ox-cart fell into a deep pothole in the earthen road and broke its axle, the captain commanding the royal escort bringing Thaneswar's annual revenue from the principality of Varahira knew that danger was brewing. The skies had darkened, suggesting an impending storm. It would make the task of reaching Anantapura, the nearest secure habitation, before dusk much harder.

Repairing the cart would cause inordinate delay, he knew, as it would take far too long to fetch an axle along with a couple or so skilled workmen needed to fix it from the nearest town. Setting aside his concerns which were growing, however, the captain got his men to start offloading with as much haste as possible the treasure from the broken cart and to try and pack the remaining four carts with its contents.

The sixth cart wasn't part of the royal convoy but could be used too. It was carrying two nubile girls and their chaperone from the professional house the captain had visited the previous night. The lady who ran the women's house had requested him to include them in his convoy heading to Thaneswar. The two were among the comeliest of girls in the province and were chosen to learn the ways of the courtesans in the capital city and to serve its aristocracy. It was a request the captain, after many suitable inducements, agreed to finally. Now the captain began worrying too about their safety, having brought them under his protection.

In ordinary times, he wouldn't have bothered too much. Accidents on the road of this nature were common, and he had previously suffered many in his long years escorting royal revenues from far-flung principalities to the capital. But lately, highway robberies had increased, and so had the number of guards in the escort. The highway brigands had been worrying parties of merchants and tradesmen but had never dared come near a royal train. He felt some reassurance also in the thought that he had twenty of the king's best swordsmen in the party.

The wind started blowing hard suddenly, and soon, sheets of rain fell on the group. The entire party was quickly drenched. But they carried on with their task as fast as they could, unloading the stricken cart and placing the precious contents in the five remaining ones, including that carrying the women who remained crouched under the cover of their cart and escaped the worst of the storm. But there was much treasure to be offloaded and it had to be done carefully, so the process took time.

When the whole task had been completed, it was already very dark, although mercifully, it had at least stopped raining. The broken cart was pushed to the side of the road and abandoned while the two oxen were freed from it to be driven along at the rear. As there was little light to see the road, the captain ordered a set of torches to be lit.

With the aid of one of the torches, the captain could inspect more carefully the portion of the road where the cart had stood previously and examine the pothole. It was then that he instantly realised that he had fallen into a carefully planned trap. The supposed pothole was actually a freshly dug-up pit covered craftily with hay and loose soil.

He immediately ordered the torches to be put out. But lighting them had already provided the perfect opportunity to the band of brigands, to pinpoint their targets. They had been hiding unobserved all this while behind a mound a short distance away, waiting for dusk to descend to commence their assault. Their first deadly arrows hit their marks accurately before the soldiers could take cover behind the carts. First one, then two and three fell as they were hit. The rest scurried behind the carts, some bleeding, some nearly at death's door. The captain was among those mortally struck. Only a handful remained unhurt.

These eight or nine waited behind the carts, their swords ready. The diminished escort realised they were badly outnumbered when the thugs lit their torches—two or three score of them could be seen, their faces covered, their swords ready. They descended swiftly on the party and, although suffering a disproportionate share of losses from the defence made by the king's highly skilled swordsmen, finally prevailed over them, the cries of the injured and dying, both of the attackers and defenders, rending apart the calm of the deathly night.

When it was all over, one of the brigands, obviously the leader, ordered an inspection of the carts and the booty they held. One by one, the carts were inspected and their contents confirmed. The fifth cart too was inspected, and as it had been packed in front and back with treasure from the broken cart, the women crouching inside were not immediately noticed and might have remained so for some more time had not the younger of the girls failed to stifle a whimper out of sheer fright, seeing a bandit peering in, his crimson sword still streaming with the blood of his victims.

The discovery of the women was a matter of great excitement for these lawless thugs living without women for months. They forgot about the treasure and crowded around the cart immediately, pulling the women out, eager to give vent to their lust, reckoning the women to be their just and hard-won trophy.

The first one fell upon the younger of the girls and ripped her clothes apart, but before he could proceed further with his vile act, the leader of the brigands intervened.

'Don't touch them!' he thundered. Approaching the girl, he took off his scarf and gave it to her to hide herself. 'I will keep these and use them for my comfort,' he said. 'Let the cowards of Thaneswar know that soon, all their wealth and their fair damsels too will be mine to enjoy!'

After securing the stolen treasure and the women, the captured convoy resumed its journey. Only the broken cart and the bleeding corpses were left behind on the king's highway. Before long, the convoy disappeared into the darkness of the night, on which had descended a troubled and uncertain stillness.

2

QUEEN GYANESHWARI

Of his four consorts, the king of Thaneswar favoured his nightly trysts with Vasundhara, whom he called Gyaneshwari after the goddess Saraswati in deference to her exceptional intelligence and learning. This became her name in the palace. She was neither the youngest nor the prettiest. When the king's amorous passions needed appeasement, he went more often to those others and often even to one or other newly recruited maid in waiting who caught his eye and whose fortune and standing in the royal household was immensely advanced by the encounter. They would satiate his quite immense desires. When he departed from their bedchambers after the delights of the night, the sweet aroma of attar or jasmine or sandalwood would linger on his limbs, depending on who was his nocturnal companion, and sometimes their sweet whispers and laughter would ring in his ears till sleep overtook him.

As he crossed over from youth to middle age, however, his ardours cooled, and he preferred spending his time more and more in intellectual rather than physical intercourse with his women. Here Gyaneshwari helped him gradually sublimate his bodily passions to those of the intellect. Not that Gyaneshwari was not physically gifted or was ignorant of the many arts of love. No royal consort of Thaneswar could ever aspire to be a companion of its spirited monarch known as much for his power and virility as for his romantic inclinations, without knowing ways of pleasing him in every way. So while Gyaneshwari was equally skilful in helping the king explore the pleasures of the night as any of the other queens, she had a gift the others didn't possess—the ability to help him ascend the path of intellectual and spiritual awakening where the vistas of pleasure and its inevitable counterpoint, pain, were limitless.

Gyaneshwari kept herself informed of the comings and goings of all contemporary thinkers and religious and spiritual leaders who happened to traverse the kingdom. On the very first information she received about any such worthy travelling through the kingdom, she would send out emissaries and invite him to the palace. They would stay as royal guests sometimes for days and often for weeks, till she had absorbed all the wisdom they could offer. Then she would pass on a distilled version to the king, who began to realise night by night what an immense fortune he had acquired in the form of his Gyaneshwari; what an immense fountain of knowledge she had turned out to be!

Of the many monks and spiritual men who graced Thaneswar by their presence, none was more favoured by Gyaneshwari than Devacharya, a monk who was a leading exponent of the Vedas, from a faraway monastery in the Himalayas. Devacharya had been responsible for restoring Gyaneshwari—earlier known as the princess Vasundhara—from a near-fatal encounter with death in early childhood, a debt which Gyaneshwari never forgot.

It happened thus: Princess Vasundhara, then a mere pubescent damsel, a princess of a small Himalayan principality, had gone hunting on horseback in the forests surrounding her mansion with a party of her similarly inclined friends and hunting companions. Loving the adventure that the jungle afforded and unaware that a man-eating tigress was on the prowl, they ventured deep into the forest, pursuing a flock of deer. They, in turn, were being stalked by the tigress, who followed, silently waiting to pounce on the unsuspecting party.

It wasn't long before the tigress rushed in with an ear-splitting roar from the shelter of the dense foliage where she had been lurking, and pounced on a straggling member of the party, an accompanying huntsman, taking all completely by surprise. With her horse about to bolt with fright, Vasundhara jumped off and rushed towards the tigress on foot, dealing it a mighty blow on the head with her sword. The animal then released her prey, whom she had grabbed at the shoulder, and jumped on Vasundhara, throwing her on the ground. By then, the party had overcome its surprise and dealt mortal blows on the demoniac animal with swords and lances. But before it finally collapsed, it had bitten Vasundhara in several places, from where she was bleeding profusely.

Luckily for them, the party had not yet travelled too far from the royal mansion and Vasundhara was carried there quickly, along with the injured huntsman (whose wounds were not that grave), and the royal physician was summoned to treat and dress her wounds. He stopped the bleeding, but Vasundhara had gone into a swoon owing to loss of blood. After a fretful night when the whole palace was up fearing the worst, Vasundhara opened her eyes. But she had developed a raging fever, and the royal physician was troubled. It was then that he suggested that the king request the monk Devacharya to visit the patient. Devacharya was known to possess knowledge of treating such wounds and had developed several potions and poultices which could work.

The king sent a party with his royal palanquin, and luckily, Devacharya responded with speed and decided to come on horseback instead, conscious of the urgency involved. Despite his haste, it was two long days before he could see the patient. The fever had not abated, and Vasundhara had fallen again into a faint. Devacharya used all the skill at his command, and before long, Vasundhara appeared to be on the mend. Her fever gradually abated, and after the night was over, she opened her eyes, to the joy of the royal household.

As she slowly recovered, Devacharya kept watch and, responding to Vasundhara's curiosity about the world and the universe, gave her the initial instructions on the wisdom of the ages that he was privy to. This included both the material world and the spiritual. Although loath to see him go when her recovery was complete, she determined to remain in touch with him, and likewise, Devacharya was keen to continue his discussions with one whom he realised was the possessor of an extraordinary mind which would grow with maturity and understanding and from whom he could also learn much.

Thus, whenever his travels to gain further knowledge took him afield and he had to travel through Thaneswar, Devacharya made it a point to visit Vasundhara—now called Queen Gyaneshwari—often unannounced, and knew he would get a royal welcome whenever he arrived. His most recent visit was a few weeks earlier on his return from Nalanda, the great centre of learning, where a new philosophical perspective propounded by Siddhartha the ascetic prince of Kapilavastu, challenging traditional beliefs, was gaining ground.

Queen Gyaneshwari was immensely curious herself about the new thinking that was being frequently talked about. She decided to convince the king that an assembly of contemporary scholars to debate on philosophical questions, particularly between the main exponents, Devacharya of the traditional school and Sanghamitra of the Nalanda *sangha*, would be particularly enlightening at the current time.

Gyaneshwari was conscious that the king, partly as a result of her exhortations, was slowly but surely entering into a philosophical phase of his life. He would often these days find time to join her in her discussions with the religious and spiritual personages who were frequent visitors at Gyaneshwari's invitations.

So that night when the king had decided to visit her bedchamber, she broached the topic. After she had tended to his needs, she said,

'My lord, the monk Devacharya has just returned from a visit to Nalanda and speaks of new wisdom that appears to challenge some of our understandings. Why don't you convene a spiritual assembly like your father and forefathers did?'

'My queen Gyaneshwari, that was exactly what I have been considering too, but I have been distracted by other concerns,' he said, surprising her with his response.

3

DISTURBING NEWS

*A*s if on cue, these other concerns rudely intervened on their conversation. The peaceful silence of the night was rent apart by the sudden shout of a sentry at the distant palace gate, challenging a horseman galloping towards it. After a brief while, there were sounds of footsteps and then a gentle knock on the door of the bedchamber.

The king understood that the matter was of utmost urgency, else no one would dare disturb him at the depth of night. Rising with him, Gyaneshwari placed the royal robes on her master and retired to the antechamber.

'The royal treasure from Varahira has been looted, sir,' said the bleary-eyed palace governor, who had been awoken from his slumbers to take the news to the king as he alone had the authority to approach the king in his bedchamber. 'The guards have been murdered. This is the work of Nagaputra, I have no doubt.'

'He has crossed all limits,' said the king. 'Summon Aryaduta and the war council tomorrow. We must put an end to this.'

'General Aryaduta has sent word that he been delayed returning from his eastern mission, owing to floods in the Magadha country, my lord, and his arrival is uncertain; but I will summon the rest of the military chiefs,' said the governor, withdrawing.

The king returned to his bed. He didn't have to tell Gyaneshwari about the news afresh as the entire conversation had been heard clearly by her. 'So that is the reason, my queen, that I had been deferring a decision on the spiritual conclave,' he said. 'The situation at this time is just not favourable for a serious philosophical discussion.'

'On the contrary, my lord,' intervened Gyaneshwari. 'When evil stalks the land, this is the best time to discuss the precepts of dharma and the ways of ennobling the soul. Much good may come of this.'

The king was not fully convinced. But as he often deferred to Gyaneshwari's judgement, having profited much from it in the past, he accepted her advice.

'I will convene this spiritual conclave soon, Gyaneshwari, my learned queen,' he said. 'But I mustn't tarry too long in dealing with the other matters,' he added thoughtfully, before falling into a slumber.

4

THE ASSEMBLY

'*T*he ultimate human quest is to conceive and realise our innate oneness with the infinite and timeless universe; just as a drop of water is part of the ocean; a tree a part of the forest. Many hundreds of births may be needed before a soul can see this, much lifetimes devoted to meditation for this to happen.' Thus concluded Devacharya, the renowned teacher from Devprayag, on the attainment of Brahmatman.[1]

His hermitage nestled high at the edge of a precipice in the Himalayan foothills overlooking the confluence of the Bhagirathi and the Alakananda rivers. Devacharya's pupils came from far and wide. They listened to his scholarly interpretations of the Vedas, the ancient collection of spiritual hymns, at the courtyard of his hermitage while it was still dark and the stars could be seen brightly in the sky and while the two rivers mingling far below were still not visible. The lessons would end just as dawn was breaking. They would toil by day with his sons in the verdant terraced fields which rose from the rivers along the sides of the valleys, until the sun had disappeared behind the mountains. Some of Devacharya's pupils had accompanied him on this long journey to the plains, to Thaneswar, at the royal invitation to discourse before the assembly of the learned. They nodded wisely, and it was clear that many of them had advanced far on the path of true understanding.

But now a sense of anticipation was clearly evident in the assembly presided over by the king himself. The many scholars and interested laymen present had studied and heard doctrines and interpretations similar to Devacharya's and would respectfully listen to such expositions from reputed masters such as him. However, new ideas were hard to come by and were sought eagerly. A monk from the sangha and monastery at Nalanda, a veritable *arahant*,[2] along with his entourage had been invited by the king to present the new ideas of the school that were being discussed there.

Aryaduta, who had been summoned urgently by the king had arrived hurriedly, travel-worn and weary, from the Magadha country. Not finding the king at court, he followed the courtiers to the assembly, where he learnt a great debate was in session. If the king needed him so urgently, he wondered, why did he convene this assembly? However, royal priorities were not his to question. Soon, however, his attention was drawn to the unfolding discussions on an area, he regretted, he had little time to spare in his life. Was it part of the royal strategy that he should be here, he wondered. This was often the king's way of introducing new ideas to his courtiers and through them to the general population. The saffron-clad monks were now often seen in the towns and villages, but Aryaduta had never bothered to find out what new messages they were propagating.

The followers of Gautama's teachings were beginning to have considerable influence among the common folk as a result of the simplicity of their ways and their advocacies. The Vedic doctrines were far too abstract and required learning to appreciate. But these more Eastern influences had not travelled yet to these fertile northern plains watered by the Ganga. The king, always ready to welcome learned travellers and monks, had heard of such new wisdom from them and decided therefore to invite Sanghamitra.

Saffron-garbed and with shaven head, Sanghamitra and his group of monks presented a contrast to the other members of the assembly, many of whom were dressed in their finery. Many wondered if a life of renunciation was essential for the attainment of nirvana, which was the goal of human existence according to the teachings of Gautama the prince turned monk from Kapilavastu, a kingdom two weeks' journey to the north, at the foothills of the Himalayas. Gautama's philosophy had gained rapid acceptance along the eastern plains of the Ganga but had not yet been formally expounded by any of his followers in these parts. Sanghamitra had many eager and questioning minds waiting to hear his words.

'The misery of human life,' began Sanghamitra, 'is the result of the usual tendency to experience existence solely through one's limited personal ego. The ability to transcend one's ego will enable a person to comprehend existence more fully and bring joy and serenity within one's life span. This consciousness is the goal of the true seeker of enlightenment.'

Sanghamitra went on to explain in detail the methods used by members of his sangha or community of monks, taught to them by one of Gautama's first disciples. Merchants and travellers had brought information about new ways to enlightenment such as the Four Noble Truths and the Noble Eightfold Path, but knowledge of these was available only indistinctly through hearsay in the marketplaces. Its popularity lay in the notion of its accessibility to all, not just persons with learning. Sanghamitra's lucid exposition held the assembly enthralled.[3]

Devacharya's senior pupil began the debate with the proposition that there was little originality in the Noble truths and that the view that suffering was caused by desire was essentially a rephrasing of the existing concept of maya or illusion, which must be overcome for the soul or atman to realise the supreme consciousness or Brahman. That it was possible to attain this consciousness by any person within a lifespan was basically an experiential issue, he felt. He wondered whether this was possible by anyone willing to join the sangha and intending to follow its disciplines. This was very ably answered by

Shraddhanada, a monk in Sanghamitra's party, who cited not only Gautama's own experience but also the experience of numerous others after him. The sincerity and confidence of their words generally turned the mood of the audience in their favour. They generally felt that Sanghamitra had brought a new vision and understanding to Thaneswar.

The king, a man of few words but of considerable understanding, heard the debate without uttering a word himself. He allowed questions from his own lay courtiers, and as the debate progressed, the day gradually turned to evening and weariness began to set in among the assembly members.

'I have a tract of woodland by the river, two hours walk uphill from here. My subjects and I will be honoured if you could set up a sangha there,' he requested to Sanghamitra at the conclusion of the discussions. A general murmur of assent rose from the assembly at this gesture of the king, known for his generosity and charity to religious people. And many were aware of Queen Gyaneshwari's contribution as well to the king's gradual turn to spiritual questionings. Thaneswar had become a spiritual centre as a result of their actions; it would gladly welcome these monks.

5

THE TASK

*R*etiring with his nobles to the inner sanctum of his palace, the king turned to secular affairs. Dismissing others, the king turned to Aryaduta when the two were finally alone together. Reports had come in that the bandit popularly known as Nagaputra had destroyed a border village and massacred its inhabitants. He had also ambushed again and looted a royal train bringing tribute from Varahira and murdered the entire company of twenty guards and its captain. His audacity was increasing day by day, and now he was demanding tax from several bordering villages.

With victory and valour in his wake, this new royal command to annihilate the upstart Nagaputra appeared to be a trifling commission to Aryaduta. But the king's solemn demeanour while revealing the task, particularly his invocation of the Kurukshetra admonitions of Lord Krishna to the reluctant Arjuna to engage in war, created a grim unfathomable foreboding in Aryaduta. Much like the creeping mist that was stealing that night of its starry splendour, felt Aryaduta while returning to his quarters.

The king's reminder of the ancient battle between the ruling dynasties of northern India and its moral lessons seemed unnecessary to Aryaduta. All of Thaneswar knew him well and his resolve to secure its boundaries; they slept in peace when he was awake and about. Thaneswar was to Aryaduta the progeny he never had. And all those who dared test his resolve in Thaneswar's defence had fallen to his sword and lance or retreated ignominiously.

Aryaduta was not one to linger when a task awaited him. Having mobilised his men overnight, he set out early the very next day. Unlike the previous night, there was no mist today, and the road and task ahead were clear. As he rode with his adjutants ahead of his company of loyal and tested warriors, he began evolving the strategy that would vanquish the foe. As always, Aryaduta looked for the path that would cause the least difficulty and the lowest loss of life and limb to his soldiers. But unlike the clarity of the task, the manner of its execution kept annoyingly eluding him.

The company had been riding since dawn, and the sun had climbed overhead. The road skirted the dense forests along a narrow stream with wide sandy shores. During the rains, this same rivulet would become an angry tumultuous torrent that would spread high up to the banks. Aryaduta declared a brief interlude for food and rest. Presently, the vanguard of the troops caught up with the party. The ace archers were summoned and a hunting party prepared to kill deer and wild boars. This inevitably turned into a contest of archery skills which Aryaduta enjoyed and liked to judge.

Surprisingly, the winner was not a recognised archer but a scout who hailed from a nearby tribal village. He quickly brought in a slain deer on his shoulders and displayed his trophy to the general and his adjutants. The ace archers were, meanwhile, still nowhere to be seen. His curiosity aroused, Aryaduta requested the youth to demonstrate his skills personally to him.

The youth guided Aryaduta on foot into the dense foliage. In a short while, the thick canopy overhead within the forest had converted the bright day outside into night. Except for occasional chinks of sunlight, there was nothing to guide the two. The youth began looking for tender bamboo saplings and, having found a clump, chose a few fresh leaves. Total silence was indicated while he put the leaves to his lips and emitted a screeching sound. Crouching low behind a shrub, Aryaduta recognised this as the sound of distress of a baby deer and understood the youth's plan. In a short while, there was a shuffle in the undergrowth, and with lightning speed, the youth shot an arrow into the direction of the sound. It found its mark, and the two made out the form of a deer which had fallen and desperately clawed the ground in a futile effort to rise. A stab from the youth's knife ended its misery. After the youth had dragged the deer back into the sunlight, Aryaduta saw that it was a doe. A hint of a tear moistened its open eye. What was it thinking when it met its end? How many mothers end up such in defence of their young?

The hunter's code demanded that animals be slain only to satiate hunger and not for sport. This required that all the meat from the animals, including that all the others had by now brought in, be prepared immediately for consumption to prevent unnecessary slaughter and that just the necessary number of animals be hunted. The slain animals were stripped of their hide and, with heads decapitated and the raw skinned carcasses cut into smaller portions, were soon transformed from living creatures of the jungle to fair and hearty food for the hungry soldiers. Trestles appeared on the bank of the river and fires lighted under the makeshift grills over which the meat was slowly turned. The light from the flames glowed stronger as the evening faded. The sputter of dripping fat on fire could be heard over the crescendo of insect noises from the jungle. The pungent odour of roast meat filled the air.

Long after the fires had died down and the sentries had taken their solitary positions over the slumbering soldiers, Aryaduta remained awake considering the day's events and planning the future course of action. War and slaughter were necessary evils which humans could not avoid. Even the state of Thaneswar, with its much admired and just monarchy, had its enemies frequently willing to test its capacity to protect itself and its system. Thus, conflict was in the natural order of things.

However, Aryaduta wondered whether there was some truth also in the new teachings being propagated by Gautama's followers advocating an avoidance of war and all forms of violence, including animal slaughter. The beat of the war drum should be replaced by the sound of *dhamma*,[4] they insisted. They were spreading ideas of a new morality. Not only did it embrace the social order among humans but included all living things. Was there a higher purpose to animals inhabiting this planet, other than to provide food? Did they have feelings which needed to be considered? Was the act of refraining from killing of animals one step towards attempting to differentiate humans from animals and from the natural order of the universe? Or was this a futile and unattainable quest?

6

THE DEADLY ENCOUNTER

*T*he mere business of living takes predominance over the resolution of essential questions about life and living in the affairs of mortals. Hardly had Aryaduta entered the realms of slumber, when he was roused and forced to consider the immediate question of survival. Nagaputra, having got a scent of the campaign, had taken pre-emptive action and attacked Aryaduta's main body of troops, which was quartered by the forest village downriver. 'I am confronting the most serious challenge of my life,' mused he. 'This is not an enemy to be taken lightly.'

By attacking at night, not only was Nagaputra displaying his contempt for generally accepted traditions of the conduct of war, he was also willing to take the risks of nocturnal combat. The terrain was tricky, and there was danger of confusing one's own combatants with the foe's. It also displayed cunning, arrogance, and a ruthless sense of purpose. This enemy was trying to prove something, not just harassing or slowing the campaign against him.

The captain in charge of the troops was an old and tested soldier. But Nagaputra's stealthy approach and the sudden unexpected attack in the dead of night had caught the night watch unprepared. Some had not even been able to utter a cry when the sharp blade or swift arrow had struck them. But the sounds of a scuffle had eventually alerted the others, who raised an alarm before the deadly rush of the enemy could fully vanquish them. Gallantry, as usual, had saved the force, a factor not accounted for by Nagaputra when devising his latest adventure. The captain had managed to rally a band of the best men and fought a pitched battle in the darkness, the enemy's dark shapes illuminated only partly by the uncertain flickering flames from the distant torches in the camp. The enemy appeared to have retreated temporarily, his retreat forced at considerable cost.

Aryaduta quickly went about the business of organising the troops and preparing them for a possible attack again by the enemy. There was little time to be lost in preparation. The enemy had tasted blood and would surely return to finish his work. This time, however, Aryaduta determined that he would use the cover of night to his advantage and deceive the enemy. He ordered a body of the force to carry torches and wait in formation by the riverbank. The rest he dispatched stealthily down river, but he asked them to wait within the forest and take up positions on the slopes of the ravine. The tribal chief who was supposed to join Aryaduta's forces the very next day with a hundred archers was asked to mobilise in haste and to aid the royal forces without delay. Should Nagaputra be lured to attack the small force by the river, he would be annihilated by the now-hidden forces that would encircle him.

That would end the campaign even before it got organised, thought Aryaduta. He had left Thaneswar with only two hundred men but hoped to gather at least three hundred more from chieftains loyal and duty-bound to Thaneswar. He anticipated little difficulty in this enterprise. Most chieftains were more than willing to prove their loyalty to the king of Thaneswar.

That is perhaps what Nagaputra wanted to avoid. By demonstrating Thaneswar's weakness right at the beginning, he hoped perhaps to disrupt the work of putting together an army against him. He had not factored in his calculation the fact that Thaneswar's strength lay not only on the might of its forces but on its moral authority to rule through its far advanced, enlightened, and fair system of governance.

The darkness slowly ebbed in anticipation of the attack that did not come. Nagaputra might have been trailing him stealthily all along, he thought, employing spies to report his every movement. He might have sensed Aryaduta's hand in the preparations after the skirmish. Nagaputra was far shrewder than he had anticipated, thought Aryaduta. He would bide his time till he found another chink in Thaneswar's armour. But before that, a strategy would have to be found to outwit this cunning adversary. What it would be Aryaduta had no idea.

The pale light of dawn allowed now a fuller discovery of the night's ravages. When Aryaduta returned to the camp, the dead and the dying were strewn all around. Thaneswar's proud standard still flew, but wilted and blood-strewn. Among the dying combatants, tragically, was his old and trusted comrade of many a campaign, the captain.

The dying man appeared, however, to be reserving his last few breaths for Aryaduta. He indicated a desire to be alone, and the others withdrew, leaving the two alone. Aryaduta drew close to the injured man and grasped his hand for the last time. Despite his acute misery, the fallen captain had a last task to perform for Thaneswar.

'I found this after the enemy had fled,' he said, giving Aryaduta a golden necklace. Its centrepiece was a dark sapphire, embedded in which, Aryaduta was shocked to discover, was the royal emblem of Thaneswar. 'How it has come into the devil's possession, I cannot imagine,' the captain whispered. In the desperate scuffle with the enemy, which had cost the soldier his life, he had stumbled unwittingly on a mystery he would never know the answer to, but realised nevertheless its immense portent for Thaneswar.

Aryaduta's world stood still for a few moments when the royal gem passed into his hands. Its lustre had not faded, he realised, since the last time he had glimpsed it, evoking memories from a time and place that had long been buried in the depths of his soul. They belonged to a different world altogether, which he had kept hidden for many, many years. Those memories of youth and incomprehensible happiness that was eventually engulfed by sadness had been buried deeply in his mind and nearly forgotten.

But the condition of the fallen soldier was more pressing than his own memories, and there was far too little time to convey all that Aryaduta wanted to say to this loyal and gallant hero of Thaneswar whom death had almost in its grasp.

'You have saved Thaneswar's pride again, my friend,' said Aryaduta, his voice breaking and his eyes clouding over. 'Go peacefully, content that you have lived and died a hero.'

7

ANANTAPURA

She had worn that necklace with the sapphire as she sat imperially near the prince and watched the dancers. It was a regal gift, and it proclaimed yet another victory for her, this time a royal one, a prince destined to be king. She did not seem to exist anymore for Aryaduta, the necklace a final testament to this irrefutable fact, a final message to him more than anyone else in the assembly that his quest of her must end.

But he had possessed this impossible-to-possess celestial being, or thought he had. He knew her innermost secrets, or thought he did. Were they shared solely with him, he wondered, or had she also revealed them to others? Aryaduta willed himself to believe that she had offered to others only the external adornments of her self; her innermost being had only been his to possess.

His heart was captivated the very first time he had seen her—even though it was a fleeting glimpse. He was leading a body of troops on one of the never-ending campaigns of those early years when disorder stalked every corner of Thaneswar. The group of tired and bloodied warriors had arrived at the town just as the sun was setting, and he decided to take up quarters for the night there. He had dismounted near a temple gateway while arrangements were being finalised.

He recalled that it was the auspicious hour between sundown and dusk—the *godhuli* hour—when the dust raised by the cattle returning from the fields scatters the day's mellowing light in an amber glow. It is the time when girls being prepared for marriage are allowed to be glimpsed by prospective grooms' families. The evening rituals at the temple had ended, and the gentle sound of the temple bells could be heard as devotees began departing. Among them was a bevy of pretty damsels. They wore dancers' anklets on their feet, which tinkled as they descended the temple steps and drew everyone's attention towards them. And one among them caught Aryaduta's eye, a diamond among the gemstones.

She carried a lotus flower in her hand, and a single plait of ebony hair fell around her neck. He remembered that unforgettable visage with its large dark shining eyes under arched eyebrows that briefly met his but quickly turned away. Was there a hint of a smile on her lips? He must have been a sight in his dust-covered battle tunic, standing among the lounging cavalrymen. He tried to see more of her, but the dancers had disappeared among the throngs in the crowded street, leaving an utter emptiness in his being.

He lay awake that night yearning to discover her. He had a day to seek her out as the following day was Deepawali—a festival and a mandatory furlough for warriors. Legend had it that on this day many centuries ago, the mighty Rama had returned victoriously to his capital, Ayodhya. Would it be Aryaduta's day of victory too?

Since fate had brought about the momentary encounter with her, Aryaduta mused, fate would also lead him to her a second time. And that was how it had turned out. How else could the two have met in a town of several thousand souls? With a yearning heart, he had set out purposelessly the next day, wandering around the town. In the marketplace, a richly decorated palanquin had halted. As usual, the sellers of trinkets and jewels had surrounded it, offering their wares. Aryaduta had been near enough to see the occupants when they inspected the wares—a bejewelled courtesan and her young companion. With a quickly pulsating heart, he realised that the latter was her! But a courtesan? Nevertheless, a smitten Aryaduta's curiosity was not diminished but in fact further aroused.

The palanquin bearers lifted the palanquin on their shoulders and prepared to resume their interrupted journey. Determining not to lose her again, Aryaduta approached the palanquin bearers and, stopping them, demanded permission to address the women. This was an unusual request from a stranger on a busy street. However, after a while, the curtain parted. 'I am Aryaduta, a warrior from Thaneswar . . . Allow me an audience,' he stated in confusion, addressing the younger woman. 'I am here only a short while and must depart tomorrow.' He thought he saw a hint of recognition in her eyes, and was there also a rush of colour to her cheeks?

'It is a bold person indeed who stops Priyadarshini's palanquin,' said the bejewelled one. 'However, we are beholden to Thaneswar and do not refuse an officer who speaks in its name. Come to my courtyard an hour after dusk tonight, and you will be well received.'

8

THE HAVELI OF PRIYADARSHINI

*T*he sounds, colours, and sensations of that night had remained vivid in Aryaduta's memory despite the passing of the tumultuous decades. Anantapura was all aglow that evening with houses lit up with earthen lamps and sounds of conch shells and gongs everywhere as the rejoicing populace celebrated yet again the victory of Rama in battle over Ravana and the vanquishing of evil from the face of the earth.

Priyadarshini's *haveli* was also decorated everywhere with rows of earthenware lamps along the floors and in every nook and cranny that accentuated the intricate sculptures on the walls and columns. The sounds of the town's celebrations disappeared the moment Aryaduta stepped inside the open courtyard and the heavy doors were closed behind him. Instead, he could hear the gentle tinkle of dancers' anklets, which kept rhythm with the *bansuri* and *mridangam* and the rich melody of the *raga* being huskily rendered by Priyadarshini. At the centre of the courtyard stood a fountain which flowed silently over a pool of water lilies.

Aryaduta was welcomed by a richly bejewelled damsel, one of those that would dance later during that long evening, but not by the one he sought. Neither was she among the dancers who were performing at the moment, watched by a small group of the town's nobility. Scented jasmine water was sprinkled on him, and being from Thaneswar, he was shown a place next to where Priyadarshini was singing a *raga* that echoed the yearning in his heart.

According to custom, the tempo of the ragas changed over the course of the evening from long invocations to more rapid rhythms that tested the dancers' skills, and other singers took over from Priyadarshini while she went around and paid her courtesies to the guests. Pretty damsels in dancing costumes came and filled the delicate tumblers with wine, but the one Aryaduta was looking for did not appear. A great feeling of disappointment welled up within Aryaduta, and he began feeling that his quest was in vain. He remembered that it was the instant when in despair, he turned heavenward and saw a shower of shooting stars streaking across the dark night sky—it was that very instant that there was a pause in the dancing and singing and she suddenly appeared.

Dressed in silk and gold and jewels of the chief danseuse, with jasmine flowers in her hair, she carried a large brass plate with betel leaves and nuts and went around offering them to the guests. Aryaduta waited with pounding heart for his turn. He could hear the rustling of her silk attire and the perfume of jasmine as she came next to him. As he took a leaf and a nut, his hand touched hers momentarily. The warmth of her touch lit a fire in Aryaduta. Her dark and sparkling eyes met his again. Was she aware of the tumult that she had created in him? He was sure that in her smile, there was more than the usual greeting of a gracious hostess. All this was over in a moment, and she was gone.

9

THE MOTH IS DRAWN
TOWARDS THE FLAME

*A*ryaduta became the moth that is drawn irretrievably towards the dangerous flame. Over the months since his first brush with his beloved, he contrived to pass through Anantapura with his body of troops as often as he could. His obsession with her grew into a madness.

Yet the moth found it onerous to approach the flame to touch its warmth. While Priyadarshini allowed Aryaduta entry into her haveli, she jealously looked after her wards and made access to them—particularly the one she sensed any ardent visitor particularly desired—difficult. This common stratagem was employed by her to raise the esteem of her haveli and to make the favours it bestowed ever more desirable and irresistible.

On several subsequent visits soon after the first, therefore, Aryaduta could not see the one he was looking for. Noting his discomfiture at her absence on one of his subsequent visits, Priyadarshini tactfully let it be known through another dancer who came around with the usual betel nuts that the chief danseuse had hurt her foot and would not dance that night. On another occasion, it was a case of women's days of seclusion and so on.

Aryaduta was deeply disturbed by these absences as he interpreted them as a deliberate rebuff from the one he desired now most passionately. After this had happened on several successive occasions, he decided during another deeply disappointing visit that he had to end his quest forever and was about to leave. However, before he could do so, one of the dancers waiting to perform quietly approached him from the shadows unnoticed while all were watching an ongoing performance and whispered before disappearing, 'Look at that window yonder, sir! Someone awaits.'

Glancing up across the courtyard, Aryaduta seemed to see for an instant that beauteous visage lit by the glow of an earthen lamp. The lamp moved away from the window, disappeared for a moment, and appeared a little later, carried by a veiled damsel in the dark corridor and then on to the staircase leading to the terrace.

There was no mistaking the signal. Aryaduta rose quickly, making out as if he was leaving for the night, and made his obeisances from afar at Priyadarshini, who had raised a surprised eyebrow, before disappearing into the shadows. He was stopped briefly by the eunuch guarding the women's private quarters, but he handed the guard a silver coin and brushed past him. He ran up two flights of stairs as stealthily as he could and then found himself entering an enormous terrace lit only by moonlight. The only light on the terrace came from the far end, where a flickering lamp was held tremulously by a veiled figure waiting in the shadows, her face turned away.

When Aryaduta approached her with beating heart, she turned towards him. The glow of the lamp lit up her alluring countenance. He beheld again those large sparkling *kajal*-lined eyes below the arched brows, the glittering nose-pin on the delicately shaped nostril, and the full lips. Her voice, which he was hearing for the first time, had a low husky tone, which sent a thrill through his already agitated heart.

She asked, 'Why do you look for me, sir, when the world outside our walls has prettier damsels from splendid mansions, any one of whom would gladly spend their life with you, if you but asked?'

'I look no further,' said Aryaduta. 'I have found my world in you, and here, fair one!' Then taking her hand, he added, 'Come with me, leave this house, and let us depart!'

'Do not be rash, sir,' she said, gently withdrawing her hand. 'You know full well that your world will never accept me. Such an act will bring misery on both of us. Let us meet, if you must, within the bounds of our destinies. Ask no more!'

With that, she walked away, leaving Aryaduta in the darkness.

Aryaduta was at least relieved that the cause of the absences of his object of desire was not her aloofness to his advances but—as he quickly fathomed—a strategy framed by Priyadarshini. In the following days, Priyadarshini made her wishes known. They were for the time being quite mundane—some favours at the royal court which Aryaduta was able to arrange quite easily, and this made access to his beloved much easier when he arrived on later occasions at the haveli. He was able to see her dance, and quite often, she came and sat near him and attended to his refreshments. But she was still holding herself aloof from him, perhaps as artful enticements for the larger prize ahead, or simply giving him time to reflect on what she had said. He could never be sure.

Aryaduta pondered long and hard at what he had heard on the terrace that moonlit night. Very reluctantly, he was reconciled to the fact that he might never be able to claim fully the person he now passionately loved. That indeed was as she termed it, his destiny. But his youthful heart knew no bounds, and he still harboured the hope that he could win her over ultimately, however hopeless the quest might appear.

He was the moth that did not care about being burnt at the flame.

10

THE NIGHTS OF THE FLOWERING JASMINE

*W*hen was it first that he came to possess her completely? After his first few visits, whatever he saw in her—either the courtesan's practised seductions and demure inhibitions, or deliberate aloofness—only raised his youthful ardour to a fever. It quickly became apparent in the haveli that Aryaduta's pursuit of her was different from the relations that other visitors normally had with the many dancers in Priyadarshini's care. What he could easily have purchased for a price he did not want. He needed from her much more than a courtesan's attentions.

On the night she finally yielded to him, the jasmines were in full flower. Although their fragrance wafted in from the garden, there was no bridal bed decked with flowers. Aryaduta wished that the flickering lamp in her room had instead been the ceremonial nuptial fire. That their feverish whisperings, caresses and longing for each other were as true as the seven eternal vows. And that the full moon and the stars who are our ancestors in the heavens witnessing the consummation of their love from afar were truly present with other well-wishers at a wedding that could never take place.

It came to pass between them that the nights of the full moon became the signal for their secret trysts. Wherever Aryaduta happened to be, when the pale full moon would emerge over the dusty horizon, he would turn his horse in the direction of Anantapura. And she would be turning from her other duties to attend to him. But he wondered whether the care she took to put the kajal in her eyes, the flowers she decked herself with or the perfume she wore on those special nights were merely the practised attention of the courtesan—or was there not a special message for him in these? Were their hearts when they caressed not equally pounding for each other in their eagerness?

But as the months passed, she appeared to be distancing herself as he desired more to possess her. There was no refusal from her side ever. That was not the custom of the haveli. But what he did possess—her body—was not his only desire. He wanted to take her being and soul away with him. He did often think that he had won her the way he wanted. At other times, she was a mystery to him, and this began to distress him. At last, the time came when he could bear this ambiguity no longer. A year or two had passed since the first time he had seen her. Yet this yielding-yet-unyielding flower that appeared to be in his hand was never fully in his possession.

'When can I truly claim you to be my own, my beloved?' he asked, half knowing the answer.

'Perhaps not in this life,' was her whispered response, 'but when we return to this world again in some distant millennium—not as nobleman and courtesan, but as simple folk who could truly give all of themselves to the ones they love.'

11

PRINCE OF THANESWAR

$\mathcal{A}$t the end of one his campaigns, successfully accomplished, the dead cremated, the wounded tended to, and a settlement arrived at with the vanquished opponent for loyalty in exchange for the prisoners, Aryaduta had set up camp and was resting beside a quiet rivulet. The messenger arrived at that time, grimy and dust-covered, with the news that the prince of Thaneswar was at Anantapura and would wait there till he was joined by Aryaduta and his forces. Any occasion to return to Anantapura was pleasant for Aryaduta and this time more so as it promised a reunion with his royal friend and patron whom he had not seen for many months. He had little knowledge then that this last visit to Anantapura would shut the door finally on any hopes of happiness he entertained with his beloved.

When Aryaduta entered once again the narrow streets of the ancient town, the sun was casting its last slanting rays through the gaps in the trees and tenements, some humble, others large magnificent mansions. Soon it would be dusk and the glow of the earthen lamps would light up the windows, and the pale moon would begin its journey through the heavens.

The news of his arrival in Anantapura had preceded Aryaduta, and soon he was joined by a body of royal scouts who would escort him to the prince of Thaneswar. Leaving the task of finding quarters for his men to his adjutant, Aryaduta rode off with the scouts, hoping that he could soon steal time away after meeting the prince to reunite with his beloved among the jasmine groves once again. The road took him past that enchanted haveli and he wondered whether she was watching him silently from one of the many lamplit windows, as the women were wont to do when a body of soldiers rode past.

The prince was ensconced in his palace in the lake a little away from the town, a place where he usually took his pleasures with many neighbouring nobles and the choicest pick of the local beauties and courtesans. The time to discuss the details of his victorious campaign, its political implications, and the bounties that it would bring to Thaneswar would have to wait till tomorrow, Aryaduta realised. Tonight's festivities would be mainly in his honour, a princely acknowledgement by Thaneswar of another victory won by its most gallant son and warrior.

As the torchlit royal vessel glided towards the island with its palace and pleasure gardens, Aryaduta could hear the faint sounds of music and merriment floating towards him. After a while as he came nearer, the music paused, and the royal party led by the prince appeared at the shore to welcome him. Shrugging aside all formalities, the prince warmly embraced his childhood friend, and Aryaduta felt all his weariness melt away as the strong royal arms clasped him tightly and refused to release him.

And then suddenly she appeared! Bejewelled and richly dressed for the dance, the payal on her feet tinkling as she approached, her enchanting eyes enhanced with kajal, a faint smile on her lips, she carried a silver dish with chandan to place on his forehead. He smelt the jasmine in her hair as she put the *tilak* with her dainty fingers. His heart beating, he looked into her eyes, but she turned away and was soon lost in the noisy crowd.

Surprised, Aryaduta attributed her unexpected diffidence to the affected shyness in public of women of her vocation. But before he could consider the matter further, the prince had drawn Aryaduta away and seated him next to himself in the pavilion and begun addressing the gathering.

'Nobles of Thaneswar,' he began, 'the victory won by our brother Aryaduta will, we hope, bring an end to the long night of strife we have suffered. Let the dawn bring an era of peace. Let us seize this happy moment, which we know is all too fleeting in the lives of mortals, and seek whatever enjoyment is possible. Let the music begin! Let us eat and drink to our merriment!'

The sound of flutes and *mridangam* playing a joyful evening raga brought gaiety into the courtyard which was further enhanced by the aroma of food that began to be served. One by one, the dancers took their turn. When she emerged, however, along with the other dancers, never once did she look Aryaduta's way. Her performance was exclusively for the prince sitting beside him; expectedly, thought Aryaduta, as that was customary.

But would she not favour him with even one glance? Aryaduta thought back to the last time he had met her and the caution and restraint that she had placed on their relationship by whispering that she could never be his in this life. Slowly but surely, she seemed to have erased the bond they had. *This is what she wants to tell me,* Aryaduta thought. *Courtesans cannot belong to any one person.* Quite plainly, her performance was for the royal personage tonight, and the prince responded with applause and praise. As the dance ended with loud applause from all sides, the prince took off one of his golden necklaces—with a large dark sapphire—and cast it at her feet.

Bowing with folded hands before the prince, she picked up the royal necklace. But did she hesitate a little before placing it around her neck? And when she turned to leave, did the glance that, for an instant, met his contain any special message for him? Aryaduta could never be sure. It would remain a mystery to him for a very long time—till many ages later when he was fated to meet her again one last time.

Later, as the oarsmen pulled the royal craft back to the edge across the silver lake, Aryaduta felt the dream world he had habited slipping away. The morning star had risen. The familiar harsh and rocky shoreline was becoming visible once again.

12

THE YEARS PASS

*T*he years rolled by, turned into decades, and these too vanished into the distant horizons of time. Aryaduta tried his best to forget the past. His duties took him to remote places; he tried to linger in these parts as far from Anantapura as possible. He roamed with his troops across parched and barren ravines, forded turbulent rivers and fast-flowing streams, traversed thick forests, and ventured through narrow and perilous icy mountain trails where a false step meant a fall many fathoms below and certain death—as happened to many an unfortunate soldier. Everywhere he pursued enemies and vanquished foes of the kingdom.

His tireless and incessant efforts as the commander of Thaneswar's armies ushered in an era of peace and, with it, prosperity in the kingdom. Travellers and tradesmen could move about freely all across the territory, without fear of ambush or robbery by brigands. Commerce flourished in the towns. The reputation of Thaneswar as a secure and safe oasis in an otherwise lawless land spread far and wide. Holy men sought sanctuary within the kingdom. The learned thronged its schools and monasteries and gave discourses.

Travellers from far and wide came to Thaneswar to enrich themselves materially and spiritually. They took back many stories with them.

And then suddenly the hard-won lengthy epoch of peace ended. There emerged a new threat—Nagaputra. The first encounter with him, which had been the result of the royal command many years ago, had left Aryaduta with a mystery to solve: how did Nagaputra come into possession of the royal necklace that the crown prince had given away that one night many years previously? Was it stolen from her? Or did she give it away recklessly to some stranger from whom Nagaputra might have obtained it by gamble, deceit, or plunder? Whatever the means, Aryaduta meant to solve the mystery one day. Perhaps by capturing Nagaputra alive, he thought. However, while there were many encounters thereafter, Nagaputra proved to be a wily enemy—a sly and vicious demon that lived and moved about in the forests and dark places, plundering unsuspecting villages and robbing travellers in the night.

Meanwhile, the past continued to haunt Aryaduta. He did not live the life of a hermit—far from it. He sought solace and forgetfulness aimlessly in the embraces of countless women—courtesans and noblewomen alike. While he made many friendships, with none could he share his soul.

Nayantara, the sister of the ruler of a remote mountain kingdom friendly to Thaneswar finally made him realise with certainty what he knew all along—that Aryaduta could never overcome his maddening unreachable lost infatuation and share his life with any other living being, however desirable.

Aryaduta had come to Nayantara's rescue after her brother was killed by Nagaputra, who sought to usurp the kingdom. After the slaughter of her brother, she had fled to the forests with her personal guards and retinue. It was fortunate that Aryaduta had stumbled upon Nagaputra's latest act of depredation when he happened to be passing by not very far away, on one of his restless sojourns along the limits of Thaneswar.

The first hint that the demon Nagaputra was around came when some villagers stopped him and his tired cavalry when it was homeward bound after a long campaign.

'We have been ruined, sir,' said a village elder. 'A horde of bandits arrived like a storm and attacked our village last night and set fire to our crops. They took whatever they could lay their hands on in our homes and did not spare the honour of our women. They said they were going to teach us a lesson for being loyal to the king of Thaneswar.'

Aryaduta realised immediately that this was the handiwork of the monster Nagaputra, whose real target must have been the ruler of the principality they were passing through, who was a Thaneswar loyalist. As the village folk could not provide further intelligence about their ruler and about their famed princess Nayantara, whose beauty was legend, Aryaduta feared the worst. He ordered his cavalry to turn around at once and head for the fortress.

On arriving a few furlongs from its grounds, he found traces of a recent skirmish. There were bodies of several of the local king's guards still bearing the kingdom's livery, lying around, rotting on the fields with vultures circling over them. Aryaduta ordered the bodies taken away and cremated. There must have been a battle which did not seem to have gone in the kingdom's favour, he feared. In that case, he realised that the fortress and its extensive grounds could still be occupied by Nagaputra and Aryaduta could try and surprise him, or the demoniacal Nagaputra could himself be laying a trap for Aryaduta—a possibility that could not be excluded.

Aryaduta assigned the task of storming the fortress to Lakshasthira, his adjutant and son of a Thaneswar courtier. Fortunately, the task did not prove too difficult, especially as the populace was friendly to Thaneswar and the few of Nagaputra's soldiers guarding the gates fled on seeing the oncoming forces of Thaneswar with battle-ready horsemen. Seeing them approaching through the dust of their galloping horses, the hostage population readily opened the gates. Nagaputra and his bandit hordes, as usual never ready to face openly the might of Thaneswar, fled from the rear without putting up much resistance. Several of them were ambushed and killed by Lakshasthira's men, but Nagaputra himself managed to flee.

Lakshasthira—and Aryaduta himself later when he entered the fortress—found a scene of pillage and destruction. The young king had been martyred while defending his fortress, and the famed princess Nayantara had been forced to flee with her personal guards to the nearby forests to avoid a fate worse than death from Nagaputra and his bandits. Such a fate had indeed befallen several of the damsels who had not managed to flee the fortress in time. All had been stripped of their clothes, ornaments, and honour and some even brutalised and left to die. The retreating bandits had taken away as much loot as they could and mercilessly slaughtered any hesitating to part with their treasures.

Aryaduta ordered the flags of the kingdom raised prominently once again from the terrace of the palace and from all the ramparts of the fort and hoped that villagers seeing this would send word to Nayantara, wherever she had taken refuge, that it was safe to return. Several parties were also deployed by the kingdom's surviving courtiers to scour the forests to locate Nayantara. Although Aryaduta and his weary troops were eager to return to Thaneswar after their long campaign, he decided to wait a little while longer for her return. The issue of whether she would take over the reins of the kingdom or whether it would be contested by another in the line of succession had to be settled. Aryaduta wanted to ensure a smooth succession here, a kingdom that had always been a trusted and loyal ally, before he left.

He wasn't ready, however, for the strange and unexpected turn of events that took place thereafter.

13

NAYANTARA

*N*ayantara returned soon after. At daybreak one day, when a hesitant sun had just appeared through the clouds, a group of dishevelled and weary riders led by the princess made their way back to the fortress. These were Nayantara and her party of bodyguards, who had fled from Nagaputra and hidden in the forests. Although her royal vestments were torn and muddy, her poise and demeanour were those of a proud, though humbled, aristocrat.

The courtiers—those that remained after Nagaputra's onslaught, along with Aryaduta—made haste to receive her. These court worthies had been determining in the last few days during her absence the matter of the succession of their late vanquished ruler and decided that as her young brother had left no issue, Nayantara had the next right to the crown. So it was as the potential new ruler of the kingdom that she was received at the entrance of the fortress. Garlands were placed round her neck when she dismounted, and conch shells were blown loudly.

Aryaduta had stood aside, allowing the courtiers to welcome their new ruler. But Nayantara sought him out and, when introduced, bowed down and touched his feet in a mark of obeisance. Aryaduta gently raised her up and the virile though greying general of Thaneswar beheld for the first time at close quarters the famed beauty, the brilliance which her bedraggled clothes and unkempt hair could hardly conceal.

'We are immensely in your debt, sir,' said the princess, 'but although we have lost much, we will endeavour to repay Thaneswar's kindness, this I promise!'

'Thaneswar's friends are never in debt to it, princess,' replied Aryaduta. 'To respond to your calamity was our duty. My abiding regret will be that we couldn't come sooner to save your brother.'

'I hope you can tarry a few days longer with us,' requested Nayantara, 'so that we could better express our gratitude to you and Thaneswar. Besides, as I hear you have been on a long campaign, you and your men must be quite weary. A few days of rest will do you a lot of good.'

Aryaduta agreed. If not for himself, he desired the furlough more for his tired men. He knew that the grateful populace would cater to all their wants and physical needs. He did not realise, however, that the courtiers—certainly with Nayantara's consent even though she might not have been the author of it—were planning something for him as well. There seemed to be considerable deliberations going on within the palace. He noticed several gatherings of the courtiers, who met behind closed doors in the hall directly across the courtyard in front of his balcony. The discussions went on till a very late hour of the night, and although the curtains were drawn, the light from torches and lamps inside shone through. Aryaduta thought that they were making arrangements for a formal *rajyaabhishekara* or coronation ceremony for the princess, who would be asked to ascend the throne as queen.

That was only partly correct. The very next morning, the chief courtier along with a few other leading nobles asked to meet him. Following the princess's example, they all bowed and touched his feet before the chief courtier explained the purpose of the visit of the delegation.

'General Aryaduta, we have come to make a request—and it is also with our princess Nayantara's consent that we speak—that you accept her hand in marriage and also accept to be our king and protector.

'As you may be aware, several times in the past, our late king has held several *swayamvaras* to choose a royal consort for our princess Nayantara—but she found none suitable to whom she could bestow her hand.

'And now providence has sent such a one, she feels, who, as the deliverer of our kingdom from the clutches of the demon himself, is the right personage to be its lord and master and also of her own heart. It is her wish that you accept our proposal and spend the rest of your life here as our king.'

Aryaduta was wholly unprepared for such a proposal. Seeing his confusion, the chief courtier assured him that he could take his time to think about their offer, but they looked forward to his acquiescence.

'It is a great honour that you bestow on me, my lords,' replied Aryaduta. 'But as you have surmised, this is not a matter that can be consented to in a hurry. You and Princess Nayantara intend to bestow on me great trust and responsibility, and I must consider deeply whether I am worthy of your confidence.'

But Aryaduta tarried long and sent no reply. Aryaduta had many responsibilities back in Thaneswar which he was loath to turn away from, although he knew that the king of Thaneswar would gladly have relieved him of them, given the great honour this neighbouring kingdom and ally was proposing to bestow on Aryaduta.

But there was a bigger reason. Aryaduta had not forgotten the one to whom he had given his heart, and he could share it with no one else in this world. The reason for Aryaduta's silence on this matter remained a mystery with the courtiers, but only Nayantara guessed its reason and felt compelled to speak to him to ease his mind.

Finding a solitary moment during his frequent walks along the battlements, Nayantara whispered to him one day, 'How long will you live in the past, my lord? Look around you. There is much to live for.

If it is not me you wish to honour, I hope someone prettier and luckier than myself will be able to claim your restless heart.'

Aryaduta was much ashamed to refuse a match from this charming princess that would have brought mutual benefit to the two kingdoms. Nayantara, rested now from her days in the forests, was like an exquisite flower in full bloom in his presence. But the gulf in years was too much, he felt, and the old wound he was carrying in his heart had not yet healed, or rather, he did not wish it to heal. He contemplated on the one hand her youth and beauty and the promise of a long and luxurious life that she held out, and on the other, the multitude of unkept promises that had yet to be fulfilled for Thaneswar, the years of struggle ahead they represented, and most importantly, his constant yearning for the one he had lost. He chose the latter.

'It is I who is unlucky, beauteous one,' he replied. 'I wish my heart was free to give to someone as desirable as you.'

However, to prevent misunderstandings with the nobles who remained quite nonplussed with Aryaduta's silence, Aryaduta arranged that Lakshasthira, his accompanying adjutant, scion of a powerful aristocratic clan of Thaneswar, take his place instead.

The kingdom set about arranging the royal marriage and the crowning of its new ruler. While this happy beginning emerging from a period of tragedy was coming about at one extremity of Thaneswar, at the other a dreadful pestilence was ending the lives of thousands, and with it, the one who was never too far from Aryaduta's thoughts.

14

A BEGINNING AND AN END

ew beginnings are never too distant from endings. As the sacred fire bore witness to the union of Nayantara and her noble lord, news reached Aryaduta that the king of Thaneswar was personally directing efforts to overcome a most sinister enemy—a mysterious ailment that was affecting thousands in the northern part of the kingdom, with most succumbing to the disease. What concerned Aryaduta most was that Anantapura was in the very centre of the outbreak.

Without wasting time, Aryaduta began his long journey north. News kept reaching him about people fleeing the affected parts—those who could. Some took the disease with them and caused others to fall ill. Towns began closing their gates to outsiders in panic. Trade suffered and shortages appeared. Famine began looming in the land.

In order to restore order under these conditions, the king had sent his nobles accompanied by his physicians and apothecaries to determine the cause of the pestilence and to devise remedies. Such things had happened before, and some knowledge existed in the royal archives about how to handle these outbreaks. Foremost among the actions was to properly cremate the dead humans and cattle, clean up the sources of drinking water, gather the town and village elders and use their offices to spread messages about basic hygiene practices, minister to the sick and dying, and most importantly, restore confidence and prevent panic.

As it became clear that the nobles themselves were hesitant to visit the blighted region, the king decided to go personally. Where the disease was most virulent, that is where the royal camp was pitched— at Anantapura. Although unbidden, Aryaduta felt compelled to be by his side at this time. And again, his path led back therefore to the town and the one he had left with a heavy heart many, many years ago. He was not sure what news would meet him there.

As Aryaduta approached Anantapura, passing travellers did not convey any news of hope. The town and the countryside seemed to be covered in a pall of misery, gloom, and death. What curse had befallen this land and why, thought Aryaduta. Had not men suffered enough misery?

As many years before, Aryaduta entered the town when dusk had fallen. But this time, there were no cheerful lamps at the windows, no sounds of children playing. Half the town seemed to be abandoned. There were sounds of wailing and lamentations from some dwellings. The king had heard of Aryaduta's coming and sent a royal escort to the gates of the town to receive him. They now took him to the royal encampment just outside the town.

The king of Thaneswar looked tired and weary. Many weeks of ceaseless toil had taken their toll on the royal visage. But he was happy and relieved to see Aryaduta. 'Why are our kul devatas not listening to my prayers?' he asked. 'Where have I failed them? Are the poor not given alms and clothed, the hungry fed, the weak protected from bandits and robbers? Are not the religious orders and sanghas given land and gifts from the treasury, and is not this holy realm bequeathed by my ancestors ably defended against our enemies?'

'My lord, do not despair,' said Aryaduta, himself troubled by this question. 'The devas have their reasons and ways we may not fathom. As mortals, our task is to ever seek the right way and, hoping we have discovered it, to tread it as well as we can. No one has followed this precept more truly than you and our Queen Gyaneshwari, and you have taught this to others.' Then he added, 'Let me now take care of the sick as I am here and allow yourself some rest, sire.'

The king heeded Aryaduta's advice and decided to leave as there was no abler person than Aryaduta in all of Thaneswar to fight the spreading scourge.

'I will journey to the holy confluence of Prayag as I have been wanting to do for many months,' he said. 'I shall offer our prayers and thanks to the ancestors for whatever good that has happened to us in this world. You are right. Despair we must not, even though we live in the midst of sorrow and calamity. Let us be happy that our efforts may have reduced in some measure the cares of a few.'

15

AN INSTANT OF ETERNITY

$\mathcal{A}$ryaduta immersed himself fully in the task of defeating the new enemy at hand. This quickly spreading scourge required different and far more difficult instruments than he was used to as a warrior. But finally, after several trials, the court apothecaries were able to develop a potion from the herbs and plants in the vicinity that appeared at last to take effect, and the tide turned.

All this while, he also made constant enquiries about his lost paramour. But she seemed to have disappeared without trace. Priyadarshini's haveli no longer existed, and all that the few of her acquaintances who could be found remembered was that Priyadarshini had returned to her village somewhere in the Avadh country but where exactly no one seemed to know.

But just as fate had brought Aryaduta to his beloved through a chance encounter, so too it was fated that Aryaduta would find her the last time by chance. So it was that when Aryaduta was organising the administration of the new drug in a village where almost nobody except the afflicted and dying remained, he received word that a very sick woman—a former courtesan who had heard of his coming—wanted to see him personally. Although he hoped that this dying woman was not the one he was looking for, he feared very much that it might indeed be her.

It was night, and the flickering lamp by her side made it even more difficult for Aryaduta to recognise her. Besides, the disease had ravaged her body, and the skeletal frame that remained carried very little resemblance to the ravishing beauty that had stolen Aryaduta's heart in his youth. And yet, there was no mistaking that noble brow and the eyes that still held their lustre despite sickness. To Aryaduta, the image of the lithe danseuse with kajal around her eyes and anklets on her legs which had filled his mind forever was not dimmed, nor would it ever be.

He asked his companions to leave, knelt down and took her frail hand and held it close to his heart, and whispered, 'Never again will we part, my beloved.'

Seeing Aryaduta, she appeared to recover a little. Gathering her strength, she motioned Aryaduta to come closer. 'Would that it were so,' she whispered back, 'but that is not to be. My time in this world is coming to a close. But I am content having seen you one last time before I go.' Aryaduta wanted to tell her those usual words of comfort humans convey to each other at such times, when she interrupted him.

'We have little time, Aryaduta. I have to tell you something before I leave this world forever,' she said.

'There has been no one but you in my heart. Only you. Others have held my body, but you have taken my heart, which has forever been with you.'

'I know the suffering I have caused you and could not forgive myself,' she went on. 'I have been praying since you left that night thirty long years ago, with the unbearable hurt in your eyes, that the gods send you to me one last time so that I can tell you this. I have prayed each day for your return. They have been kind.

'I have been fortunate in many ways. Lucky indeed is a poor girl like me to have become a courtesan, with princes and nobles as companions, and luckier still to have lost my heart to you and been loved immeasurably by you in return. What more can humans hope for?'

Tears welled up in Aryaduta as he heard all this. The dying courtesan he had loved immeasurably had fulfilled his life with her parting words, telling him that their affection was mutual. He gathered up her frail body in his arms and held her closely. The flood of emotions that Aryaduta had kept at bay all his life burst finally, and he wept openly.

But there was something else he needed to know that could not be deferred, even at this time. He took out the royal necklace which he always carried and held it near her. 'We seized this from the bandit Nagaputra. How did you lose it, dear one?' he asked.

Her face hardened, and she was quiet for some time. 'I didn't lose it,' she replied finally with great difficulty. 'I gave it to the son that I had with the prince, now king of Thaneswar. I gave it to the one who is now called Nagaputra.'

Aryaduta was too startled to speak, but he felt that the terrible secret that had been revealed to him was true. The effort to pass on this information had drained her of her last strength, and she went into a swoon.

Her spirit departed as the hint of dawn appeared outside the window and as the first *kokila* birds had begun their plaintive calls.

Aryaduta carried her limp, lifeless frame to the riverbank and placed her body on the funeral pyre that he prepared with the help of his companions. And while the priest chanted the ancient Vedic prayers, he lit the flame that ended their earthly bonds forever.

While doing so, he recalled her words whispered quietly to him a very long time ago when she had talked of another lifetime at some distant future when they could come together again—not as courtesan and nobleman but as common folk who could give themselves to each other fully.

Whether the gods would ever fulfil this desire in another lifetime, he was not sure. He felt content that at least he had found in this world his unfathomable love not unrequited, and his soul felt replenished in some measure. He subdued his immeasurable grief with this thought.

16

THE TERRIBLE SECRET

*H*owever, Aryaduta's anguish was compounded by the shocking new intelligence she had left him with.

Over the next few days, Aryaduta tried to resolve in his mind several of the questions that confronted him. Most importantly, was the king of Thaneswar aware that Nagaputra was his own illegitimate son? As he mulled over this question over and over, Aryaduta became convinced that the king indeed was aware. Wasn't that the reason he had invoked the famous instructions of Krishna to Arjuna before the great battle of Kurukshetra when he ordered Aryaduta to annihilate Nagaputra? Arjuna had been reluctant to slay his near and beloved in battle even for a just cause, but Krishna had prevailed. But why did Nagaputra turn against his father as Ajatashatru had against the great king Bimbisara?[5]

Was it possible that Nagaputra was claiming more from the king as his natural son than the king was willing to gift? The king, Aryaduta was certain, would not be willing to entrust even a small part of the realm of his ancestors to a vile and demoniac person—a veritable *asura*[6]—whose true nature began to show as he was growing up. The king would rather engage in battle with him and eliminate him if need be, and it did not matter whether it was his own son that was his adversary.

And why did the king choose to keep this a secret from Aryaduta, his most loyal and trusted friend? Did he feel that Aryaduta's resolve to destroy Nagaputra would falter if he discovered that Nagaputra was the king's natural son and, by that token, likely—if revealed—dear to Aryaduta also? Was the reminder about Krishna's teaching to Arjuna a deliberate message to forestall the eventuality of Aryaduta discovering this secret?

These questions gradually began to resolve themselves in Aryaduta's mind. Although some doubts still remained, the king's conduct in this matter had become clearer. The task of defeating and slaying Nagaputra had become, indeed, much harder with this new information, and Aryaduta realised why the king had been so circumspect when sending him on his first mission to annihilate Nagaputra.

However, none of these conjectures could be confirmed without the king's word on them. Aryaduta decided to find out from the king of Thaneswar himself before engaging in a final campaign against Nagaputra.

The opportunity soon arose when he received royal summons to attend court. The king, he was informed, had decided to forsake his temporal life and abdicate in favour of the crown prince. Thereafter, he would embark on pilgrimages to the holy sites. Not many returned from these arduous journeys and so the king wanted to see his friend before he departed.

17

PRAYAG

*A*ryaduta was able to reach Prayag at the confluence of the three holy rivers of Ganga, Yamuna, and the mythical Saraswati, where the king of Thaneswar had come to offer sacrifices to the gods before he began his spiritual journeys. After days of *havans*,[7] the king began undertaking charity by distributing a large portion of his personal wealth to the poor and needy. In three days, his personal coffers were empty. Much of the gold and jewellery he had acquired in his lifetime he gave away. In this, he was following the footsteps of his father and his forefathers.

Thereafter, he began making preparations for his holy pilgrimages that would take him in the first instance to the holy temples of Kedarnath and Badrinath, tracing the river Ganga to its source and then beyond, over the Himalayas to the lake Mansarovar, where all the holy rivers originated and over which the majestic Mount Kailash sat, its crown soaring into the clouds, the abode of the gods. Although saddened to leave his many friends and followers behind, the departing monarch looked back with satisfaction on an immensely fulfilled existence. Indeed, Thaneswar had witnessed a golden period with peace and prosperity under this ruler, a flowering of arts and learning, spread of ethical and moral thinking, growth of many religious orders, great admiration by its friends and equal fear from its enemies, who now kept their distance.

'Do not regret my leaving you, my friends. I leave happy and contented,' he said to those around him. 'On you now rests the mantle of preserving and protecting Thaneswar's future, and I cannot think of worthier shoulders on which it can rest.'

To the crown prince, who could be forgiven for not being soothed by these words and who soon would be the new monarch, he had only a few words: 'Rule with honour and compassion. Bring glory to Thaneswar.'

His last words were in private to Aryaduta. 'Good friend, Thaneswar owes an immeasurable debt to you which it can never repay,' he said. 'But there is still a last task you have to perform, and that is to destroy Nagaputra, whom you have been pursuing now for several years. An Ajatsatru has again emerged in our time, and so long as he lives, Thaneswar will never be safe.'

Aryaduta noted the king's reference to Ajatsatru, who had slain his father Bimbisara to wrest control of the eastern kingdom of Magadha. Was the king, then, aware of Nagaputra's relationship with him? Aryaduta wondered whether to bring the subject up. But this was the last opportunity to clear up the mystery. He took out the royal necklace he had been carefully looking after so long and showed it to the king.

The all-knowing king did not appear too surprised. 'Aryaduta, my friend, you were bound to find out Nagaputra's true relationship sooner or later,' he said. 'I have tried to keep it from you as long as possible so that your task is less painful. Many years ago, he sent secret emissaries to me, demanding that I part with half my kingdom. Although our *sastras* do not endow any rights to children of courtesans, even if they carry royal blood, there are many instances of such children distinguishing themselves. I would gladly have embraced him had he shown inclinations and capability of good rulership.

'Soon after birth, his mother gave him away to Priyadarshini, who raised him like a mother, and whom, I believe, he still has regard for. But from his childhood and youth, he showed inclinations for violence, malice, and diabolism. In fact, he has turned into a veritable monster.

'I have tried to negotiate secretly with him several times, asking him to consider giving up his path of pillage and violence, but he has had the audacity to reply by murdering my emissaries,' said the departing king. 'Therefore, the death of an *asura* awaits him and only you can overcome his cunning and deceit. I go confident that this undertaking is in your safe hands.

'And this is now yours,' said the king, handing back the necklace to Aryaduta. 'I have no more need of these. Keep it to remind you of your task.'

'My lord,' replied Aryaduta, 'I will accomplish this, whatever it may take.'

18

THE STRATAGEM

*T*he king, now an ordinary mortal, left incognito on horseback, clothed in simple garb and accompanied by Queen Gyaneshwari, his favourite queen, who decided to brave the privations of a wandering pilgrim's life to stay with her husband. A few loyal servants disobeyed the royal command to stay behind and also elected to be with their master, giving up the comforts of courtly life.

The newly crowned king, along with Aryaduta and all the courtiers, saw them off at the steps of the palace. Not an eye was dry. But the party of pilgrims never looked back and was soon lost from sight in the rising dust from their horses' hooves and the gradually engulfing dusk.

Aryaduta set about devising a way of accomplishing Nagaputra's annihilation, with determination. He was not one to be swayed from or delay a promise made, and especially one made on the last instructions of his departing friend and former king. The usual method of engaging an enemy in open warfare would not do in Nagaputra's case, he realised. He had to overcome stealth by stealth and cunning with cunning.

While he was thus engaged in thought and gazing out to the nearby forest, one evening soon after the abdicated king's departure, he noticed a group of hunters emerging with a slain deer. His mind went back to the time when, on his first campaign against Nagaputra, he had organised a hunting contest. The tribal youth who had won it had done so by enticing and trapping a doe by mimicking the cry of a fawn in distress. Aryaduta's plan was made. Rather than hunting Nagaputra, he would trap him. This time it would be the doe which cried for help and the fawn that responded.

The departing monarch had passed on a most valuable piece of information—that Priyadarshini was Nagaputra's foster mother and he still had much affection for her. Could she not play the role of the doe and entice Nagaputra to come to her? She might not if she knew Nagaputra's designs against all of Thaneswar's court. But what if Aryaduta were to convince her that he had come to offer a last chance to Nagaputra to abandon his heinous path and make peace with the king? Being the worldly-wise person she was, would she not see that this was indeed Nagaputra's only hope?

Of course, this would involve seeking Priyadarshini's cooperation and then ultimately deceiving her as well. But then sacrificing the interests of near and dear ones if necessary was a small price to pay to serve justice and the greater good. Many lives would be saved if a battle were avoided. But he would have to live out his life with Priyadarshini's curses on him. This was yet another burden—like many others—that he would have to bear.

The first task was to find Priyadarshini. He had learnt that she had retired to her village somewhere in the Avadh country. He would have to make discreet enquiries to locate her, but given the king's formidable army of informants, it was not a difficult task. He would then have to meet her and convince her to send an invitation to Nagaputra that he was unlikely to refuse. He would take a trusted aide along with him to Priyadarshini, who would presumably negotiate with Nagaputra after Aryaduta had left but actually direct the operations to destroy and kill him.

A party of assassins would fall on the unsuspecting Nagaputra when he appeared and deliver him from his present existence. That was the stratagem. Of course, Priyadarshini would be told an entirely different story. The whole operation would have to be conducted in the strictest secrecy from beginning to end as Nagaputra had spies of his own and, given his cunning, could discover and foil the plot at the slightest hint he got.

19

PRIYADARSHINI'S VILLAGE

$\mathcal{T}$he day finally came when Aryaduta had to journey to the tiny village in Avadh where Priyadarshini now lived. He had with him the prince of a neighbouring principality—Nayantara's husband, Lakshasthira, who had both the stature and the neutrality to be considered a credible negotiator in Priyadarshini's eyes. They both travelled incognito—two ordinary horsemen among hundreds going about their business.

A party of twenty of his skilled and fiercest fighters were also following, singly and in pairs in ordinary dress with their daggers well concealed. They were to keep a close watch on the only entry point to the village—a small wooden bridge over the dirt track that led to it. All were from the locality, and if the wait were to take even as long as a week, would be able to find shelter without being suspected. Soldiers routinely came home on furlough and stayed around for several weeks loitering around, visiting women of the night and drinking till their money lasted.

If all worked to plan, Priyadarshini would, after Aryaduta convinced her, send out an urgent message to Nagaputra to visit her.

What would suffice as a compelling enough cause for Nagaputra to appear would have to be left to Priyadarshini's judgement. Fortunately for Aryaduta, Nagaputra had been seen recently in the vicinity. News of robberies and murders which were typical of him had been received from nearby towns and villages, including another attack on a revenue convoy. Given his proximity, the whole operation could be over in a few days.

Considering it wise to reach Priyadarshini's home in the darker hours, Aryaduta and his companion entered the village after sunset and arrived at Priyadarshini's homestead unnoticed. The glow of a lamp from one of the inner rooms meant that it was inhabited. Presently the sound from the blowing of a conch shell, thrice repeated, emanated from the inner recesses of the dwelling, indicating that whoever was inside had completed her evening prayers.

Aryaduta knocked gently and waited. The lamp moved from room to room, and finally, the woman carrying it appeared in the courtyard. Priyadarshini was wearing a simple red-bordered white sari. The lamp in her hands showed she wore no jewellery and that her majestic looks had not faded despite the years, although her hair, which fell on her shoulders, had greyed.

'Who is it that comes this late at dusk?' asked Priyadarshini, not making out Aryaduta's features in the dark.

'It is I, Aryaduta,' he replied, 'a warrior from Thaneswar.' It was thus that he had addressed her the first time, ages ago. 'And this is my companion Lakshasthira,' he added without elaborating further.

Her hand trembled on hearing this, and she quickly covered her head with a fold of her sari—not wanting to be seen unveiled by men. However, recovering her composure but clearly much surprised, she said, 'Aryaduta? What brings you here? My life of music, dance, and laughter is over. And the dancers have left one by one, some such as the one you could not forget, gone forever from this world.

'But you must be tired. Let me get you some water.' And she bade them come inside.

'I come to seek your help on Thaneswar's behalf,' said Aryaduta.

'There can be only one reason since you have come in person—it must be Nagaputra,' replied she, anticipating the obvious cause.

'Since you raised him as your own son, Thaneswar desires to offer him a last chance to mend his ways and seek our friendship,' said Aryaduta.

'Yes indeed, I did raise him as my own son,' said Priyadarshini. 'But how could we have ever known what he would grow up to become? Had we known that we were rearing a demon, he would have been throttled at childbirth as is the custom among us courtesans. We do not bring children into this world. But he was special, and that's why he lived.

'I am glad you have come, Aryaduta,' she continued. 'Perhaps you will succeed where the king's earlier missions failed.'

Aryaduta explained his strategy—the version he had made up for her. He was surprised that she did not require any persuading—deceit was not something she expected from him. Her hospitality to him and his companion and the complete trust she reposed on him made Aryaduta feel far guiltier than he had anticipated.

20

THE TRAP

$\mathcal{T}$he trap was set. Priyadarshini sent out word through one of the village youths known to have contact with Nagaputra that she was on her deathbed and would wish to see her wayward foster son for the last time and that he must come immediately if he were to see her while still in this world. It was a simple but effective stratagem which had been employed by countless mothers, and she was confident would work also with him. Thereafter on discovering that he had been deceived, Nagaputra would be furious, of course, and could turn violent. But she expected to pacify him when the peace proposal was revealed. At least that was what she understood and hoped would be the outcome. She was prepared to take the risk.

The youth brought back word that Nagaputra was indeed preparing to come soon, but would not disclose when. He would obviously have to come disguised and stealthily, knowing that Thaneswar's spies were constantly on the lookout for him. Aryaduta surmised that this would be on Amavasya night (when the moon is absent from the night sky), which was falling two nights hence.

Accordingly, he sent out word secretly, and his combatants were ready. All arrangements for Nagaputra's assassination—a justified and necessary execution, in Aryaduta's mind, planned meticulously over several month—were in place.

The fateful day that would rid the world of its present *asura* finally came. Priyadarshini had no hint of Nagaputra's fate being planned by Aryaduta.

No mother can ever fully disown a son, however evil he may have turned out to be, and Priyadarshini was no exception. She began preparing a special meal for Nagaputra and began stirring over the fire the auspicious *kheer* made from milk drawn from her own household cattle.

Aryaduta's uneasiness grew as the day progressed. He realised that however good the cause, the heavens would not forgive him for this horrible deception that he was forced to commit on Priyadarshini. Even the completely irreproachable Yudhisthira, the eldest of the Pandavas, was forced to visit hell according to the legends of old because of a very minor untruth he had uttered—the only instance in his life. He tricked his main adversary into thinking that his son had fallen in battle, when only the elephant Aswathama by the same name had been killed—which broke his adversary's morale and totally changed the course of the Kurukshetra war. Yudhisthira had said, 'Aswathama is dead,' and added in a whisper not heard, 'the elephant.'

His own deception was far more deliberate and sinister, perpetrated on the woman whose very home he was living in, and likely to be less forgivable, realised Aryaduta. But his mind was made up. Like Yudhisthira, he was prepared for any punishment the gods would mete out to him.

Having satisfied himself that all preparations were fully ready, Aryaduta sent off Lakshasthira when it was almost dusk to the predetermined place from where he would set the whole process in motion, before returning.

The time came finally for Aryaduta to take leave of Priyadarshini. Seeing him making preparations to depart, which she had not expected, Priyadarshini came up to him and said, 'Aryaduta, I know that you cannot forgive Nagaputra in your heart for all the evil he has done. But why don't you stay back and see him at least and speak to him personally. He may heed your words more than those of Lakshasthira.'

She was silent briefly thereafter, hesitant and struggling inwardly, wanting to say something but faltering. An uneasy feeling was growing in Aryaduta as well.

'There is something on your mind,' he said. 'Tell me now as we may not meet again.'

'I must reveal this truth which we have kept closely guarded from you all these years, but cannot any longer. Nagaputra is no son of the king. You, Aryaduta, are his father!'

21

THE DISCOVERY AND
THE DILEMMA

*A*ryaduta's world spun around him violently on hearing Priyadarshini's words. 'It was a secret she never wanted revealed,' said she. 'She was carrying your child when the prince—the former king of Thaneswar—came to Anantapura. She wanted to bear your child but felt that the only way we could allow him to live was if he was presumed to have royal blood. The child would also have had a much better chance in life that way. Besides, she wanted to end forever her relationship with you—the only person she ever loved. This would never have happened if the child was known to be yours.

'We kept this secret between ourselves. Later, she made over the child to me, and I reared him as my own. We passed on the news of his birth to the king in due course, but it remained only in the knowledge of the three of us. But that Nagaputra was your son and not the king's was concealed from the king as well.

'The king sent gifts to us secretly, acknowledging his progeny as is the custom, and Nagaputra lacked nothing. However, as he grew up, he assumed through the king's munificence that a special relationship existed between him and the monarch, although no such intelligence was formally ever conveyed to him. Gradually as the years passed, his demands for recognition were far greater than could be met by the king.'

Through the physical and emotional turmoil that Priyadarshini's revelations had caused him, Aryaduta recalled the sudden diffidence that his dying paramour had felt when she saw the royal necklace. Even in her last moments, she wanted him to be spared the ignominy of having an enemy and traitor as a son, even if that meant not revealing the living bond that existed forever between them.

22

KURUKSHETRA REVISITED

*T*hat Thaneswar's mortal enemy could be his own son appeared totally incredible to Aryaduta. But recalling the last moments of the royal courtesan, his lost beloved, he didn't doubt the truth of this revelation. Now he had to confront the fact that this monster was the only link to the person whom he held most dear and whose being had now sublimated into memories and abstractions. But then all beings, as the philosophers held, were part of the mind's creation and make-believe and did not exist beyond that, thought Aryaduta.

If that were indeed so, why do we struggle to improve the illusory environment that we as non-real beings exist in? Why do we revere the great teachings emanating from the Kurukshetra battlefield? Why indeed glorify the battle to change the course of human conduct? Why have humans engaged in the constant and ceaseless effort at change and improvement since conscious life emerged in this universe?

It had to be because there must be a bigger truth—an immense point to the apparent pointlessness, Aryaduta was convinced. But what was it? And did pursuing that unknown reality require him to put an end to his only progeny—his just discovered woefully errant son, but his only certain link to that he held most dear? Could Nagaputra be given a last chance to reform—or must he fall by the righteous sword? Aryaduta realised that he might not have considered mercy if he had remained ignorant of Nagaputra's true relationship to him. But did not even the last and most errant citizen of Thaneswar deserve to be given such a choice? Aryaduta agonised over this dilemma long and hard as the night wore on.

The gradual suffusion of the morning's light brought clarity to his tortured mind. Aryaduta conveyed his decision on Nagaputra's fate in clear terms to Lakshasthira and knew that it would be carried out as instructed. But had he done the right thing? The answer was ambiguous; the propriety of the most difficult decision of his life would remain forever poised on the knife-edge separating right from wrong.

23

THE MONASTERY

*T*he journey home was a long one. Aryaduta felt weary, and the heaviness that had settled on his soul would not lift.

He brooded over the decision he had made. Humans since countless aeons past have had to confront choices such as he had faced and would do so limitless aeons after. The course of mankind was fashioned by dilemmas resolved by solitary souls with no guidance except the voices of their inner souls who followed their lonely paths according to their own limited understandings of truth. Ages hence, Aryaduta realised, someone might stumble upon the choice made by him and ponder over its correctness. They too would, in turn, be judged by others. And so it would go on, endlessly.

For the first time in his life, Aryaduta did not look forward to the many challenges that faced Thaneswar and demanded his attention. The road he had been taking for the past week came to a fork, and he remembered that the narrower path emerging from it led to the mountains and the monastery high in the Himalayas. A long time back, a certain wise king had made a gift of land to Sanghamitra the Buddhist monk, but Aryaduta had never had the time to visit it.

Aryaduta decided to leave his worldly cares behind him for the time being and seek comfort in Sanghamitra's cloistered sanctuary. Dismounting from his charger, he handed over his sword and armour to his escorts and asked them, despite their protests, to proceed to the capital without him.

The path he trod became a narrow trail, and as it climbed higher, the air became cooler; soon it began to skirt the rocky banks of a swiftly flowing stream. Aryaduta realised that he had already climbed quite high into the mountains, and his exertions had tired him. He decided to take a break. Disrobing, he plunged into the icy waters of the stream. He allowed the current to take him midstream but soon found that he had to use all his strength to counter the torrent, whose power he clearly had underestimated. Although a powerful swimmer, he realised that he was losing this battle.

He hadn't noticed that a fisherman was beginning to row frantically towards him in a dinghy till the man was near and had flung him a rope; with the fisherman's help, he was able finally to climb aboard.

'That was a mighty foolish thing you did just now, my friend,' said the man. 'The currents here are treacherous, and you were about to drown.'

Thus, Aryaduta who had saved thousands of others' lives in his lifetime found himself saved in turn from certain death by the fisherman. He thanked the latter profusely for saving him and was embarrassed that he could not reward the man, having sent off all his possessions with his escorts. 'Tell me, how I can repay you, my friend?' he asked.

'You already have,' said the man. 'It is not every day that you get the satisfaction of saving a drowning man.'

As Aryaduta continued on his way, he was struck by the man's words. He was indeed a drowning man in more ways than one.

But no longer.

As he climbed higher on the trail which clung precariously to the edge of the massive mountain on one side and fell sharply on the other, down to the gurgling stream far below, his despondency began to gradually leave him. The verdant rice terraces on the other side of the valley, the thick canopy of conifers on the mountain slopes, and the bracing mountain air combined together to revive him. As the trail took a sharp turn, Sanghamitra's monastery and the shimmering snow-capped mountain peak that overlooked it came suddenly into view.

Aryaduta felt an overwhelming sense of exhilaration. The last rays of the sun cast the snow-peaked mountain in an amber glow.

This extraordinary world in its animate and inanimate forms was the truth, felt Aryaduta. Life was nothing but a fleeting experience of this bliss. This was his to see, struggle in, and cherish momentarily— as the endless flow of women and men since aeons past had likewise seen, struggled in, and treasured before him; and his to fight to protect and preserve as ably as he could for the infinite stream in ages hence that were to follow.

Nilghat District

LAST FEW YEARS
OF THE 1970S

1

THE MIDNIGHT KNOCK

$\mathcal{R}$anjit didn't respond to the first few knocks on the glass panes on his front door. However, when they became louder and more insistent, the deep dreamless sleep he was in was finally and rudely interrupted. Squinting groggily at his bedside clock, he saw that it was 12.30 a.m. This had to be an emergency as no one would normally awaken the subdivisional officer at this time. He roused himself and went to the front door.

It was pitch dark outside, but Ranjit's front lobby always had a dim 60-watt lamp burning throughout the night. The police messenger saluted him and handed over a copy of the wireless message just received at the Sadar Police Station. It was directly from the state chief secretary, addressed to the commissioner Central Division and all district collectors and subdivisional officers under him, conveying instructions that the Central Government desired in no uncertain terms that the road and railway blockade enforced by the Confederation of Tribal Student Unions in four of the ten districts through which the national highway and the railway trunk line passed must be lifted immediately—repeat immediately—with the use of force if necessary according to the prescribed procedure in the administrative manual on the use of force etc. Action should be completed before noon and conveyed to the chief secretary.

The message had also been copied to the subdivisional police officer, Ranjit's police counterpart. Ranjit had visited the railway station and tracks near the town the previous evening with the SDPO before winding up for the day, and several thousand students were massed on and around the tracks. They were in a pretty belligerent mood. Talks between the students and the state government had been continuing for a long time but had reached an impasse. Meanwhile, all transport of goods and traffic between that region of the country and the rest had effectively ground to a halt. This included almost the entire nation's coal resources, and the blockade was threatening to shut down the northern and eastern power grids in the country. Time was running out; hence, the Central Government had intervened and tried to negotiate and, noting what they felt was irrational obduracy on the part of the students, had decided to act.

Ranjit's immediate problem was how to remove the protestors with the insufficient police force in the town. He had never before had to resort to use of force in the short year or so since he had been posted as SDO, his first assignment since joining the civil service. The tribal students' agitation had been growing, however, and taking often a violent character. But there had been few incidents thankfully in his subdivision so far.

He walked into his small residential office room next to the front lobby and switched on the table lamp, and before he could call, the telephone began ringing. It was Sudarshan Rao, the SDPO. He had also received orders to take action without delay from his boss the district police superintendent.

'So what do we do now—how many armed police personnel do we have?' asked Ranjit.

'Just one company of riot police. After taking away the cook and his helpers and those on leave, only eighty-five men. Not enough to disperse the 5,000 or so agitators, I'm afraid.'

'Should we ask for reinforcements from district headquarters?' asked Ranjit.

'I have done that already, but the SP and the DC have to act against the agitators in headquarters also. "Can't spare any" is the line they gave me.'

'The usual response,' mused Ranjit.

'Our only chance is to take the agitators by surprise,' suggested Sudarshan. 'If we are the first to act in this province, the students not expecting any action will still be sleeping.'

'OK. Let's go for it, then, and hope it succeeds,' said Ranjit. 'Pick me up on the way to the station,' he ended, hanging up.

While he conducted this conversation in a somewhat casual manner, Ranjit tried not to betray the growing nervousness that was welling up within him. The small force that he had was grossly outnumbered, and if attacked by the students, the only way they could survive a lynching was by using live ammunition—the one action any executive magistrate like him would like to avoid during his or her entire civil service career. The ultimate responsibility for use of force rested with the civilian magistrate accompanying the police force—Ranjit himself in this case. If the action flopped or there were unacceptably large casualties, given the increasing trend of weakness in the top echelons of the administration on whom he could hardly rely on for support, he could very likely end up being the scapegoat, with his entire career ruined forever.

However, he set aside these thoughts. What had to be done, had to be done, and he was only a small link in a vast administrative machinery which would grind on towards its mission, regardless of the doubts or hesitations of any individual member.

By the time he was ready, it was already 3 a.m.

2

EARLY MORNING ACTION

$\mathcal{R}$anjit stepped down from his old Jeep near the football field adjoining the railway station being blockaded by the tribal students. In the Jeep behind him was Sudarshan Rao, his police counterpart, and the commandant of the armed police contingent, who came with his company strength force in four trucks. All had switched off their lights as they neared the field. Although still very dark, the sea of makeshift tarpaulin tents was visible, under which the students— mostly boys, but also some girls—slept unaware of what was coming their way. This comprised the main body of the student protestors; there were other small groups scattered elsewhere too, but they were a lesser problem.

The police constables jumped out of the truck noiselessly. Their rifles were kept in reserve in the trucks, except for two policemen who had brought their weapons. Others had large *lathis*, or solid bamboo truncheons. Ranjit hoped that only these and not the deadly rifles would be needed today.

The commandant approached Ranjit with the regulation form that the magistrate must sign, seeking to record formally the permission granted to use force to disperse an unlawful assembly. Ranjit signed it, hoping no one would notice his nervousness, using the torchlight provided by Sudarshan.

On the form, he wrote, *'Assembly declared unlawful. Follow standard procedure to disperse by making announcement, then use minimum force if needed.'*

All this was happening at one end of the football field while the students slept on peacefully under their tents. Lulled into the belief that nothing would happen, as before, they had not even taken the precaution of placing a watch—or more probably, those on watch had also dozed off.

For the rest of his life, Ranjit would recall vividly those moments that transpired immediately after he signed the form: the sudden floodlights coming on, police banners unfurling, loudspeakers blaring, asking the assembly to disperse peacefully—nothing happening initially, a few students peeking out, a few slogans and shouts from the gradually awakening students, another request from the commandant for lathi charge, the thuds of the policemen raining lathi blows, a few cracking sounds as lathis fell on heads and backs, students fleeing pell-mell, the several-thousand-strong student contingent scattered into the countryside, running for their lives, several injured students, one with a bleeding nose helped on to a police vehicle.

It was all over in a few minutes. Ranjit and the police party made their way through the empty smashed tents to the railway station where the staff had been under siege for several weeks. A very relieved Sudarshan shook hands with the company commandant, who confirmed that the railway tracks were now clear and his company had taken positions all around and would repulse any attempt to block the station. However, no more than another lathi charge would be needed, felt the commandant, even if the students tried to regroup.

For the moment, there was nothing further to do than wait, and Ranjit hoped that the students would not attempt any new adventure and risk their lives. However, given their commitment to the cause and the hundreds of young lives already sacrificed in this agitation, he was not sure that it was all over.

The rescued stationmaster invited Ranjit and the police officers to his office for a cup of tea from the station canteen, which had started functioning already. Outside, the sun had risen, and the mist from the grounds was lifting. While they were sipping their very welcome tea, the stationmaster's phone rang. 'It's the district collector, asking for you, sir,' he said, handing over the line to Ranjit.

'Ranjit, great job!' came the DC's voice over the trunk line. 'It's better to disperse a mob with an effective lathi charge as you have done, even if there are a few minor injuries. I was worried that there could have been firing. Some extremely bad news is coming in, however, from our neighbouring district. You can hear it over the radio now.'

The stationmaster switched on his old radio set. The newsreader was reporting already the news of the morning action by the state administration all over the province. Five students had been killed in police firing, he reported, in one of the districts. The district collector had apparently tried to negotiate with the angry students but the negotiations had dragged on and the number of students had swelled immensely, some resorting to violence, following which firing had to be ordered to stop the mayhem.

On the way back home, Ranjit kept thanking his lucky stars that Sudarshan's strategy of a surprise strike had succeeded splendidly and helped avoid bloodshed in his subdivision. The few broken noses and limbs suffered by the students would heal in time. He had been very fortunate, and there would no doubt be a good mention of this in his career dossier.

But lives had been lost in the same statewide action, precious young lives. Were their deaths futile, wondered Ranjit. Sure, they had become martyrs already to the students' cause, but would their loved ones be comforted by this? In every war or conflict, it is always the young that have to sacrifice their lives while the so-called leaders work from behind the scenes. Unfortunately, dying is often the only way to bring change. He wished that there had been more understanding between the two sides, the students and the government, so that it did not come to this.

Ranjit asked himself, Were the students wrong? This was a backward province, and the students were asking for a just share of the resources being extracted by the central government, more jobs and development. But blocking railway lines and shutting down the country's economy was no solution, either. Who was right?

Returning to his bungalow, Ranjit sat down in the veranda to read the morning dispatches. His gaze moved over to the large turquoise expanse of the lake spread out in in front of him. The first group of colourful migratory Siberian ducks had arrived, floating placidly and leaving long wakes behind them on the otherwise still water. All was quiet, and the hustle and bustle of the day and its daily grind was yet to begin.

When would the unnecessary violence and turmoil that had destroyed the peace and tranquillity of this sublime land finally end, he wondered.

3

MEETING AT DISTRICT HEADQUARTERS

$\mathcal{T}$he pile of files on his desk never diminished, Ranjit noted with frustration. It was mainly land acquisition cases, and as the subdivision had one of the largest number of acquisition cases in the country owing to the hyperactivity of central government agencies to extract coal and other minerals, the onerous duties of 'collector'—usually performed by the district collectors—had been conferred on the SDO by some sadistic chief secretary in the past out to spoil the lives of young civil servants who came out to the subdivision. In earlier years, he was told by some old timers, this subdivision was considered a honeymoon posting where newly married officers were sent and left undisturbed for months by the administration.

Honeymoon indeed! Ranjit muttered to himself while putting his signature on yet another land acquisition case. The case law was complex, and decisions had to be made with great care as any excessive land acquisition award was viewed with suspicion by audit parties. When they came out to his subdivision, it was the practice to put them up in the *dak* bungalow and place half the subdivision's staff to minister to their every whim and fancy. These included, apart from the usual sumptuous meals, placing a few bottles of whiskey—seized by excise officials from tax dodgers—discreetly in their rooms at night. All departments cooperated in this effort, putting local rivalries on truce while the audit team remained.

Not that these helped. Apart from the new land acquisition cases he had to handle, there were hundreds of audit notes from the distant past that he had to find credible answers to. Each Saturday, he would make an earnest effort to dispose of all the week's accumulated files that he couldn't attend to owing to the growing law-and-order situation in the state, which took up most of his time. These would be tied up in large green cloth bundles and head-carried by his personal staff from the subdivisional court to his bungalow. And each Saturday also, most of the morning and afternoon would go by—stretching often into Sunday—till the last file was cleared. And each following Saturday, he would find an even bigger pile awaiting him. It was as though he was fighting an endless battle with an unseen *rakshas* wanting to gorge on more and more files without ever being satiated.

When his last file was done, he would look forward to his afternoon game of tennis with Sudarshan or the subdivisional judicial magistrate in the tennis court at the circuit house next to his house.

He got up looking forward to this sport, when his telephone rang. It was the district collector. 'Urgent meeting at my bungalow office at 7 p.m. to discuss the next phase of the agitation,' he said. 'Sorry for the late notice, but try to be on time. We'd like to end early.'

The district headquarters were more than fifty miles away, and they would take about two hours to reach, given the road condition. When he set out it, was nearly five, but Ali the driver was confident they would make the meeting in time. Usually, Ali didn't wear his regulation uniform when called out on the weekend, but today he was well turned out as they were going to the DC sahib's meeting.

As soon as they left the town with its cycle rickshaws, crowded bazaars, and pedestrians, the road became less cluttered, and the surrounding countryside with vast stretches of paddy fields came into view. The monsoons had arrived, and the fields were green with recently sown paddy seedlings. Occasional clumps of thatched or tin-roofed huts, with coconut palms around a pond, would mark a village settlement. The fields stretched out to the horizon on both sides reaching up to the hills, their tops covered with clouds. On the northern horizon, snow-capped mountains could also be seen sometimes. On either side of the road, the *gul-mohur* trees, some red and some yellow, were still in bloom.

After an hour's drive, they came on to the bridge over the Kenduli River, which marked the boundary of Ranjit's subdivision and the *sadar*[8] headquarters subdivision administered directly by the DC. The river which at other times was a placid stream had swollen into a wide fast-moving body of muddy water. Soon the flood warnings would be up, and the seasonal relief and rescue operations would have to begin.

There were so many different types of problems facing the state, thought Ranjit, even without the possibly unnecessary human-made aggravations that they were all plunged in. But again, if protests on development-related problems did not take place, would the huge central monolith that controlled development across the country wake up to the issues confronting the state?

He had to postpone his musings, however, which always preoccupied him on long trips such as this, as they had already arrived at the headquarters town. The DC's bungalow was in the 'civil lines' area, a term the former British rulers of India had used to indicate a part of a town where the European officials lived, in contrast to the 'native quarter'. While nearly four decades had elapsed since the British had left, this demarcation between the modern well-laid-out part of town from the original settlement remained in most small towns of India still, particularly in less-developed parts of the country.

The Bara Bungalow, as the DC's residence was called, was a double-storied wooden structure within well-manicured lawns and gardens amid a large number of *neem* and *peepul* trees. A line of cars and Jeeps were parked on the driveway already, including one carrying the insignia of the local army brigadier.

The meeting room was already full. All of DC's executive magistrates in headquarters, as well as the other outlying SDO, Vijay Gautam, Ranjit's counterpart, were there. After a little while, the DC along with the local army brigadier, the deputy inspector general of the Central Range and the superintendent of police came into the room. They had been huddled together, discussing possibly the strategy to adopt to tackle the new problem that had arisen. Along with the DC was a young lady appearing to be from north-east India, whom Ranjit had not seen before, wearing a blue *salwar kameez*. The waiting officials stood up as was the custom, before they were requested to be seated.

'Good evening, everybody, and thanks for being able to come at short notice,' began the DC. 'All of you know each other well, so there is no need for introductions. I would only like to introduce Brigadier Naveen Dar, who is the new commandant of the 19th Brigade attached to the army's 6th corps. He is here at my request, as part of the army's assistance to civil authorities in case the need arises. I hope it doesn't come to that.

'Also newly arrived in our district is Evelyn Syiem,' he said, turning to the young lady who was sitting one row behind, taking notes. 'She is the new assistant collector on training assigned to this district. Although we are all preoccupied with law and order, I hope we can show her a how a district is run well, so please give her all your support and cooperation when she comes around.'

He then turned to the main order of business. 'The student agitation has now taken a new turn,' he announced. 'After the death of the five students in police firing, an indefinite statewide *bandh* has been called by all student unions in the state – both tribal and non-tribal – beginning Monday, demanding a complete shutdown of all educational institutions and government offices, transport, and business establishments. Several government employees' and trade unions have joined the movement,' he informed the meeting. 'The protestors have announced that they will set up pickets to prevent government staff and workers from joining work. In other words, they have declared a complete shutdown of the state regardless of the consequences. The government, meanwhile, has declared the *bandh* illegal and the chief secretary has sent out instructions ordering all government offices and institutions and all essential services to function normally with help from the police and paramilitary forces.

'As a critical first step, you must all ensure that all district and subdivisional offices open regularly and the national flag is hoisted and brought down at dawn and dusk as usual without fail. The chief secretary wants a daily report of compliance from all offices,' he said. 'The Central Government is sending additional armed police contingents to the state, and by afternoon tomorrow, we will receive additional forces here which will remain in reserve. Meanwhile, call up all forces from other duties, cancel leaves, and see that picketing doesn't take place.'

The government mood seemed belligerent, and a tough no-nonsense stance was palpable. What steps the protestors were considering was not known, and Ranjit wondered whether all this was leading to a spiral of violence which would be difficult to recover from.

4

DINNER ON THE TERRACE

*B*efore ending the meeting, the DC invited all participants—as was usual—to dinner at his house. The meal was prepared by the circuit house *khansama*,[9] whose culinary accomplishments were known far and wide. He was one of the few remaining *khansamas* from the British times and had helped prepare numerous meals for the *bara sahibs* and *memsahibs* during the days of the British *raj*.

The buffet table was laid out on the large covered terrace on the first floor of the bungalow, and the participants had to climb the broad wooden stairs to reach it. All around were tall shady trees through which the well-maintained garden spread out around the bungalow could be glimpsed.

Although the cook's repertoire was known to be immense, the menu tonight was modest in keeping with the government's austerity drive, and meant to be simply a working dinner for guests, some of whom, like Ranjit had travelled from afar and would return the same night. There was cream of spinach soup to begin with, followed by an entrée consisting of grilled chicken served with lightly sautéed vegetables, an alternate baked cheese cabbage dish for vegetarians, salad and bread on the side, and ending with assorted fruits served in small delicately made fruit baskets. Alam the *khansama* personally supervised the servings and graciously accepted the compliments on his cooking from the guests with salaams.

It was the last dish—the fruit basket—which was the subject of much curiosity. Evelyn, who, as the officer responsible for hospitality and protocol, invariably the first assignment of officer trainees, had decided the menu, was busy explaining how it came about. 'I was told to organise the dinner in a hurry, but Alam rose to the occasion as usual,' she said. 'We had a little problem only with the desert, but Alam asked for an unusual ingredient for it—an eggplant!' As she learnt later, it was to serve as a base to make the caramel fruit baskets. What would have been an ordinary desert—the fruit platter—turned out to be an interesting dish instead with these little delicately made works of culinary art.

The junior officers got together over coffee. Ranjit sought news about the training academy from Evelyn. Most young officers who spent two years of training at the hill station in Mussoorie had many pleasant memories and a host of anecdotes to share, especially about their favourite horses and riding classes.

'How's Rani doing?' asked Ranjit. Rani was a particularly timid mare whom Ranjit usually picked for riding as she was easier to handle. Every morning before getting on the saddle, he would feed a little jaggery to her, and they had become fast friends.

'She's doing fine. But my favourite was Chetak,' said Evelyn. This indicated immediately to all that Evelyn was a good rider, as it was well known that this black spirited stallion was extremely frisky and difficult to handle except by the best equestrians. It came out that she had also bagged the riding trophy and the shooting and tennis ones as well. 'Wow!' exclaimed Vijay. 'You're quite the sportswoman.'

Ranjit and the others began observing Evelyn now with some interest and deference. She had short hair, was fair and taller than average Indian women, and had features common to women from India's north-eastern hill states. Although dressed in a plain *salwar kameez* and without much make-up, she was quite obviously

attractive. Not many women had so far joined the civil services—
given perceptions about its rigours—and in this province, there were
only a handful so far. Those that did had to struggle against centuries
of gender stereotyping in every aspect of their work. There were
superiors who were overprotective and didn't expose them to law-
and-order work, district staff who looked on them as an aberration
and not very comfortable working with. Most were generous in giving
gratuitous advice but not in taking instructions.

As it was getting late, the guests started leaving one by one. Only
the core district officers remained. The DC was sitting on a sofa,
sipping his favourite post-dinner liqueur and asked the others to join
in. It was past 11 p.m., and Ranjit looked at his watch.

'Bothered over Ali?' asked the DC. 'Don't worry, I have asked all
drivers to be fed well and sent to the dak bungalow to sleep. You and
Vijay must stay over, I'm afraid. I can't let you leave at this time of
night, certainly not given the current situation. You can leave early
tomorrow.

'Meanwhile, let us put the world and its affairs behind us and have
a pleasant time while we can.'

5

TOLERANCE AND INTOLERANCE

$\mathcal{T}$he DC asked his junior colleagues to help themselves to liqueur from his bar, which had a good collection of wines and spirits. The district headquarters also had an air force station and an army base, and his friends from the forces would frequently help restock his bar with foreign liquor from their ample canteen supplies. It was well known that the DC was fond of his liquor, and Ranjit had heard stories of how he would spend whole nights binge-drinking with the SP and visiting officials. But somehow, he was up and functioning as usual in the mornings. So long as he went about his work efficiently, the bosses in the state capital turned a blind eye.

No one doubted his leadership qualities. He was the most senior DC at that time, and in fact, some of his batchmates were already secretaries at state headquarters. For reasons unknown, perhaps because of his wild, unorthodox ways, he had been bypassed by junior colleagues on his district assignment. Rumour had it that the chief secretary had summoned him and asked him to complete his mandatory field assignment requirement, even if was very late, before allowing him to head a department. One of the benefits of being sent at a very late stage was that he outranked all field officers in the state and had little difficulty in handling them as most looked upon him with awe. Vijay and Ranjit were way below him in seniority and he treated them—particularly on matters not related to work—with a total lack of seriousness.

The conversation began with a discussion of the recent events. Now in a more relaxed mood and environment, the DC put forward his own take of the course the student protest was taking.

'The agitation is taking the form of extreme sub-nationalism,' he suggested. 'The demand for all resources to be retained locally, all jobs to be reserved only for locals, throwing out migrant workers from other states, and so on are not supported by our Constitution. I don't see how any agreement can be reached with such unreasonable demands being made.'

'The root problem is a lack of jobs,' said Ranjit. 'The only long-term solution is more development so that a larger space is created for all groups. I think the Centre should focus urgently on more rapid development of the state.'

The DC gradually changed from liqueur to his favourite brand of cigar. Taking a few puffs, he said, 'Development can't come about quickly, and certainly not in a climate of violence. The students must calm down and see the larger picture. But what I suspect is that it's not entirely a development issue. It also stems from a lack of understanding and toleration. And this is not confined to this state. It's becoming a general phenomenon all over our country.'

'Absolutely correct, sir,' said Vijay. 'There is no limit to regional chauvinism. How many divisions and subdivisions of our country can we make? The other day, students in my subdivision lodged a petition asking for all jobs in the new paper mill to be reserved for local workers from the subdivision. Even those outside the subdivision but from within the state are now considered outsiders!'

The additional DC, who hailed from the area and therefore could be termed local, tried to bring some levity into the discussion which was turning too serious. 'At this rate, the Siberian ducks that are arriving in our district will soon be called outsiders too,' he said. 'But our feathered migrant friends bring colour and diversity too.'

'That's exactly the point,' said Vijay, who was warming to his argument and didn't want to get distracted. 'Migration of races and people from outside our country and within it has always been part of our history and culture. We have been enriched by this experience. Tolerance has always been our creed. When did we get to be so intolerant and give up the principles of universalism of Tagore and Gandhi? Every state in India consists of populations that represent a mingling of races, cultures, languages, and religions. Then why is this feeling of "us" and "them"? If we slice the population of each state by time, every segment will have an even earlier migrant group who settled there. Who then are the true inheritors of the land?'

'If we want to divide, there are unlimited ways that divisions can be made,' said the DC. 'We can divide by rich and poor, space, time, language, dialect and subdialect, religion and divisions within the same religion, and by race—and sub-racial characteristics that are infinite. We can also divide by caste, political affiliation, and innumerable other ways. Each group can then begin to consider others as different and breed intolerance on the basis of imagined differences. Why can't we look for what is common and focus on those things that unite us rather than those divide us?'

'Let's not forget the growing intolerance concerning gender,' said Evelyn, who was sitting quietly, listening to the conversation. 'Such intolerance leaves half of our population deprived and subjugated!'

'And that we discriminate against her is clear as we have left Evelyn out of our conversation altogether,' said the additional DC, always trying to lighten the conversation but often without much success.

'Fault admitted,' said the DC, 'and gender intolerance is certainly no trivial matter. And to make amends, I am making Evelyn responsible forthwith for bringing about improvements in the working conditions of our women staff in the district offices. Evelyn, you have a year before you finish training with us, and that will be your major assignment.' This was one of the DC's old habits—anyone who brought up a problem was tasked with resolving it.

There was much mirth at this. Evelyn, being new, had yet to learn the DC's traits. Ranjit remembered how he had raised the issue of insufficient sports facilities for district staff once with the DC and was promptly made the chair of a committee to set up sports clubs in each subdivision for district staff. Of course, the DC supported each of these tasks with resources and advice.

But the issue of intolerance was nagging Ranjit. 'Since we must reach a conclusion on this subject and the district magistrate must pronounce on this issue, let me present my final arguments,' he said.

'We must ask ourselves why this country which was based on the lofty principles of universalism, secularism, and tolerance is becoming gradually an intolerant society. The answer may lie in economics, I feel. When there is enough for all, there's always peace and understanding. The population expansion, growing unemployment, the lack of jobs is creating an explosive situation. Only if we can develop fast enough to provide space for all and importantly create sufficient jobs for our youth will intolerance come to an end. When there's scarcity, there's a scramble for resources, there's hunger, there's anger, and there's violence.'

'Now that you've heard the economist, let the historian provide his take on the matter,' said Vijay. These two young SDOs were always found arguing on some esoteric topic or another, but often, there was a tone of seriousness in their supposed banter. Tonight was no exception.

'Go ahead, Mr Historian,' said the DC. 'Present your arguments to the learned court.'

'Very well, Your Honour,' began Vijay. 'Intolerance is not caused by scarcity of resources, but a scarcity of values. Whatever the bounties development may bring, history has shown time and again that human greed knows no limit. Our wants grow faster than any technology or development process can deliver. How could a Ram *rajya* exist in the ancient times when there was little development in our sense of the term? But greed and vice existed then, also creating the Kurukshetra wars of the past.

'Leaving mythologies aside, our own history tells us that there were periods of great prosperity and peace in ancient times as well as periods of war and strife,' continued Vijay. 'In my humble opinion, the truest form of development is one of the development of principles, and ethics. The goal of such a state is not prosperity but happiness.'

'I must ask two questions to both learned counsel,' interjected the DC. 'First, is it possible to achieve an ethical state in the absence of material progress? And secondly, in your learned opinion, is humanity progressing towards the ethical state, stationary or regressing?'

'I am afraid, Your Honour, I must call for a recess,' said the additional DC. 'Your humble petitioner must leave very early morning tomorrow on very important business.'

'Which is?' enquired Evelyn. Everyone else was well aware of the ADC's business.

'To watch more of our feathered friends who are arriving from Siberia!' the additional DC replied. He was an avid birdwatcher, and nothing could stop him from this Sunday morning pursuit.

This broke up the discussion. Ranjit noted that it was well past midnight.

6

THE ANCIENT URN

*W*hen Ranjit woke up in his room at the circuit house, it was a little past sunrise. He called for his cup of morning tea and opened his window to look out at the garden. It had been turning cool in the night, and the lawn was glistening with dewdrops touched by the early morning sunlight. In the middle of the lawn around the flagstaff was a rose garden without many roses, however. He noticed that the flag had already been hoisted.

The turbaned bearer brought tea in a shining stainless-steel teapot on a tray covered with a spotless white tray cover. In a separate plate were two biscuits. Noting Ranjit's obvious appreciation at the vast improvement in the service—the turban, the tray cover, the shining teapot—compared to his previous visits, the bearer said, 'Sir, it's on orders of the new assistant collector madam. She has tightened things up a lot since she came here.'

That explained it, thought Ranjit. Evelyn had taken charge of the circuit house and insisting on running it by the rule book. As in most districts, the trainee AC was billeted in the circuit house for the whole year and was usually given charge of its upkeep. In his own case, he did not pay much attention to the circuit house in the subdivision with so many things on his hands. He made a mental note to attend to it when he went back. There were so many things one had to look after, including the garden, which was now overgrown with weeds.

Obviously, the garden here was being well tended. The gardener—also wearing his khaki uniform—came into view and started hoeing the soil in the rose garden. Soon after, he noted that Evelyn had also turned up and was no doubt coercing the gardener to produce more roses. She was in a tracksuit and probably returning from her morning walk. He had no doubt that like the entire circuit house staff, even the rose garden would start blooming soon on the new AC madam's orders!

Ranjit realised that the whole district establishment was already up and he was in danger of missing breakfast. On calling the reception, he was told that although the timings had been advanced an hour, on Sundays, breakfast would still be served till 9 a.m. That gave him sufficient time to get ready.

At the dining room, Vijay was still lingering over his coffee and reading the morning newspaper. They decided to leave at the same time and, since a part of the journey was common up to a forest inspection bungalow about forty miles away, to travel together till that point and part ways thereafter.

Ranjit ordered his breakfast. The usual fare was cornflakes with warm milk, a choice of how the egg was to be made, toast with butter and jam, and papayas and bananas on the side. This was the standard 'English' breakfast menu possibly served in all circuit houses across the country since the British *raj*. Vegetarians could have vegetable cutlets as an alternative. Some circuit houses, however, had started serving *puris* and *subjees*, but this was still considered somewhat heretical in these parts.

Ranjit's egg order was well known, and it soon arrived—scrambled egg on toast. He noted that the paper napkins had been replaced with regular serviettes and mentioned this to Vijay. 'Ask the magician yourself,' said Vijay, turning in the direction of Evelyn, who had just come in for breakfast.

'Can I join you?' asked Evelyn, sitting down at their table. She had washed her hair, and it was still wet. A fragrance of an exotic perfume wafted over from her. When asked about how she managed to bring in the transformation in the circuit house, she had a simple explanation. 'Just followed the manual,' she said. 'Serviettes, for example, are part of the standard inventory, and *dhobis* are on the rolls. I had to merely ask the DC for supplying the full inventory. It helped a lot, of course, that the governor is paying us a visit and will be staying here for a night. The DC was able to get an increase in his admin budget from headquarters because of this and wants to put up a good show.'

'Aha!' said Vijay. 'So the real trick is to invite the governor to visit.' That matter settled, they turned to Evelyn's training schedule. It transpired that the DC had drawn up a yearlong series of attachments for her, and for training in land acquisition, she would be visiting Ranjit's subdivision for a month. She would have another month with Vijay on other aspects of revenue administration.

It was soon time to leave. They settled their bills, and Ranjit noted with satisfaction that the charge was well within his daily allowance. He often marvelled at how this happened—regardless of what he had eaten and however many meals he had had, the circuit house bill never exceeded his DA. Some guardian angel at DC's office was obviously whispering to the caretaker to see that this was taken care of.

Ranjit got into Vijay's Jeep, who decided to take the wheel himself while his driver took the rear seat. Ranjit's Jeep followed, driven by Ali.

The common route that would allow Ranjit and Vijay to enjoy each other's company a little longer involved taking a different route from the one Ranjit had used coming to district headquarters. It took a somewhat northerly direction towards the hills and meant a dozen or so miles more for Ranjit, but there was so much to discuss that he was glad to make the detour. They had decided to have lunch at the forest inspection bungalow, which was in a picturesque place within the forest, next to a stream. Vijay had called up the caretaker to make arrangements.

After a little while, the road started skirting the stream leading to the forest and their destination. It also began climbing a little. Little by little, the cultivated land gave way to trees and shrubs, and before long, they were already in a forest. The inspection bungalow was on a hilltop, and the road had to take a number of sharp twists and turns to reach the summit.

Turning towards the final ascent leading to the inspection bungalow's driveway, they discovered that they had company. The additional DC's car was there along with that of the district forest officer, better known as the DFO. In fact, there seemed to be some sort of a commotion on the front porch, with a number of villagers talking animatedly with the two sahibs.

Vijay parked his Jeep, and the two of them went up to the additional DC, who had apparently arrived quite early at the IB. This was one of his favourite birdwatching spots, and he had been able to identify quite a few species he hadn't photographed earlier. But the additional DC's birdwatching was somewhat rudely interrupted a little while back when the DFO had arrived with a set of excited local villagers led by the village headman.

The object of the commotion was an old earthenware urn. Apparently, a forest villager had found it while digging near his hut. It was now sitting on a table surrounded by the villagers, and the DFO was not allowing anyone to come near it. 'It seems to be an ancient cremation urn,' said the DFO. 'We found some remains of bones and some ancient jewellery.'

'Be very careful,' he told Vijay, who wanted to inspect it. 'The contents could crumble on touch.'

Vijay was a history student and had some knowledge of these things. 'If it has survived so long, it will a little longer,' he said. He carefully opened the lid, and both Ranjit and he had a peek inside. The contents were ash grey and had solidified. Some small bone fragments seemed to be sticking about here and there. But what was most remarkable was that it contained a necklace which appeared to be of gold and some precious gems.

'The villager claimed the urn as it was found on his property,' said the DFO. 'But the village headman retrieved it from him and sent word to me. As the whole village falls in a government reserve, they do not have rights over it.'

'Well, they may have some traditional rights,' said the additional DC, 'but we can determine the ownership later. It's more important that we take steps to preserve this urn and find out more about it.'

Vijay interjected at this point. 'It looks like a royal cremation urn,' he said. 'The ancients used to bury the ashes of royalty along with some of the deceased royal's favourite personal belongings. The necklace is an invaluable find. Let's send this urn to the Archaeological Survey of India to carbon date the contents and try and discover whose ashes these are.'

Vijay's suggestion was accepted, and the additional DC explained to the anxious villager and the headman that their rights as finders of the urn would be investigated according to law and duly compensated by the government. He made the DFO prepare a receipt, stamp it from the IB office, and handed it over to the villager. The villagers departed not yet fully satisfied despite the reassurance from the district authorities that proper care of their valuable find would be taken and the discoverer rewarded.

The caretaker announced that lunch was ready, and the party retreated to the small dining room. The lunch was a simple fare of chicken curry with *chapatis*, which Ranjit and the others ate with gusto. The discussion on the urn continued uninterrupted.

'I have often been told that there used to be an ancient monastery in these parts which appears to have been destroyed by an earthquake sometime in the past. It's possible that the urn belonged to a cremation ground for the monks. But why a monk would have his remains in a royal-looking urn with a very valuable piece of jewellery in it beats me,' said the additional DC.

'Of course, it's a mystery which would be interesting to get to the bottom of,' said Vijay. 'But it's possible that this was no ordinary monk, but a royal personage who became a monk and was therefore cremated according to his position.'

The ADC had the urn wrapped in newspaper and secured with strings. 'I'll have it sent to the Archaeological Survey tomorrow,' he said, waving and driving off. His car disappeared soon after taking a sharp bend while descending.

A mist was rising gradually, its swirling fingers slowly covering the trees. It was time to leave.

7

PREPARATIONS

*W*hen Ranjit returned to the subdivision, the entire set of officials—most ex-officio executive magistrates—along with Sudarshan the SDPO were waiting for him at the circuit house for urgent discussions on arrangements to counter the student agitation starting the next day.

He briefed them about the latest announced phase of agitation involving picketing of government offices to paralyse government functioning. He also informed them of the government's determination to counter their designs. Many of them were already aware from newspapers or radio.

A number of steps had to be taken. Ranjit issued orders prohibiting gatherings within the town and near government offices. He assigned territorial responsibility to all executive magistrates to enforce these orders along with police forces. He instructed the government publicity team to inform all government staff to attend offices without fail or suffer a pay cut.

'I suggest we take pre-emptive action to prevent any gathering taking place,' said Sudarshan, who had become an expert on early action. 'So we start early at 6 a.m. tomorrow and disperse any students trying to gather.'

'Good idea!' agreed Ranjit. 'Please send regular reports of any untoward incident to our control room,' he said, turning to his officers. 'We will rush more police forces if you need help. Please remember, use as little force as you can.

'Most importantly, provide all help to heads of offices to attend. All flags, at the very least, must fly from all government offices here.'

These instructions were routine but necessary. Ranjit liked Sudarshan's idea of early action. It could work, he thought, given the reputation that they had established, and prevent any bloodshed.

On reaching his bungalow, he found that his orderly had already prepared his dinner. He decided to call it an early night as it would be a long day tomorrow.

8

CUPS OF TEA AND WAITING

$\mathcal{I}$n fact, the next day went off better than Ranjit had expected. Well before sunrise, all of Ranjit's designated executive magistrates were in place in the town as well as in the outskirts along with police contingents. Ranjit and Sudarshan went around inspecting their preparedness. With all the hustle and bustle of the administration's *bandobast*[10] evident since early morning, and with Jeeps and trucks loaded with armed policemen whizzing about, the students were hesitant to group. A few students tried to gather near the veterinary office, which was located in the outskirts of the town but were soon shooed away.

After going around the town, their final stop was at the *sadar* police station where the control room was set up. The sentries on duty presented arms. The officer in charge of the police station and his deputy saluted the duo smartly. The OC briefed them on the latest reports. It seemed that the situation was completely peaceful so far and no untoward incidents had taken place. On his part, the OC had hauled in all the usual known 'bad characters' as a precautionary measure. These small-time thugs, pickpockets, and snatchers were languishing in the lock-up—some sitting on the bench and some sleeping on the ground. They had all come to expect this usual harassment that took place before any program of agitation was announced and had reconciled themselves to becoming the police *thana*'s guests for the day, knowing that they would be released before sundown. Many of them were police informers.

Without being asked, two cups of tea appeared for Sudarshan and Ranjit. It was made in the usual style—steaming hot syrupy sweet with strong tea liquor and milk. To Ranjit, it was most welcome after the build-up of tension and a wonderful relaxant. All in all, the students' picketing program turned out to be an anticlimax. All government offices were able to hoist the national flag without any hindrance. Attendance at the offices was, however, thin or, in some cases, non-existent, with most staff not turning up, being afraid of trouble.

The OC called up all the police stations in the subdivision one by one. Reports were also coming in over the police wireless system from Ranjit's *tehsil*[11] officers. There was nothing much to report from anywhere. Ranjit decided to make a symbolic visit to his own office.

In Ranjit's office apart from the officers not assigned law-and-order duties, the head clerk, the *nazir*[12], and a few of the senior clerical staff were also present. There was little work transacted, obviously, with the general public and the usual throng of petitioners staying away. The staff hung about, discussing the political situation and sipping endless cups of tea from the canteen. Somehow, the canteen always functioned in government establishments whether other public work was transacted or not. There was always the blackened tea kettle being carried about by Raju the ubiquitous tea boy and tea served along with hot samosas—the basic minimum any government office canteen was expected to produce, whatever be the circumstances.

Ranjit sat down at his desk and drafted a message to the chief secretary as required, informing him that all the subdivision's offices were open, the national flags flown, all officers present but with less than 10 per cent clerical staff in attendance, and there were no law-and-order incidents to report. As the office messengers were playing truant, he stamped and sealed the draft personally, and gave it to Ali his driver to take to the police wireless office and ensure that it was dispatched immediately.

The few officials present in the subdivisional officer's court gathered together in Ranjit's office room. This was a small, somewhat informal room next to the formal courtroom where mostly land-related cases were taken up. With the separation of the judiciary from the executive branches of the government, the main magisterial functions performed by the executive magistrates—as they were called—were few and related only to the maintenance of law and order. The bulk of the judicial functions were now performed by the subdivisional judicial magistrate from a separate establishment. The SDO's main remaining judicial work related to land revenue administration involving civil disputes. Ranjit had entrusted the routine land revenue matters to Sunder Mohan Biswas, his senior executive magistrate, who also acted as his second in command. Biswas was a veritable institution in the SDO's office who was now nearing retirement. He liked the pomp and show associated with court work, and Ranjit was glad to delegate this entire load of revenue matters to him. Hence, he hardly ever used the courtroom except when a particularly complicated issue came up, and spent most of his time meeting people in his informal office which had become the de facto SDO's office.

With no work to be transacted, the officials sat around gossiping, sipping tea, and discussing various bits of information. In course of time, the head clerk, dressed as usual in his spotlessly clean dhoti and kurta, came around with the dak[13]—the official memos, letters and telegrams, and public petitions—received on Saturday. He had carefully stamped and initialed them and docketed them in the official ledger, a task he had been doing assiduously since he became head clerk, which was long before Ranjit had arrived as the SDO.

'How did you manage to come to work, Chowdhury?' asked Ranjit, knowing that the head clerk lived in a village quite some distance away from the town and eager to know if some public transportation was working.

'Sir, I took no chances and stayed last night in town with my sister whose husband works in the Public Works Department. The bus that comes from my village hasn't yet arrived and may not today.'

Though he didn't show it, Ranjit was very grateful for the diligence shown by the head clerk and thought of some way to reward him. Unfortunately, government salaries were woefully low and that of clerical staff lower still. Yet many such staff—particularly those belonging to the older school—performed their duties with unusual sincerity purely because of the social status that a government job conferred. This was an important consideration, particularly in rural societies from where they came. Many detractors would sometimes sarcastically remark, however, that the 'diligence' shown by such staff was not to their public service but the opportunities for 'additional income' that dealing with the public presented. However, Ranjit felt that this wasn't always the case, and there were shining examples such as Head Clerk Chowdhury.

'By the way, sir,' said Chowdhury, handing Ranjit a wireless form marked URGENT, 'I thought you should see this, which has just arrived from the police station.' The wireless message read:

FROM: CHIEFSECY
TO: SUBDIVISIONAL OFFICER RANJIT GUPTA
COPY: SECY TO GOVERNOR/ COMMISSIONER
          CENTRAL DIV/ DISTCOLL NILGHAT/ SUPDT
          POLICE NILGHAT

= HON'BLE GOVERNOR ARRIVING YOUR SUBDIVISION WEDNESDAY 20TH OCT FOR DEVELOPMENT MEETING WITH TRIBAL STUDENT FEDERATION AND POLITICAL LEADERS ON THURSDAY 21ST AFTER CONCLUDING MEETINGS AT DISTRICT HEADQUARTERS STOP DETAILED PROGRAMME FOLLOWS STOP PLEASE MAKE ALL NECY ARRANGEMENTS FOR MEETING AND GOVERNOR'S STAY=

9

PREPARATIONS FOR VIP VISIT

$\mathcal{I}$t was evening when Ranjit received the call he was expecting from the DC about the governor's visit. He was sitting outside on his veranda that overlooked the lake at his bungalow. Sundar his orderly had just given him his small peg of rum, and he was sipping it and munching the hors d'oeuvres Sundar had concocted, consisting of peanuts seasoned with onions and lime juice. The fireflies were flickering quite brightly in the dark and the crickets outside had set up such a loud racket that it was after the phone in his office had rung several times that he finally heard it.

The DC helped solve the puzzle as to why the governor had suddenly decided to add his subdivision to his itinerary instead of returning after his meetings at district headquarters. Ever since the government had collapsed and the state brought under president's rule, it was now directly administered by the Central Government through the governor. It had become the governor's practice to hold development coordination meetings with all the state's district collectors to sort out issues facing major development programs. The meeting at Nilghat was intended for this purpose.

'That was the stated objective for the consumption of the press,' said the DC, 'but the real reason was to quietly meet with the office bearers of the state tribal students' union and the tribal leaders, most of whom come from your subdivision. Therefore, keep it as low-key as possible. The line to any inquisitive reporters is that the governor wants to discuss the special development issues concerning tribals and that is the only agenda.'

Quiet talks on development indeed, mused Ranjit. It was crystal clear for all to see that the governor, as the Central Government's interlocutor on discussions with the students, was trying to divide them on tribal and non-tribal lines. This must have been the brainwave of some disingenuous joint secretary in New Delhi, a supposed expert who understood very little of what was really happening on the ground. The move—the standard one which the British had employed for two centuries to divide and rule over India—would be hugely unpopular and help in further solidifying the student movement rather than weakening it.

Although the two weeks left to prepare for the governor's visit appeared too little to spruce up the subdivision, Ranjit was truly surprised at the speed the creaking government machinery could achieve if it needed to. It helped that the students had temporarily suspended their agitation to allow for negotiations with the government to proceed. This allowed the government departments to resume their normal work.

While for a year, Ranjit had been pleading with the Public Works Department to paint and repair the decrepit circuit house, which had been neglected for years, all of a sudden, he found the entire engineering department working round the clock re-plastering and repainting the modest structure. It consisted of two large guest suites and a somewhat spacious dining space which could also be used for fairly large meetings, apart from a kitchen and pantry, and large verandas at the front and back. There was a porch in front with tall columns. Surrounding the structure were large grounds now overgrown with shrubs, almost a jungle, a garden in front and a tennis court at the side.

Looking out from his veranda one morning a few days later, he found that the building had taken on an entirely new appearance. The walls were white and sparkling, and the freshly painted green roof looked new. The floors, which were of red patent stone, had been polished. The window frames and doors had been re-varnished. There was a truck depositing red *morrum*[14] gravel to spread on the long driveway and the tennis court. The bamboo fencing had also been given a fresh coat of dark-green paint.

On his part, Ranjit obtained more money for furnishings by calling up the additional DC. This was sanctioned instantaneously, and he used it for laying new carpets, buying new cane sets, and replacing the worn-out curtains. He also called up the forest department and got them to send an army of gardeners to restore the limp and dying lawn and weed-infested garden. He was determined to give the district circuit house and Evelyn some competition.

A couple of days before the governor's visit, the colonial-era structure had been fully restored to its old glory. The additional DC who came on the Sunday preceding the governor's visit (along with his birdwatching binoculars), to see the end result, seemed genuinely impressed with the transformation. 'This can host even the president!' he said.

'Not a bad idea,' said Ranjit. 'Now that we have president's rule, we can invite him for a visit too!'

They were sitting on the circuit house veranda and discussing the details of the visit. Asaram, the sole cook cum bearer of the circuit house served tea to them in the new crockery that Ranjit had ordered, wearing his new uniform.

The invitations to the tribal students had been sent, and most had confirmed. Additional chairs for the dining room, which was now a full-fledged conference hall, had been purchased. Security arrangements had been completed, and the security convoy coming from district headquarters along with the governor would remain and return with him. The governor would be provided with a guard of honour and a gun salute and the police contingent for this, and a bugle detachment would arrive a day before the visit. A new flag had been purchased and would be unfurled at dawn each morning and lowered at dusk punctually.

The final item on the checklist was selecting the menu for the governor's meals. Ranjit pulled out the wireless instructions from the governor's secretariat. 'No restrictions,' it stated blandly but both of them knew that bad meals could ruin a visit and good ones add many brownie points informally for the district and subdivision. They had found out that the governor, who belonged to the old Indian Civil Service cadre set up under British rule, was a *pukka*[15] brown sahib as far as his meal preferences were concerned. Now it was up to Asaram to deliver.

'Asaram, are you confident, or shall we ask Alam to come over?' asked the additional DC.

'Sahib, there is really no need,' said Asaram, appearing to take offence. 'I will cook *pukka* English *khana*[16] for you tonight, and you will see for yourself whether Asaram or Alam is better.'

They both laughed at this, but they knew very well that a lot rested on Asaram to turn the visit into a success.

10

THE INCIDENT AT GOLMUNDA

$\mathcal{T}$he governor's convoy left Nilghat, bound for Ranjit's subdivision after the day's long development meeting with its very full agenda had ended. The governor was accompanied by the DC and the governor's personal security officer. There was a police pilot Jeep in front and behind the governor's car the convoy consisted of the DC's car, which had the DC's security officer and his private secretary, the SP's car, in which the governor's secretary was also travelling, and an armoured vehicle with armed policemen at the rear.

Evelyn, whose training attachment with Ranjit was to begin once the governor had left, and who was to help provide support for the governor's meeting on tribal development (another of her training assignments), left a couple of minutes later in her car. She had to finish packing, which was taking longer than usual as she had to be away for a month, which delayed her departure a little. She was about a couple of miles behind but was making good progress and rapidly reducing the distance to the governor's convoy, which naturally couldn't travel as fast as a single car, needing to keep tightly together for security reasons.

The distance to the subdivisional town could usually be covered in about two hours, and the DC had suggested that the governor reach his destination well before dusk set in. Also, the usual welcome dinner with the officials and the town's principal citizenry had been scheduled, and there had to be time to freshen up before that. However, with the festival of Diwali round the corner, the roads were more crowded than usual with families going back to their villages, with buses packed and other vehicles such as small trucks and Tempo vans also pressed into service. This slowed down the convoy quite a bit.

Despite the delay, Evelyn managed to leave Nilghat before sunset. There was a good hour and a half before nightfall set in. This was her first trip to Ranjit's subdivision, but the driver was an old district hand and very familiar with the roads and towns. He managed to clear Nilghat town quite quickly although the roads were crowded with shoppers buying all sorts of trinkets and gifts from the roadside stalls, some of which mushroomed seasonally with the festivals. A few crackers were going off occasionally, startling the shoppers as some impatient children could not wait for Diwali to use their stocks. Once they hit the national highway connecting the two towns, the going was much faster.

The Kenduli River, which demarcated the subdivision's boundary, soon came into view. After crossing the bridge, one passed the town of Golmunda, which had a police outpost and was also a *tehsil* headquarters. The OC's Jeep was parked outside. A number of policemen who had been assigned traffic duties in the town which was a little distance away were returning to the outpost after seeing off the governor's convoy.

Golmuda was a small town with just a few houses and shops along the national highway, a small temple, and a high school. Small neat bungalows of the *tehsildar*,[17] the OC of the police station, and other government officials completed the town's collection of buildings. Evelyn's car had just crossed the town when she saw a small crowd by the side of the road. A solitary policeman was among the onlookers. Evelyn asked the driver to stop and find out what was happening.

The driver came back somewhat excited. 'Madam, you should have a look!' he said. 'Someone seems to have just been killed.'

Evelyn got out of the car, and the crowd made way for her to take a look. A man's body was lying face down in a pool of blood in the gravel skirting the road. Half his face was blown away, and there were severe injury marks all over his body as though a bomb with numerous splinters had been thrown at him.

The policeman at the site explained that just after the governor's convoy had cleared the town and he was about to go back to the outpost, there was a loud blast, and some people came rushing to him, saying that a man had been killed.

Evelyn guessed at once that there had to be some connection with this killing and the governor's convoy. The SP had to be informed immediately. She asked the policeman to stay and instructed her driver to head back immediately to the Golmunda police outpost. On reaching it, she found the OC preparing to go home, about to get on his Jeep. On seeing her car drive in, he stopped. Evelyn quickly narrated the incident to the OC and suggested that he contact the SP at once before going back to the spot where the dead man lay to investigate.

The OC went to the wireless room, and after a while, came back saying that the SP wanted to speak to her and that she should step inside the radio officer's room. The wireless officer gave Evelyn a set of headphones. She could hear the SP faintly over the crackle of the radio. The SP was using the mobile radio set in his car and was hardly audible.

'Evelyn, what's this I hear?' asked the SP. 'Are you sure this was a bomb blast, or was the man killed in a road accident?'

'No question that this was a blast, sir,' said Evelyn. 'Didn't you or anyone in the convoy hear it?'

'Well, I didn't, but we'll have to ask the others when we get to town. But wait a bit,' he said, pausing. 'I did hear a loud sound quite a bit behind us and didn't bother as I thought it was a cracker. That could have been the bomb!'

The SP rang off hurriedly, thanking Evelyn for alerting him. 'I'll put the pilot and the security staff on high alert at once. We are about to reach town soon. Meanwhile, I'll ask OC Dutt to get to the bottom of this.'

The OC left immediately for the blast site, and Evelyn followed in her car. At the spot of the incident, the crowd had swollen. The OC got off and went near the body. When Evelyn came up, he was looking carefully at the corpse's right hand. Half the hand was missing, and the entire body was blackened.

'From the look of things, it's clear that this was a would-be assassin. He was killed by the grenade he was carrying and that probably went off before he could lob it. There is no doubt in my mind that the target was the governor.'

11

THE BEGINNING
OF EXTREMISM

*T*he development discussions with the governor passed off well as far as the logistics were concerned. Asaram's culinary skills appeared to have met with the governor's approval, and Ranjit learnt that His Excellency had partaken heartily of the five-course dinner (soup, salad, roast mutton, grilled vegetables, and custard pudding) that Asaram had prepared the night before the talks, as well as of the more modest working lunch with the tribal delegation. He also seemed to appreciate the *bandobast* with honour guard and gun salute that Sudarshan, the subdivisional police officer, had organised.

While the talks were going on, OC Dutt of Golmunda PS quickly investigated the matter of the grenade attack. Further discussions with the personal security officer of the governor revealed that he had heard a sound that appeared to be a stone hitting the hub of the left rear wheel of the governor's car. He hadn't thought much of it as several sections of the highway were being repaired and loose stones and gravel sometimes struck cars, making similar noises. A search of the road near the incident by a contingent of policemen led to the discovery, however, of an unexploded grenade lying buried in the soft clay of the roadside ditch near where the stone was heard hitting the governor's car.

It was clear therefore that the failed assassin had come prepared with two grenades. He had lobbed the first one at the governor's car, but luckily, it failed to explode. The pin of the second was then taken out, but it had exploded in the assassin's hand. Obviously, it was an amateurish handling of ordnance by a first-time user that saved the governor's life. It was also very apparent that this person wasn't acting alone. The grenades were from army stock that was being increasingly used in domestic anti-insurgency operations. There had to be a ring involved in the procurement, supply, training, and what now appeared to be meticulous planning of the attack.

The remaining visage of the dead man indicated that he was of tribal descent. Although this alone was not enough to suggest that there was necessarily a tribal connection to the attack, Ranjit felt certain that the students' agitation overall had now taken an extremist turn. This was bound to happen sooner or later if the main body of the agitation failed to obtain the necessary concessions they were seeking from the government. The attempt by the Central Government to woo the tribals away from the agitation also appeared to be a flop. The governor's offer of more development of the tribal areas appeared to have come far too late. The districts with high tribal populations had continued to be neglected following independence. The tribal delegation cited statistics showing how the tribal population had been left behind in all areas of development such as schooling, health care, roads, electricity, communications, and ultimately, jobs.

'I am the only college graduate in this delegation, Your Excellency,' said the leader of the delegation, breaking off the discussions. 'Our people live with the hope that at least our children will live a life of dignity that we haven't lived. Unfortunately, we see no such hope right now. What we have been offered instead are just the same empty promises that government after government has made in the past but never fulfilled.'

Ranjit couldn't help glancing at Evelyn when the tribal leader was making his observations. Although from a different part of the country, Evelyn was of Khasi descent, a hill tribe in India's far-off north-east. No doubt this was striking a sympathetic chord with her. However, she betrayed no emotion and kept taking notes assiduously.

Evelyn's quick reaction to the failed attack on the convoy had enabled the SP to make a hurried change in the route and take a detour while coming into town. There could have been other assassins lurking on the way, waiting to attack, and no one could take any chances. The diversion they had taken was slightly longer, but it went through less-crowded areas.

The district bosses decided to wait till some definitive news of the investigation was available before informing the governor. The DC did so after the tribal delegation had left and sought the governor's permission to contact the air force to arrange for a helicopter as the road route back to the state capital could be hazardous under the changed security circumstances.

Ranjit spoke to the air force civil liaison officer, Squadron Leader Mukherjee, about an hour after he had sent a written wireless message to him. He was surprised at the quick response, but considering that the state governor was to travel, the air force bureaucracy had been double quick—not their usual hemming and hawing over parting with their prized assets for civilians. The fact that the governor played golf with the chief of the Central Air Command at the air force golf greens might have also been a factor, but this Ranjit was not aware of.

Luckily for all, the time of day and the weather were within the safe flying parameters, and the helicopter arrived with a loud whirring of its rotors at the circuit house tennis court, which also doubled as a makeshift helipad in times of emergency. The rotors slowly came to a stop, and the pilot opened the main cabin door, jumped out, and saluted the governor smartly. The DC wished the governor a safe flight, and the governor, his ADC, and his secretary went in. The door was closed, and the helicopter took off with its powerful main and tail rotors creating a mini dust storm and, rising rapidly, soon disappeared from sight.

Ranjit and Evelyn saw the DC off at the front porch. Ranjit could hear the DC's personal security officer speaking over the wireless set to alert police stations on the way that Delta Charlie—the DC's code name—was on way back to district headquarters. Suddenly, the security atmosphere in the state appeared to have changed, and the good old days of worry-free travel were over.

The DC himself seemed to have been affected by the incident at Golmunda. 'I have asked the SP to assign personal security officers to both you and Evelyn,' he said, getting into his car. 'Take good care!' And then he was off, with the flashing red beacon of his car disappearing quickly among the town's motley traffic.

12

FIRST DAY OF TRAINING

$\mathcal{E}$velyn went for an early morning walk around the big lake that fronted the circuit house where she was billeted. The lake was rectangular in shape and was dug many centuries back by the local raja. Apart from the circuit house, it had the SDO's house at one corner and SDPO Sudarshan's house diagonally across at the other corner. The third corner was occupied by the bungalow of the other important local dignitary that completed the triumvirate, namely the subdivisional judicial magistrate. Occupying almost the entire east side was the jail. Evelyn felt that this was a travesty in architectural planning in that a dismal and forbidding edifice with tall grey walls should have been built on the side of such a serene and pretty lake and in the midst of the residential area. However, this might have been a deliberate policy of the long-departed *Raj*[18] to remind the natives to keep the peace, or else. A girls' college and a large Shiva temple fronted half of the lower west side, the other half being occupied by the SDO's courts, beside which was the SDO's residence occupying a large corner.

Passing by Ranjit's house, Evelyn noticed that it had also benefited from the governor's visit. Apart from a fresh coat of paint, it had been newly thatched with freshly cut golden-coloured hay. The colonials had obviously wanted to create a residence to remind them in this very distant place of their pretty country cottages back home on which this was fashioned. There were two medieval Indian cannons fronting the entrance, and several different varieties of flowering bougainvillea creepers had crept up the sides untidily. Large trees occupied the compound, and there was a badly tended garden and lawn in front and a large disorganised vegetable patch on the side, on which maize and various other vegetables were growing. Evelyn surmised that the government-salaried gardener was more interested in growing vegetables than tending a garden, and the young—usually bachelor—SDOs busy with their work had neither the time nor inclination to supervise him.

This morning, her first day of training, Evelyn was to report to the SDO's office as soon as it opened at 9 a.m. and would be attending Senior Executive Magistrate Biswas's court as he heard a few land-related cases—to familiarise herself with the local laws and procedures. In the afternoon, she would accompany Biswas to an acquisition site nearby where actual surveys and measurements were being made.

This was a pretty boring exercise, but this part of the training was essential, she realised, given the importance of land acquisition in the state. The mining companies were expanding their operations rapidly, and the state government's land acquisition officials were always under pressure to work quickly to clear their cases. One had to have all the laws and regulations at one's fingertips not to fall foul of accusations that one or other party was being unduly favoured. Ranjit had reminded Evelyn that one of his predecessors had in fact been accused of favouring a mining company and was now under suspension, fighting a battle for many years to clear his name.

As the final case of the morning was being heard, the monotonous drone of the lawyers' arguments about bylaws and precedents made

Evelyn almost doze off. She was glad, therefore, when a peon brought a note from Ranjit asking her to see him in his office.

The peon made way for Evelyn to pass through the crowd of petitioners waiting to see the SDO. Inside his tiny room, Ranjit was sitting at his table with a large stack of papers in his in-tray and hardly anything in the 'out'. Sitting across him was a smart young lady in a lawyer's black gown and white collar.

'Meet Advocate Susheela Gautam,' said Ranjit, introducing Evelyn to the lady. 'She is representing a large number of tribal peasants affected by a recent notice of land acquisition issued by us.'

He handed over a petition on stamp paper signed by a large number of people, some with thumb impressions. 'Take a look at this,' he said. 'The petitioners have asked for cancellation of the proceedings started by us on behalf of the National Mining Corporation. If you are going on a field visit this afternoon, I suggest you meet these people and hear them out. Advocate Gautam can meet you at the site with some of their representatives.'

Biswas came over to the circuit house after Evelyn had had a light lunch, and they set off together in Evelyn's official white Ambassador car provided by the DC. The armed personal security officer newly assigned by the SP sat on the front seat next to the driver. The acquisition site was about an hour away towards the mountains where the National Mining Corporation had already acquired hundreds of hectares of land for its operations, displacing a large number of families of cultivators.

Biswas explained that although the law allowed for compensation, the cultivating families really got very little as the Land Acquisition Act did not lead to a fair deal for displaced families. It did not require, for instance, that the state provide alternative land for cultivation. Thus, poor peasants losing land effectively lost their livelihoods as well since they didn't know how to invest their compensation money or possess skills to look for other non-farming jobs. The policy required that enterprises acquiring land provide jobs to at least one member of a displaced household. But this was rarely implemented or monitored. The law was thus harsh on the poorest.

It would take many decades far into the future before the law would finally be changed, but meanwhile, it continued its oppressive course and helped spread despair and discontent.

13

THE FIELD VISIT

$\mathcal{A}$s they neared the mining site, Evelyn noticed that the topography of the countryside kept changing fast. The flat, well-irrigated lands were slowly giving way to more rugged and hilly terrain. The road began passing through patches of forests, and they went by small settlements consisting of mud and thatched huts. After a while, the paved road gave way to gravel. The vestiges of civilisation started departing one by one. After the road, it was the turn of the electricity lines, and then the primary schools and health centres. After a while, Evelyn couldn't find a single brick structure anywhere. No regular cultivation was visible any more. How did the tribal folk living here subsist, wondered Evelyn.

Presently, they came across a large clearing where the National Mining Corporation was engaged in quarrying. Parts of the surrounding hillocks had been levelled and deep cuts and gashes made on others by the giant claws of the mammoth mining machines moving slowly on caterpillar tracks. The field office of the company consisted of a set of barrack-like structures that stood at the far end of the clearing beside the road. When Evelyn's car drove up to the office, she noticed that Advocate Susheela was already there and talking with an obviously agitated crowd of people whom Evelyn assumed were the peasant folk being dispossessed of their land.

Biswas and Evelyn walked up to the group. The local *Patwari*, the keeper of village land records in the *tehsil*, had been alerted by Advocate Susheela and was also present. He was a young man possibly on his first job, and had arrived on the scene on his bicycle and was ready with the revenue maps and land records of the village.

'I've heard that the tribals are planning a demonstration, sir,' Evelyn overheard him whispering to Biswas. 'I suggest we make our meeting short and leave before it gets nasty.'

Biswas turned to Evelyn with this intelligence. However, Evelyn, fresh from training at the Academy and drilled with ideas of responsive government, was not willing to cut short her critical field visit. 'Let's hear them out and report back to Ranjit,' she replied. 'After all, we've come to listen and help them.'

At Evelyn's suggestion, Susheela requested the village headman to take them to the nearby village where land had been notified for acquisition. This required a climb led by the headman through a meandering village path up the hillside and through thick vegetation, mostly scrub and degraded forests. The whole group of villagers followed in single file. The group began swelling with curious villagers joining them. Soon, a young man who stood out from the group, wearing glasses and in a khaki outfit, also joined the group. The party had to stop for a short while to allow a long snake which had come on their path to slither away.

In a short while, they reached the village. The headman took them to his hut and brought out an old worn-out mat and laid it out for the visitors. After the group had settled down, he explained the whole issue at length. It transpired that the government was planning to acquire the entire village along with some of the contiguous area for the mining project. The villagers all made a living by collecting and selling forest produce and growing maize and vegetables through the old traditional practice of shifting cultivation, which consisted of slashing and burning the degraded forests, cultivating on the cleared land, and moving on to other areas while the previously cultivated land remained fallow and recovered its fertility.

'What can we do if we lose our traditional work? How will we feed our families?' asked the headman.

He was very rudely interrupted by the young man in khaki outfit. 'We will not give up our land!' he shouted. 'Our comrades will fight and oppose this with full force and defeat this oppressive move!' As if on cue, a number of other village youths in similar khaki fatigues made their appearance and stood behind the crowd, which had swollen to over a hundred persons.

Evelyn decided that the time had come to placate the group, which could soon turn into a violent mob. She stood up and addressed the villagers in broken Hindi, a language she had tried hard to master at the Academy, but she had not yet fully succeeded.

'We have come to hear your problems,' she said haltingly. 'The SDO has only issued a notice for acquiring this land, and he has sent Mr Biswas and me to listen to what you have to say. No action will be taken without informing you.' She paused and added, 'Believe me, I understand your problems. Like you, I too belong to the tribal community, although from a very distant part of the country.'

These few words from a strange-looking and even more strange-speaking young tribal woman from far away seemed to work. The youth in military outfit appeared less piqued but approached Evelyn with what appeared to be a pointed message. 'Please tell your SDO to take us seriously. The mood in the tribal villages in these parts is getting restive,' he said gruffly.

When Evelyn finally returned to the circuit house, it was well past midnight. The lake in front was pitch dark. All was quiet, and the town had gone to sleep. The SDO's bungalow was also dark, except for the single lamp shining through the window of his bungalow office, indicating that he was still at work.

14

THE REPORT

*A*saram brought in Evelyn's bed tea as usual at five thirty in the morning. 'Madam, SDO sahib called last night when you were away and said he will come by this morning before going to office and would like to meet you,' he said, before withdrawing.

At nine thirty, Ranjit's Jeep came down the gravelled driveway and stopped under the front porch. After Ranjit got out, Biswas, who was in the rear seat, also emerged. Evidently, Biswas and Ranjit had already been discussing yesterday's events. They sat down in the wicker chairs on the veranda.

'I've asked Sudarshan to join us,' said Ranjit. And soon, Sudarshan's Jeep also trundled in and the SDPO dressed in civvies waved them good morning and joined them at the table. A little later, Asaram came in with a pot of tea and the standard set of Marie biscuits.

'Biswas came in early this morning, and we discussed the tribal opposition to the acquisition,' Ranjit began. 'But this is not a routine objection to a state acquisition. Those we receive hundreds of and settle quite quickly. This is taking on a different colour altogether,' he said. 'This looks like the beginning of a tribal revolt.'

'I had information last week from the OC of Nahargram where the National Mining Corporation is acquiring land,' said Sudarshan. 'He says some tribal youths have begun indoctrination of affected villagers. I've asked him to give me a full report by today with the names and backgrounds of these individuals and what their objectives are and who are backing them.'

'Sir, this looks like the repetition of the Naxalite movement,' added Biswas. 'These tribal youths are certainly being incited by the Maoist elements from other states. They feed on discontent and illiteracy in rural areas. They begin by indoctrination, promising a future they cannot deliver, then proceed to formation of village resistance groups, and then violent opposition to the state. It inevitably leads to futile armed insurgency without end.'

'But why don't we nip the situation in the bud and stop the tragedy from repeating here by looking at the genuine complaints of the tribals,' interjected Evelyn. 'They appealed to me yesterday to consider their situation and stop their meagre livelihoods from being destroyed. I promised that the SDO would look into the matter.'

'Yes, we cannot be unfair,' said Ranjit. 'I wish the matter could have been resolved by me. The acquisition process with strong lobbies involved has progressed too far for us to stop at this level. And perhaps such acquisition is also needed for the overall growth of the country. However, we must look at both sides. The rates of compensation are clearly insufficient. We need to put in place a support mechanism that enables the dispossessed land owners to gain a better livelihood. We just don't have it now.

'What I can do is of course get them the best compensation that can be given legally and do it fast. But this will be too little. Their land is infertile, and their dwellings and other assets such as trees and ponds would fetch very little market value. Whatever little compensation is given is likely to be consumed quickly rather than invested.

'Perhaps we can begin here by trying to set up a model process,' he continued thoughtfully. 'Let me discuss this with the DC. We shouldn't proceed headlong with the acquisition and evictions without putting in place some kind of safety net. I don't know how long we can delay the acquisition process with the constant pressure on us and the accusations of delay from the higher ups.'

The meeting broke up, with Ranjit deciding to report to the DC on the matter. He asked Biswas to inform him of the latest progress on the Nahargram mining acquisition case and Sudarshan for a copy of the intelligence report from OC Nahargram which he asked to be rushed.

When Ranjit entered his small office at the SDO's courts, there was already a crowd of litigants with their lawyers in black coats and ties and general petitioners waiting to see him, waiting outside. Inside the room, his files were stacked up high in the inbox despite the herculean efforts he had made to clear the backlog last night. His personal peon came in with a glass of water. As usual, the first person to meet him was the head clerk in his spotless attire and lips red with betel juice. He handed the important messages and set it on a pile on the table.

The first message was from the chief secretary to the DC and copied to him also. It read:

> FROM :   CHIEF SECY
> TO :   DISTCOLL NILGHAT
> COPY :   SUBDIVISIONAL OFFICER RANJIT GUPTA

> = GOVT OF INDIA (MINISTRY OF MINES AND MINERALS) SERIOUSLY CONCERNED AT DELAY IN ACQUISITION AT NAHARGRAM HOLDING UP ANNUAL PRODUCTION TARGETS OF NATIONAL MINING CORPORATION AND INTERNATIONAL EXPORT CONTRACTS STOP TAKE NECESSARY MEASURES TO EXPEDITE ACQUISITION AND SEND REPORT WITHIN WEEK =

Exactly the type of pressures he was just talking about, thought Ranjit to himself. He would have to get cracking on his report. After going through the other urgent papers (hint of trouble at the local college, report of a major bus accident on the national highway, latest announcements by the student leaders on their intention to resume the agitation, and miscellaneous similar things), he called in Biswas, who brought with him the bulging Nahargram file.

The case was stalled, owing to the objection filed by the tribal settler group represented by Susheela Gautam, who had taken up the case on behalf of a national NGO. The tribals were opposing any acquisition and not willing to accept the usual rates of compensation. The field visit and direct discussion with the affected persons Biswas conducted yesterday confirmed this. Complicating all this was now evidence of a militant uprising.

After a number of reminders, the police report also arrived, in a brown envelope marked URGENT/CONFIDENTAL, brought by a uniformed inspector of the special branch. It now confirmed that left-wing extremists had indeed become active as Sudarshan had mentioned. The area had been visited by two prominent underground Maoists belonging to the Central Committee of the banned organisation who had organised a number of indoctrination camps and set up local village action groups. Their next step was resisting any 'anti-people' actions by violence and simultaneously attacking police personnel, capturing arms, and carrying out assassinations of prominent public officials and 'exploiters'.

Ranjit called in Dikshit, his personal assistant and stenographer, and dictated a first draft which he edited a couple of times in between eating his lunch, which consisted of a mixture of fried vegetables with *puris* which Sundar, his bungalow peon, had prepared for him and brought in a tiffin carrier.

The final message he sent to the DC late in the evening when all commotion around him had died down, the courts and officials and all petitioners had left for the day was simple but carefully worded out:

URGENT/CONFIDENTIAL
FROM :   SUBDIVISIONAL RANJIT GUPTA
TO :   DISTCOLL NILGHAT

= NAHARGRAM ACQUISITION CASE LA75/2038 STATUS IS THAT NOTICE ISSUED AND IS PENDING FORMAL HEARING OF OBJECTIONS RECEIVED BY TRIBAL GROUP AND ALL INDIA NGO SAMATA STOP FIELD VISIT CONDUCTED YESTERDAY BY SR EXEC MAGISTRATE STOP AFFECTED GROUPS HAVE REPRESENTED STRONGLY AGAINST PROCEEDING WITH ACQUISITION STOP INTELLIGENCE REPORT SUGGESTS AFFECTED GROUPS BEING INDOCTRINATED FOR ARMED RESISTANCE IF NECESSARY BY MAOIST CADRES FROM OUTSIDE STATE STOP (PARA)

TRIBAL UNREST PARTLY RESULT OF GRIEVANCE AT INSUFFICIENT COMPENSATION WHICH NEEDS TO BE CAREFULLY EXAMINED STOP NEED TO PROVIDE ALTERNATIVE LIVELIHOOD OPTIONS THROUGH STATE DEVELOPMENT INTERVENTIONS STOP PENDING THIS SUGGEST STATUS QUO BE MAINTAINED STOP COPIES OF DETAILED REPORT DISPATCHED =

A late night yesterday with the files and an exhausting day left Ranjit quite weary. He decided to call it a day. Asking his peon to pack his pending files and send them to the bungalow in his Jeep, he decided to walk home. The narrow road by the lake was nearly empty except for the occasional cycle rickshaw or a roadside hawker returning home with his wares on his head. The infrequent municipal lamp posts, some with missing bulbs, kept the road mainly in shadow; the few which were dimly lit had halos of dust and swirling insects around them, not allowing much light to penetrate through.

Strolling slowly through the shadows, Ranjit had nearly reached his bungalow, when he found himself overtaken by a more determined walker. It was Evelyn on her evening constitutional around the lake. They both stopped.

'Do you walk here often?' queried Evelyn, surprised.

'Normally don't, but felt like stretching my legs,' replied Ranjit. 'Been sitting all day. Why don't you come in for a cup of tea? I need to hear what you've been up to today.'

They entered through the small wooden gate in front of his bungalow which led to the front veranda. A couple of wicker chairs and a table were always kept there for visitors. Sundar, the bungalow peon, turned up on hearing them, salaamed the new lady officer about whom he had heard but not yet seen, and took orders for tea.

Evelyn's day had been spent helping Biswas write the report on the Nahargram acquisition case, which Ranjit had already dispatched to the DC.

Sundar brought tea and his signature onion *pakoras*. This was the time sahib liked to have his rum and ruminate over the day's happenings, but with the lady officer present, alcohol was out, he presumed.

'I see we've kept you quite busy on your first couple of days,' said Ranjit, sipping his tea. 'But before you become only a land acquisition expert, you should get acquainted with other activities which keep us busy, often pointlessly, I think. Why don't you study the confidential files on the local college? There's some trouble brewing there, and it's likely to blow up soon.'

'When do you get time to relax?' asked Evelyn.

'Some of my colleagues think that work is their relaxation, their *dharma*.[19] Probably the government thinks so too. They keep dumping us with more and more useless tasks. Take the local college, for example. The Education Department, in their infinite wisdom, decided to disband the governing body, which was apparently siphoning off government grants, with the principal also on the take. Without consulting anybody, the government constituted an interim executive council in its place and appointed the SDO as its chair. Now the crooked old principal is pulling out new tricks from his bag of tricks and blocking the executive committee from working. The college problems have now become my headache. As though there weren't other things to think of!

'Anyhow, let's forget work for a while,' continued Ranjit. 'Why don't we do a round of tennis tomorrow afternoon? Let me call up Sudarshan and Agarwal for some compulsory tennis lessons from the expert! Will get them to relax and refocus too.'

The crickets in the shrubbery had meanwhile turned up their racket considerably. They almost drowned out the phone ringing faintly in the office room. Ranjit left to answer it, leaving Evelyn with her tea and *pakoras*, the dark vista of the lake in front, and flickering fireflies all around.

Ranjit emerged after a while. 'That was the DC. We'll have to postpone our little tennis party, I'm afraid,' he said. 'Meeting tomorrow morning at DC's bungalow in Nilghat to discuss land acquisition issues. He wants you to come too. So let's leave at eight thirty in the morning. I'll come around to pick you up.'

15

A SHORT INTERLUDE

*W*hen Ranjit stepped out on his veranda, he found the morning was bright and clear, and a much larger number of colourful Siberian ducks was swimming placidly in the lake. The personal security officer who had been assigned to him had already reported and was sipping a cup of tea provided by Sundar, sitting on the stump of a tree sawn off ages ago. Sundar and the PSO had already become fast friends. His weapon was balanced carefully on the other side of the stump. He got up immediately on seeing Ranjit, and cup in one hand stood rigidly at attention, providing quite a comic spectacle thought Ranjit. He much doubted whether this fellow would be able to provide any security to him when the crunch came.

Ali was ready, properly uniformed for a change, for the journey to district headquarters, which he tended to take more seriously. As Ranjit was planning to take the Ambassador car allotted temporarily to Evelyn by the DC, Ali would have to drive that car rather than the old but pretty well maintained Jeep assigned to the SDO. He was looking forward to this prospect and had done a couple of trial runs with Evelyn's driver already in the morning. The car, white in colour, was now standing in front, spotlessly cleaned, waiting to begin the journey.

Evelyn was waiting at the circuit house porch, her hair washed and untied and dressed in a green salwar suit, when Ranjit's car drove up. The PSO was sitting in front with the driver, and this allowed Ranjit and Evelyn to sit comfortably in the rear seat of the capacious Ambassador. They couldn't have all fitted into the Jeep.

'I'm quite jealous of your car,' Ranjit joked. 'I'll tell the DC to allot it to me when you finish your training.'

'According to the DC, this car is reserved only for married or lady officers so that they can easily get in and out in their sarees,' Evelyn replied. 'So the chances of you getting this are somewhat remote at this stage, I'm afraid.' And then she added, 'Of course, you can try your luck when a Mrs Ranjit appears on the scene!'

'Wedding gift from the DC! Big incentive to find someone quickly, then.' Ranjit chuckled.

Ranjit found it refreshing to be out of the office after a number of days of drudgery with the endless stream of petitioners and boring files. He was thoroughly enjoying Evelyn's company.

'Hasn't someone been lined up for you already?' asked Evelyn. 'Almost all my male batchmates are either married already, or are fairly advanced in their matchmaking by now. The women are usually not that lucky. So what's your story? I'm sure you've had hundreds of enquiries from families of suitable women.'

'Sorry to disappoint you,' said Ranjit, 'but obviously women haven't considered me a hot item. I don't suppose I was too popular with the women probationers at the Academy. Thereafter, all possible social interactions have vanished.'

Evelyn wasn't too convinced with the Academy story. She decided to quietly find out by contacting one of her women batchmates who specialised in this kind of gossip. There must have been an affair which might not have worked out for some reason. There were plenty of those too. But she was sure that Ranjit's family and friends were looking for a suitable match for him.

'And what is *your* story? I am sure a number of people have their eyes on you!' said Ranjit.

'Of course, the whole Academy is after me!' joked Evelyn, trying to change an increasingly embarrassing line of conversation that she had blundered into.

The fact was that given her obvious attractiveness, although many of her batchmates had made initial overtures, their ardour inevitably cooled when their families came to know that a tribal girl from the north-east was involved. Despite supposed changes in attitudes towards people from the north-east, underlying prejudices remained. There was the Shillong college friend, of course, a great singer with his guitar, whose family ran a large transport business, but stopped contacts after Evelyn went to Mussoorie. Men not in the services generally felt women like Evelyn too snobbish for them. She had bumped into him a couple of times along with other college friends when she went home on leave, but he usually feigned being very busy and rumour had it that he was going out with somebody else. So Evelyn was pretty much on her own now.

They were nearing the halfway mark, and the small revenue circle headquarters of Golmunda was approaching with its set of small but neat houses along the road front. Ranjit had a favourite *dhaba*[20] just beyond town where he stopped often for a quick meal. Their spicy chicken curry with *naans* was quite famous, and long lines of trucks were usually parked near the roadside establishment. In the night, liquor was known to be illegally sold, and other types of illicit entertainment for the truck drivers were also quietly provided. So long as the establishment managed to conduct these activities discreetly, the local *thana* turned a blind eye to them—their vision also blurred by the frequent spicy meals served to the *thana*, gratis.

Ranjit asked Ali to stop at the *dhaba*. On seeing the SDO's car, the owner ran out and greeted Ranjit. 'What can I offer you, sir?' he asked.

'I'm in a hurry, so we'll only have your *masala chai*. Make it quick, please,' said Ranjit, getting out of the car. Evelyn also emerged and they sat down at a table nearby. A light breeze kept blowing Evelyn's open hair on to her face. She tied it up into a ponytail with a hair band and felt much more comfortable. From somewhere a koel was calling. Rows of flowering trees lined the highway on either side. They were both quiet for some time, savouring the pastoral scene.

'What's the latest on the grenade attack investigation?' asked Evelyn, breaking the silence when the tea arrived, recalling the incident vividly, now she was at Golmunda again.

'Well, we had asked that a high-level police investigation be conducted to determine the group involved and apprehend the culprits. An inspector from the state detective branch came around and met a number of people and took notes. Police informants have also been contacted and are supposedly feeding him information. The fellow looked to me very much like the blundering Inspector Lestrade. I doubt anything will be discovered.'

The brief interlude ended soon, and they continued with their journey to district headquarters. They crossed the Kenduli River and drove on to the *sadr* subdivision mostly in silence. As they approached Nilghat, Ranjit's cheeriness began leaving him. He was back to his brusque businesslike nature.

'What do you think about your training so far? Are you learning enough? The DC is surely going to ask me that,' he said.

'Well, I am up to my ears in land acquisition, which is my main assignment with you, I suppose, so no complaints on that front. But considering that there are so many things going on in the law-and-order front, maybe some exposure there will be useful,' said Evelyn.

'Certainly no dearth of learning opportunities there!' remarked Ranjit, laughing. 'There's something brewing at the local college which I spoke about yesterday. Maybe you could go over with Sudarshan and take a look.'

Soon they were in Nilghat, its roads still empty, the town yet to begin its bustling day. Ranjit noted that they had made it exactly on time. At five minutes to ten, their car drew up at the porch of DC's bungalow, and Ranjit noticed that Vijay too was getting off his Jeep.

16

DELAYING THE INEVITABLE

*T*he DC saw Ranjit and Evelyn in his bungalow office with its wood-panelled walls and large French windows looking out into the garden. He sat behind his large desk, and behind him on the wall was a long wooden board which listed the names of all his predecessors right from British times. On either side of it were portraits of Mahatma Gandhi—a permanent feature in all government offices—and Indira Gandhi, the current prime minister.

'We have quite a problem, don't we?' remarked the DC. 'I don't think we can defer the acquisition. There are too many pressures from the top. We have to complete the process. But we can try making it as humane as possible as you suggested in your report. And while we are at it, secure as much time as we can to work on the rehabilitation part.

'So I agree that you slow the process,' he continued. 'Call for objections, hear as many opinions as possible. Adjourn whenever requested. No need to provide short dates. You get the point, I'm sure. Meanwhile, we gear up the development machinery to help the affected families. Get the departments to show results, for once.'

After this short briefing, they proceeded to the meeting room which adjoined the office. The DC had summoned all heads of departments who could contribute. Although Ranjit's report had been circulated in advance, he knew from long experience most hadn't read it. There was a story about how the DC had found a newly arrived officer fumbling for his facts at an important meeting and told the hapless man, 'Shinde, why don't you go home and finish all your unpacking and then come back.' He therefore began by requesting Ranjit to provide a detailed update to all participants.

Ranjit did so in full. 'We can't proceed the way we have so far,' he concluded. 'This appears to be leading to resistance and extremism. The affected families are really poor and have no other means of livelihood. We must do something for them and do so fast,' he said.

'Unfortunately, there is pressure on us to complete acquisition speedily,' added the DC. 'I discussed it with the chief secretary, and he was a little annoyed with what he called dithering on our part. Yes, that's the word he used—dithering! According to him, we have to separate the acquisition issue from the issue of growing extremism, which the intelligence agencies are fully aware of and acting on appropriately. He feels that the displaced families have to get compensation according to law and whatever else we can provide, but that's all.'

'In other words, the government doesn't seem too concerned with the plight of the displaced persons,' remarked the additional DC.

'Well, I didn't say that!' said the DC. 'Although there's some truth in what you say. But let's make the best effort we can at our level. To begin with, compensation must be as high as legally possible. At the same time, let's focus development support to the displaced families immediately. Let's start by allotting new homesteads from unused forest and other government land and help them build new homes through our relief funds. These may not go too far but might cover cost of roofing, for example.'

'Sir, the Integrated Rural Development Project is just the right scheme for them,' said Suresh, the IRDP project officer, the first to speak up. He was known as a keen type, in the parlance of the time, ready to impress superiors at meetings. He and his white Jeep were well known in the district, turning up unexpectedly at remote places. 'We will find them alternative livelihoods. Our livestock project is doing well here and may help.' The DC looked at him a little sceptically as livestock had failed almost everywhere, but he let the matter rest for the moment.

'I also request bankers present to encourage the families receiving compensation to place them in fixed deposits. Can't we also organise livelihood loans for them?' asked the DC.

'We will look into it, sir,' said the bank representative. Realising that the response was terribly inadequate, he continued, 'I'll suggest a special line of microcredit to my superiors for the displaced families. This will be a new scheme, but it can be pilot-tested here.'

'Thanks, Anand!' the DC said to him, though a little unconvinced, but pleased on the whole at the response he was getting.

'We can also step up health and education support from the nearest primary health centres and schools,' said the additional DC, not to be left behind. 'I can also request our district employment exchange to find jobs with local industries for one person from each of the displaced households.'

The DC turned to the executive engineer of the Public Works Department, who had not said anything. 'What about employment in road maintenance? We have a large budget which wasn't spent fully last year. Can't we use it?' he asked.

'Sure, I can offer work immediately on maintenance jobs to those who are able-bodied,' said the executive engineer. 'There are also a number of roads projects under the employment generation scheme where work can be offered.'

'Wonderful!' remarked the DC. 'But I hope the promises you are making today don't remain just promises,' he said. Then glancing behind, he located Evelyn and enquired whether she was recording the minutes. 'I lost Evelyn temporarily to Ranjit's subdivision,' he said jokingly, 'but she is back at work as usual and will send round the minutes.

'Our additional DC will act as special development officer for the displaced families,' the DC added. 'He will henceforth coordinate all district level activities for them.'

This was good news for the additional DC—many more opportunities for combining his birdwatching excursions with work.

'And now, ladies and gentlemen, lunch awaits!' said the DC, concluding the discussions.

17

THE URN BEGINS REVEALING ITS SECRETS

*A*s usual, lunch was served in the DC's large covered terrace upstairs. Vijay picked his way through the diners towards Ranjit and called him away from the buffet queue. Ranjit had just finished piling his plate with the savouries that Alam had drummed up from the kitchen, and Vijay had done the same, but only the vegetarian ones as he was a strict vegetarian. They walked out to the uncovered part of the terrace, pulled up a few wicker chairs lying around, and sat down with their plates for a chat.

'I heard back from the Archaeological Survey of India yesterday,' Vijay informed him. He had found the ASI letter buried in his mountain of *dak* and could easily have overlooked it as the letter was addressed to the additional DC and he had only received a copy. His head clerk would certainly have buried it in the miscellaneous file, and there it would have remained, gathering dust till eternity. But luckily, it had caught his eye.

'That was fairly quick!' said Ranjit. 'It's been barely a month since encountering the antique urn which you thought had a royal connection. They must have dashed your historical flight of fancy, have they not?'

'Quite on the contrary, my friend,' replied Vijay. 'They probably replied fast as we have something significant. Anyway, I'll show you the letter after lunch. I've brought it with me.'

Spying the two SDOs in the open terrace, the additional DC also came up. 'You two must be talking about the ASI letter,' he said between mouthfuls of salad. 'I saw that Vijay was copied and, as our historian, the most qualified to unravel the mystery.'

'So the ADC sahib is also interested in getting to the bottom of this,' said Vijay, 'I almost missed seeing the letter, and it might have gone into oblivion—but obviously you wouldn't have let that happen!'

'Please read the Antiquities and Art Treasures Act of 1972, my friend,' said the additional DC. 'Although a somewhat obscure law and not necessary for our general functioning, one should be aware of *all* our legislations which our hardworking MPs spend hard-earned taxpayers' money to devise. I ask you to read it as I too have some responsibility for your training. I am sure you haven't, else you wouldn't have made such a callous remark about my being interested,' he continued jocularly. 'Apart from being very interested, I am *duty bound* to attend to it. The said Act gives powers over handling of antiquities to the DC, and as management of these obscure laws are passed on to me by him, it has become my task to get to the bottom of it.'

'So what do you think of their reply?' asked Vijay.

'The reply suggests clearly that the urn and its contents are ancient and therefore will need to be registered by us,' said the additional DC. 'A lot of bother, really. Notifying the public, calling the finders, seeing if there are other claimants, deciding whether we allow the finders to keep it or deposit it at a museum etc. etc.'

'Apart from the obviously important issues about who the urn belongs to and whether it should be kept in a museum to prevent it being sold to unscrupulous antique dealers or smuggled abroad, I am infinitely more interested about the story that this urn may hold,' said Vijay.

Evelyn strolled in, eating a dessert. 'If you people keep talking and not eating, these *gulab jamuns* are going to get cold!' she said. 'What is it that is so secretive?'

'We are discussing about a rare piece of jewellery about which, if I may be allowed a sexist remark, you probably may have more expertise than us!' said Vijay.

'Ah, thus the privacy!' said Evelyn. 'If it is meant as a present for someone special, I certainly don't want to intrude.'

'It may have been, two thousand years before, who knows?' said Vijay. Then adding to her bewilderment, he continued, 'It could have been a present from me to you many, many previous lives ago, for instance.'

'Like Arjuna to his Manipuri princess Chitrangada?[21]' Evelyn retorted.

'Don't listen to him,' said the additional DC, laughing. 'I'll explain over our *gulab jamuns*, which certainly shouldn't be allowed to get cold.'

The three got up and joined the dessert queue, and the strange story of the urn was told to Evelyn bit by bit by the additional DC.

'Let's go to the circuit house for tea after this, and I can show you the ASI letter,' said Vijay to Ranjit and Evelyn.

The three along with Evelyn decided to drop in to the circuit house before leaving for their different destinations. Bidding goodbye to the DC, they asked their drivers to follow them and strolled down to the circuit house, which was next door to the DC's compound. Evelyn noticed that the garden was still in good trim and was happy that the maintenance routine she had set up was working. When the tea arrived, it was in the shiny well-polished stainless steel teapot and tray, and the cups were spotlessly clean. Ramu, the circuit house waiter, was also well turned out in his white uniform with brass buttons gleaming. He *salaamed* the group and had a special smile and *salaam* for the officer memsahib, glad to see her back, but was informed by Evelyn that the visit was temporary and that she would return for a longer stay only after another few weeks.

Vijay took out the copy of the ASI letter from his briefcase and laid it out on the table for Ranjit and Evelyn to see. It was addressed to the DC Nilghat and said:

> This refers to your letter no. DO/NGT/ADC/ Misc/1979/2036 regarding carbon dating and valuing the contents of a package accompanying the said letter, containing one old urn and old pieces of jewellery and human remains within the said urn.
>
> Our findings are as under:
>
> (i)   Carbon dating of the human skeletal remains indicates that they belong to approximately 280 BCE (+) or (-) 50 years. This would place them in the immediate pre-Ashokan period.
>
> (ii)   The necklace is made of gold with an attached sapphire gem. Necklaces of this type were usually worn by princes or high nobility of the period. This suggests that the skeletal remains also belong to a person of nobility in that period.
>
> (iii)   The place of the urn and the time profile of its contents indicates that they in all probability belong to an ancient Indian principality called Thaneswar about which not much is known currently. However, recent references to Thaneswar have been emerging in certain ancient Buddhist scrolls which have made their way from China through the government of the Republic of China (ROC), Taipei, Taiwan.
>
> (iv)   In fact, coincidentally, our office has been contacted by one Dr Biswajit Banerjee, former professor of Benares Hindu University (BHU) and now a research scholar with the government of ROC in Taipei, Taiwan, who has been enquiring whether there have been any excavations from our side in this area that would provide further evidence about this principality, its nobility and people, and their political, social, and

religious activities. The discovery of this urn is in fact the first major archaeological finding concerning Thaneswar and based on the accounts in the Buddhist scrolls (about which we may have to learn more from Dr Banerjee) and this important archaeological find we are considering undertaking a program of excavation around the area of your discovery in the next financial year. Before this is done, we will be inviting Dr Banerjee for a detailed presentation of his research relating to Thaneswar so that we can be better guided on our archaeological works.

(v)   As to valuation of this find, it is hard to place a price on such antiquities. But suffice it to say, it is the first major discovery on this ancient kingdom, and there would be a large number of institutions and individuals who may not have a bona fide interest in the urn and its contents. Our recommendation would be to have it registered and committed to a museum, after due compensation to its owners, where it would be well looked after. But DC Nilghat may like to proceed according to the provisions of the Antiquities and Art Treasures Act, 1972 in this matter.

We are returning the package by registered and insured post to your office. We have removed the human remains for better preservation with us but returning the necklace along with the urn. Please feel free to contact us in case of any clarifications that you may need.

Yours sincerely

s/d D. K. Das
Chief Archaeologist

'Well, well, well, we now know where the learned additional DC picked up his archaeology laws from!' exclaimed Ranjit. 'At least that part of the mystery is solved, isn't it?'

They all had a good laugh over this. Evelyn, who was a recent entrant to the episode, was intrigued.

'Well, there are a number of possibilities,' she mused. 'It could indeed have been a gift of a nobleman to his lover, or part of a royal ensemble, or a gift of a prince to a danseuse. But naturally, it must have been a matter of great importance to the person who had it till he died, important enough to have it buried with his remains.'

'The strange thing is that it looks like that it came from a monastery,' said Vijay. 'My hunch is that it belonged to a nobleman who joined the monastic order in his later life and brought this with him. One piece of worldly attachment he couldn't give up for some reason.'

'You were spot on as far as the noble origin of the artifact is concerned,' said the additional DC to Vijay. 'Why don't we try and unravel the mystery fully? I suggest that since you are our historian, you write informally to this Dr Banerjee and find out what he knows. We can get his address from the ASI, with whom he appears to be in touch. Meanwhile, I'll go about the official closure of this very interesting case.'

That ended the tea session. The urn and its contents had become an interesting diversion for this group of district officials. They dispersed with Vijay promising to inform the rest of any reply he got from Taiwan. It was already four when Ali brought the car around to the porch for Ranjit and Evelyn to get back to the subdivision. Just barely time to reach before sunset, thought Ranjit.

18

REMINISCENCES

$\mathcal{T}$he trip away for the day had done Ranjit a world of good. He had not felt this good for a long, long time. While sitting on the veranda, sipping his rum, he recalled the conversation he had with Evelyn on the way to Nilghat when she wanted to know a little bit more about him, especially if he had any romantic commitments. As always, he had diverted the question with some light-hearted banter. He had allowed no one to trespass into his past—not in the Academy nor anyone since he arrived in the district. His diffidence was assumed generally by others to be a sign of his preoccupation with work, and they were partly right as he kept deliberately busy to try and forget.

But he was surprised that tonight, those memories were somehow less painful. These were mainly of Suneeta, his fellow college lecturer at St. Augusta's, where he taught a couple of years before taking the civil services examinations. She was also his one-time betrothed. The two were to get married after Ranjit's field assignment was over so that he could negotiate with his superiors for a common place of posting. The government was pretty accommodating in this respect and provided help if feasible.

But that was not to be.

A telegram about four years back when he had just joined the Academy had summoned him in the middle of the night to a hospital in the town Suneeta was living, stating that she was in a critical condition and asked him to rush. He took an overnight bus to Delhi and managed to get on a flight to her town the next day. When he reached the hospital, Suneeta was in the ICU on a ventilator. The doctors said that she was sedated and in an induced coma.

But when he held her hand and called out her name, she seemed to be responding. Was there a slight tremor that he felt in her fingers? He thought so in his heart and believed it to be so—but could never be sure.

The next few days were sheer agony. Her condition was diagnosed as malignant malaria which had spread to the brain and then begun attacking all her organs one by one. Every day, Ranjit and Suneeta's parents, who were also there in the hospital, waited to see a flicker of life. But there never was one.

The day finally came when the attending doctor came up to them and spoke the dreaded words that they had all feared—that Suneeta was determined to be brain dead by the hospital medical team and he suggested that she be removed from all life support systems. They merely sought permission from Suneeta's father, and Ranjit was not even consulted as he was technically no relation of hers.

'Can't we try for another week to see if she revives?' asked Ranjit.

'We can, but we think it's pointless,' was the doctor's reply.

Nevertheless, Ranjit got Suneeta's parents to agree. The ICU bills were piling up and had already depleted all of Suneeta's parents' savings. Ranjit didn't have much in his bank account but transferred all of it to the hospital so that his beloved Suneeta could have a chance, however slim, at recovery.

Suneeta spared them all the moral dilemma of deciding to take her off life support. The call came the same night they had decided to continue support for another week. The curt message from the hospital desk was that Suneeta's heart had stopped beating and that she had passed away at 2 a.m. They were to come immediately and collect her body etc. etc.

With this ended two years of an intense and passionate relationship. After the initial months of her passing away, there was an acute and almost unbearable sharpness to the pain he felt.

Ranjit kept his personal loss closely to himself. He devoted his energies to his courses at the Academy, but people did notice his serious demeanour and would often try to enquire if anything was amiss. He usually dismissed these with some levity or other. Over the months, the pain had dulled but was still present. But gradually as the days passed, he was able to dwell on the brief period of their lives together, especially the happier moments.

Suneeta taught chemistry and Ranjit economics at the same college they worked in. It was an old Christian institution with a solid reputation built over the years. It was quite a privilege to be a student or faculty there. Suneeta had joined the college as a lecturer a year later than Vijay. It was the year the college had first opened up admission to girls from being a males-only bastion. It also therefore began hiring women faculty and initially Suneeta in the chemistry department and another woman lecturer in the economics department joined. The two were quite a curiosity in the teachers' common room when they first appeared.

Ranjit recalled that it was winter and Suneeta was wearing a red cardigan. She had just come in after a long ride in the cold on her moped which had given her cheeks a rosy tinge. He noticed that she had large eyes and showed a dimple when she smiled. Although he disliked the hackneyed phrase of 'love at first sight' and would have chided anyone who attempted to attach it to him, he had to admit that was exactly what happened. Thus, when the male teachers—all nothing more than overgrown children—were discussing among themselves as to who should go up and ask the two women huddled together alone at the corner of the common room to join them, Ranjit took up the challenge willingly. He went up and introduced himself and later all the others.

Their relationship blossomed over the year they were in the college. As the college teachers' common room became too public a place, they found several reclusive spots on campus. The law faculty coffee house, where they served South Indian coffee with its rich aroma and signature *masala dosas* was a favourite place for their trysts—away from prying and over-curious eyes. The coffee house had tables on an upstairs balcony which often provided more privacy.

Unfortunately, however, their romantic interlude came to an end after Ranjit announced to all in the common room at the beginning of the next academic year that he had qualified for the civil services and would be leaving the college.

Suneeta, of course, had known that Ranjit was appearing in the civil services examinations, and was hoping that he would succeed. She was a little afraid, however, that someone else in the Academy, more glamorous than her, might steal Ranjit away. Ranjit sensed this dormant nervousness and did his best to remove it.

'Come over to Mussoorie as soon as you get some leave,' he remembered shouting to Suneeta standing at the door of his compartment as the train to Dehra Dun slowly pulled out from the station. As the train gathered speed, Suneeta, wearing the yellow sari he liked, kept waving frantically, till finally she was lost in the crowd.

19

JEEP BREAKDOWN

*V*ijay got into the driver's seat of his Jeep. He liked to drive whenever he could, his driver Bhagat taking the passenger seat next to him. Vijay had seen to it that the Jeep, although old, was well maintained. He liked the power the vehicle contained and its ability to take on all types of terrain—rubble, slushy soil, fording shallow rivers, going up steep gradients—with ease. It was also relatively easy to fix. Vijay had taken a course on motor mechanics at the Academy and was quite adept at the simpler problems.

When, therefore, the engine started stalling a bit, he wasn't too bothered. The road to Vijay's subdivisional headquarters took a climb most of the way. The headquarters town itself was in the midst of the hills, and the subdivision was for the most part generally thickly forested except for village settlements where vast expanses of land had been cleared for terrace cultivation since ancient times. Shortly after leaving Nilghat, it began following a stream with the road cut from the side of the mountainous valley, meandering along its course. On a clear day, one could see the Himalayan peaks from certain lookout points.

Vijay hoped that the Jeep would behave at least till they were near the forest inspection bungalow where he usually made stops on his way home. This was also where Viay and Ranjit had met the additional DC unexpectedly the last time on their return from another meeting at Nilghat and they had come across the mysterious ancient urn.

Luckily, the Jeep managed to chug its way up to the Inspection bungalow. Vijay got off, and Bhagat opened the bonnet. He asked Bhagat to check the air filter, which might have got clogged. Meanwhile, he took a stroll on the grounds to stretch his legs.

The Inspection bungalow was on a hilltop and commanded a view of the valley and the hills and the forest around. The clear evening sky had touches of scarlet and pink near the western horizon. Vijay liked to stop here often. It fell just inside his jurisdiction, and when he had just been appointed as SDO a year back and needed to go around meeting his circle staff, he had spent a week alone at this place. He remembered that he had been rummaging through the small public library in the subdivisional town and come across a book on the *Upanishads* translated by a Harvard professor. It must have been donated to the library by one of his predecessors wanting to offload unnecessary luggage on a transfer. He doubted that the local library committee would have had such interests. Not knowing much Sanskrit, he had never been able to read the text and so borrowed the book and kept renewing it till he had the leisure for serious reading which it demanded. It came during his weekend sojourns at this Inspection bungalow.

He would wake up at four and take a chair and sit with his book in the lawn under the open sky high above all habitations and far from all human contact. Bhagat his driver and the *chowkidar* would depart after serving him his dinner. They lived in the outhouse which was a short distance below, reachable by a *pagdandi* or a narrow mountain path across the scrub. All would be completely still except for the chirping of the waking birds.

The book gave him a beginner's guide to the Upanishads and concepts such as Brahmatman, which is when the human soul merges with the collective consciousness of all creation. Here was the infinite universe—the earth, the sky and the stars—spread out around him, and for a moment or two, he was able to feel himself part of that infinite space and time. It was strange that the book had come his way and compelled him to consider issues he had not thought about. There was something mysterious about this place too, Vijay felt, that threw up ancient secrets for him to unravel.

The *chowkidar* came out and broke his reverie. 'A cup of tea, sir?' he enquired.

'Sure, make it quick, please,' said Vijay. He walked over to Bhagat, who was still fiddling about with the tangle of machinery under the bonnet. Bhagat pulled out the air filter, and they both had a good look at it. Unfortunately, it didn't seem to be the problem. Regrettably, Vijay realised that the knowledge required to fix the Jeep was beyond his limited learning at the motor mechanics class. Neither did Bhagat seem to have any clue as yet, although he did not admit it right away and continued tinkering with the parts.

It was clear soon, however, that more serious work was needed on the vehicle. It was much after dusk already, and to get a mechanic with spare parts to come over would be difficult. The alternative was to get one of his senior magistrates to send him the subdivision's pool vehicle so that at least he could get back home and attend to his work by the morning. Unlike Ranjit, who could reach his headquarters within two hours, driving along level road the entire distance, Vijay needed almost double the time as the terrain was hilly and difficult and it was not easy to negotiate the hundred or so kilometres in less than about three and a half hours. So although a car was organised with some difficulty—as getting a call through the local exchange proved quite a challenge—and Vijay asked it to be sent out at once, he decided to leave in the morning when the sun was up.

Darkness had enveloped the small bungalow, and the crickets had set up their cacophony. Vijay's thoughts went back to the urn they had discovered here earlier and its contents. What was so special about the necklace that had drawn him and the others to it? Was there an ancient story of love, happiness, and heartbreak attached to it? Vijay hoped indeed there was one—and the historian and romantic in him felt compelled to unearth it.

'Dinner is ready, sir,' announced the chowkidar. Vijay sat down alone at the dining table and allowed himself the simple vegetarian pleasures of *dum aloo* and *parathas*, spiced up with *achaar*.

20

THE BURIED MONASTERY

*H*e woke the next morning, hearing voices outside on the veranda. It was still quite early. Peering through the curtains, he saw that the headman of the nearby village along with the same villagers who had claimed to have found the mystery urn had turned up. It was not unusual for villagers to be up and about early. Their activity level by long habit and custom was based on the daily solar cycle, and most were fully awake well before dawn.

Word spread very fast in these parts. Someone might have seen his Jeep going up the hill and, not seeing it descend, must have surmised that the SDO sahib was spending the night at the Inspection bungalow as was his wont. Vijay realised that the headman might have come to find out about the urn and its precious contents and was glad that he could give him some news on that score.

The chowkidar also came in with the cup of morning tea. 'The villagers learnt that you are camping here, sir, and have come to see you,' he said. Then setting the cup down on the bedside table, he added, 'The pool Jeep has also arrived, and the driver is ready to leave. I am making some egg-*bhujia* and *chapatis*—will that do for your breakfast?'

'Also add some achar, yaar[22],' said Vijay, and he assured the man that that would do very well indeed. The fare at Inspection bungalows was quite basic compared to circuit houses, and Vijay couldn't complain much. Besides, he liked eggs as they were the only non-vegetarian stuff he permitted himself.

After a quick shower and breakfast which he ate with gusto, Vijay was ready to meet the villagers. Apart from the headman, there was the principal discoverer and several others who had joined the company out of curiosity. Vijay asked the chowkidar to find some chairs, although when they came, the headman was reluctant to sit down. The British rulers had always treated villagers as subjects, and they could not be seated at the same level as the English sahibs. Old photographs showed English civil service officers sitting regally on camp chairs with village folk sitting on carpets—or their local variants, *durries*—spread out on the ground. Although in independent India, such practices had been given up, old customs continued even several decades after independence.

At Vijay's insistence, the headman sat down gingerly on the chair offered. A couple of others also joined the sitting party, but as there weren't enough chairs to go around, the others remained standing.

Vijay informed them about the reply he had received from ASI headquarters. 'The urn you found is very old, over two thousand years old, and priceless. The necklace is made of solid gold, and the gem is pure sapphire. According to the specialists at the ASI office, the discovery you made is extremely important,' he said.

'When can I have it back?' asked the villager who had found it, already perhaps dreaming of the money he would make selling it.

'Unfortunately, because it is so important, it will take some time for us to complete the paperwork. The ADC sahib will call you to Nilghat, and you will hear more of this from him. I am sorry to disappoint you, but because of the risk that it could be stolen, the government may decide to keep it at a museum. Of course, they will determine a fair compensation for you in return if that happens.'

The village elder who had found it in his land was not very happy. Vijay made a mental note to tell the ADC that he should at least pay the market value of the necklace, which, given its weight in gold, would certainly make the poor man much richer. In addition, some value as an antiquity should also be added. He would have to really read the Act and the rules now and check the practices on valuing such findings.

'But tell me,' said Vijay to the headman, 'the last time we met, you mentioned that you believed there was an ancient monastery in these parts. What led you to think so?'

'This has been a traditional belief with us. But now and then, we come across pieces of old stones and bricks while ploughing the ground. These may have been part of some large building. There is one place, particularly, where the village boys have been finding many such stones recently.'

Vijay's ears pricked up on hearing this. Maybe there indeed was a major archaeological discovery waiting to be excavated here. 'Can you show me the spot?' he asked.

'It's about a mile or two down the hill towards the river,' said the headman. 'If the SDO sahib can spare an hour or so, we could go there. The road is a little further down, and we could ask your driver to go ahead and wait there, then you wouldn't have to climb back.'

The arrangements were made. Bhagat would wait till a mechanic with spares came to fix the Jeep, and Vijay asked the pool driver to go ahead with a villager who would know the right place to stop and wait till he came down. He paid the chowkidar's bill, thanked him, and the party set off. It was difficult clambering down the hillside on the narrow *pagdandi* which twisted and turned and wound its way down through the scrub interspersed with tall trees. There were sometimes sharp drops, and Vijay had to watch out. His patent leather shoes were not helping, either. The others were moving with alacrity, and Vijay was slowing them down.

Gradually, the path came on to more level ground, and presently, they came upon the village playing field. The party stopped, and the headman came up to Vijay. 'This is where the boys have been picking up these strange stones,' he said.

'Hey, Chhotu!' he shouted at a curious boy who had turned up, seeing the group of people with what looked like an important personage. 'Show sahib what you found the other day. Do you still have it, or have you lost it?'

The boy ran off to fetch what he had found.

Meanwhile, one of the villagers who had a piece of land adjoining the field asked Vijay to follow him. The hillside was extensively terrace-cultivated. At the edge of the field, there was a fall of about a metre to the farmer's plot. On the side of the hill, there appeared to be a row of old bricks jutting out. Centuries of soil erosion had uncovered it. Vijay inspected the bricks with growing interest. These villagers could be absolutely right, he thought. This could indeed be the site of an ancient monastery.

More support for this idea was evident when Chhotu returned with a shiny stone which appeared to have been carved into a lamp. He gave it to Vijay, who inspected it carefully.

Vijay returned it to the boy and said, 'Keep it carefully and don't use it for target practice, OK?'

The boy smiled shyly and grabbed the stone piece back from Vijay's hand. Vijay decided that there was enough material for an ASI team to make an exploratory visit. He kept the thought to himself, however. Any announcement of the possibility of it being an archaeological site, even informally, would spread, and there could be reckless digging by treasure hunters to unearth anything they could find, which could destroy any remaining archaeological relics.

He walked to the edge of the field and could see the hill rolling steeply down to the stream flowing over the rocky bed and the winding road alongside, keeping it company. The clouds were moving slowly, and at times when they lifted, he could catch a fleeting glimpse of shimmering snow peaks of the distant Himalayan ranges.

'Very well,' said Vijay generally to the villagers clustered around him, 'I've seen what I have to.' And then to the owner of the precious urn, 'I will ask the ADC sahib to act and decide on the matter. Don't worry—we'll do what is best in your interest. Your urn is in safe hands with the government.'

He wasn't too sure about the last bit though, he thought to himself, as securing the best compensation from the government is usually not an easy task. With the exploitative ways it had gotten used to, this man's claim might well not fetch what it really deserved.

Reaching his substitute Jeep required a further descent downhill through equally difficult terrain. Vijay was glad when he could finally set off for the remaining portion of his interrupted journey. He noticed, with some trepidation, that among the group that came to see him off was Chhotu the urchin, nonchalantly twisting and turning in his fingers his little new-found toy, the stone lamp, neither he nor the villagers around him knowing how precious it was.

It took Vijay more than an hour to reach his destination. Unlike Ranjit's subdivisional headquarters, which were in a bustling plains town sitting smack on the national highway, Vijay's headquarters were in a somewhat remote location lying in a valley surrounded by hills. Road communications relied on this long and twisting road, but it was also served by a railway line.

Vijay's bungalow in fact looked out over a wide valley, and the railway line could be seen downhill in the distance. The line crossed a tall viaduct over the river that passed by the town a little after leaving it. The trains travelling over the viaduct presented a pretty sight, and often, they would blow a whistle that echoed all around the surrounding hills. It was convenient to take the train to the state headquarters, but the closest the line came to Nilghat was at a station called Nilghat Road, about forty kilometres away from Nilghat town. Vijay preferred therefore to travel by road by his own allotted Jeep although it took longer, but it gave him the freedom to travel at his own convenience, to stop wherever he pleased, and not be dictated by the railway timetable.

Vijay was a carefree individual enjoying his freedom and bothered that he had to abandon his broken-down old Jeep and worried whether it could be fixed. It took him wherever he wanted and had become like an old friend. Getting a substitute in the government system could take ages. So, when late that night he heard it being driven, noisily spluttering into his garage, he felt happy.

21

A NORMAL DAY

$\mathcal{T}$he much-postponed tennis match was finally taking place at the circuit house tennis court near Ranjit's bungalow. It was a warm late afternoon but clear with a light breeze blowing in from the lake. The foursome had converged from their respective workplaces at closing time, straight to the tennis court for the game so they could have a good hour and a half before it became too dark to play. Evelyn was in her tennis outfit—white short-sleeved blouse and skirts. The others were in white shirts and shorts. Asaram had prepared some local variant of lemonade—sweetened *nimbu pani* with ice cubes—and laid it out in a jug with glasses on a table by the court. The ball boys had been summoned—made up mainly of drivers' and peons' children who were glad to volunteer in return for some Cadbury's chocolate eclairs and leftover snacks later. All was set before the players arrived.

It was decided to team up Evelyn with Aggarwal the SDJM while Sudarshan and Ranjit comprised the opposing team. This was on the clear knowledge—not overtly mentioned—that Aggarwal was the weakest player in the lot and this combination of players would make it a more balanced game.

Aggarwal indeed posed quite a handicap for Evelyn. Team Evelyn lost the first set 4-6, while she was adjusting to the quirks of her partner. But the second set was closely contested and finally went her team's way at 8-6. The final set was no contest and was easily won by them at 6-2. It was mainly Evelyn's show throughout.

'Well played, Evelyn,' said Ranjit, 'I've never had to work this hard on a game before! We all have to take lessons from you.'

'Thanks, and with pleasure!' said Evelyn with a mock bow.

The group finished up Asaram's lemonade at the court and gathered on the wicker chairs Asaram had placed on the front lawn.

'Let's do this at least once a week,' said Sudarshan. 'To stretch out the playing hours, why don't you arrange some lights?' he asked Ranjit. 'That will give us some flexibility to plan out our playing time.'

'Good suggestion,' agreed Ranjit. 'However, I can ask the PWD to fix new lights if we can get some more players interested in tennis. The executive engineer may not agree if only a few of us use the court.'

Aggarwal volunteered to start an officers' tennis club. 'If Evelyn acts as coach, there will be no problem getting new members!' he joked. Evelyn and the others all laughed at this.

'Don't tell the new members that she has only a week or so left of training here,' said Ranjit. He saw that all of them looked a little disappointed. 'It's true,' he told them. 'She has been assigned only for a month and then she is off to Vijay's subdivision for her last month of district training before she goes back to the Academy for the final year before posting.'

'Too bad,' said Sudarshan. 'Ranjit was saying the other day that he'd like me to take you on a law-and-order situation, but things have been quiet somehow, after you've come. A sort of lull. What you could call an unusually normal period.'

'I hope it stays that way,' said Ranjit quickly. 'We've had too many situations lately, and soon, I hear, the students' agitation is resuming.

Let's enjoy the break till it lasts, and Evelyn can get all her law-and-order exposure with Vijay.'

'Oh yes!' said Sudarshan. 'Actually I am using this break trying to bolster our riot preparedness. I have asked for at least another company of armed police. We should not be caught napping like the last time. Looks like bad times are round the corner.'

'I got a wireless from the chief secretary that the talks with the students have collapsed again and that they are planning their next phase of agitation,' said Ranjit. 'This time, according to the wireless, the agitation will be less Gandhian in nature. That is the general feeling. There has been intelligence also that some are acquiring arms and explosives.'

It was always difficult in these times to get the talk even at social events like this away from work. The mood had turned a little sombre. However, the appearance of Asaram's piping-hot *samosas* lifted spirits a wee bit.

'Great samosas,' said Sudarshan, helping himself to a couple, 'but we will be losing our appetite for your barbecue.' It had been decided that after tennis, they would all take a break, wash up, and meet again at Ranjit's place for a barbecue dinner.

'Don't place much store on that!' said Ranjit. 'You may be disappointed.'

All of them knew that Ranjit was being modest. His culinary accomplishments were widely known and appreciated. He had repaired an old charcoal grill he had found among a heap of rubbish, used perhaps by some English SDO long before and then forgotten, soon after he started living in the old SDO's bungalow. He experimented with it a couple of times and then got the heating and grilling conditions right. Thereafter, his barbecue invitations had become much-awaited events among the officer circle. Right then, there was a set of chicken and mutton pieces being marinated in his fridge, waiting to be put on the grill.

When they reconvened later that evening at Ranjit's bungalow, it was a bigger group. In addition to the four, Biswas the senior executive magistrate, the local PWD executive engineer, the latter two with their spouses, and visiting police circle inspector Jamaluddin had turned up.

The grill was set up under the old mango tree in the lawn, which had been swept clean for the occasion. The group sat in a small circle on a set of miscellaneous chairs which Sundar had brought out and arranged under the tree. The lone electric lamp from the front veranda provided some light apart from the red glow from the charcoal grill.

While Ranjit arranged the chicken on the grill, Sundar brought out his onion *pakoras* and served orange juice to the ladies. The men were offered rum, either neat or with ice and water.

Evelyn was in a bit of a quandary as to whether she should take the orange juice or the rum with ice. The last time she was at Ranjit's place, he had offered her only tea, she recalled, and wondered whether it would look too scandalous if she took a hard drink in front of the ladies. But throwing all caution to the winds, she picked up a glass of rum in time to acknowledge Ranjit's toast. If she saw Ranjit's slightly raised eyebrows at her glass, she chose to ignore it. She determined to have a good time and didn't care what the local gossip circles were going to discuss. She surmised that she had provided good material for them for at least a week.

For once, the outside world was forgotten, and the jokes and banter flowed along with the perfectly barbecued victuals and drinks. The chatter drowned the usual racket from the crickets. The glow of light from the charcoal grill reflected on the happy faces of all the invitees. The darkness outside was interrupted once in a while by the flitting fireflies and the glow of an occasional cycle lamp passing silently by on the road outside.

22

PARTING

*W*hile sipping rum in this company somewhat clandestinely, Evelyn recalled the relatively uninhibited drinking parties that her friends at home sometimes dragged her to. One of the last ones was when her civil services results were announced and she discovered in a national newspaper her roll number among those called for interview. It was initially total disbelief resulting from a wholly unexpected outcome which she clearly had not anticipated, and she was thrilled beyond measure. It gave her a good chance—one in two—to secure at least a stable central government job, if not to the most-coveted foreign or administrative services. Those were also within reach if she could do well in her interview. That was to be a month or so later, the schedule for which she would be informed by post.

At home, her mother and younger sister were in raptures. The three of them comprised her entire family. Her father had died while Evelyn was still a child, and she had hardly any memory of him. Her mother worked hard to bring up her two children. She had a very modest income as a schoolteacher in the local government high school but had taken on private tutoring to augment her income and to pay for her children's education and, when it became apparent that Evelyn had a knack for sports, for her tennis coaching lessons as well. Her hard work had slowly taken her from a junior to a senior teacher's position and, finally when Evelyn had gone to the university, to the headmistress's position. The news of Evelyn's success had changed her entire family's fortunes.

'Lyn, I wish your father was here to see this day!' She wept, on hearing the news from Evelyn on phone, the large burden of raising two girls alone all by herself already appearing to lighten although the uncertainty of the interview still remained. She left her work in the charge of her most-senior teacher and took her two daughters to the nearby church to light some candles to thank Mother Mary for her blessings.

Meanwhile, Evelyn's close friends decided to organise a bash. Not that too many excuses were necessary for parties, but still it was rare for candidates from the north-east to qualify for the central services, and this was an event that couldn't go un-partied. Evelyn wasn't really part of the partying crowd. Her classes and tennis took up most of her time. When not studying, she was busy in the university tennis courts, practising for some upcoming championship or other.

'No excuses, Lyn!' said Peter, who was known as Evelyn's steady. 'This could be among the last times we see you in these parts and so we must make it a rocking event.'

Evelyn agreed for precisely that reason as she was fairly confident that she would secure some job at least, but kept these thoughts to herself. Her protestations that the interview hurdle was still to be crossed found no takers. 'Rocking event' meant a lot of booze and smoking grass, among other things, which college students across the country had begun experimenting with. Having agreed, she finally found herself along with a dozen or so friends of both sexes, mostly pairs, driving down one evening a week before her interview in Delhi, to the guest house of a hydroelectric power company, which was situated at a picturesque dam site not too far out of town. Peter's uncle worked for the company and was able to arrange booking of the whole guest house with its four rooms for them.

The guest house was located amid a forest of pine trees and looked out on a vast body of water created artificially by the dam, ringed by hills in the distance. Although it was a spring day, it always became quite chilly in the mountains as the evening turned to night. The rugs were pulled out from the Jongas, the provisions carried out carefully as there were lots of beer bottles, and the ubiquitous guitars brought out of their cases. A crackling bonfire lit up its immediate surroundings in the dusk and later the pitch-black night.

Far below in the plains, there was turmoil. The hills were also in the grip of sectarian violence with frequent riots between hills and plains people created by narrow political ambitions. A sinister era of intolerance had taken root everywhere. People thought nothing of setting off bombs in crowded marketplaces, killing and maiming dozens of innocent people. So, when after much tuning and plucking of his guitar, Peter began singing quietly one of the veritable hymns of the time, 'Where have all the flowers gone?' it struck a deep chord within everyone. The chatter stopped, and everyone listened intently to Peter's deep baritone. He followed it up with 'How many roads must a man walk down before you can call him a man?' Lighter songs along with beer, grass, and eats followed, with the singing being taken up by others also. Almost everyone had a knack for singing in these parts.

Thus the night moved on with song, and the magic and light-headedness of grass. Through a dizzy haze, Evelyn found that Eddie had the guitar and he was singing quite aptly, 'Lucy in the sky with diamonds . . .' Once in a while during the breaks in the singing, the crowd around the bonfire thinned, with some leaving in pairs to walk along the lake front. But Peter made no move nor glanced her way, which Evelyn thought puzzling.

What not-so-subtle message was he sending her, wondered Evelyn. Was this night organised by Peter not only as her send-off but also as a signal of the end to their relationship, which had begun from high school? If so, so be it, thought Evelyn. She realised that their paths had turned away from each other. But she had to find out.

She got a chance when at one point, all the others had left temporarily, either knowingly to give them some privacy or by chance.

'Peter, what's got into you?' she asked. 'What's the cause of this heavy indifference?'

'Look, Lyn, don't you see your making it to the Civil Services has changed everything? While of course I'm happy for you, don't you realise the practical problems this has caused our relationship? I can't give up my family business, and you will have to take up postings at other places. Let's enjoy this last party and remember all our good times.'

Evelyn was not yet that practical a person. The images of the many days of walking hand in hand at the little lake in the municipal gardens, the many meetings alone and with friends at the momo and tea shops in the bazaar—all flashed through her mind. But she realised that she had to leave these behind.

Soon the others returned. The night was giving way to dawn. Someone was singing, 'Morning has broken, like the first morning; blackbird has spoken, like the first bird . . .' Almost everyone had sung their various pieces, the renderings of joy, sorrow, or protest. There was finally a request that Evelyn must close the proceedings. She wasn't a good singer but could hold a tune a little, like everyone else in these parts. She tried to think what would be apt for this nostalgic occasion. With Peter accompanying her on the guitar, she sang quite emotionally the Joan Baez break-up song:

> You, who are so good with words
> And at keeping things vague
>
> 'Cause I need some of that vagueness now
> It's all come back too clearly
> I once loved you dearly
> And if you're offering me diamonds and rust
> Well, I've already paid . . .

23

INTERVIEW

$\mathcal{E}$velyn had dressed simply in a yellow-and-white combination *salwar kameez* for her interview as some friends had advised her. She was given to understand that the intention of the interview was not to discover how much she knew—this had already been tested in the written exams—but to gauge her overall personality for the job. Despite this knowledge which had reassured her somewhat, when her name was called and she entered the large interview room, the interview panel—all looking solemn and serious—looked formidable. It consisted of six members: apart from the chairman, there were five national experts from various fields. There was only one lady panellist. Evelyn tried not to look nervous.

After the preliminary questions about where she was from and her background, the committee warmed up to the real interview business.

'How do you propose, as a woman, particularly one from the north-east, to command respect from your male subordinates?' asked one of the panellists.

'Mrs Gandhi has shown the way for all Indian women,' Evelyn began. 'If one is good in one's work and can handle difficult situations well, I think one can gain respect from all those around.'

'But how can you be sure that you will be able to handle situations well?' was the follow-up question.

'Well, I don't right now. But I suppose that is what I will be taught during my training,' was Evelyn's reply. She noticed that there was a nod from the questioner and smiles all around.

Questions followed on foreign affairs (such as what was the US position on Kashmir), on current affairs, and on her particular subject, botany. She wasn't too sure that she had answered all questions well. But she was happy that in botany, she had answered fairly well. She was asked, for example, to explain very simply in layperson's terms Mendel's discovery on genetics and how it was different from the prevailing theories of the time, such as Darwin's. She explained about Mendel's background in the monastery and the experiment with the peas. Occasionally there were follow-up questions to her answers.

She had heard there were questions on Indian culture and particularly on the epics. So she was prepared when the culture expert asked, 'Since you are from the north-east, tell me, who was Chitrangada?'

'A Manipuri princess whom Arjuna met during the period of exile of the Pandavas and married,' said Evelyn.

But she was stumped by the next question, 'Who was their son?'

Evelyn smiled and said she didn't have the answer. The interview was going well, although she knew that no one expected her to be an encyclopaedia; still, she had hoped she knew the answer. But she was reassured, however, when the chairman picked up on her major extracurricular activity, tennis and asked, 'You say that you have won prizes and medals in tennis. Can you tell us a little about your accomplishments?'

'I am the current state champion and have held my championship trophy for the last three years. I am also seeded fourth in the national ranking among women players,' she said modestly.

'That's excellent, and I am sure it will stand you in good stead in the future. Thank you and that will be all,' he said, closing the interview.

When Evelyn got outside, she checked her watch and was surprised that forty-five minutes had elapsed. Successful candidates she had consulted while preparing for her interview generally said that if it went on for more than half an hour, it signalled that it had gone well. She had hardly noticed how fast the time had flown.

Evelyn called up her mother on reaching her friend's flat where she was putting up. 'There's no way to tell how it's gone, Mama,' she said. 'More than a thousand candidates have been called for interview for just four hundred openings in all the services put together,' she added, trying not to raise any expectations.

Having come all the way to Delhi, Evelyn decided to stay on with her friend till her results were announced. It was a small flat being shared by three other girls from the north-east, near Delhi University, where the girls were studying. She had brought her sleeping bag with her, and it sufficed; although the others wanted to give up their beds for her, she declined their offers. These girls were studying hard for their final exams, and she didn't want to disturb them.

About a month remained still for the big day. The days were long and hot, especially so for her, used to living in colder altitudes. The wait seemed endless. She would occasionally get called to parties where some north-east girls who had made it to the services were invited. She heard a lot of stories about the Academy, the great times they had there and at Mussoorie, the picturesque hill station where it was located, and dared not dream about such possibilities for herself. Instead, she focused on her life after college, trying to secure a job with some local establishment in her town or coming to Delhi to look for one, focusing more on her tennis, and so on.

The results were to be announced in the end of May after the university had closed for the summer vacations. The last week of her wait was in a completely deserted university campus. Of the three girls, two had left for home, but one, Joanna, stayed on and would be leaving with her. The building which took on a lot of boarders had stopped their common meal facilities, so Evelyn and Joanna had to go to a local *dhaba* to have their meals. Seeing the campus, which otherwise would be swarming with students, totally empty was weird. The loud conversations and banter, the long lines of buses emptying loads of students on the teeming pavements, the overcrowded grounds and cafes—all disappeared in a day, and a deathly silence took hold.

After a particularly hot day, a dust storm hit the campus. The sky darkened, and the wind blew viciously, tossing the trees and upsetting flowerpots and covering everything in dust. A few drops of rain also fell, bringing a welcome drop in the temperature. Although not superstitious, Evelyn secretly wondered what this darkening of the skies portended. That evening after the *aandhi*,[23] when the skies had cleared again, Joanna and Evelyn took a walk through the main road that bisected the campus, skirted the lawns, and came out the other side without finding a soul, although the offices and libraries were apparently still functioning.

The day finally arrived when the results would be put up on the walls of the Union Public Service Commission building in New Delhi near India Gate. With beating heart, Evelyn and Joanna got out of their scooter taxi and made their way through the crowds of worried candidates.

At a few minutes past noon, a couple of staff came out with sheaves of paper and started pasting them on the walls. When they were done and left, all the waiting candidates surged forward. Evelyn started scanning the list called Central Services and didn't find her name. Disappointed, she moved to the list called Indian Administrative Service. There were a hundred or so names, and going down the list, she saw *it*! Her name was 94th on the list, but this did not matter—she was now a member of the very-coveted administrative service! Joanna came up and hugged her, and Evelyn had to go and sit down at a nearby bench to get over her overwhelming feeling of relief.

When she returned to her lodgings, she found that the landlord had disconnected the phone line. So the next day, while Joanna and she waited at New Delhi station for their train to roll in, Evelyn went to the post office at the station and sent off a one-line urgent telegram to her mother:

GOOD NEWS. SELECTED IN INDIAN
ADMINISTRATIVE SERVICE = LYN

When the train set off finally on its long journey home, Evelyn hoped that the telegram would arrive earlier than she did. When after a day and a half, she finally got off the train and then her bus and started climbing the hill up to her home, after her long and exhausting journey, she saw that it had. There were balloons and streamers outside the door, and celebrations were in the offing.

24

VIJAY

Vijay's days were usually quite full, like Ranjit's, but his set of challenges were different. For a long time, his subdivision was basically a part of the *sadar* or headquarters subdivision of Nilghat district and had only lately been carved out as a separate subdivision. In fact, it was Vijay's particular distinction to be the first subdivisional officer of the new subdivision, and one of his major tasks was to get it up and running. The government had constructed the subdivisional courts and the SDO's bungalow and renovated existing quarters of the circle office to provide housing for some of the officials. But construction was still going on to provide accommodation for offices and staff. This gave Vijay the opportunity to be creative to plan out roads, locations, and choice of designs of buildings and staff quarters. Since land was plenty, he tried to see that all staff buildings and quarters had ample grounds and had good views such as his own bungalow, which had a grand panoramic vista.

So, a lot of his time was spent with the executive engineer of the Public Works Department. Unfortunately, this man had a dubious past, with rumours that he was corrupt big time. Officials such as him deliberately sought out postings in remote places away from public gaze and with considerable contracting work to make money in. He lived lavishly with his dollish wife and several large Samoyeds which kept prancing about on his lawn. He also owned a shiny new Fiat, white like his dogs. This was a subject of particular envy among his colleagues in the subdivision, who could hardly dream of owning a car till mid-career. Vijay kept receiving anonymous complaints from failed bidders that he passed on regularly under confidential cover to the man's boss, the district superintending engineer in Nilghat, which did not appear to make any palpable difference. Vijay was convinced that the whole department was on the take. He merely tried to ensure that the quality of work did not suffer, although not being an engineer himself, he had no way of being certain that the buildings being built would not start cracking and tumbling down in a few years.

Another major project in the subdivision was surveying the land and registering land rights. With growing population and spread of settled cultivation, more and more tribal people were being encouraged to give up the traditional *jhum* or slash-and-burn method of farming and settle down and take up terrace cultivation. The land therefore had to be properly surveyed, including the boundaries of plots, and registered under the cultivator's name. This conferred the all-important title to the plot holder, and it could be used for obtaining bank loans and improving the lot of poor farmers. Although it was a very slow process, Vijay gave the task high priority and would often go out with survey parties.

Vijay recalled how the chief secretary had played a funny joke on them when he along with his batchmates paid a courtesy call on him upon arriving at the state for their first posting. The chief secretary was in a nostalgic mood which newly appointed officers always induced him into, causing him to recall his younger days three decades or so earlier. After giving them some sage advice on how to conduct themselves and so on, he said that they must take their training very seriously, particularly training in survey school as land surveys and records had been historically the chief work of all civil service officers right from the time of Todar Mall, the famous minister of Akbar the Great who introduced the revenue system during Mughal times which later the British adopted and that continues even today.

'And don't forget to pay Mr Gunia my respects when you meet him in survey school,' he concluded.

So, when Vijay's batch was assigned to the survey school for a month of intensive training, the first person to meet them informally before the course was to begin was the principal. One of Vijay's batchmates blurted out, 'Very pleased to meet you, Mr Gunia, the chief secretary sends his respects!'

The principal took out a small brass scale from his pocket calmly. 'Let me first introduce him to you,' said the man, totally unperturbed. 'This is Mr Gunia,' he said, holding up the tiny scale for everybody to see. 'I am sure he is happy to meet you and likewise sends his respects. As for me, I am Chowdhury, your principal.'

'But don't be embarrassed in the least,' he continued. 'The CS has been playing this joke regularly with all batches that have called on him since I don't know when!'

Mr Gunia was a constant companion during the entire course and an invaluable measuring device needed for all survey drawings, along with the theodolite. Vijay never failed to chuckle to himself whenever he saw the gunia in the hands of his survey staff. He liked going out with them to camp in remote locations and meet the local villagers. It was a critical anti-poverty process, and he valued the idea of slowly empowering the countryside through this slow but steady work of measuring, plotting, mapping, and recording.

The other set of challenges related to Mother Nature. The stream that ran through the subdivision often turned into a swollen torrent during the rains, causing havoc in its way, washing away tenements near the shore, breaching the embankment and the road that ran along its course, cutting off communications, and inundating low-lying villages for days.

That Mother Nature took on an angry countenance often was due partly, Vijay realised, to the harm that humans were causing her. All around him, there was evidence of this. The green hills were turning gradually and—as though inexorably—to brown. Wanton illegal felling was going on, and all the government functionaries except a few were party to this looting. Among the honest and sincere ones, he counted his friend the divisional forest officer, who was fiercely involved in the fight to save the forests.

Vijay soon engaged himself wholeheartedly in this effort too. When the survey party had completed survey of two ten-mile-long stretches of degraded forest land along either side of the riverbank adjoining the town and had classified it as a 'revenue village' for settlement, he cancelled the classification and converted the stretches to 'forest' and personally trekked the entire stretches on both sides along with the DFO to hand over the long stretches to the forest department for reforestation. This was very soon after he had joined as SDO, and now the young trees had taken root and what was earlier barren rocky lengths of mountain terrain had turned into young forests again, the tender branches swaying with passing winds.

Looking out from his high veranda perch, Vijay enjoyed seeing this view each morning. He also liked often to climb up the mountain path behind his bungalow which led to a thick forest of conifers. Buried within its luxuriant verdant depths and reassured by the rough but strong and solid feel of the tall tree trunks, he could never consider the forest without some awe.

This massive forest had been here since ancient times, far longer than even the ancient monastery he had discovered, he told himself. 'Longer than your tribe and mine, my friend,' he told a bemused langur which had stumbled on to his path. 'And if we don't mess up, it will still be there millions of years after we are gone!'

Bhagat, who had caught up with the SDO meanwhile and saw him talking to a langur, wondered whether loneliness was finally getting to his boss. He had heard that Evelyn memsahib, the new assistant collector, was coming soon for training and wondered whether that was the antidote his boss needed.

25

THE INCIDENT AT
THE COLLEGE

$\mathcal{I}$t was again a dull day with routine land acquisition work that Evelyn had fairly mastered. Her final task was to finalise the status of the detailed brief that had to be sent to the DC, with a copy to the chief secretary, on the State Mining Corporation acquisition.

Yesterday was more interesting, although in a sinister way. Ranjit had heard all parties and turned down any plea for stay of the proceedings. Evelyn was present in Biswas's courtroom when he (on behalf of Ranjit) had announced the scale of compensation that the SDO had proposed, and suggested that the SDO would make this the final award. There was a lot of commotion when Biswas announced this, but he mentioned that the petitioners were still free to appeal to the DC, who could call for the records and make a decision himself. He informed them that he was prepared to wait for the Hon'ble DC to satisfy himself, if the parties so wished his intervention to further scrutinise that due process had been followed and the scale of compensation was appropriate.

This was particularly so as the SDO had been given final authority under the law in the matter and his award closed all proceedings. This meant that the dispossessed tribal people had to vacate their land within a period of thirty days, and if they failed to do so, would be forcibly evicted. The compensation that Biswas announced was about double that awarded earlier in similar cases. He also informed the petitioners that the ADC of the district has been appointed as the rehabilitation coordinator to provide adequate additional support from state development agencies to the families affected by the acquisition and that it was the state's aim to ensure that these families faced as little hardship as possible.

The courtroom was full as apart from several villagers and their headman whom Evelyn recognised, there were their lawyers as well as Susheela Gautam, the lawyer on behalf of the national NGO supporting the villagers, along with several of her juniors. There was also a fairly big crowd outside. On hearing the announcement, a couple of young people who had been standing outside rushed in. One of them shouted, 'Down with the SDO and DC! *Murdabad! Murdabad!*'[24] Another ran up to Biswas, who looked on in astonishment as the man attempted to snatch away the papers on the table. One of the court peons engaged him in a scuffle and, with the intervention of the constable assigned to the court, managed to subdue him. However, the papers were scattered all around, a cup of tea was overturned, some of which fell on Biswas's white shirt. The two men were arrested and taken away for disorderly conduct and assault.

That was yesterday, and now all was quiet as Evelyn put the finishing touches on the report, thinking that she could leave early when office hours were over. The report had to go out to Ranjit by close of business for his final review. The matter was getting out of hand, and that major discontent was brewing had to be communicated to all superior authorities so that they were aware of the consequences of the state's decisions.

Ranjit's office peon came in, saying that he wanted to see her. Probably wanting to know how the report was coming along, thought

Evelyn. She found Ranjit at his desk with Sudarshan, the SDPO opposite him smartly turned out in his Indian Police Service uniform.

'Are you done with the report?' asked Ranjit, exactly as Evelyn had expected.

On hearing that she was, he went on, 'There is a problem at the local college, as you are aware,' said Ranjit. 'Now matters have come to a head. We just heard that the students are protesting the removal of the principal and the governing body by staging a *gherao*,[25] preventing the executive committee members from moving out of the meeting room they are in. Obviously, this is being directed by the ex-principal.'

'I just got a call from the secretary of the executive committee to rescue him and the committee members,' he added. 'Sudarshan is going to the college with a platoon of policemen in case needed to clear the way to rescue the committee and wants an executive magistrate to accompany him. This will give you finally some exposure you wanted to our law-and-order functions. Sudarshan will fill you in with the details while you are on your way. Get in touch with me over radio if any force has to be used. If that is necessary, I will come in myself, although I don't think it'll come to that.'

Evelyn deposited the draft report with Ranjit and took her car, and Sudarshan got in with her; his police Jeep and the riot police led by a sub-inspector in a covered police truck followed. The local college was on the outskirts of the town, and it took a little time for the three vehicles to negotiate the crowded streets.

Sudarshan explained that the college principal and the sacked governing body had been found by an audit party to have been misusing government grants that the college had been receiving for several years. Pending an enquiry into the matter, an executive committee had been appointed, with the SDO as the chairman. Ranjit left routine matters to be tackled by the secretary, and he had attended only one meeting so far of the executive committee. Nevertheless, he was in charge. The principal didn't want the SDO and the executive committee to find out more of his misdoings and wanted the committee out by hook or by crook. He had instigated a section of students, particularly some tribal students on scholarships, to start a protest program to oust the committee.

Normally the police avoided entering academic institutions as it would, in the words of student critics, 'destroy the sanctity' of the campus. On the other hand, when the college authorities sought their intervention to prevent a crime—which holding people against their will amounted to—they were duty-bound to intervene as now.

On reaching the college, she found a large number of college students—almost two hundred—with over half of them girls, outside the principal's room and in the corridors. Some of them, mainly girls, were sitting in front of the principal's room, where the executive committee members were being gheraoed. On seeing the police party, they rushed towards them.

Sudarshan and Evelyn got off the car and approached a bearded tribal youth who seemed to be the ringleader. He held out his arms, barring the way to the room, and a number of students started milling around them. Some were a little surprised at seeing what appeared to be a woman official in the police party.

'Do you realise that you are committing a grave offence by preventing the executive committee members from leaving?' Sudarshan told them. 'Please disperse peacefully or else—'

'Or else, what?' shouted another student. 'We are going nowhere until the executive committee members all resign. Use whatever force you want, we are ready!'

The sub-inspector commanding the platoon pushed his way in and saluted Sudarshan. 'Platoon ready, sir,' he said. Meanwhile, the platoon of about fifteen policemen with their *lathis* and riot shields had got off the truck and arranged themselves in an open space near the principal's office.

The show of police strength did not seem to deter the students, however. In fact, they seemed to have gotten more belligerent. At a cue from the ringleader, they began shouting slogans such as 'Executive committee shame, shame!' and 'Resign, resign,' and 'Get out before we boot you out.' This went on for a long time.

The sub-inspector had meanwhile gotten hold of a few students he knew and tried to reason with them. They went into a huddle. Sudarshan and Evelyn stood apart, waiting. The discussions continued for a long time, but the sub-inspector persisted. Finally, however, he gave up. 'They are in no mood to give in, sir,' he told Sudarshan. 'We may have to use force.'

Sudarshan went to the group and tried his brand of persuasion. He explained patiently that this nonsense had gone on long enough, and as a police officer, he couldn't allow this to continue any longer. The students were not prepared to yield. He gave them five minutes to disperse. Then he called the sub-inspector and asked him to get ready. The party got hold of their megaphone and started unfurling the red flag which was a signal for an unlawful assembly to disperse. He came back and looked at Evelyn to see if she was ready to declare the assembly unlawful and sign orders to that effect. As the executive magistrate present, she had to authorise the use of force. But before doing so, Evelyn would have to consult Ranjit as instructed by him.

'Let me talk once more to the ringleader,' she said, and she walked up to the bearded youth.

'Look here,' she said. 'I am the magistrate here, and the police want me to authorise use of force.' The youth was taken aback a little at this young tribal woman who claimed to be a magistrate addressing him. Before he could say anything, she continued, 'These men are about to begin a *lathi* charge to make way for us to get the committee members out. It may end in very serious injuries to you and other students who resist. We have orders to get these people out peacefully if possible and by force if necessary. Why don't we reach a compromise? You offer peaceful resistance, and we will arrest all of you peacefully also. That way, no one gets hurt or killed. You can tell the people who are advising you that you resisted and had to court arrest, and we can also get our job done.'

Whatever be his show of bravado, Evelyn realised that the youth must have been feeling some trepidation, especially when he realised that the police party was deadly earnest about their intent. This administration, he knew, had often resorted to force in recent times. He decided that Evelyn's offer was a good enough face-saving compromise. Besides, being arrested would also turn them into heroes.

He went back to the others and, after some time, came back to Evelyn, telling her that the students had agreed to her proposal. 'We will come up in batches of ten, and you can then arrest us,' he said. Evelyn went up to Sudarshan and explained what had to be done. This required some logistics—buses to get this large a group of arrested students away from the scene. But once the plan was agreed on by all parties, there was a palpable sense of relief everywhere. This had gone on for hours; it was nearly ten in the night, and everyone had to go home.

The students continued their slogans for quite some while, till the private buses commandeered by the local *thana* trundled up to the college grounds. As agreed, the students came up in batches of ten continuing to shout their slogans, were arrested and asked to board the buses peacefully. One by one, the buses left. Finally, Evelyn and Sudarshan went into the principal's room and met the secretary and the committee members.

'Wish you could have done this faster,' said one of the distraught committee members, not at all grateful to his rescuers. 'We have been sitting here since morning and haven't even had a drop of water to drink!'

But Evelyn was happy that the matter had been resolved somewhat amicably without force and no one was hurt even though these worthies had been inconvenienced. She wanted to brief Ranjit about the outcome.

'May I use the phone?' she asked the secretary and called up Ranjit from the office.

After the first ring, Ranjit picked up the phone. 'Evelyn, thank goodness no force was needed, but did you send all two hundred students to jail?'

'Well, isn't that what you are supposed to do when you arrest people?' asked Evelyn, incredulous.

'No, no, we will have a situation in our hands. Come over and I'll explain,' Ranjit said, ringing off.

26

A BAD SITUATION

$\mathcal{R}$anjit was in his bungalow office when Evelyn arrived. It was nearing midnight, and he was busy dictating the report on the college situation for the DC, and all others concerned, to his confidential assistant and indicated that she should sit down. Evelyn was able to catch the last part of the message:

> SITUATION HANDLED ABLY BY ASSISTANT COLLECTOR UNDER TRAINING WHO LIFTED THE ILLEGAL OBSTRUCTION OF THE COMMITTEE MEMBERS BY ARRESTING THE STUDENTS ON MY ORDERS STOP EXPECT TO RELEASE ALL STUDENTS TOMORROW.

After he was through, he turned to her.

'The correct procedure in such arrests is to take those arrested some distance away from the place of incident and then release them,' he said. 'Unless it is a very serious offence, sending them to jail is not resorted to, particularly in the case of students. Besides, the jail superintendent called me up, saying that he wasn't prepared to receive such a large number of under-trial prisoners.

'Of course, this isn't your fault. I should have told you about this before sending you out. But I didn't think that the students would resist our attempts to free the executive committee members. There seems to be a sinister mind behind all of this.

'I am fairly convinced that someone wanted deliberately to create a nasty situation, which you prevented. But I hope we can resolve this complication quickly.'

While Evelyn waited, a little upset that her intervention hadn't gone off fully satisfactorily, Ranjit picked up his phone and called Aggarwal, the subdivisional judicial magistrate.

'Aggarwal sahib, I need your help,' he said, explaining the situation. It was agreed that the SDJM would hear the student' cases the first thing next morning and free all of them on the basis of personal recognisance bonds.

'That should do it,' he said, replacing the receiver, relieved finally. And then he said, turning to Evelyn, 'Why don't you have something to eat before you go? You must be famished.'

They went out to the veranda and Ranjit asked Sundar to fetch his bottle of rum and glasses. Sundar realised that the officer memsahib had graduated to drinks from tea, after serving her at the barbecue. Ranjit also asked that his dinner be heated up and served for the two of them outside as well.

'I am beginning to figure out what's happening,' he said while they drank their rum. 'The principal knows that this student agitation is soon reviving, and to save his skin, he is trying to get the students who are already quite worked up to discredit us to serve his own narrow interests. But we have to be a step ahead of him. I only hope we have not played into his hands by sending the students to jail.'

It was well past midnight when they finished their modest but what appeared to Evelyn a delicious dinner prepared by Sundar of chapatis, dal, egg curry, and fried vegetables. Evelyn had sent her driver home, and Ranjit took out his Jeep and dropped her the short distance to the circuit house. 'Have a good night, and let's see what's in store for us tomorrow,' he said before driving off.

Unfortunately for them, events unfolded in the next few days according to Ranjit's pessimistic but—as it turned out—realistic view about the principal's intentions, and the wily man had indeed been a step ahead of him. When the students were produced next morning in batches before the SDJM, they refused to sign personal recognisance bonds that would have freed them. Instead, they all— one hundred and ninety-seven in total—returned to jail, demanding that the administration withdraw the cases against them.

By the afternoon, he was receiving calls from angry parents who wanted their children home. He explained that they had all been offered liberty on personal undertakings but were refusing to sign them. He asked them to persuade their wards to do so and end the matter amicably. The girls' parents were able to take them all away, but the ninety-five boys were determined to stay on in jail. It was becoming quite a game for them and their controller, the principal, Ranjit felt.

Late in the evening, the jail superintendent called Ranjit to say that a new problem had arisen. The boys were refusing to have chapatis served to them as they were complaining that they were of poor quality. 'Do they think that they are in a five-star hotel?' he asked.

On day three, Ranjit was informed by the superintendent that the students were now all on hunger strike, refusing to eat the jail food. Privately, he learnt from Sudarshan that the boys' parents were quietly supplying them food, so he wasn't too worried. However, a news item appeared in a local paper that the arrested boys were all officially on hunger strike. He realised that the opposition was now trying to whip up sentiment using the press, who had printed the item without checking with him or Sudarshan about the facts.

That evening, Ranjit paid a visit to the jail. He found all the students lying on mats or playing cards or chatting. They didn't seem to be too affected by the fast. He had taken the subdivisional medical officer, who checked them up and said they were all OK.

'We want the cases against us withdrawn without condition. Till that happens, we will fast unto death if necessary,' said the bearded ringleader, on Ranjit's request to give up fasting.

Afterwards, the subdivisional medical officer said that young people could easily survive without food for long periods and there was no need to worry for at least a week so long as the students kept drinking water. As they were doing that, there were no health risks so far.

On the fourth day, the national papers picked up the story. Reporting was factual without comment. In the evening, he got a call first from the DC, who wanted to know the latest situation.

'It's rather extraordinary, isn't it, that students go on hunger strike for withdrawal of minor cases against them, merely to defend their principal?' he said. 'The problem is that the principal is a well-known literary figure and murkier facts about him are not known generally. That's why the Education Department is taking a cautious approach to build up a case against him. But this is not a battle that we should fight. Let the Education Department, who got us involved, solve their own problem.'

An hour or so later, the Education Secretary called him up from state headquarters. 'Ranjit, the Department of Personnel and the chief secretary are quite upset that we did not consult them when setting up the executive committee. I have decided to restructure the committee, and the government would not be involved any more with this private institution. Sorry that we landed you in this mess.'

Ranjit was happy that as far as his superiors in the administration were concerned, they were solidly behind him. He needed that as things started getting uglier.

On the ninth day since the arrest, the hunger strike had entered the sixth day. The All-State Students' Union announced support for the students as reported in a statewide newspaper. As usual, no one bothered to check the administration's side of the story.

Condemning the callousness of the district administration to the condition of the ninety-five students on hunger strike now for a week, the general secretary of the All-State Students' Union has extended support of the union to the college students and demanded immediate withdrawal of the cases against them. Our Nilghat correspondent was informed by jail authorities that the students' condition was precarious, and two of them had fainted and had to be revived.

Ranjit called up the jail superintendent on reading the story. The superintendent was not aware of any student fainting. But he said he would check and call back. After a while, he did. 'The medical officer has been regularly checking the condition of the students. Two of them said they felt light-headed and went to sleep. Their blood pressure is a little lower than normal, but otherwise, they are all OK,' he said.

On the morning of the tenth day, the Nilghat police superintendent along with Sudarshan came by Ranjit's office. Over tea which Ranjit's peon had promptly provided, he said, 'The DC asked me to come around as the chief secretary is getting worried. The papers are now all reporting this situation on their front pages prominently. The problem is that even if we wanted, we don't have powers to withdraw cases of this nature once they are filed in court. Only the state government has those powers. I am reluctant to recommend any withdrawal as it would set up a bad precedent.'

Where will you get another case where such a precedent would come into play, thought Ranjit, but he kept the thought to himself. Instead, he said, 'That is a matter for you to decide. Meanwhile, I want to take away any initiative from the principal, who has been dictating this matter for far too long.'

After they had left, he called Evelyn. She had another two days of training left in the subdivision. 'Evelyn, let's complete what we started before you leave. I want you to visit the government hospital and meet the subdivisional medical officer and get ninety-five beds ready. We are going to force-feed the strikers. Meet Sudarshan and get the police to take over a ward and convert it into a temporary jail with adequate police staff. No reporters or visitors allowed. There will be medical bulletins put out twice a day on the condition of the students, who should be looked after properly by all doctors and nursing staff. Get our publicity officer to put out these bulletins to the papers and also the entire set of facts of the case. I want you to take charge and have the students in the hospital by five this evening.'

Evelyn rushed out to make these arrangements while Ranjit called up Sudarshan and the subdivisional medical officer. He was confident that things would be in place now that Evelyn was in charge. He wanted her to leave with some feeling of accomplishment and decided to talk to the DC to hold her transfer to Vijay's subdivision on training until this blew over.

When he visited the hospital along with Evelyn that evening, the students were all in the temporary jail hospital. The medical officer said that the students had agreed to being fed intravenously. They all looked well, and the first medical bulletin along with the complete facts of the case had gone out to the media both local and national. The doctor in attendance confirmed that there was no danger to the health of the students, who were getting all the essential nutrition they needed.

This farce continued for another four days. After the administration had put out all the facts and the regular medical bulletins confirmed that the students were in good health, the press lost interest and stopped reporting the case. Finally, the students—and very likely on advice of the principal—decided en masse that they would sign the bonds. This was also perhaps as they started getting bored in the hospital with nothing to do, and the whole episode ended as quickly as it had started.

When Evelyn was ready to leave the next day for Vijay's subdivision, Ranjit dropped by at the circuit house. 'This is a temporary victory,' he told Evelyn. 'The battle lines are clearly drawn, and the students' mood is aggressive. Worse still are things I hear happening underground. We are in for a long period of uncertainty and turmoil, I'm afraid.'

Rising, he escorted her to her car and added, 'You've been a great help, Evelyn. I hope you learnt some things despite all of this.' Then before waving her off, he laughed and said, 'And finally, don't forget to brush up on arrest laws and procedures!'

27

TRANSFORMATION BY WHEAT

The circuit house in Vijay's subdivision was new, Evelyn discovered, and so was the staff. The latter aspect implied, among other things, that the caretaker had very few culinary skills. Although she wasn't too fussy about food, Evelyn at least wanted her omelette not half burnt or her fried egg not so messed up that it resembled an omelette. Or the staple elements of all meals, *dal* and rice, at least cooked tolerably well, instead of the watery souplike substance that the *dal* turned out to be, and the sticky gruel that was served as rice in nearly all meals during the initial weeks of her stay. And the less said about the vegetable curries, the better: they were either too salty or too spicy. She asked the caretaker therefore to focus on just simple fries. By the time she left, at least these basic items in the menu had been brought up to minimum standards.

Similarly, the gardener's skills were confined strictly to cutting grass—in which he was aided by his cow, whom he allowed to graze on the lawn—and planting rows of marigolds. Raising flowers other than this was not part of his repertoire. By the time Evelyn had left, at least the range of flowers sown had increased, although she was not able to see them bloom.

Despite these shortcomings, Evelyn was happy to be there. Life in this small subdivisional town was quiet, a wonderful respite from the frenetic pace at which events unfolded one after the other in Ranjit's subdivision. Her days of training, mainly with the survey teams, learning cadastral survey techniques and record and registration of land titles, were routine as training was supposed to be. There were no law-and-order problems, and the tribal agitation had not as yet touched the villages in these hills. The little subdivisional town was pretty and neat, with its collection of newly constructed houses with brightly red-painted corrugated iron roofs. The circuit house was situated on the same part of the hill as was Vijay's bungalow and commanded the same grand prospect of hills, the forests, the river valley, and the rail line over the viaduct. In the early morning, the mist would rise from below, sometimes covering and sometimes uncovering the view. It reminded her very much of home.

One morning, Suresh, the project officer for the Integrated Rural Development Project arrived from Nilghat in his white Jeep. Vijay had arranged that he would take Evelyn to meet some innovative farmers who were being encouraged to introduce wheat as a new winter crop to augment their meagre incomes.

On the way, Suresh explained that most local peasants had been growing only rice as a single crop on their terraced plots for centuries. In the dry winter season, their land lay fallow. The government was now introducing quick-maturing and low-moisture-requiring varieties of wheat, which could be grown in winter. This additional crop meant doubling of incomes and could transform the lives of farmers. This was palpable in some villages through which they drove.

'The first thing you notice is the way the children going to school are dressed,' said Suresh, pointing to a large group of children walking to school. 'These children have proper uniforms and appear also to be in better health. In single-crop villages, you won't find this.' And indeed, that appeared to be the case, the contrast striking.

After some bumpy driving on steep and winding dirt tracks, near a much-poorer village, they arrived at a small farmer's land which had been selected for demonstration. Wheat saplings were already growing at a lush green demonstration plot, which contrasted strikingly with the innumerable dusty brown terraced fields running down the valley. A small group of farmers had gathered to hear about the quiet revolution that was taking place and how they could be part of it.

While Suresh and an agricultural extension officer explained the process of wheat cultivation in detail, Evelyn recalled the debate after dinner many months back in the DC's bungalow when Ranjit had strongly argued about the benefits that development can bring and how it could resolve strife and misery. Things like this silent transformation in the countryside never made it to the news as much as bomb attacks, student hunger strikes, and police *lathi* charges did. Yet there were few things more worthy of being heralded and publicised than these.

'Why didn't you tell us about this earlier?' one of the farmers asked Suresh. Evelyn was curious to know how Suresh would answer this very pertinent question. She knew that several complex factors were involved: ingrained cultural practices that for centuries had made rice cultivation a way of life, for one. Resistance to eating *rotis* made from wheat in place of rice had made wheat cultivation pointless. The slow progress in agriculture research to develop high-yielding varieties of wheat mainly due to the government's insufficient attention to rural development was perhaps the most important factor.

Instead, Suresh said, 'This program was introduced in our state only two years back. We are trying as much as we can to spread wheat as a second crop. Please tell everyone about what you saw today. We are here to help in every way possible.'

Evelyn felt that Suresh's reply was apt but obviously left many questions unanswered. It was a decade or so since the green revolution had arrived in the country. When so much could be gained by changing the lives of the poor, why didn't the state put in more funds? What prevented the politicians who, in a democracy, were supposed to respond to the needs of the electorate from making the right decisions in their interests?

On their way back to town, Suresh gave his simple take on the matter. 'Without education, it is too difficult to expect the poor majority in our country to be capable of holding the politicians to account for their condition. But wait for a few more decades. Things could change radically!'

The tribal students in the state were not waiting for those many years and had already taken matters into their hands, thought Evelyn to herself. When democracy dies, protest can jerk it back to life, else in desperation or mischievous ambition, extra-constitutional extremism takes over.

When they reached the circuit house, the caretaker had a message from Vijay. He handed over an envelope in the SDO's stationery, which had a small hand-written note. It said,

Evelyn,

Please come over for dinner along with Suresh at around 7.30 p.m. We have a surprise guest. Only vegetarian fare, though, I'm afraid. But I promise you good company and conversation! See you both soon.

Vijay

28

THE ENIGMATIC BIRD

*A*s Evelyn and Suresh drove up to Vijay's bungalow, who the surprise guest was no longer remained a surprise. The ADC's black Ambassador car was parked in the driveway, his official designation displayed on it in bold red letters. However, when Suresh and Evelyn entered the drawing room, Evelyn made the usual exclamations expressing surprise so that the host and surprise guest were not disappointed.

The ADC was already seated on the sofa, with a glass of rum in his hand and his bird-spotting binoculars and camera resting on the side table beside him.

'Ah, here is the iron lady of Nilghat herself!' he exclaimed on seeing Evelyn. 'Madam, your fame has spread far and wide. Two hundred students sent behind bars on your very first law-and-order assignment!' he said jokingly.

'I should have known better than put those students behind bars,' said Evelyn, a bit embarrassed. It appeared that her little tryst with the college students had been much discussed at district headquarters, and she was not very comfortable with the thought.

Realising her discomfiture with the topic, the ADC added, 'That's a matter of detail which we should have warned you about. But no harm's done, mission accomplished with no noses left bleeding, nor any heads broken. And we have another law-and-order expert in our district. The DC feels that we, most certainly, must place you in the vanguard of our next encounter with student protestors!'

'Hear, hear!' said Vijay, entering the room. He had gone to his bungalow office room and had a wireless message in his hand. He gave the message to the ADC and asked Suresh and Evelyn what they would like to drink. Suresh asked for a rum, and Evelyn hesitated a little and then decided to go for a Thums Up cola with ice. She wasn't sure whether the ADC would approve her joining the boozers' club.

But the ADC would have none of it. 'What, the iron lady with a glass of Thums Up? I thought you were more spirited than that!' he said.

Evelyn acceded willingly. Glasses of rum were handed out. Rum, rather than any other liquor, seemed to be the favourite by far over all other drinks and was the standard fare in these parts. Very few even thought of stocking anything else.

'Cheers and welcome!' said Vijay when all had glasses of rum in their hands. 'A toast to our chief guest for all his wisdom and advice over the years, to Suresh for helping us with our development work, and to Evelyn for exposing our own numerous shortcomings while training with us.'

'And likewise, to our kind host, for pulling our legs!' said the ADC amid general laughter.

Since it was a Saturday, the ADC was combining his work with his hobby. He had come to chair an interdepartmental survey and settlement meeting on behalf of the DC and would be staying on for much of Sunday to look around for exotic birds in the forests around the town. In particular, he said to Vijay and his guests that he was looking for a rare species of an Indian bird—the great white-bellied heron, a near-extinct species which some said were not seen any more in these parts, although there were accounts from some villagers that a few were seen recently.

'Here is a picture of one,' he said, pulling out a cutting from a magazine from his wallet. It was a magnificent-looking creature with a long grey neck, black beak, white belly, and black legs. 'It is more than four feet tall and the second largest heron on earth,' he explained. 'Unfortunately, rampant deforestation has destroyed its habitat. But thanks to Vijay and his forester friends who have been bringing the forests back, we may have a few surviving and maybe even multiplying.' His goal was to make a positive identification of one and send its photograph to the national birdwatching association of which he was a senior member.

'Why don't you both join us?' asked Vijay of Evelyn and Suresh. 'That way we'll have two more pairs of eyes to look out for the creature, if there are any still around.' He was particularly eager that Evelyn would join as he considered her very jolly company.

Luckily for him, both readily agreed to participate in the effort to find the near-extinct bird. It promised some exciting trekking and, if they were lucky, a sighting of the enigmatic heron itself.

'And what, may I ask, ADC sahib, would be our reward for waking up at a godforsaken hour tomorrow and stumbling about in the forests with you the whole day in search of this creature?' asked Vijay.

'I'll enlarge a photo of the bird for your office, and you can keep looking at each other all day!' replied the ADC.

Vijay served dinner early so that the party could leave well before sunrise. Early next morning, when it was still pitch-dark outside, the circuit house caretaker knocked on her door and served tea to Evelyn. She emerged in a little while, in her running shorts and shoes, which she felt would be most appropriate for the trip, and waited for Suresh outside in the veranda. It was still dark and very quiet, but she heard a first solitary bird begin its hesitant call. When they left in Suresh's Jeep, dawn had not yet broken. The party was to meet near the railway station and then follow the assistant conservator's Jeep.

They found that the other group was already waiting. The forester led the way, followed by Vijay's Jeep in which the ADC was also riding, and Suresh's Jeep took the rear. On leaving the station, the road went steeply down the hillside, taking several sharp twists and turns till they reached the bank of the river. In the near darkness, they could still make out the shapes of two rubber dinghies that the forester had organised, bobbing up and down gently on the river a little distance away from the riverbank.

Boarding the dinghies was a bit of a challenge—or fun, depending on the perspective—as it required wading out to them. Except for Suresh, all had come ready in shorts and running or trekking shoes. The shoes could be taken off easily and held in the hand but negotiating the cold water of the river with its sandy bed strewn with prickly pebbles was not easy. Suresh's trousers got a little wet despite his attempts to roll them above the water line. He was not prepared for this sudden excursion. The ADC handed over his precious birdwatching binoculars and photography kit somewhat reluctantly to the dinghy driver and waded tentatively to his dinghy and clambered on.

The group divided themselves in the two dinghies, with the forester, Evelyn, and Vijay in the first and the ADC and Suresh in the second. The forester had arranged to get spare binoculars for the party. Soon the drivers started the motors and they were off. The morning quiet was broken by the gentle hum of the motors and the noise of the swirling waters rushing by the dinghies. The first few streaks of dawn could be seen in the eastern sky above the line of the mountains.

The plan was to go upriver for about half an hour till they came near the village where the apparent sightings had been reported. The dinghies picked up speed, and Evelyn found the cool morning breeze now blowing strongly on her face quite refreshing. She had tied her hair tightly into a ponytail, but a few stray strands kept coming on to her face. They were already in mid river and making good speed, and the forested shoreline slipped past quickly. As the light brightened, more of the details on the shore could be seen. She noticed that some of the forests were young, obviously results of past afforestation efforts, which Vijay confirmed. Here the trees were spaced evenly in neat rows. These were interspersed with older, more mature forests with tall thickly growing trees and diverse foliage. And then there were also areas where the forests had been destroyed and Mother Nature had tried to cover her harsh wounds with shrubs and various types of ferns and bracken.

After what looked to Evelyn only a short ride, the dinghy drivers cut their motors and suddenly all was still. The dinghies glided silently towards shore and then came to a stop gently near the bank. Evelyn got off, balancing her shoes in one hand while wading to the shore. Suresh made a worse job alighting, and almost the entire length of his trousers became fully wet. They had a good laugh on seeing his state, but at least his shoes were dry. The ADC looked at them sternly and whispered that they had to keep very silent from now on. Soon the entire party was ready, and they set off walking along the sandy shoreline and talking only in whispers. All trekkers trained their binoculars to the surrounding foliage, trying to discern animals and birds along the riverbanks or sheltering in the trees bordering them.

They spotted many birds but not the great white-bellied heron. Many common herons were about, and the party kept a good distance away so as not to disturb them while they happily caught fish and flew in or away with much fluttering and beating of wings. After about a couple of hours or so of this fruitless endeavour, they got down to having their picnic brunch as all were hungry. Thanks to the forest department, they feasted on vegetable sandwiches and boiled eggs and washed them down with hot and very flavourful South Indian coffee.

Vijay sat down on a rock on the river near the shore which he had to get to by jumping over a few boulders. The river swirled around him. He had brought some scraps of bread from his leftovers and started feeding the fish with them. He also threw a few scraps on the sand and watched sparrows, crows, and miscellaneous jungle fowl come forward tentatively and later, when no great danger was seen, start picking on the scraps.

All of a sudden, there was a loud flapping of wings above them, and the very bird they were looking for swooped in to take its share of the spoils just a few feet away from them. It was soon joined by its mate. They looked much taller than the four feet usually attributed to them. They were there for all of them to see, with their dark-grey plumage and white bellies, elegantly strutting about while picking up the scraps, unperturbed by the shock and surprise they had occasioned.

The whole party became deathly still on seeing the birds, but Vijay calmly kept throwing his scraps as though he was feeding crows. Everyone looked around for the ADC, but he was having a peaceful nap with his head resting on his photography kit. Suresh, who was nearest, silently nudged him for a while before he woke up and looked around, a little dazed. Without saying a word, Suresh pointed quietly at the birds. The ADC gazed at them unbelievingly. But just as he tried desperately to bring out his camera from its bag, the birds flew off, first one, and then the other, with their large wings flapping directly over them and then disappeared into the jungle.

Despite spending the whole afternoon looking for them, the birds didn't show up again. Finally, the birdwatchers gave up, exhausted.

'Never mind that we couldn't photograph the creatures,' said the ADC sadly, 'at least I have four credible witnesses who will vouch for my having seen them!'

29

EVELYN, TRAINEE
HEAD CLERK

$\mathcal{T}$he local newspaper arrived in the subdivisional officer's courts in the afternoons, being dispatched early each morning from the state capital by train. The national newspapers came later towards the evening. Apart from the infrequent news from the radio, these were Evelyn's primary connections with the world outside. The local paper mainly contained news from around the state and traditionally tended to take a somewhat parochial slant. Lately its views had begun veering towards extreme regional chauvinism—perhaps under threats from local students and other political interests or owing to the growing intolerance of its editorial staff to 'outside' groups which were considered generally to be exploiting the locals, extracting their wealth, taking their jobs, and so on. The element of subjectivism was so severe that any outside reader could be forgiven if she or he considered it nothing but blatant yellow journalism.

Thus, while an incident of violent assault on 'outsiders' by some people in the factory premises of a paper mill, which led to the hospitalisation with severe injuries of the manager and some senior staff, who were all outsiders, was reported prominently on the front page, the main editorial on that incident took the view that the management was really responsible and had brought the incident on themselves by not employing locals to the extent they should. It sent a warning to other establishments in the state that a similar fate could follow them too, should they ignore the writing on the wall.

The papers now all reported that the student-led agitation had resumed in earnest. It had been joined by the aggressive local regional party and possibly under their coercion by the state government employees' union. At the call of the agitation mongers, the government employees had gone on an indefinite strike, including the vast majority of Vijay's clerical staff. So, with no land record and registration work to learn from, or development projects to visit, Evelyn found a lot of time on her hands. In order to use her training period meaningfully, Vijay was making her look at some intricate appeals files and asking her to help out in the office with miscellaneous work, now that apart from the officers, no staff was attending office. But the basic urgent public functions had to be maintained.

After finishing reading the papers, Evelyn turned to what had become now one of her prime functions—taking on the role of head clerk and opening all the mail, marking each with the official stamp and date of receipt and forwarding it to the concerned officer to handle. Those she considered more urgent were to be taken to the various officers personally. It gave her excellent understanding of the main functions of a subdivisional officer, which would be her first job after her training was completed.

For example, as soon as she had finished reading the papers, she received the following message delivered from the police wireless office:

FROM: CHIEF SECRETARY
TO: ALL DISTCOLLS/ALL SUBDIVISIONAL
               OFFICERS/ALL POLICE SUPERINTENDENTS/
               ALL SDPOs

YESTERDAY'S INCIDENT OF ASSAULT AT JAYANAGAR
PAPER MILL HAS LEFT MANAGER AND THREE STAFF
FROM OUTSIDE STATE SERIOUSLY INJURED STOP
GOVERNMENT VIEWS THE INCIDENT WITH UTMOST
CONCERN STOP STATE INTELLIGENCE HAS WARNED
THAT MORE SUCH INCIDENTS LIKELY IN FUTURE AS
AGITATION INTENSIFIES STOP SUCH INCIDENTS WILL
NOT BE TOLERATED AND MUST BE PREVENTED WITH
USE OF FORCE IF NECESSARY AND IF OCCURRING
PERPETRATORS   IDENTIFIED   AND   PROSECUTED
PROMPTLY WITHOUT DELAY STOP PREVENTIVE
DETENTION CAN BE USED AGAINST KNOWN AND
LIKELY OFFENDERS AND RECOMMENDATIONS TO
THAT EFFECT SENT TO HOME SECRETARY

Evelyn immediately put the red URGENT stamp on the message and took it to Vijay. She had brought her pencil and notebook with her, expecting Vijay to dictate a draft to her. Instead, Vijay asked her to draft one herself.

'And don't forget to instruct SDPO sahib to detain all the langurs in this subdivision as they are the only known and likely offenders in these parts!' said Vijay.

They had a good laugh over this.

Luckily for Vijay, although his subdivision had felt the impact of the statewide agitation in terms of absence of staff and the virtual non-functioning of public offices, its uglier manifestations such as large-scale protest actions and violence which DC Nilghat and Ranjit, his counterpart in the other outlying subdivision, were experiencing were largely absent. His main functions at this time were to see that law and order and essential services were maintained. And with most of his staff reporting absent, and schools closed, the overall situation in the area under his charge, unlike in the plains, was quiet.

As the agitation dragged on, the government had to take increasingly unpopular measures. Apart from preventive detention of some agitation leaders, it started acting against its own employees who had joined the agitation en masse. To begin with, instructions were issued to withhold salaries of state employees not reporting for work. This was bound to sooner or later force employees back to work. But meanwhile, it was another measure that reinforced the divide between locals and the outsiders, with the government under president's rule increasingly considered acting against local interests.

Evelyn noticed that the mail traffic coming to Vijay's office increasingly reflected a situation apparently spiralling out of control. There were reports of protests mostly non-violent but some clearly designed to motivate use of force and add to the spiral of hatred, more reports of sectarian violence against outsiders, various reports predicting further disturbances from state and central intelligence agencies, and the inevitable stream of instructions on how to sternly deal with the agitation from the chief secretary.

In the midst of such gloomy correspondence, Evelyn found one letter pleasantly distracting, evoking a different world and a distant millennium. It was from the Archaeological Survey of India and said:

> This is with reference to your letter no. DO/SDO/Misc/1979/2120 regarding further findings of archaeological interest in Bamurin Circle in your subdivision.

> The apparent discoveries appear to confirm that there are subterranean archaeological structures relating to the Thaneswar principality circa BCE 280 approximately that could be confirmed, however, only through a pre-exploratory trial excavation in the area. In order to conduct this, we propose to send a team headed by Dr Shyam Chandra, deputy archaeologist, and comprising five other staff.

> Dr Chandra and the team will need accommodation initially for a day or two in the nearest available government circuit house or dak bungalow before the team sets up a camp office and temporary living quarters at the site. In order to prepare for the

team's visit, we propose to send Dr Chandra for a preliminary visit next month to meet you and discuss the logistics. Please let us know when it would be convenient.

Finally, it may be of interest to you to learn that we have invited Dr Biswajit Banerjee, who, as I mentioned in my previous letter to DC Nilghat, is an expert on ancient Buddhist scrolls and on Thaneswar as a panellist at our seminar 'Ancient India in the Immediate Post-Ashokan Period' to be held in Varanasi on 5/1/1980. We would also like to invite you to the event.

Yours sincerely

s/d D. K. Das
Chief Archaeologist

When Evelyn took the letter to Vijay and suggested that she draft a reply to the ASI, suggesting that the visit should be put off for the time being, given the current disturbances, Vijay had a good laugh.

'No, no, let him come. These archaeologists are immersed only in the ancient past and don't seem to know what's happening around them. Let him come and see that the same mayhem of the Kurukshetra is playing out in its modern form right around us!'

Evelyn, therefore, drafted the following reply which, after a few modifications by Vijay, was dispatched. It read:

Thank you for your letter No.ASI/1979/2934. We will be pleased to receive Dr Chandra in this subdivision for his preliminary visit. As you are aware, because of an ongoing illegal agitation in the state, Central Government officials travelling to the state will be provided security to facilitate their movements. Please let us know the proposed detailed itinerary of Dr Chandra so that we can make necessary arrangements for his visit.

As far as Dr Biswajit Banerjee is concerned, it is good to learn that he will be in India soon, and we thank you for your invitation to the seminar. While it will be difficult to spare district officials at the present juncture for the seminar, should Dr Banerjee be also interested to visit the proposed excavation site in this subdivision, we will be happy to provide him the same courtesies and facilities as to the members of the ASI team.

Yours sincerely,
Vijay Gautam

30

THE INCIDENT ON
THE TRAIN

The agitation intensified. As it lengthened, it started adversely affecting the state employees themselves who had joined the agitation. Some of the poorer employees could not afford to go without their salaries and attempted to come back to work. They were prevented by picketers. In many instances, this led to violence.

A couple of days before Evelyn's training with Vijay was to come to an end, she read from an incoming wireless from Ranjit to DC Nilghat and copied to Vijay that a serious incident had occurred in Ranjit's subdivision. A large body of student picketers led by state-level student leaders had gathered in front of the SDO's courts. As orders not to assemble were in force, the police asked the picketers to disperse. This went unheeded, whereupon a mild *lathi* charge was resorted to. However, on hearing about this incident, other students gathered in large numbers, exceeding a thousand, by the SDO's account. The stand-off turned ugly when some miscreants from the crowd started pelting stones on the small force of policemen keeping the large crowd at bay. SDPO Sudarshan was hit in the head, and several other policemen sustained injuries. It was at this time that SDO Ranjit had to order firing. Two students, including one of their prominent leaders, were injured, with bullet wounds in the leg. The crowd dispersed, and both students were hospitalised. They were reported to be in stable condition and likely to be released in a few days.

The account in the *Daily Herald* which arrived in the afternoon of the next day after the incident took an altogether different slant, however, when reporting on it:

> Our Nilghat correspondent reports that SDO Ranjit Gupta ordered firing without provocation on a group of students picketing the SDO's offices peacefully. As a result of the heavy-handed police action and the unprovoked firing, nearly twenty students received injuries, including two who were shot at from close range and are now in hospital in a precarious condition. One of the students fighting for his life is the general secretary of the All-State Students Union. The incident has created high tension in the subdivision apart from providing a further instance of provocation for those so far participating peacefully in the agitation.

'A very difficult situation indeed!' said Vijay when discussing the incident with Evelyn. 'I think Ranjit was lucky again. It could have been much, much worse. None of the injuries are very serious. But the situation is certainly getting grimmer by the day.'

A day later, Evelyn was scheduled to leave. But as a result of the incident of police firing, the student leaders had called for an indefinite *hartal*, which meant that all life would be brought to a standstill. In addition to the call for closure of educational institutions and government offices, all shops would be forced to close; the students would also not allow vehicular traffic on the roads. Of course, the government promptly announced that the *hartal* was illegal, but given that its resources were stretched, it hardly had the means to prevent it.

Vijay discussed the options with Evelyn. She could, of course, stay on for some more time till the situation improved. But it wasn't certain whether that would happen soon, and things could in fact get far worse. There were essential aspects of her training at district headquarters she had to get on with, also. Besides, knowing Evelyn, he surmised that she wanted to be more involved with learning how the district administration in Nilghat, probably the worst affected by the agitation, was handling the situation—an invaluable opportunity to learn which she was missing at Vijay's placid subdivision.

As the roads were blocked, Vijay suggested that she take the train and make the short journey from Nilghat Road with a police escort, which the SP could help arrange. Although there were occasional obstructions to the railway track too, DC Nilghat had so far been able to successfully remove them and keep the rail traffic moving so that essential rail movement was not affected.

Vijay came to see off Evelyn at the station. 'The survey team had prepared a parting gift for you,' he said, taking out an envelope. 'They couldn't give it to you personally as they are on strike; they asked me to be their messenger. Looks like copies of some maps which you were involved in developing.'

'And here is something more exciting from my side,' he said, giving her another envelope. Inside, Evelyn found a photo of the birdwatching group, with Evelyn in the middle and the ADC and Vijay on either side. 'It will help you remember the great white, which I am sure you will never go after again!'

It was taken, Evelyn remembered, by Suresh using the ADC's camera meant for taking a shot of the great white-bellied heron but used instead to photograph the group who had seen the birds but weren't able to record the event.

The signal turned green, the engine blew its whistle loudly, and with the stationmaster waving the green flag, the train started moving slowly away. Vijay stood on the platform, waving, and Evelyn could see his solitary form for quite some time in the deserted station till the train took a sharp bend blocking the view as it sped towards the viaduct.

From the bridge, Evelyn could see the little subdivisional town spread out over the hill, the circuit house, and the SDO's bungalow with their red roofs looking tiny in the distance. The afternoon sun flashed briefly on a few of the windows before suddenly, the view was gone as the train entered a tunnel and was enveloped in darkness, the compartment lit only by its dim electric lights. When it emerged soon on the other side, the view was replaced by that of a blur of fast-moving hills and thick jungle.

The journey was to take only two hours or so. Evelyn settled in on her bunk. With the agitation on, the passenger traffic was light, and there were only a few people in the coach and only one other passenger in her compartment. She was curious to see what Vijay's survey team had prepared for her. The contents of the envelope were a detailed Survey of India map of the subdivision and part of the neighbouring areas which contained the geographical features of the area. In the map, a small rectangular part was demarcated in red ink. Evelyn recognised this as the area where the survey party she was training with was preparing detailed cadastral maps. Attached to it were the survey maps that she had contributed to. This was very useful, she thought, putting them back in the envelope.

With nothing much to do, she picked up a conversation with the only other passenger in her compartment. It transpired—and this was not obvious as he was not in uniform—that he was an army officer, a Lieutenant Colonel Raghav with the Jammu and Kashmir Rifles, travelling home on a fortnight's furlough. Evelyn had spent two weeks on training with the army in Kashmir, essential for training of civil service officers as the army often came out in support of the civil authorities in emergencies.

So she had a ready topic of conversation for Colonel Raghav. She recounted how the army had assigned an army doctor as the liaison officer for the brief period she spent at a forward location. He was an instant hit with the trainee group as he allowed them a much more relaxed schedule compared to their previous liaison officer, who insisted that they wake up each morning at 4 a.m. and be ready to play basketball against the army team. Of course, the dazed and sleepy civilians were no match for the army and lost all games, usually without scoring. On the other hand, when Doc allowed them time till 8 a.m. to get ready and began each morning with a briefing over a sumptuous breakfast at the army mess and ended each day with a debriefing over gallons of rum and whiskey, he became a great favourite. Not that they didn't go through the usual rigorous training of rifles and small arms, which was compulsory.

'On the last day before leaving, it was Doc's birthday, and we all lifted him up and gave him bumps in the mess. It was quite a sight!' said Evelyn.

When they were nearing Nilghat Road, there was a sudden loud screaming of brakes from the undercarriage, which interrupted their conversation. This was followed by a sharp slowdown. Finally, with a big jolt and shudder, the train came to a halt. The stop was so sudden that Colonel Raghav had to hold on to the straps behind him with all his might to prevent himself from falling off the bunk. He survived without damage.

'What was all that about?' he exclaimed after regaining his balance. Then saying, 'Let me take a look,' he went out to investigate the reason for this emergency halt.

A very long time later, he came back with some grim news. 'Some miscreants have removed the fishplates and rails on a bridge about a mile away,' he said. 'Luckily, a rail patrolling party detected it in time and signalled the train to stop. Else we could have been in the middle of the river the train was about to pass over.'

31

ANOTHER TREK

*I*t took some time for Evelyn to realise the near-miraculous escape she and the other train passengers had experienced. She was quite shaken. Although the railway staff on this section must have been conducting more daily patrolling, given the current situation, they could have missed detecting this sabotage attempted by obviously trained extremists. As Colonel Raghav and Evelyn concluded, it must have required several persons to remove the bolts from the two pairs of fishplates on both the rails on either side of the track, and to remove the rails and then vanish quickly. Some of these deadly saboteurs could still be lurking around in the vicinity, trying to see the result of their efforts. This gave Evelyn the creeps, especially when, looking out of the compartment window, she saw that they were still in the midst of thick forests.

The guard and several railway staff came around a little while later, explaining that the authorities were already on the job and were arranging a relief train. This could take an indefinite amount of time, however. Evelyn did not like the prospect of spending the night stranded in the forest. Obviously, Colonel Raghav was also thinking the same. His wife was expecting him home soon, and he didn't want his short furlough further shortened by this unfortunate incident. After the initial shock had worn away, both, particularly Colonel Raghav, were highly incensed at the audacity of the extremists.

'How far are we from Nilghat Road, do you think?' asked Evelyn.

'Just twenty-five kilometres, according to the railway staff,' replied Colonel Raghav. And then more angrily, he added, 'I can't allow a bunch of —ers to spoil my plans. I wish I could get my hands on them!'

Evelyn remembered that she had a Survey of India map with her. She pulled it out, and the two of them located the railway line and the river they were about to cross. The map indicated that the next station was only about ten kilometres away if they went by foot through the forest, but more than double that if they followed the railway line as it meandered about to maintain a steady gradient. Although they were in a forested area, if they walked along the banks of the nearby river—the same one which the train would have plunged into—and took a westward course along it, they would arrive very near a railway station that was connected by road with Nilghat Road Station, her destination. It would be possible to get to the next station and alert SP Nilghat and ask to be picked up from there instead of her original destination.

'Let's go for it,' said Evelyn.

She was used to jogging over ten kilometres often, so this would not be a difficult trek. She assumed Colonel Raghav would not have any problem either, given the much more arduous tasks army personnel were trained for. They had a detailed map of the area, and Colonel Raghav revealed that he had with him his personal revolver and a pencil torch for reading. There was still a good hour or so before sundown, and so there would be enough light for another hour. The only problem was their luggage. Evelyn had a suitcase, and so did Colonel Raghav. They decided to persuade the guard to keep them in his custody and deliver the items to the stationmaster at Nilghat Road, from where those could be picked up.

After both had identified themselves to him, it didn't take long for the guard to be persuaded about taking custody of their luggage. But he was a bit sceptical about their plan to trek to the next station.

'Do you think it's a good idea? The *badmashes*[26] may be around,' he said. 'Considering what they were planning, they seem to be a very dangerous lot!'

'Send a search party out for us if we don't reach the next station by 9 p.m.!' said Colonel Raghav, half in jest.

The two set off for their destination. It was better than doing nothing and waiting indefinitely for the promised relief train to arrive. They followed the railway line initially on to the bridge, and Evelyn saw the missing rail sections which had been pulled out and thrown on either side of the track. What diabolical minds must have been at work here, she thought.

They found that they couldn't simply walk over the bridge as it didn't have a pedestrian walkway and there were no guard rails. That was the first surprise. Anyhow, they could still go down to the river and find some other way to cross it. The way down to the river wasn't difficult. One only had to be careful to avoid slipping on loose rocks that could have led to a nasty fall. Evelyn had taken the precaution of changing into her running shoes before handing over her bag, and Colonel Raghav was not in any difficulty despite his leather shoes, which he was forced to wear as he had not brought his drill shoes.

On reaching the riverbank, they tried to explore whether the river could be forded. Although the sandy banks were wide, there was a deep channel where the river was running swiftly, and it wasn't fordable. They would have to find a boat. That meant they had to look for a village, whereas in this dense jungle, no habitation seemed likely. Evelyn took out her map.

Unfortunately, the map wasn't helpful either. If there were small informal settlements, it didn't show them. They decided to walk downstream towards the outer limit of the forested area as they were more likely to find villages beyond it. That was also the route to the next railway station, although they needed to cross the river at some point. However, it was now beginning to get dark, and they had to hurry.

They set a brisk pace along the riverbank, which took a bend, and quickly, the railway line and the bridge were far behind them. Evelyn began to doubt whether it had been a good idea to enter into this foolish adventure when they could have waited it out in the stranded train.

But soon, it looked as though her misgivings had ended. They noticed a couple of figures in the distance on the bank of the stream, crouching near a double dugout made of coconut trunks. It wasn't clear from the distance whether they were removing some loads or trying to push the dugout on to the stream. Colonel Raghav clapped and shouted at them to draw their attention and hold the boat till they came up. They stopped and looked their way and immediately halted whatever they were doing and scampered into the jungle, drawing something wrapped in gunny bags with them.

Colonel Raghav and Evelyn stopped in their tracks. This behaviour looked very suspicious to both. They realised that they had interrupted some clandestine business. They cautiously approached the dugout, and when they reached it, they couldn't find any trace of the two. Colonel Raghav shouted a couple of times, trying to draw the attention of whoever was listening—and they were sure they were—and indicating that they merely wanted to cross the stream and wanted to use the dugout.

Well trained in these matters, Colonel Raghav quickly heaved the dugout into the stream with Evelyn's help. When they got on it, they found a long pole lying on the hull to steer the boat by, which however rapidly moved ahead unaided. When they were midstream, Evelyn found that there was a small gunny bag filled with some things near her feet, tied carefully with strings. Colonel Raghav helped her untie it.

'Hand grenades . . . looks like foreign ordnance,' said Colonel Raghav, carefully examining the contents. 'The stuff they carried away were probably guns, and they may have left these behind in their hurry. Our enemies are no longer at the borders. They are here among us.'

32

BANTER AND MUSINGS

'There were some anxious moments certainly, when you didn't show up after the relief train arrived and the police party sent to pick you up learnt from the guard that you were trekking across the forest!' said Vijay. 'But luckily while the SP was still organising search teams to send after you, news that you had surfaced came through.'

'I told DC sahib not to worry as most likely, you were looking for exotic flora and fauna again!' was the ADC's weak attempt at a joke. 'Were you trying to get another look at the great white?' he asked. Nevertheless, everybody laughed. After all, they were all guests at his party.

This was several days after the train incident. There was a mini-gathering of Nilghat district officials at an informal dinner at the ADC's place. A temporary halt in the agitation had been announced after the student leaders had been called by the Home Ministry to New Delhi for talks. Hopes had arisen of an agreement that would end the state's rapid downward spiral into violence and destruction. Taking the opportunity of a lull, the DC had called a security meeting to take stock and chart out the strategy for the next phase of the agitation, which he felt was inevitable.

Both the outlying SDOs, Ranjit and Vijay, along with Evelyn the assistant collector and, of course, the DC, were invitees to the party. The DC had sent word that he would be a little late, but everyone was aware that he intended to stay late too, lingering over his drinks and philosophising. The ADC's wife Aruna was the hostess, and she had supervised what was commonly anticipated would be a great meal as her culinary capabilities were well known in the district. While they waited for the DC and his wife to make their appearance, the guests were treated to a variety of drinks from the ADC's bar and a delectable stream of hors d'oeuvres from Aruna's kitchen.

Soon the DC and the first lady of the district arrived. The DC had married very late, and although he himself was quite senior among the officer cadre of the state, his wife Nivedita was just about a little older than the SDOs. They had no children. She was a very pretty and lively person, and soon, the party also livened up with their presence. The big topic of discussion of course was Evelyn's adventure in the forest.

'It turns out that the grenades you found had the same markings as the ones that were used in the attack on the governor,' said the DC to Evelyn.

'And isn't it strange that the only times the grenades have showed up in our district, it was Evelyn who first saw them?' said the ADC. 'Evelyn, you have a lot of explaining to do!'

'Thank heavens police work is in safer hands,' said Vijay, 'as with this line of inference, we wouldn't be going too far with the case!'

'Don't worry,' said Evelyn. 'After the grilling session that the SP subjected me and poor Colonel Raghav to, he seems to have cleared us. At least there are no further inquiries from his side.'

'Maybe for now, but don't overrule the possibility of a midnight knock on your door anytime soon,' said Ranjit, carrying on the Evelyn-teasing project.

'Jokes apart—and pardon me, Evelyn, for saying so—owing to what many would term your foolhardy adventure into the forest after the sabotage attempt, we have now a valuable lead into what could be a den of extremists,' said DC Nilghat. 'The problem is that the forested area is too large to search. It would be like looking for a needle in a haystack. The SP is therefore relying on intelligence mainly. So far, nothing has come up but soon may.'

The ADC attempted to break the sobriety that had crept into the conversation. 'Ladies and gentlemen, a toast to Evelyn for her stunning discovery and safe return to our midst, not forgetting her reprieve from the clutches of our SP!'

After that toast was drunk, he raised another one. 'To our brilliant Home Ministry negotiators—may they have wisdom to succeed with the negotiations and finally lead us to peace!' This was met with loud cheers. Everyone longed for normality to return soon and was weary of the continuing turmoil.

'And now, ladies and gentlemen, to dinner!' the ADC said with a flourish.

Aruna's dinner spread turned out every bit as anticipated. The aromas of cooking had been wafting in from the kitchen and had whetted everyone's appetite. Although simple, there were both vegetarian as well as non-vegetarian delights. Among the former was a dish of baked cauliflower with cheese. The high point of the latter was roast *raan* of lamb. The main dishes were rounded off with an equally splendid dessert spread—*rasa malai* and an assortment of the season's best fruits. Nivedita, whose expertise in the culinary arts was somewhat limited and who was therefore forced to employ Alam the circuit house *khansama* on occasions such as these, was the most vociferous in praise of Aruna's sumptuous menu.

'Aruna, we have to force you to reveal your delightful secrets!' said Nivedita. 'Why don't you start cooking lessons? There is a large group of gastronomic illiterates like me who would be eager to learn.'

'Aruna has a repertoire that would surpass Julia Child any day!' said the ADC, overhearing the conversation. 'But I am concerned that her cooking classes may turn into a sharing of more than just culinary secrets among the Nilghat ladies!'

'Aren't you a champion of public transparency?' retorted Nivedita. 'We have nothing to hide. Or do you have some dark secrets that you are afraid may come to light?'

'You are right, there. The skeletons in my cupboard are banging to get out!' said the ADC to general laughter.

After dinner, while Aruna and Nivedita continued a private conversation at the dinner table, the rest settled back around the sofa set in the living room, and the DC ceremonially picked out a cigar from the cigar case that the ADC had materialised especially for him and carefully lit one. A glass of his favourite whiskey was also placed by the ADC at the side table next to him. The others took glasses of their favourite Old Monk rum.

'Ranjit and Vijay have been very hospitable each time I've visited them. Aruna has been pestering me to organise a party in return, but the students have been conspiring so far to prevent it,' the ADC said, beginning the post-dinner conversation.

'We have subjected you to the very limited fare churned out by our untrained bungalow peons. This is not a return but a feast!' said Vijay. 'Please don't compare them.'

'Very true,' Ranjit agreed. 'I will gladly provide ten of Sundar's meals for a return treat such as this!'

Although the ADC wanted to keep the conversation light and away from the grim outside world for once even if for a short while, as was inevitable, however, it turned to the situation they were all facing. And it was initiated unwittingly by the ADC himself.

'I have been dwelling often on the conversation we had at DC sahib's bungalow one evening in what seems ages back,' he began. 'After my last visit to the two of you, I couldn't help but feel how ironic it is that Vijay the historian and believer in values as critical to shaping society is reaping the benefits of development. While Ranjit the believer in development is seeing the divide development is causing and the intolerance it is breeding,' he said.

Reflecting on this uncharacteristically philosophical observation from the ADC, Evelyn couldn't help thinking how true it was. It was Vijay's subdivision which remained like an oasis of peace perhaps owing much to the social transformation that was silently taking place there. This was largely due to people like Vijay and his survey team's efforts, Suresh and his double-cropping initiative, and the afforestation efforts of the forest officials that were restoring nature to its pristine state. On the other hand, Ranjit's subdivision was in the eye of the storm raging in the state with exploitation of the state's natural resources vitally needed for national development directly in conflict with local interests.

Taking a puff on his cigar, DC Nilghat addressed the ADC and said, 'Sitesh, you've provided us an opportunity to observe the world objectively. We are like eagles flying calmly in a clear sky while the storm clouds are spread threateningly below us.'

He paused to take a sip of his whisky and then added, 'If you recall the conversation we had many months ago, I asked our young colleagues here to reflect on two important questions. The first one, if I recall correctly, was whether it was possible to achieve an ethical state in the absence of material progress. The second one was whether humanity is progressing towards the ethical state, is stationary, or is regressing. Have we reached any conclusions so far?'

'I doubt whether after imbibing three double *patialas*[27] I can seriously address your questions, Your Honour, but let me take a shot at the first one,' ventured Ranjit, standing up a little unsteadily to deliver his speech, rum glass in hand. 'Let's take our two subdivisions. I can't say whether an ethical state has been reached in Vijay's subdivision, but clearly, it hasn't been swayed by violence and xenophobia affecting the rest of the state. Three cheers to Vijay for focusing development where really needed!

'On the other hand, the bigotry and divisions we see elsewhere, I think, can be largely attributed to a false vision of development when such a vision causes benefits to some but leaves others behind in poverty, illiteracy, and deprivation. That's what is clearly evident in mine. Why can't our superiors come down and see what's really happening on the ground?

'Your Honour, war and strife will continue to plague humanity if such absolute scarcities and wants remain,' he concluded to loud applause.

There was a long pause after that. This was broken by the telephone ringing in the ADC's bungalow office. The ADC left to pick it up. He returned in a short while.

'The chief secretary is on the line, sir,' he said, addressing the DC.

DC Nilghat left the room. When he returned, he looked glum. 'The news from Delhi is not good,' he said. 'The students have called off the negotiations and announced an immediate resumption of the agitation. I'm afraid Ranjit and Vijay will have to leave immediately for their subdivisions.'

33

INDEPENDENCE DAY

*R*anjit got up early. Looking out from his bedroom window, he saw that the day was clear. That seemed at least to be a good sign. The whole country was celebrating Independence Day with singing of the national anthem and other patriotic songs, speeches, festoons, sports activities, and distribution of sweets for schoolchildren. It was a day of festivities as exactly thirty years earlier, while the country's late prime minister made a historic midnight speech to parliament, the Union Jack was brought down, and the Indian tricolour replaced it.

But in this state, the situation was joyless and grim. The students' agitation continued unabated, and the Students' Union had called for a boycott of all official celebrations. Ranjit looked at the message lying on his table from the Secretary of Education which asked the district authorities to inform the government school principals within their respective jurisdictions that they ensure, on pain of dismissal, that all their students attend the official flag-hoisting ceremonies. Ranjit had duly copied the message to all principals and ensured they were received.

It was now a quarter past ten, and with no elected government in office as the state was under president's rule, the DCs and SDOs were to hoist the tricolour at their respective headquarters. In normal times, this task was performed by local ministers. The official ceremony in Ranjit's case was traditionally organised at the main sports stadium in the town. He donned his formal wear—black Nehru jacket and trousers—and set off with Ali as soon as Sudarshan arrived to officially escort him to the stadium.

Arriving at the stadium, Ranjit noticed that although attendance was thin, all government officials had braved the boycott and arrived at the venue. Each was eager to catch his eye so that his or her presence was officially acknowledged. Also sitting on the first three rows all around the stadium were the schoolchildren from the local government schools in their respective school uniforms. He noted that the children who were attending were mainly in the primary grades, who could perhaps be coaxed to participate while the older children were mostly absent. Other than the front rows, most of the stadium was, therefore, empty.

At exactly ten thirty, Ranjit hoisted the tricolour which, when unfurled, scattered a bunch of marigold flowers around the pedestal. The entire audience was on its feet, and the children sang the national anthem with gusto. The freed flag fluttered cheerily against the blue uncluttered sky and did not acknowledge the hostility that had accompanied its unfurling.

Because of the boycott, the official flag-hoisting ceremony had been confined to the bare essentials. The platoon of armed policemen that was at the venue conducted a brief march past. When marching past the podium, the platoon commander saluted Ranjit smartly, and Ranjit returned the salute. Following this, Ranjit walked up to a bust of Mahatma Gandhi near the entrance of the stadium followed by district officials and placed a garland consisting again of marigold flowers around it and paid his respects, along with the others, with bowed head and folded hands, to this simple man who had overcome one of the mightiest nations on earth to win India her freedom through non-violent means.

That ended the brief official celebrations, which appeared to have passed off smoothly. Ranjit climbed onto his Jeep, and Ali drove it out of the stadium, with Sudarshan and the police contingent saluting him smartly. Sudarshan, thereafter, left too.

When Ranjit's Jeep turned on to the road by the lake, heading towards his bungalow, he heard a loud muffled sound coming from the distance. He hoped that it was nothing more than a burst tyre from a passing truck, which often caused quite a loud noise. He tried to dismiss it from his mind but couldn't.

On reaching his bungalow, Ranjit could hear his office phone ringing. It stopped and started ringing again. When he reached the phone, it was Sudarshan at the other end.

'There's been an explosion near the Gandhi statue at the stadium,' he said. 'Seems like an attempt to get at us. Thank goodness we finished our event quickly. The timer was set for 11 a.m., which was the exact time we were expected to be at the statue for the garlanding, according to the official schedule that you had distributed. But we had left by 10.53 a.m.'

'Was anyone hurt?' asked Ranjit, interrupting him.

'Yes, unfortunately. Two girls around six years old. While everyone else had left, these two continued playing near the statue. I have had them moved to the hospital. One of them caught a shrapnel in the head, and her condition is quite serious.'

Ranjit took off his formal wear and changed into everyday clothes. Without wasting any time, he asked Ali to take him quickly to the hospital. Although the traffic was thin because of the holiday and the continued agitation, it still took a good half an hour or so—unacceptably long, he felt—to reach the government hospital. Throughout the journey, Ranjit hoped that both the girls would be safe. He couldn't get over the feeling that he was responsible for getting the children to participate, even though in fact he was carrying out orders from his superiors.

Ali dropped Ranjit at the hospital entrance, and he rushed in. The duty nurse at the reception informed him that the medical superintendent himself, who was a surgeon, was in the operating theatre, attending to the girl who had sustained a head injury. He read from the patient list that the girl's name was Sujata Verma, aged 6 years and 4 months. Ranjit ran up the stairs to the OT which was on the first floor. A red light was on at the OT entrance, which indicated that surgery was in progress.

After an inordinate wait, the superintendent came out looking grim. On seeing Ranjit, he came up to him.

'Bad case,' he said. 'I've tried to stop the bleeding and have put her on transfusion, but there is severe damage to the brain.'

'Dr Nath, you have to save the girl whatever it takes!' Ranjit pleaded. 'Is there anything I or the DC can do?'

'Her only chance is to get her specialist attention at state headquarters,' replied Dr Nath. 'She needs to be operated on, and we don't have the necessary capacity here. I am sending her by ambulance with an emergency doctor and staff to the state hospital, which unfortunately is a good six hours from here if there is no traffic. If you can ensure that the appropriate medical team receives and attends to her there, that will be useful.'

'I'll also organise a police escort to see that there are no hold-ups on the way,' said Ranjit.

He talked to Sudarshan from the reception and organised the escort. It would be at the hospital within twenty minutes. Meanwhile, Dr Nath made preparations for the girl to be moved by ambulance. Ranjit decided to make the rest of the arrangements from his bungalow.

When he spoke to the DC over phone, the latter had already heard the news. 'I know the chief medical superintendent at the state hospital very well. I'll ask him to get his team ready to attend to the girl. Leave that to me,' said the DC.

There was nothing further to do than worry. Ranjit couldn't get rid of the feeling of guilt that had taken hold of him. How would he face the parents, he wondered. The day slowly turned to evening and then to night. Ranjit couldn't do a spot of work. Finally, he went on to his veranda, sat down wearily on his wicker chair, and asked Sundar to fix him a strong drink.

Well after ten at night, a constable from the police wireless office came by on his bicycle, lifted the latch on the front gate, walked in, and saluted Ranjit. He handed over a sheaf of wireless messages. The one Ranjit was looking for was buried among them. Its terse message read:

FROM: CHIEF MEDICAL SUPERINTENDENT,
          GOVERNMENT STATE HOSPITAL
TO: DISTCOLL NILGHAT
COPY: SUBDIVISIONAL OFFICER RANJIT GUPTA

PATIENT SUJATA VERMA AGE 6 YEARS 4 MONTHS WAS OPERATED ON BY SPECIAL MEDICAL TEAM ON ARRIVAL BUT DESPITE OUR BEST EFFORTS EXPIRED AT 2125 HRS. BODY RETAINED FOR POST-MORTEM.

34

DISCUSSIONS BY
THE RIVER

'$\mathcal{I}$sn't it ironical that despite the happenings around us, some feel that violence is on the decline in our world and we are progressing towards peace?' said Vijay.

Vijay, Ranjit, and Evelyn were at the state circuit house in the state capital and discussing the recent events in Ranjit's subdivision. They had all arrived at the state headquarters for a security conference called by the chief secretary. Evelyn too was invited as an observer as assistant collector on training. All three of them were billeted at the state circuit house.

This colonial edifice was situated on the banks of a wide-bodied and slowly flowing river. Although the monsoon season was over, the river was still swollen but no longer its restless self. On the other bank, very far away, chains of distant hills stretched out on either side east and west interminably till they disappeared among the clouds. A garden and lawn extended from the main building and a recently built more modern and totally incongruous annexe, to the river. Well-tended beds of multicoloured Canna lilies—mainly oranges and yellows—bordered the garden, while bushes of roses were planted at its centre. Verdant *kadamba* trees could be seen with their resplendent round yellow blossoms from where they sat, while from somewhere near but unseen, the *bakul* trees made their presence felt, the sweet fragrance from their tiny white florets occasionally wafting in.

Ranjit had a corner room with a veranda overlooking this serene view. He had stretched out there on an 'easy' chair—a vestige of the colonial past on which British officers used to take a siesta or smoked their hookahs. Vijay and Evelyn were sitting on comfortable wicker chairs nearby. The conference was over, and they were due to return the next day and enjoying their brief interregnum from work. Naturally, the talk mainly concerned the recent events they had been involved in. Ranjit was still tormented with the Independence Day blast although it had taken place several weeks previously. Vijay tried to get him to look at the event philosophically.

'Although it is difficult for us here to imagine a future without violence, I have no doubt that violence is gradually abating,' Vijay began in a serious tone, imagining perhaps that he was back in a classroom. Vijay, like Ranjit, had briefly taught in his university before joining the civil service.

'Take the wars and scale of casualties in ancient and medieval Indian history. Ashoka's defeat of the Kalinga forces left, for example, a field of over a hundred thousand dead from a single battle. In medieval times, northern India witnessed bloodletting on a far more horrific scale than we see now. Wars which took place relentlessly caused unimaginable slaughter of soldiers and civilians. The three battles of Panipat which established Mughal supremacy over India, to take another example, each left over fifty thousand dead. The sacking of Delhi by Timur in the fourteenth century and by Nadir Shah as late as the eighteenth century left probably an equal number of innocent citizens of Delhi massacred over a few hours of slaughter. Surely, we have transcended those times, and although we do see violence, the revulsion it generates in present times prevents any large-scale recurrence.'

'But hasn't the rise of lethal technology increased the risk of large-scale casualties? I believe more than a hundred thousand civilians died in Hiroshima and Nagasaki alone in the atomic bomb blasts,' countered Evelyn.

'Exactly,' agreed Ranjit. 'I think the relative peace after the carnage witnessed during Second World War may have lulled us into the belief that violence is declining,' he said.

'There is no denying that after the two world wars, which killed tens of millions all over the world, there has been relative calm as the world must have understood the futility of war,' persisted Vijay, trying to advance his argument. 'This is similar to what Ashoka experienced after seeing the scenes of the dead and dying at Kalinga, causing him to shun violence forever. There is now a general feeling all over the civilised world that war is unacceptable. That may also have contributed to the growing feeling that weapons of mass destruction must be eliminated.'

'Notwithstanding which the number of countries who have covertly begun seeking such weapons is on the rise,' said Ranjit. 'Also, while the scale of slaughter that the world experienced in the first half of this century may have abated, there are new threats that could lead to bigger conflicts. Religious extremism is on the rise. Looming scarcities of natural resources such as mineral oil and water could be another source of violent competition between countries. I have been reading about the growing disquiet of environmentalists about global warming and scarcities it could exacerbate. We could soon be engaged in deadly struggles over water, for instance.'

'But when have scarcities of the past not been mitigated by technological improvements?' asked Vijay. 'No, my friend, the question that needs to be asked is not whether increasing physical scarcities will cause war and violence but whether absence of ethical thinking and civilised conduct and institutions will.'

'I don't see much ethics and reason right now,' remarked Ranjit ruefully.

'I think if one sees the bigger picture, we obviously get a better perspective than our microscopic experiences suggest. Thankfully, from that perspective, we are seeing positive developments taking place globally.

'Just as in the past, avatars such as Buddha and Christ appeared from time to time, to bring about changes in thinking and attitudes to prevent humanity careering towards self-destruction, in the present time too, transformations in thoughts and ideas are emerging. The evil of colonialism is ending. Independent countries are responding better to the needs of their citizens. Democracy is spreading, although with fits and starts, and even where it appears to have taken root, may still be far from perfect. Increasing education and awareness is forcing governments to pay closer heed to the voices of the people. Even the misguided extremists in our midst may be—using their own distorted logic—trying to bring change in favour of the people, although they may be quite wrong in the way they are going about it.'

'Quite wrong?' exclaimed Ranjit. 'The death of an innocent child can never be forgiven, whatever be your rationalisation, Vijay!' said Ranjit, quite agitated.

'I fully agree with you that adoption of violent means for any cause, particularly when innocents are harmed, cannot be condoned,' said Vijay. 'In fact, Mahatmaji showed the world that empires can be overcome through non-violent means. His emergence as a beacon of peace at a time of upheaval and violence all over the world may have been one of the turning points in world history and is another instance of the rise of reason and ethics.

'Of course, there are also those who are scared of the light that is spreading across the world—such as tyrants, dictators, zealots, obscurantists, feudal thinkers, and their ilk, who would rather dwell in darkness and persuade others to do so to protect their interests. But I feel that their end is certain, although they will not go out with a whimper and will cause considerable suffering to all before they do.'

'Bravo!' Evelyn said, clapping her hands. 'That was quite a speech!'

'Very well put, indeed,' agreed Ranjit. 'But just to interject a small contrary position into the debate, isn't this all a little on the optimistic side? Aren't there always people whom you consider to be in darkness who feel that it is they who represent the pinnacle of truth and reason while the opposite groups are those who are living in the dark? Will that not mean that mankind is doomed forever to facing war and conflict?

'I am sure such issues must have been debated time and again ever since mankind emerged from the caves into civilisation. I do hope very much, however, that you are right,' said Ranjit.

There was a pause in the discussion as a uniformed and turbaned bearer brought in tea and biscuits. Evelyn looked at her watch and noted that it was exactly half past four. The state circuit house was maintaining its traditions scrupulously, she noted to herself with satisfaction. At Ranjit's request, the bearer poured out the tea and passed around the steaming cups to them. Outside, the day was waning, and Vijay suggested they go for an evening stroll on the bank of the river after finishing their tea and snacks.

A set of steps led down from the garden to the riverbank. The sun was just above the horizon, its aura of gold spreading out to the sky and reflecting over the placidly flowing river. Groups of people were strolling on the riverbank. Children were running around and shouting playfully. From far away, the plaintive notes of a folk singer could be heard once in a while above the din. Evelyn bought a packet of peanuts from a vendor who was roasting them on a charcoal stove. The three of them kept shelling and munching on the nuts and walking leisurely. It was a normal, peaceful scene. Why couldn't it go on like this forever, thought Ranjit.

Early next morning, they got ready to go their separate ways. Each had a long way to go.

'By the way,' said Vijay, about to get on to his Jeep, 'I heard back from the Archaeological Survey of India. They are sending a survey team for preliminary excavations at Bamurin. I've asked them to come despite the agitation. Unravelling the mysteries of the past is far too important to wait, I feel. The good news is that Dr Banerjee—the Thaneswar expert—will be joining the team. Can you make it when they are here, even for a day?'

'I don't see how I can, especially now,' said Ranjit.

'I thought of that,' said Vijay. 'The students are likely to call a truce during Janmashtami. Both of you can take a day off then, can't you? I've invited Dr Banerjee to be present then.'

Ranjit agreed to come if there was indeed a truce.

Janmashtami, the day Lord Krishna was born—Evelyn remembered that it was the same day a year ago when she had received news of her assignment at the Academy as assistant collector, Nilghat. Her year of training—with its almost bewildering array of experiences—was nearly over, and she was not sure whether she was happy or sad about it.

'I must try and make it,' she said.

'I am sure you won't regret it,' said Vijay, very happy at her response to his invitation. 'We must hear what the voices from the past can tell us about the present.'

35

THANESWAR RECALLED

$\mathcal{T}$he agitation was called off temporarily as expected for Janmashtami. Not doing so would have been unpopular. This enabled families to travel and be together on this auspicious occasion. It also allowed Vijay to play host to ADC Nilghat, Ranjit, and Evelyn and his chief guest, the very erudite Dr Banerjee. The ADC had brought the excavated urn and the necklace with him, which Dr Banerjee was examining very minutely.

Dr Banerjee looked every bit the renowned scholar he was. As they learnt over the evening, his first doctorate degree was in philosophy from Heidelberg University. He had followed this up with doctorates in Sanskrit from Benares Hindu University and then in Chinese from Rabindranath Tagore's famous Vishwabharati University in Santiniketan. He was dressed very simply in white shirt and trousers. He was in his mid-forties but already had thinning hair and the furrowed forehead of a deeply thinking man, a long nose, thick lips, and bright eyes that peered out of thick black-rimmed glasses.

'These do look very ancient,' he said, 'and the necklace very likely belonged to the mythical nobleman the Buddhist records talk about.'

'Dr Banerjee, where did you come across these Buddhist texts you refer to?' asked the ADC. He was voicing the curiosity of all those present.

'That's a long story,' replied Dr Banerjee. 'About five years back, the Buddhist scholars at Taipei University decided to begin an international search for someone who could help them decipher the ancient Buddhist scrolls retrieved from Tibetan monasteries and written in Pali, a derivative of Sanskrit. The Kuomintang had brought these scrolls with them when fleeing mainland China. As I had dabbled in Buddhist philosophy and taught Sanskrit and Pali, I may have fitted their bill,' he began.

Vijay requested a pause before the interesting story began, to serve refreshments. Dr Banerjee accepted only a lime juice. Seeing the others hesitate taking stronger stuff in his presence, he requested them to not emulate him.

'I have been living in a remote monastery these last five years quite far from Taipei, and leading a near-monastic life,' he said by way of explanation for his modest choice. 'But I have no issues or prejudices of any kind and do understand the needs of a secular life, to which I hope to return soon. But not yet.

'This monastery has the largest collection of these Buddhist scrolls, and I have been trying to make sense of them along with some other scholars and the monks,' he continued. 'Despite the somewhat Spartan existence, I have gotten accustomed to it and in fact begun enjoying it. It has provided me with the right environment to enable me to fully focus on the work as many things are emerging which weren't known to the modern world before.

'One of these is about the principality of Thaneswar, which holds a very enigmatic story. Its rulers appear to have been attracted to Buddhism after a certain monk came into their midst and discussed the new Buddhist thinking. One of the reasons, there are several references in the scrolls to this particular principality, is that the dilemmas its nobles faced appeared to raise some theological questions that the Buddhists took keen interest in and were interested in resolving.

'Thaneswar was subjected to attacks by hostile forces although the rulers themselves appeared to be wanting to live in peace. The scrolls indicate that it was able to defend itself because of a very able military commander who is variously referred to as Ajyatutha in some places, Alyatita in some, and other similar-sounding names elsewhere, which all probably refer to the Sanskrit name Aryaduta.

'One particular issue which appears to have been debated a lot concerns a particular royal commission which this Aryaduta was asked to undertake by the ruler of Thaneswar near the end of his rule. This had caused considerable inner turmoil to this very hardened commander. He confessed his inner turbulence to the senior monks at the monastery he finally took refuge in and where he spent the remainder of his life—and that is how we have come to know about it—and it is possible that his remains were in this very same urn we have here.

'When I heard about the finding of this urn and the necklace, I began to feel that such a possibility existed because the scrolls also talk about this person's involvement with a royal courtesan. This necklace which he seems to have treasured and retained with him, quite uncharacteristically for a man who has renounced the world, I feel, may have some link with this woman. So this urn may indeed have contained Aryaduta's remains, which now are in a sealed packet in the ASI headquarters.'

'But what's there in his story to have so interested the ancient Buddhists?' asked Ranjit. 'General falls for royal courtesan, can't get her, renounces the world, and dies clutching the necklace he meant to give her. Makes a good romantic story but why are the Buddhists interested?'

Dr Banerjee and the others laughed at this.

'I was coming to that,' he continued. 'Apparently, Aryaduta was in a terrible moral dilemma of some sort. The accounts in the scrolls hint at a kind of Kurukshetra dilemma similar to that faced by Arjuna that Aryaduta too had to confront as a result of the royal command. It is not clear why this is so. On the one hand, it appeared that there was some kind of existential calamity to the state of Thaneswar that he was duty bound to overcome. On the other hand, this particular commission involved possibly the killing of a very near relative—which is the Kurukshetra angle. The scrolls don't seem to go beyond this.

'The fact that Aryaduta took shelter in a Buddhist monastery appeared to indicate to the Buddhist scholars that he took the Buddhist way out of this impasse. But at the same time, the accounts also indicate that the menace to the state of Thaneswar appears to have been removed and a period of relative peace had been ushered in. So it is not determined that he did not take a militarist route either.

'The Buddhists at that time, very naturally, must have been discussing the dominant theological debates of the time, including the central theme of the Mahabharata and the choices before Arjuna. In Aryaduta's dilemma, they found an echo from that theme and a contemporaneous example of attempts at its resolution.'

'Very interesting indeed,' said ADC Nilghat. 'Isn't it coincidental that we are discussing Arjuna's dilemma today, which is Lord Krishna's birthday? All of India seems to support Lord Krishna's resolution to the issue.'

'Very interesting, indeed!' echoed Vijay. 'Let us consider, however, that if instead of Lord Krishna, Arjuna had the option of consulting Lord Buddha about how to resolve the demands of the Kauravs, would the story of the Mahabharata been different?'

'That must precisely have been the type of debate that may have arisen among the scholars at the time and why they felt a resolution was needed,' said Dr Banerjee. 'But that it caused a lot of discussion is apparent in the scrolls.'

Dinner was served. It was a strict vegetarian affair, which also meshed in with the spirit of Janmashtami. The guests continued talking after they sat down to eat at Vijay's dining table.

Evelyn was quite taken up with the story. 'One of the major gaps in the story you have not filled, Dr Banerjee, is how close to Aryaduta was the person against whom he had to act. The closer it was, such as to a son or wife, the bigger must have been his dilemma,' she said.

'I have a feeling that the enemy must have been a very close relative—probably a son,' mused Dr Banerjee. 'Women normally did not take up arms. Killing of brothers was quite common, such as by Ashoka himself when competing for the throne and would not have evinced too much concern in those days. But eliminating one's own son is quite another matter. It must have led to immense sorrow if it did happen.'

36

THE APPEAL

$\mathcal{F}$inally, Evelyn's year of district training was over. She was leaving by train for the long journey to the Academy at Mussoorie next morning for the final four months of training which would complete her two years of probation before her first posting on a full-fledged job. She had completed all her packing. She looked out of her room and noted with satisfaction that the garden was really blooming. That, at least, was a tangible contribution from her training period. As she had to take the train from Nilghat Road Station, which was some distance away from the town, she had to leave very early the next day.

She was about to leave the state at a time it was still in turmoil. The student leaders had announced a week's break in the agitation, following announcement of yet another round of talks at Delhi with the Home Ministry. But Evelyn was sceptical about the outcome and did not believe that any agreement would be reached within the next four months that she would spend at the Academy. As she had already been assigned this state as her parent cadre for the rest of her working life in the administrative service, she was expecting her first posting anywhere in the state, as either a subdivisional officer like Ranjit and Vijay, or an undersecretary in a desk job temporarily in the state capital till a subdivision fell vacant. Her posting orders, she had been given to understand, would soon be sent to her at the Academy.

But she still had a full day ahead. It was an important day as the appeal from Ranjit's contentious land acquisition case was to be finally heard by the DC in the afternoon. There was also a farewell function organised for her by the DC later in the evening. Ranjit had come ahead with the papers from the subdivision to brief the DC fully about the case. The DC had also invited Vijay to hear the case. It was rumoured that Ranjit was likely to be promoted either as an additional DC to some other district or as a joint secretary in state headquarters and Vijay likely to take his place. It looked now all the more probable as the DC wanted Vijay to be involved in the case.

As this was her last day in the district and as she was unlikely to have time to change before the farewell event where she was chief guest, Evelyn decided to dress more formally. She put on a dark-blue-bordered off-white cotton saree and blue-coloured blouse. When she walked in wearing this outfit with her high-heeled shoes clicking on the stone floor, all eyes in the courtroom turned towards her.

'You're looking great!' said Ranjit smiling appreciatively when she sat down on the bench behind him. Vijay also raised his eyebrows admiringly.

'Oh, it's you!' said the ADC jokingly. 'If Ranjit and Vijay didn't identify you, I wouldn't have known.'

Evelyn recognised Advocate Susheela Gautam, one of the lawyers representing the petitioners among the group of lawyers near the DC's high bench and waved out to her. Apart from the petitioners and the district officials, there were members of the press and some tribal student leaders from the district. Outside the DC's courts, quite a crowd had gathered, hoping that DC Nilghat would set aside the acquisition order rendering hundreds of families homeless. The SP had taken the precaution, however, of posting a platoon of policemen in riot gear should the decision not be to the liking of the petitioners.

The chatter in the courtroom subsided, and all stood up as DC Nilghat entered the courtroom and took his place on the high bench. He nodded to Susheela Gautam and her colleague lawyers, who were quite well known to him.

'This hearing is under Section 15A of the Land Acquisition Act of 1894,' he began. 'Petitioners have represented to the state government to set aside the order of learned SDO, and the state government has delegated the responsibility of hearing the petitioners to this office and making a decision on its behalf.

'But let me be quite clear at the outset as to the limitations of this hearing. All that this office can look into is whether due process as per law has been followed in making the proposed award about which the petitioners have been informed already by the SDO. If there is anything you wish to place before me within these parameters, I would be glad to hear. As you all know, once the award is made, there is no going back,' he concluded.

Advocate Susheela Gautam rose to speak. 'Your Honour, a great injustice is being done,' she said. 'No government in a civilised society can expunge the homes and livelihoods of hundreds of families in this way. This draconian law under which this is being carried out was enacted in 1894 by the British colonial administration. But we supposedly live in a democracy. How can one public-sector corporation be allowed to have its way despite the opposition of hundreds of men, women, and children?' she asked.

'Ma'am, you are arguing issues which you know well are quite outside the competence of my office to decide,' replied the DC. 'Besides, you are also quite aware no doubt about the opposing argument. The minerals that this land holds are needed sorely for our industry and for our exports. Thousands can benefit from the surge in growth and employment that this can provide. Besides, my administration has taken particular care to see that the compensation is appropriate—in fact, it is historically the highest we have awarded so far. In addition, our ADC sitting here has been charged with the task of coordinating a whole slew of development measures to see that the affected families do not lose out from this process of acquisition and ultimately suffer no hardship. This too is a first, as far as I am aware, in the whole country.

'Thus there are strong arguments on both sides, but as I said, this hearing cannot go into questioning the law. Hundreds of such legislations enacted during the British times have been carried over by our parliament. What we can look at is whether there were deficiencies in the process of acquisition. I would request you to please argue on that basis alone.'

Advocate Gautam knew very well that the DC would not allow such extraneous issues to be raised, but she was mainly speaking to the press members, knowing that her speech would get prominent reporting the next day. But she was also prepared with other arguments.

'There are a number of deficiencies in the process, Your Honour,' she said. 'Notices have not been delivered properly, there has been insufficient care taken in preparing the list of assets, some names are missing from the list of affected landholders—to name just a few. I will submit a detailed annexure to my main petition pointing out the irregularities.'

'How much time will you need?' asked the DC. 'The state cannot wait indefinitely.'

'Two months, Your Honour,' replied Advocate Gautam.

The DC realised that this was a ploy to get some more time. The whole set of files would have to be checked again once Advocate Gautam's detailed list of deficiencies to the proceedings was received. He knew that most of her objections were unlikely to hold up to scrutiny. However, he couldn't leave any stone unturned. He motioned to the ADC, who went up to the bench, and the two consulted for a while in whispers.

'OK. I can agree to a two-month adjournment of the proceedings. The petitioners will provide necessary documentation within that period. No further adjournments will be allowed under any circumstance,' he said, closing the hearing.

The news of the temporary reprieve was greeted with loud cheers by the crowd outside. A lot could happen within that time. The DC took upon himself the responsibility of making a decision which his boss the chief secretary would be highly critical of, but one that could be justified politically, given that the talks were on once more and it was wise to keep the matter pending.

The officials and Evelyn accompanied the DC to his chambers. They completed some formalities relating to the case. The DC was quite relieved that the difficult decision was postponed, even if for a short while.

'Who knows, in two months, I may not even be here,' he said. 'Then my successor would have to decide. What a convenient exit that would be!' he said, laughing.

'But now, time has come to bid our assistant collector farewell,' he said, turning to Evelyn. 'Although we couldn't devote too much time to you over the year, I hope you've picked up a few useful things along the way, despite our preoccupations!'

37

END OF TRAINING

It was past sundown when they stepped outside. The farewell was to be in DC's bungalow, the scene of many such gatherings that had taken place during her year of training, thought Evelyn. But this was to be her last, at least for the time being. Many assistant collectors had returned to their districts as DCs themselves—and who could foretell what the future held for her?

When the group arrived in their separate vehicles, the lights on the DC's bungalow, which had all been lit up for the occasion, could be seen glimmering through the canopy of trees on the driveway. A number of guests had already turned up, and there was a long line of parked government cars. Apart from her immediate district colleagues, the DC had invited the SP, and Evelyn found that Sudarshan Rao the subdivisional police officer from Ranjit's subdivision had also turned up—reflecting also perhaps Evelyn's popularity.

Also present were Suresh the IRDP project officer and all heads of district agencies with whom Evelyn had interacted in some way or other, such as the divisional forest officer, the executive engineer, the district agricultural officer, and so on. Their spouses had also been invited, so it was a fairly large group. Aruna, the ADC's wife, was also present, and Nivedita, of course, was the hostess of the evening's function. When the DC's group and Evelyn arrived at the upstairs veranda where the farewell was being organised, the chatter subsided.

'The time has come to bid farewell to Assistant Collector Evelyn Sing Syiem,' said the DC after the invitees had all settled down. 'This is the first time a lady assistant collector has been assigned to this district for training—in its entire history since 1869—and so its successful completion is almost a historic moment for us.'

There was hearty applause at this. After it died down, the DC continued his speech somewhat light-heartedly.

'Therefore, those of you who have helped train her can take credit that you have contributed to supporting the cause of women in this country. But Evelyn herself personally needs no supporting, as those who have come in contact with her know. Those who have tried their luck at tennis with her, for instance, have all suffered defeat quite ignominiously.

'She has proved to be a strict disciplinarian. The staff of the district circuit house and of the two subdivisions, who are probably heaving a sigh of relief now, do not realise that we will continue to hold them to account to the new standards she has set.

'In the couple of assignments she was asked to handle, she has shown her mettle. I am sure the students in this district, for example, will not forget her easily.

'I much regret that we were not able to devote as much time and effort to her training as we would have wished. But I think just being here and observing what has been happening and how we tried to handle them may have given her some exposure to the areas of administration that this state will be facing in the future.

'Those of you who are not familiar with Meghalaya's history may not know that the Syiems of Shillong confronted the British and suffered under their rule. But they remained defiant, and some Syiem leaders are remembered with pride as true revolutionaries. Being a descendant of this clan, I see in Evelyn a representative of this glorious past, and I am sure she will go on to great things. I wish her, on behalf of all of us, a successful career and a magnificent future!'

After the clapping had died down, Evelyn rose to speak. Her response was very brief. 'My posting in this district has been a stroke of fortune for me. Quite contrary to what DC sir has said, I have probably seen and learnt more here than any of my batchmates across the country. Thank you, sir, for your help and support from the very first day of my arrival.'

Then glancing particularly at Ranjit, Vijay, and her immediate circle of district functionaries, she continued, 'More than just providing training to a colleague, you have given me your warmth and friendship and made me feel at home. This is something I will always treasure.'

There was enthusiastic applause at her short speech. That ended the formal part of the farewell function.

Vijay came forward, trying to imitate a rider on the trot. 'Back to Chetak and the cool climes of Mussoorie now!' he said. 'How I wish I was back!'

'Living up in the hills, you should be the last to complain of the weather, Vijay,' said Ranjit. 'We will soon experience the heat and the dust of the plains and then you'll see how fortunate you are!'

'How I will miss these quarrels,' said the ADC, coming up to the group. 'If the rumour mills are correct, Ranjit is soon up for a promotion, but no one knows where he is going. With Evelyn also leaving us, what's going to happen to our debating club? We still haven't resolved fully the questions that the mystery urn has placed before us.'

'What questions?' asked the DC, who had come to invite Evelyn to the buffet dinner and had overheard the last part of the ADC's remark.

'That's a long story that is still without an ending,' replied the ADC. 'With our little debating society going their separate ways, it may now never find an end.' He appeared genuinely disappointed.

'Well, the debating society is still intact as of now, isn't it?' said the DC. 'The night is still young, and we may yet reach a conclusion well before Evelyn has to leave to catch her train.

'And meanwhile, let's have dinner!' he said, leading the way.

The menu, prepared again by Alam, consisted of a simple affair with an entrée which was one of Evelyn's favourites: chilli chicken served with fried rice. There were in addition a mixed vegetable curry to be had with *naan*, salad, and a desert which was also favourite of hers: banana fritters in custard. Alam served Evelyn her favourite dishes personally. Evelyn noted that he had prepared the dishes exactly as she liked them. The chilli chicken was moist and savoury, the fried rice wasn't too oily, and the banana fritters had just the right amount of sugar.

'Excellent food, Alam,' said Evelyn, and Alam accepted the compliment with folded hands. He had seen many assistant collectors come and go, but Evelyn had taken particular interest in his work.

'Evelyn madam, I hope you come back here as the DC,' he said. 'And I wish I am still around when you do.'

38

THE DEBATE CONTINUES

After the invitees had finally left and the DC and his most immediate colleagues repaired to the sofas for a quieter interaction over drinks from the DC's bar and he to his favourite cigar, Evelyn felt a feeling of déjà vu come over her. A very similar meeting had taken place when she had just arrived in the district, when everything was unfamiliar to her. It was difficult to comprehend that so much had happened within this year which had passed incredibly fast. And she had been in the thick of events as they unfolded.

'So, what are the questions you are seeking a closure on, Sitesh?' asked the DC, turning to the ADC. 'Mind you, not all questions can be answered.'

The ADC recounted the entire story from the finding of the urn and the mystery behind it to the discussions they had had with Dr Banerjee, the scholar from Taiwan who helped unravel much of the enigma associated with it by telling the strange story of the nobleman and his dilemma that had evoked so much interest in the ancient Buddhist scrolls.

'Putting the pieces of the jigsaw puzzle together and through logical deduction, we have come to surmise that matters of considerable spiritual interest were being debated in this very district several millennia ago,' said the ADC. 'And the issue was whether this nobleman who was forced to make a very difficult decision that involved sacrificing someone very close to him personally—perhaps his own son—did do so in the interest of the kingdom, as part of a royal commission he had promised to undertake, involving the annihilation of this person, or did he try and find a pacifist solution to the issue that would have required him make peace with the enemy of the state and to disobey his monarch?'

'Hmm . . . that's a difficult question indeed,' said the DC, taking a puff of his cigar. 'I feel that to some extent, this kind of moral dilemma is felt by every generation some time or other in a big or small way. But why don't I open this up to our debating society to arrive at a conclusion ourselves? Isn't that what you wanted, Sitesh?'

'Exactly,' said the ADC. 'I suppose there are no absolute truths. Each generation, community, or group must find its own solution, in keeping with the social needs and requirements of the times. But let's see what this group feels and agrees on.'

'Right, then let's call on the rationalist Ranjit to have a go first,' said the DC, turning to Ranjit. 'What is your conclusion?'

'Well, from the story that we've pieced together, it looks like this nobleman, a general of some sort, was asked to carry out a personally difficult project by his sovereign. His entire life's reputation as a loyal soldier was at stake. Would a person who recognised the need to protect society and generations after him give in to a personal frailty? I doubt it very much,' said Ranjit.

'Even if it meant murdering his own son?' asked the DC. 'Isn't a progeny a living sign of one's continuity, in some sense one's possibility of immortality?'

When Ranjit replied, he and all others around realised that in addressing the DC, he was responding to a person who himself did not have any children. 'For a person like Aryaduta, I think he would have been considering all of the citizens of the kingdom as his own family, his own parents, his own brothers and sisters, and his own children. Preserving the immortality of that society must have been for him a bigger goal than the life of his own son who had turned an impediment to the very existence of that society.'

'And what does our historian and philosopher think?' asked the DC, turning to Vijay.

'It is easy for us to take a somewhat objective view of the issue, separated as we are in time and situation from the events of that time,' answered Vijay, carefully choosing his words. 'But consider the terrible personal dilemma that this man has been facing. The contemporary teaching of his times reflected in the Mahabharata gives a pretty clear set of guidelines: no matter how great your personal sacrifice, follow the path of truth and justice. But the dillemas in the Mahabharata do not consider filicide—that is one sacrifice it did not discuss. There isn't any instance of it in Hindu mythology either, as far as I am aware. On the other hand, there was the growing influence of more pacifist teachings. It is just possible that Aryaduta may have worked out a compromise. Gautama Buddha, for example, did turn around the great terrorist of that time, Angulimala.[28] It is possible that the reason the Buddhist scrolls show such interest in this man's story was that it could have presented them with another example of the possibility of redemption of that most terribly lost soul.'

'That's an interesting take on the matter, I must agree,' said the DC. Then turning to Evelyn, he asked, 'What is your view, Evelyn?'

'Well, I haven't really given it as much thought,' said Evelyn. 'However, my understanding is that although the gods are known often to test humans with requirements of personal sacrifices of this extreme type to demonstrate their devotion to them, the scriptures rarely condone such practices. I am thinking of the well-known story of Abraham, for example, who was asked by God to sacrifice his only son Isaac. But when Abraham agrees, the killing is halted by God, thus clearly indicating that such a sacrifice was unacceptable at that time. I don't think it is ever sanctioned by any ethical doctrine at any time or age.

'But I think that if the nobleman had followed his instincts and reached a compromise, it would not have generated such a debate at that time. The story may in fact have become prominent because he did what was unusual and unexpected.'

'So you bring us around again to an impasse,' said the DC. 'Maybe such issues can only be resolved when one faces an actual dilemma. The circumstances of each situation we are called upon to resolve are usually unique, and therefore, there are no general principles that can be drawn upon. It is the burden of every society in every time and age to find their own answers to the predicaments that they face.'

'Such as the one, DC sahib, you are facing now,' said Vijay light-heartedly. 'On the one side is the greater national interest in the land acquisition case, and on the other, the interests of the soon-to-be displaced poor tribal households.'

'Somehow, I have been thinking exactly the same way, Vijay,' said the DC. Then he added, laughing, 'Why is it that I get the eerie feeling that this man Aryaduta's spirit is stalking us right now and watching every move we make critically?'

'But I must admit that this quandary I am placed in is nothing in comparison to that faced by Aryaduta. Of course, my sympathies do lie very much with the tribals whose interests we are here to protect and which are in no way subordinate to the interests of the state, I feel. And as you all know, I have been trying to ease their losses to my maximum abilities. But we are separated by absence of contiguity with the affected persons and can therefore still take a somewhat objective view of the issues at stake. Aryaduta wasn't as fortunate.'

Unknown to all of them, however, events in the near future would force the DC to confront a much more severe test, not much unlike Aryaduta's.

'Anyway, it's getting late, and we must let Evelyn go,' said he. He got up, and everybody rose along with him. 'But it's a long journey by train to Dehradun, and you can catch up on sleep then. Enjoy the last bit of your training!' he said, shaking hands and waving her off.

'And for heaven's sake, don't get off the train and venture into the forests again!' were the ADC's words of farewell.

Evelyn went downstairs, accompanied by Vijay and Ranjit. Her allotted white Ambassador car was waiting in the porch.

Vijay first considered giving her the formal handshake as he had done all along but then said, 'What the heck, you aren't our trainee officer any more, Evelyn!' and proceeded to give her a comradely hug. Ranjit, the more reserved, followed suit, somewhat stiffly. At that moment, all formalities had disappeared.

Getting into her car, the last thing Evelyn noticed was that the light was on in the wireless room in the corner of the DC's bungalow and the lone police operator was still busy at this late hour receiving and transmitting messages. The routine work of the district continued without a pause, not waiting for the comings and goings of people. As it should, thought Evelyn, waving goodbye to her two colleagues and Nilghat district.

39

A SURPRISE CALL

$\mathcal{R}$anjit felt the days dragging on, lifeless and colourless, like the scorching summer heat that had descended on the land. Yet he plodded on, mechanically disposing the hundreds of cases that kept piling up on his table. Although the agitation seemed to have ebbed a little, with some hope generated by the rounds of talks which appeared endless, armed militancy was on the rise. One group, predominantly the tribal students, simply refused to go along with the main student body and appeared to have broken off from it, adopting violence and refusing to accept that anything short of revolution would bring them justice. After the incident of attempted sabotage on the train, there had been reports of some encounters with police forces which left several policemen dead while the militants had disappeared into the forests.

Ranjit couldn't help feeling that Evelyn's departure had something to do with his general feeling of despondency. Had he developed some kind of bond or attachment with her? He refused to believe it. Even if he had, there was clearly no evidence of any reciprocal feeling from her side, he felt.

Ranjit was yet to overcome Suneeta's loss. Mourning her, he had maintained what others thought a mysterious aloofness from his women batchmates while at the Academy. When Evelyn was sent for training in his subdivision, he remained friendly enough, courteous and correct, but no more. Thus, although he liked Evelyn well enough and thoroughly enjoyed her company, he maintained a clear distance emotionally from her, particularly as she was a trainee officer.

But now examining his own feelings, Ranjit realised that Evelyn had somehow made a difference. Through the dark, gloomy clouds that filled his inner existence as well as the external environment, he saw Evelyn's company bringing in delight and freshness. But anyway, he realised, there was no point in thinking such, and he had to continue with his life and work and go his separate way as he had always done.

Trying to shake off this stupid feeling, Ranjit called up Sudarshan for a game of tennis at the circuit house after work. They played three sets, which Sudarshan won narrowly. Ranjit felt much refreshed after the vigorous exercise it afforded. But their standard of play again reminded Ranjit of the classier brand of tennis they had witnessed when Evelyn was around.

Asaram served them lemonade on the veranda as before, while they discussed the current developments. The circuit house was now completely empty. Official tours dropped dramatically in the height of summer. The lake beyond the wilting garden was completely still; there wasn't even a ripple.

'I think it may be wiser for you take an armed escort when you travel, Ranjit, rather than just the PSO,' said Sudarshan. 'We've received intelligence that there may be more attacks on police forces and government officials by the extremists. The SP has ordered an escort to accompany me as well. I've requested a platoon of armed police for you too, and they will be ready at the police station to accompany you. Just let the OC have your day's itinerary in advance, and he will organise the escort.'

'Well, I won't be around here in this subdivision too much longer, as you may have heard. Vijay is tipped to take my place. Besides, the tribal folk are well aware of my sympathies with them, and I don't think they want to harm me.'

'They aren't a homogeneous group,' said Sudarshan. 'From what we've learnt, they have a lot of divisions among them. There are totally irrational elements among them also. You shouldn't take any chances.'

'OK, agreed,' said Ranjit, not entirely convinced. He detested the idea of a Jeepload of policemen with bayonets following his vehicle everywhere he went. They would curb his freedom of movement and slow down his functioning as a public servant who needed to be in close contact with the people. Regretfully, Ranjit felt that they were moving into altogether different and dangerous times and the much-vaunted days of the civilian administrators of yore were over.

At least he wouldn't be around much longer here, Ranjit mused, and that was a comforting thought. He had completed over three years in the subdivision without a break, and now he felt weary. It was time to take a break, he felt.

After Sudarshan left, Ranjit sat around for a while. He called Asaram and drew his attention to the withering cannas and the drooping marigolds. The lawn had also developed brown patches in places.

'Just because Evelyn madam is gone doesn't mean you'll stop looking after the garden, Asaram,' he said. 'If the gardener isn't doing his job, you have to pull him up. You are the caretaker of this circuit house, and you have overall responsibility for its upkeep!'

Asaram was apologetic, and Ranjit felt remorseful at his outburst. But these fellows needed tightening up once in a while, he reasoned. Or was he losing his cool? He told Ali to take his vehicle back and took the short walk back to his bungalow.

He dreaded going back to his office room and the files, more of which must have piled up in the in-tray while he was gone. He decided to put off doing any work altogether for the day and sat down in the wicker chair on his front veranda, with the cup of tea Sundar brought for him.

The phone started ringing in his adjoining office room before he could take a sip of his tea. He got up, wondering what new problem was in the offing.

'Congratulations, Ranjit!' came the DC's cheerful voice over the line. 'You have been promoted as additional district collector right here in Nilghat in Sitesh's place. Sitesh has been promoted also and moving to our neighbouring district as DC. And of course, Vijay is taking your place. Looking forward very much to your joining my team here, although I will miss Sitesh a lot.'

Ranjit thanked the DC. He had been expecting the promotion but didn't realise that the DC wasn't prepared to let him go altogether.

'And by the way, just to give you a break before you join here, I have organised a two-week refresher training course for you at Mussoorie,' continued the DC. 'It starts next week, so you have to begin preparing to leave immediately. You can hand over charge to Vijay after you return. Biswas will act as the SDO meanwhile.

'Go take a good break—you've been looking a little tired lately,' he concluded before disconnecting the line.

40

CONTEMPLATIONS
AT THE ACADEMY

$\mathcal{D}$inner was over—the finale to the Kerala Nite, one of a series of state cultural evenings that the course director for the final training course of the Civil Services Academy had begun so that probationers could be more familiar with the cultures of the states they would be working in.

The Kerala dinner was preceded by a cultural evening where the trainees from the state had organised a variety show including instrumental music and dances and the famous Kathakali dance by a troupe all the way from Trivandrum. The dance was a great hit, with the colourful costumes and make-up of the dancers, and the lively song and musical accompaniment, which helped transport the altogether brilliantly exotic environment of Kerala into the quiet mountain campus. The troupe enacted an episode from the Mahabharata: the one where Arjuna and Duryodhana vie for Lord Krishna's support for the impending war between them, and the latter wins Lord Krishna's invincible army, while Arjuna is overjoyed to receive Krishna's personal support, which to Arjuna, surpassed all else.

The dinner too was a great success. It consisted of lemon rice and appam, cabbage thoran with coconut, Kerala-style sambar dal, an exquisitely spiced prawn curry, fish molee (a fish curry with coconut milk), and semiya (vermicelli) payasam for dessert. Each item had subtle Malayali flavours, stewed as they were with the whole spectrum of Kerala's spices and ingredients.

After dinner, the probationers hung out in the lounge, listening to music or reading books or chatting. It was a Saturday evening, and with a holiday next day, there was no hurry to go back as there was no early morning PT. Some went out in groups to have *paan*[29] from the *paan*-shop just outside the campus. As Evelyn was not a *paan* addict, she was left to herself, and she decided to saunter out to the balcony.

As soon as she had closed the lounge doors behind her, the quietness enveloped her. It was quite chilly outdoors, and she had to button up her cardigan. The night was clear and the entire vista of snow-capped mountains receding either side from the twin peaks of the Nanda Devi could be seen clearly in the bright moonlight, standing majestically above the wave upon wave of the nearer Terai ranges. Manna Dey's melodious voice singing 'Zindagi Kaisi Hai Paheli', the popular song from the Bollywood film *Anand*, was wafting in softly from the lounge. The song dealt with the enigma that life presented and the comings and goings of its players. It made Evelyn also recall the recent events from her life and the principal players in it, with whom her own life had become intertwined within a short space of time.

She remembered the DC and his wife and how they had tried to make her welcome in every way. The DC, a very senior officer in the cadre, stood tall above all the others, his advice and opinions sought by all, including the state's chief secretary. A childless couple, they looked at all the junior officers as part of their large family. On the other hand, the ADC, although quite senior too, was more like a friend, with his interesting hobbies and his penchant for attempting to make light of everything around him, encouraging the district officials to work and live normally even though the environment around them was tumultuous.

Evelyn's principal contemplations, however, were about Ranjit and Vijay. She wondered particularly whether they had remained merely colleagues or had come to occupy a closer position in her heart. She had never had the time to really consider her feelings for either of them before now. The days in the district had been too hectic, and she had gotten immersed in too many things to think clearly of such matters.

She much admired Ranjit, and she was attracted to his boyish looks. Though he was several years her senior, and more also than Vijay, he too was very young. But he had acquired the wisdom of a far older person. This might have come about, thought Evelyn, through the sudden onset of responsibilities that the job placed on him and the difficult situations he had had to confront—much more than his batchmates in similar positions in other states, most of whom, she knew, were having a rollicking time in their districts. He was practical and firm but also judicious and compassionate. More than anything, he was a very decent soul. The land acquisition case that was causing so much stir in the state revealed his traits clearly.

She was aware that Ranjit liked her company and enjoyed their time together. When she had travelled with him on official trips, he appeared light-hearted, and his formal official demeanour disappeared. But this, she reasoned, could be because of the distractions she provided—tennis, for one. She wasn't, therefore, sure about what he felt about her. There was also a mysterious aloofness about him that prevented her coming too close emotionally. Having been rebuffed herself a number of times in previous relationships because of her tribal background (although Ranjit never gave her any hint of any such feeling on his side and was in fact openly appreciative of her), she was wary of any fresh trauma that could ensue from an emotional adventure from her side and so remained somewhat hesitant herself.

Vijay, on the other hand, was an entirely different personality. He was jovial and informal and extremely fun to be around. Although a deeply thinking person, unless compelled, he kept his quite-substantial learning to himself and would prefer to make light of everything. Without much fanfare, he had quietly brought about a massive change in his subdivision. Vijay also seemed to be less reticent than Ranjit in reciprocating her warmth and friendship. She recalled that at times, although in banter, he might have been dropping hints—or so she imagined. She remembered, for example, the time when the antique necklace was discovered and Vijay had suggested jokingly that in a previous life, it could have been a present from him to her. She had retorted that that was like Arjuna and the Manipuri princess Chitrangada. While they all had a good laugh over it, she wondered whether the remark meant something to Vijay. It certainly did to her.

But now, several weeks had passed since she had arrived in Mussoorie, and there was no word from either of them. But wasn't that natural? They must have gotten engrossed with their busy schedules, and after all, Evelyn was just another trainee officer like many others who came and went, in an endless stream.

Evelyn decided to banish these idle thoughts from her mind and savour the remaining weeks of her training. This was likely to be her last break for a long, long time. She should soon learn where her posting as SDO would be and then it would be back to the turbulent atmosphere of the state. Meanwhile, she determined to enjoy her time at the Academy.

Tomorrow, for instance, would be the tennis championships, which she expected to win easily. Her riding tests were also coming up, and she had to practice her hurdles with Chetak a bit more. She also had to do some catching up on her coursework, particularly criminal and constitutional law, where she was falling behind.

The night sky had gradually clouded over while Evelyn was immersed in her reveries. The snow view was lost as rising mists from the valley soon engulfed the mountains. Returning to the lounge, she found that it was practically empty and the music from the record player had stopped. There were only one or two probationers around, chatting on the sofas. She waved goodnight to them and walked up the hill to the ladies' block.

41

SURPRISE ENCOUNTER

❧

*T*he week went by quickly. The tennis championship was a woefully one-sided affair, and Evelyn won it in straight sets 6-3, 6-2. Her opponent tried to put up a fight in the first set but could not make much headway in the second. She also cleared her riding tests quite easily, and Chetak cooperated wonderfully in the effort. A trained horse always recognised a good rider, and that was the case with Chetak and Evelyn. She patted him on the neck and gave him a lump of jaggery in appreciation.

There was a funny incident during the constitutional law class. The teacher, Prof. D. C. Mishra—called DCM for short—was very particular about punctuality and usually turned away probationers who came late. The classes were held in the auditorium, in front of the stage with thick maroon-coloured satin curtains that were kept drawn to conceal the stage. When the class was well in progress and over ten minutes had elapsed, one of the probationers, Dilip Rathore (nicknamed Late Rathore), a habitual offender, tried to sneak in quietly from behind the curtain while DCM was at the blackboard writing out some weighty propositions relating to India's Constitution. A

snigger from some in the audience unfortunately drew his attention
to the hapless Rathore, who had just stuck his head out from behind
the curtain and was looking for a quick unobtrusive entry.

'What is this? What is this?' thundered DCM.

'This, sir,' said Rathore, now coming into full view and pointing
at the parted curtain, 'is the loophole in the Constitution!'

The audience was in splits, and even DCM couldn't hide his
mirth. Rathore was let off with a warning. It became the joke of the
week.

And now it was Friday with a long weekend ahead as Saturday
had turned out to be a holiday. Everyone was looking forward to
the last of the cultural evenings to be staged on Saturday night—
Punjab Nite, being billed by the Punjab contingent as 'The Nite to
End All Nites!' With the prospect of a long and relaxed weekend
ahead, Evelyn and Sujatha, her roommate, decided to hit the town for
the Friday evening. There was a popular restaurant and bar at Kulri
called Tavern, where probationers usually flocked, and they opted
to have a pre-dinner session there along with the others. Sujatha
also wanted to visit an old antique shop she had discovered in Kulri
market which Evelyn hadn't visited and she said she'd explore too.
The shop sold various old items collected by the former English
residents of the Landour cottages, which were getting sold one by
one as the occupants either passed away or left for England or other
countries. There were thus many interesting items one could get at a
throwaway price if one could rummage through the collection and
strike a good bargain with the shopkeeper—himself a bearded and
bespectacled ancient.

So, they left early as soon as the afternoon classes were over,
hurriedly drinking their tea served in their room, eager to get away
from the campus. The Kulri market was at the other end of town,
and one had to cross the entire length of the Mall, which began at the
municipal library, itself a good mile and a half from the Academy,
which was tucked away on a remote part of the hillside.

The entire length of the Mall was lined on both sides with houses,
some elegant villas and others more modest tenements. They all had

a grand unhindered view, however, of the Doon valley, and at night, the flickering distant lights from Dehradun town far below were often clearly visible, unless obstructed by mists or clouds rising from the valley.

At this time, the Mall road was very crowded with tourists walking about or buying wares from the assortment of hawkers: Bhutias, Tibetans, and Garhwalis selling colourful hand-made woollen garments, necklaces and other ornaments made from beads and semi-precious stones, and sundry other handicrafts. They soon came to a fork on the road and had to decide whether to continue on the crowded Mall road or take a longer circuitous and less-traversed route to Kulri which ran around the other side of the hill. They decided to take the latter. At once, the crowds thinned out, and they came to a nearly deserted stretch of the road passing through forests of tall pine trees interspersed occasionally with old colonial-era cottages with sprawling grounds looking out to the mountain ranges.

A sharp bend in the road brought them away from the pine forest and on to a clear stretch of the road where a lookout point offered tourists a completely unfettered view of the forested valley below and the mountain ranges above crested with a grand line of snow peaks. Here there was the usual crowd of people, some taking photographs, others merely gazing at the view. Sujatha and Evelyn stopped for a while to also take in the breathtaking view and inhale the cool pine-scented air.

'Grand view, isn't it?' said someone just behind Evelyn.

Recognising the voice, Evelyn turned around, totally amazed to see Ranjit sporting a wide smile. He was dressed like a tourist in a red pullover, white cord trousers, golf cap, and sneakers, and that was perhaps why she hadn't noticed him among the group of people. Like the tourists too, he had apparently begun his purchases and was clutching something wrapped in a brown paper bag.

'What a surprise! How did you turn up here?' asked Evelyn, puzzled.

Ranjit mentioned his promotion and transfer and the DC's insistence that he take a training break at Mussoorie. Evelyn made the necessary introductions.

'I arrived just last night and was planning to come up to the Academy to see you later this evening,' said Ranjit.

'Well, it's lucky we took this route, then,' said Evelyn, 'else you would have missed seeing me at the Academy,' said Evelyn.

'This is my favourite route too,' said Ranjit. 'Especially this lookout point. Anyhow, looks like you are heading to Kulri. I'm just returning from there. Matter of fact, I found something at an old antique shop there we used to frequent.'

'You're not referring to the Old Curio and Book Shop, are you?' said Sujatha. 'That's where we are going.'

'Yes indeed!' remarked Ranjit. 'Some things never change. In fact, I bought an interesting item from the same shop. An original 1888 edition of Kipling's *Plain Tales from the Hills* published by Thacker, Spink, and Company of Calcutta. It is a collector's item.'

Ranjit had bought the book as a gift for Evelyn after spending a lot of time ruminating over what to give her. But he hesitated handing it over publicly at this time. Besides, he had yet to write out a short message for her. He decided to give it later privately.

'Why don't you join us for our evening outing—that is if you have the time and don't mind going back to Kulri?' asked Evelyn.

'I don't see why not,' said Ranjit, happy at the invitation. 'There's not much to do back at our training institute in any case.' The institute he was referring to was for in-service training of civil servants. It was a much smaller establishment and was located not too far from the Academy.

The lookout point wasn't too far from the Kulri bazaar, and very soon, they were in the midst of the holiday crowd again. Sujatha very considerately, thought Ranjit, suggested that Evelyn skip the curio shopping and go ahead with Ranjit to Tavern while she did the antique hunting solo, there would be many opportunities for Evelyn to visit the shop later etc. etc. She would join them as soon as she was done.

42

TAVERN

Ranjit found a table near the window and ordered two beers and a set of shrimp *pakoras*. It was still a little early for dinner, but the place was filling up fast, including with trainee officers, many of whom waved out to Evelyn, but some discreetly ignored them, not knowing who the stranger with her could be.

Ranjit noted that Evelyn had changed her style of dress from the somewhat correct *salwar* and full-sleeved *kameez* she usually wore in the district to jeans and a top over which she was wearing a loose beige cardigan. She had also altered her hairstyle and had tied her hair into a bun. As the atmosphere inside the restaurant was getting quite warm, she took off her cardigan, and Ranjit saw that she was wearing a short-sleeved black top exposing her long neck line and arms. She had also worn lipstick, which was another change— looking altogether very comely, Ranjit concluded.

'So, tell me all the news,' said Evelyn, trying to initiate conversation with a Ranjit who appeared to have become more silent than he usually was. 'Are you looking forward to being Sitesh's replacement at Nilghat?'

'Well, I must confess, I was expecting a transfer to a quieter low-key district. But obviously the DC has other plans!' said Ranjit.

'The DC is looking for support from you at this difficult time, Ranjit,' said Evelyn. She was aware that apart from his dependability, the DC was also personally very fond of Ranjit. It was good to have people around whom you could trust and were comfortable with; hence, the choice was obvious.

'Tell me about yourself,' said Ranjit. 'What have you been up to these last couple of months? Has a lucky someone come into your life?'

'Not yet, I'm afraid,' said Evelyn, laughing. Ranjit had guessed this to be so when he saw her with Sujatha. But he was glad to hear her confirm this.

The restaurant had filled up, and the chatter from the tables was making it difficult to continue a conversation without talking very loudly. The DJ had started off with some dance numbers, and a few people—mostly the officer trainees—had taken to the dance floor in couples. Presently, Sujatha came in, her shopping over for the moment, and showed Evelyn the few items she had found—a porcelain cat, a Moghul miniature, and an ornate picture frame. These were for her parents and sister, she explained.

Ranjit ordered another round of beer and *pakoras*. After taking a few sips, Sujatha joined the group on the dance floor, having found a partner from one of the tables. The beers had made Evelyn quite cheerful, and she also stood up and asked Ranjit to join her too.

'I don't dance, Evelyn,' said Ranjit. 'I'll make quite a fool of myself in front of your friends.'

'You think they'll notice? They are all half-drunk already! Just get up and let yourself go and try and swing to the beat!' she replied, half dragging him to the floor.

Ranjit got up reluctantly. The DJ was playing a number from Boney-M's just released album. He paired off with Evelyn and tried copying her steps. Beginning very awkwardly, he found that gradually his stiffness was disappearing, and he began to quite enjoy himself.

As with other things, Evelyn was an expert dancer and more than made up for his deficiencies as part of the dancing duo.

After a few more fast numbers, the DJ, noting the mood on the floor, switched to a slow waltz. Evelyn took Ranjit's hand in hers and asked him to hold her waist with the other, imitating the dancers on the floor. They moved awkwardly around the floor initially, but later Ranjit slipped into the rhythm of the dance. He found Evelyn's closeness enthralling. The perfume she wore, her narrow waist, and the soft touch of her body when the dance brought them close, all bewitched him. He wished the evening could go on.

Unfortunately, however, the music stopped as the DJ had to take a break. It was also a signal for the officer trainees to call it a day and take the long walk back to the Academy, else they would miss their dinner.

On the way back, it was difficult to have any private conversations as Evelyn introduced Ranjit to her colleagues as the ADC, Nilghat, and everyone was eager to talk to her senior colleague from the state which was constantly in the news the past year. Some even started addressing Ranjit as 'sir', and he had to remind them of the convention that such an honorific was reserved only for colleagues more than five years apart in seniority, which was not the case here.

So Ranjit could hardly talk to Evelyn. He was a little disappointed that she hadn't invited him to the Academy, although he would have to go over on his own sometime to call on the director and meet those of the faculty from his time who were still around. But still, he was hoping for some indication from Evelyn that she would like to meet him again. He wanted at least to present her the book he had bought for her. He was glad, therefore, that a little before they reached the training institute, which was a short distance before the Academy, Sujatha and the two of them fell back a little.

'Well, I have to take off from here,' said Ranjit. 'Thanks for a great time. I haven't enjoyed myself like this for a long time!'

'Me neither,' Evelyn said. 'If you're not busy, why don't you join us for the Punjab Nite around 6 p.m. tomorrow?' she added. Ranjit was glad that finally Evelyn had invited him.

'You mustn't miss it,' said Sujatha, laughing. 'It's going to be a night to remember, they say, A Nite to End All Nites!'

'In that case, I have to be there,' Ranjit agreed readily.

'Goodnight, and see you, then, tomorrow evening!' said Evelyn, waving goodbye.

Ranjit walked up to the dining room of his training institute. A few late diners were still around. He helped himself to the buffet and found an empty table near the tall glass doors, which were kept shut to keep out the cold. He brought out the book he had bought for Evelyn and was glad of the purchase. He had found an old silver bracelet which was embedded with rubies which he liked very much but felt it might be too personal. He had finally settled on the book. He began wondering what he would write as a message. He wanted it to be more than just a formal note.

Ruminating over this issue, he finished his dinner and went to his room. He was glad that the administration had given him a room with a great mountain view. There were several new renovated rooms but Ranjit had asked for anything which looked out over the mountains, and he was given this. Although it was part of an old cottage which badly needed repairs, he didn't mind that.

He switched on the table lamp and sat down at the old teakwood desk. Opening to the title page of *Plain Tales from the Hills*, he wrote:

> To Evelyn:
>
> Hope reading these tales in the hills will make you forget the torrid times you experienced with us in the plains! But while those narratives may fade with time, I hope you remember the players.
>
> Take good care,
> Ranjit

43

BACK AS A VISITOR

*R*anjit arrived at the Academy a little before he was expected and took the time to explore the main campus buildings where visitors were permitted, for he was now a visitor—the front lawn and the grounds around the main block which housed the lounge, the officers' mess, and the library. Nothing had changed in the five years he had been last there. The buildings were magnificent double-storied Swiss-style wooden structures with gabled roofs which had once been the famed Charleville Hotel built in the late nineteenth century, being in fact the first regular hotel built in Mussoorie. One of the queens of England had apparently been among its famous visitors.

The buildings were uniformly green in colour, with red gabled roofs, and formed a semicircle around the grounds in front with its tall pine trees and a well-kept lawn and garden. These main buildings stood on the crest of a hill which descended quite steeply on all sides. On one of the sides, the Academy had a series of hostel buildings which led to a small level ground surrounded by forests, known as Happy Valley, where the riding ground and the sports complex with outdoor tennis and indoor badminton and squash courts were located. There were also some cottages for the senior faculty.

The library was one of Ranjit's favourite haunts, and as he climbed the wooden stairs of the main block, he recalled the many pleasant hours he had spent there. The reading area extended along the windows from where a grand view of the northern hills and, on clear days, the stunning snow view could be seen. It was a wonderful place to study and do course assignments rather than in his hostel room. It remained exactly as he had seen it the last time, and Ranjit felt that the intervening years had just vanished.

It was about time for his meeting with Evelyn and so Ranjit decided to stand around the ladies' block till she emerged. It was getting to be time for the cultural evening to begin, and the trainees started appearing in ones and twos from their hostel blocks and began milling around the auditorium entrance. Ranjit was wearing his old blazer which he had hardly used after leaving the Academy and had carefully kept the book for Evelyn in its inside pocket, to present to her at the first opportunity of a private moment with her. A carefully knotted Academy tie complemented the blazer, and as he looked around, Ranjit found himself overdressed a trifle, compared to the chattering group of trainees around him, who were dressed casually. But he remembered the etiquette course where the instructor had advised that it was always better to be overdressed than underdressed, and didn't bother.

The ladies' block also happened to be right next to the director's cottage and who should be emerging from it, Ranjit saw, but the man himself! The director's eye immediately turned to the somewhat formally dressed man, and he instantly recognised him.

'Ranjit, wonderful to see you back!' he exclaimed. 'Are you at the refresher course at the institute?'

Ranjit was very pleasantly surprised that the director remembered him from the thousands of probationers that had come and gone. But that was one of the traits of good leaders, Ranjit thought, and no wonder, therefore, that he was the director of this prestigious institution.

'Yes indeed, sir,' he replied, 'I made an appointment to see you in your office on Monday, but now that won't be necessary.'

'It's lucky we met as that wouldn't have happened, I'm afraid,' said the director. 'I've had to cancel all appointments next week as I am leaving for Delhi tomorrow for an urgent meeting. But tell me how you've fared and whether the stuff we drilled into you has come in useful.'

They talked for a bit, and while deep in conversation, Ranjit noted from the corner of his eye that Evelyn had emerged from her room alone, without Sujatha her roommate and was slowly walking towards them. She stood around a little way off so as not to intrude. But the director noticed the waiting lady officer and ended his discussion.

'I see you've set up a meeting with the lady and I mustn't keep you waiting!' he said. Then turning to Evelyn, he said, 'Ranjit was one of our finest officer trainees, and if I remember correctly, won a medal too! Please look after him and see that he joins the cultural evening and dinner.'

He left, giving Ranjit a pat on the back. Just before leaving, he turned to Evelyn. 'By the way, Evelyn, there's a wireless message that came in from your chief secretary this morning to all probationers in your state about your postings. Pick it up from your mailbox.'

Evelyn was eager to find out where she had been posted. The mailroom was just next to the auditorium, and Ranjit waited while she went to fetch her message. She came out looking quite disappointed and handed Ranjit the wireless message. It read:

FROM: CHIEF SECRETARY
TO :   EVELYN SING SYIEM (IAS 1980)
COPY : DIRECTOR ACADEMY, MUSSOORIE

=YOU HAVE BEEN POSTED AS UNDERSECRETARY (POLITICAL) AFTER END OF PROBATION STOP PLEASE REPORT TO OFFICE OF CHIEF SECRETARY ON COMPLETION OF YOUR TRAINING=

Noting her disappointment, Ranjit tried to console her. 'Don't worry, Evelyn,' he said. 'There must have been some administrative glitch, and the subdivision you are eventually going to may require a little time to be vacated. It happens frequently. Besides, you will directly be under the chief secretary in the Political Department, which he oversees and is the nerve centre of the state administration. It is an equally important assignment, if not more important than an SDO.'

Evelyn perked up at this. 'Very well, if you say so, Ranjit,' she said. 'I trust your judgement. I'll soon find out when I reach state headquarters.'

'Meanwhile, let's join the Nite to End All Nites!' she added.

Ranjit realised that this posting imbroglio had cost him the opportunity to present Evelyn with her book and he would have to wait till the evening festivities ended. Meanwhile, the auditorium was filling up with probationers waiting for the much-anticipated super entertainment, and he joined Evelyn to look for vacant seats.

44

HIGHS AND LOWS
ON PUNJAB NITE

$\mathcal{T}$he Punjab Nite began on a sombre note with one of the talented trainees, Jaswinder Singh Gujral (Jassi for short), rendering a couple of bhajans accompanied on a harmonium while a lady colleague held the scale gently on the *tanpura*. From the serene semi-classical melody of the bhajans, the mood of the music then moved to the modern, with a few popular Punjabi folk numbers sung by a gifted lady trainee, Bhupinder (Bunty) Randhawa. Bunty was a close buddy of Evelyn, and she clapped loudly after each of Bunty's songs. No Punjabi cultural evening is complete without Punjabi jokes—made all the more humorous by being both narrated and directed at the Punjabi *sardarjis* themselves. The audience was regaled with a number of these by the jester in the Punjab contingent, Raminder (Joker) Singh. The mood of the audience had changed quickly, and everyone was shouting for more.

And then from somewhere behind the stage, the *bhangra dhol* began its inimitable drumbeat, slowly at first and then building up the tempo. At last, the Punjab Nite was delivering on its promise, felt the now-restive audience.

Then quite dramatically, a professional *bhangra* troupe from Ludhiana made its appearance. The men were dressed in gaily coloured *chaddars* and *kurtas* with traditional headdresses—the *paghs*. The women dancers were in equally colourful *salwars* and *kameezes*, with *chunnis* on their heads.

They first performed a folk dance—the men and women together—and then the women did a lively *gidda* by themselves. The next item consisted of a number of rousing pop numbers from a member of the invited troupe, accompanied on synthesiser by another member. Those were the days when Punjabi pop music was just beginning to create a sensation, and this was an early example. After that, the *dhol* picked up a frenzied beat once again, and the male dancers came on stage and presented a series of lively *bhangra* numbers. The last one was the most rousing of all, and a few of the trainees couldn't resist the heady beat and joined the *bhangra* group on stage themselves while those who couldn't be accommodated on stage nevertheless did an impromptu performance on the aisles. At the end, the Ludhiana troupe got loud applause and a standing ovation with many encore requests, but the performers were done and the cultural evening ended far too quickly, most felt.

But the biggest attraction of the evening was yet to come—the Punjab dinner. In this, Jassi again had a big role to play. Not only was he a talented singer, but he was a man of many parts and was famous also for his qualities as a gourmet and amateur chef. He had been advising the kitchen staff all along in the Academy on the proper way to cook Punjabi dishes and had come to acquire a somewhat legendary stature in this respect. It had therefore been widely advertised that the Punjab menu was to be Jassi's creation and prepared under his direct supervision.

After the cultural program was over, the officers therefore gathered in the lounge, waiting in keen anticipation for the mess doors to open. As there was still a little while before dinnertime, Evelyn decided that Ranjit must view Jassi in full flow in the kitchen, before the dinner itself. She had filled him in about Jassi's renown, and although Ranjit was curious and went along, he was still looking for a private moment with Evelyn, which again this would postpone.

The large kitchen was in the basement below the mess and had to be accessed by a winding staircase. A wonderful aroma wafted up from the kitchen stoves as they descended. They found Jassi engaged in stirring four large cauldrons of butter chicken, occasionally tasting the curry to see if the taste was correct. He was hurrying all the cooks as they were getting a bit delayed for the dinner. On another set of clay ovens, the tandoori *rotis* were being made. The rest of the dishes were ready.

'Hi, Evelyn, I see you've brought a visitor,' said Jassi, seeing the two while continuing his work.

Evelyn made the introductions, and it turned out that Ranjit was in the same batch as Jassi's elder brother Jagmeet.

'What a small world!' remarked Ranjit. 'Then I must have I met you at Jagmeet's wedding in Delhi last year. Let's chat more over the delectable dinner you are making. We shouldn't distract you from your very crucial enterprise.'

'Before you go, I must make you sample some of this,' said Jassi, picking up two plates and serving Ranjit and Evelyn each a portion of the chicken from the boiling cauldron and *rotis* from the tandoor.

'This is the best butter chicken I've ever had, Jassi, and I mean that seriously,' said Ranjit. 'Somehow I'm getting the feeling you're in the wrong profession!'

They left Jassi to his last-minute preparations and went back to the lounge to wait for the mess doors to open. The lounge was full with a number of trainees standing near the closed doors of the mess so that they could be the first in line. The flavours of the butter chicken had been drifting in, and some impatient trainees could wait no longer for the doors to be opened and started knocking loudly and asking the mess staff to open up. When the doors finally did open, there was a near stampede as the hungry horde rushed for the buffet tables. The butter chicken was the most popular item, and although there were sundry accompaniments such as an Amritsari-style fish, *mutter paneer, gobi sabzi,* stuffed *bhindi* and *rajma,* the chicken was the most sought after, with most coming back for seconds and even thirds. Ranjit and Evelyn let the crowd settle down at the tables and waited till the buffet line had shortened. They were among the last to get to the buffet, and Ranjit realised how lucky he was to have had a good sampling of Jassi's butter chicken as while fairly good portions of other items on the menu were still available, the butter chicken tray was empty, scraped clean of even the last drops of gravy.

Dessert consisted of *gulab jamuns* served in hot syrup. Ranjit took his plate to the lounge, where he sat down in a comfortable sofa. Evelyn brought hers too. The magnificent voice of Nusrat Fateh Ali Khan, the rising Punjabi Pakistani *qawwali* singer who was getting increased attention in India was playing on the record player. Ranjit noticed, looking out from the French window next to him, that it was a clear night and he could make out the dark languid shapes of the mountains and tops of the pine forest in the valley below and thought that now would be a propitious time to go outside with Evelyn.

'Why don't we go for a *paan* and then I can be off to my institute?' he said.

'I don't have *paan*, but I'll keep you company and see you off at the gate,' she replied.

When they got up to leave the lounge, Evelyn noticed that a few of the probationers were carrying letters and some were sitting and reading them. The evening *dak* had obviously arrived.

'Ranjit, can you wait for a minute here and I'll check my mailbox and come back in a jiffy. I'm expecting a letter from my mom,' said Evelyn, leaving him temporarily.

The last two days had gone splendidly, thought Ranjit while he waited in the lounge. Evelyn had seemed genuinely pleased to see him, and they'd had a jolly good time together. Perhaps the future held more promises for both of them.

Evelyn returned. She had an opened letter in her hand. She was flushed and appeared confused. She sank back on the sofa and exclaimed, 'It's from Vijay, and would you believe it? He's proposed to me!'

Ranjit's imagined edifice of dreams and aspirations built around Evelyn and himself collapsed around him. How could this happen, he thought. Vijay had given no indication, he felt, that he was serious enough to consider proposing to Evelyn. Of course, he was aware of his jokes and the banter between them, but he had not the slightest clue that there could be anything of a serious nature going on between them. If he had, Ranjit would obviously have stepped aside—as he had done so many times before.

Careful, however, not to show the swell of emotion that had engulfed him, he said, 'Wow, Evelyn, that's great news! I couldn't think of a better pairing than the two of you.'

'Of course, Ranjit, I agree that Vijay is a swell guy,' said Evelyn, 'but this is all too sudden! Why couldn't he wait for me to get back at least?'

'You know how impulsive Vijay is. But often it's better to be,' said Ranjit, thinking ruefully about how his procrastination might have cost him.

He got up to leave. It would be completely out of place now, he felt, to present his small gift to Evelyn. Evelyn also got up. They walked down the long path to the Academy gate, mostly immersed in their respective thoughts.

'I hope we'll meet before you leave?' asked Evelyn before they parted.

'I'll try but can't promise. I am here only for a week and don't know how busy I'll be,' said Ranjit, appearing not to sound dejected. 'Anyway, you'll be back soon, and we'll bump into each other sometime or other. And thanks for the wonderful time I had both yesterday and this evening,' he added, waving goodbye and disappearing into the suddenly cold and fog-engulfed night.

45

HANDING OVER

$\mathcal{T}$he day had finally arrived, when Ranjit was to bid goodbye to his subdivision and move to Nilghat as the new additional district collector. It was several weeks after he had returned from his short break at Mussoorie. The matter regarding Evelyn had faded a bit as he immersed himself in work. The intervening days since Mussoorie had disappeared in a flash, with the business of winding up taking most of his time, including the rounds of farewells at the outlying circle offices, and police stations, the latter accompanied by Sudarshan.

For his last day, Ranjit had only two important remaining items in his agenda: handing over the cash at the treasury and the evening farewell at the office. Vijay had already turned up for the takeover and was putting up at the circuit house. Ranjit had invited him for dinner at his bungalow, and the two of them had sat around on the veranda, chatting over drinks before Sundar served dinner. Vijay had not spoken even once about Evelyn, and Ranjit too had kept off the topic.

Ranjit planned to leave as soon as the farewell was over. He felt it would be in bad form to linger when the new SDO had formally taken charge so that the staff could focus fully on him rather than the departing one.

He had already sent his few boxes and trunks—containing mainly clothes and books—along with Sundar to Nilghat. While packing his books in his bungalow office, he had kept the book meant for Evelyn aside on his table several days, unable to decide what to do about it. He decided finally to send it to Evelyn by post as after all, he had bought it for her and he didn't expect her to attach any significance to it other than the simple gift it was meant to be. He had no furniture, the SDO's residence being fully furnished with spare or discarded items from the circuit house, and he was spared having to move any.

The treasury handover was a tedious exercise but essential. In many subdivisions and districts, large amounts of the government's cash kept at the treasury often went missing, discovered only at the time of change of guard. Ranjit had therefore instructed his treasury officer to verify the cash balances regularly, but in the three years since he had taken over, this was the only time that he could spare for a thorough personal inspection.

Ranjit requested Vijay to start the check, and Vijay had been at it since the treasury opened in the morning but was not yet done by lunchtime. So he ordered some *aloo parathas* and *dum aloo* from the canteen and walked over to the treasury, which was just next to the main building.

He found Vijay at the dingy inner room of the treasury, next to the currency chests, with thick wads of large-denomination rupee notes spread around him. A huge pile to his left had been counted, but there was a sizeable pile on his right yet to go. The treasury officer kept removing the finished piles and storing them back in the iron safes.

'Time for a break!' Ranjit announced, arriving. A little later, Raju the tea boy from the canteen turned up at the treasury door, balancing the plates of *parathas* in one hand and his blackened tea kettle and cups in the other and shouting, 'Chai, *parathas*!' loudly. Ranjit realised that he would quite miss seeing Raju, although all these years in the subdivision, he had hardly taken note of the fellow.

Raju, however, had played a vital unobtrusive role, reducing the daily boredom of the office with his cups of tea and *samosas* and helping overcome his hunger pangs when occasionally he worked late, with impromptu tiffins from the canteen. He therefore handed Raju a big *baksheesh* while settling the bill.

'I heard you are going away, sir. Please do something for me before you leave,' entreated Raju. Ranjit had been hearing this persistent plea the last few days, what with the acute unemployment situation in the country and particularly this state with its stalled development. 'Do something' meant induction to a government job at the lowest echelon as a peon. But providing such largesse was getting increasingly difficult with the government tightening the rules regarding such hires.

'Which class have you studied to, Raju?' asked Ranjit. The minimum requirement was sixth pass, which meant having cleared primary school and being literate (the former not necessarily guaranteeing the latter).

'Sir, only class four,' said Raju dejectedly.

'Well, in that case, I'm afraid you'll have to clear class six somehow before you can get a permanent position in the office,' Ranjit replied. 'But . . .' He hesitated as a thought came to him. 'Check with the new SDO sahib. He may need a new bungalow peon, as mine is coming with me to Nilghat,' he added. The hiring criteria for temporary bungalow staff was much more lenient.

Raju was overjoyed, and he salaamed Ranjit profusely. Ranjit made a mental note of speaking to Vijay about it before leaving. Returning to the treasury's inner sanctum, he found that their tiffin had been laid out and Vijay and the treasury officer were waiting for Ranjit's return. They devoured it quickly, and thereafter, Vijay and Ranjit took up counting the remaining currency bundles, sharing the work between them. This quickened the process, and in about another hour, they had finished and the accounts were found to be perfect. Thereupon, they formally signed the handover in the ancient ledger.

It was nearly time for the farewell, so they decided to walk over to Ranjit's office and wait there till all staff had assembled. While visitors kept Vijay busy, wanting to meet the new SDO, Ranjit looked around, surveying his small office room fondly. He had spent much of his last three years here. Looking around, he noticed that the room had become quite unkempt and untidy. He had hardly had time to look at the details. The curtains needed replacing. Some of the paint on the walls was peeling off. The green tabletop on his large desk was frayed. What with the paucity of funds always cited by the PWD, he hadn't been able to have the room even repainted. He realised that Vijay would have to do some serious renovation work before moving in.

After a short while, the head clerk came in, in his spotless white *kurta* and *dhoti*, inviting them to main clerks' hall. The head clerk's table, which he had surrendered for the occasion, had been covered with a white tablecloth, and a vase of flowers—mainly marigolds—had been placed at the centre. There were three chairs, one each for the departing and incoming SDOs and another for Biswas, the senior executive magistrate who was the master of ceremonies for the function. The entire staff sat at their respective tables, while some chairs had been placed in front for the few officers. After a brief introduction, Biswas invited Ranjit to speak.

'I dislike farewells and would have much preferred that my welcome three years back had continued,' began Ranjit. 'That is, however, not possible, and all good things must end and so also my journey here. It is difficult to realise that it was three years ago that I stood here as the new, quite inexperienced SDO. The time has flown fast, too fast, and it appears to me as though it was just the other day.'

Ranjit noted that the entire staff was hearing him with rapt attention. Most appeared genuinely unhappy to see him go—this despite the various unpopular actions that he had to enforce, such as ordering pay cuts for absences during the agitation. They obviously realised that these were actions he had no discretion over. Given the various crises they had ridden out together (law-and-order emergencies, natural calamities, the long-drawn-out agitation, the major land acquisition fracas, and so on), a bond had grown between them, and they were all survivors of the many storms they had weathered.

'I thank you for all the help, support, and cooperation you provided to me and the government,' he concluded. 'This was my first job as a public servant, and you helped me learn the ropes from the first day onwards. Our many successes have been the result of our joint efforts. I am sure I could have done many things better and will take valuable lessons with me. It has been a privilege to have worked with you all.'

Vijay, as the new SDO, was also asked to say a few words. Afterwards, light snacks and tea were provided. And then it was all over. Ranjit felt an immense freedom, suddenly shorn of all his responsibilities. Although he would be taking charge as ADC the next day, it was basically a supportive role, with the DC calling the shots.

The air outside appeared fresher, the sky bluer, and the placid lake in front immensely lovelier. Ranjit savoured all the sights around him with a sense of novelty mixed with a tinge of sadness, not having had time to really appreciate them fully and regretting having to take leave of them.

His car, a black Ambassador, sent by DC, Nilghat, was ready. The title 'Additional District Collector, Nilghat' was prominently displayed in bold red letters in front. A PSO also from Nilghat was to accompany him. Ranjit had declined the armed escort that Sudarshan had offered as unnecessary as he was no longer SDO and so did not perceive a threat.

The entire officer group, along with the head clerk and the *Nazir* came out to bid him goodbye. They had seen many SDOs come and go, but had he been different? Ranjit wondered. He shook hands with all of them and finally with Vijay, who gave him a warm hug.

'Take care . . . see you soon in Nilghat,' he said simply.

The driver held open the door and Ranjit got in. And then waving goodbye to all, he was off. Looking back, he saw Vijay now a lonely figure on the steps of the SDO's courts still waving. But he too was lost soon as the car turned and entered the crowded main street of the town.

It was early evening, and Ranjit expected to be in Nilghat well before nightfall. They negotiated the crowded streets of the town slowly and then, reaching the outskirts and the open countryside, speeded up. Ranjit's thoughts, unbidden, turned to one of the countless trips he had taken to Nilghat when Evelyn was with him. After he passed Golmunda, he looked out for the dhaba where they had stopped for *masala chai*. Ranjit decided to take a break, asked the driver to stop, and got out to stretch his legs.

As before, the dhaba owner came running out to meet him. He ordered tea for everyone and sat down alone at the same table Evelyn and he had shared—and although the picture of Evelyn with her hair open, sitting across him that morning not too many months ago came to him, he decided to banish those images from his mind and instead think ahead. He realised with dismay that he had forgotten to mention Raju to Vijay. It had to be done quickly before Vijay appointed someone as he would need to.

He walked up to the owner, who was only too glad to allow Vijay to use his telephone, which was in a room inside. However, getting through to Vijay took a long time with the small exchange in the subdivision unable to locate the new SDO immediately. However, finally, the connection was made, and Vijay was surprised to get a call so soon from Ranjit.

'I was surprised, thinking that you had reached Nilghat in record time,' said Vijay. 'Of course, I'll get Raju. In fact, I had asked Asaram the circuit house caretaker to look for someone, and this will be a great help. You know what a miserable cook I am!'

Ranjit felt relieved. The call had delayed him a good half hour, but he was glad that his final chore was over. The skies were darkening when he got into the car. The driver switched on his headlights, and they drove off.

No one noticed the two motorcycles that were following them till they came alongside, and a shot rang out, smashing through the front window and catching the PSO in the left shoulder. He was immobilised and bleeding profusely and couldn't retaliate. The other motorcycle shot ahead and forced the car to a stop at gunpoint. Then things happened very quickly. The gunmen, all with faces concealed and heavily armed, ordered the driver and the PSO to get out, and one of them got in the driver's seat and another first blindfolded Ranjit and then sat next to him, with his weapon jabbing his ribs.

Ranjit then heard the car starting and driving off while he could hear the motorcycles following the car.

'What do you want and where are you taking me?' he shouted at his captors.

'Keep quiet and you won't be hurt, at least not just yet,' said Ranjit's captor menacingly in the local vernacular as they drove away into the night. 'You'll come to know soon enough.'

46

KIDNAP AND 'TRIAL'

~~~

*T*he night had been difficult. After a while, Ranjit couldn't make out where he was headed. His captors had taken several twists and turns and then abandoned his office car and forced him to get into another vehicle while still blindfolded. After driving on level ground for some time, they seemed to take a slow hill track which kept climbing and meandering. Another hour or two passed—Ranjit had lost track of time—when they made him get off and, after finally taking off his blindfold, began a long, unending walk through dense forests. Then the track started going downhill until they came near a stream. Ranjit was made to get on a country-boat, and his captors pushed off with him and started rowing. Ranjit realised that his captors were obviously very familiar with the terrain. The boat kept stealthily going upstream in the night for what appeared a very long time till they halted at the other bank. Then another trek in the dense forest began.

Finally, they arrived at their destination. It was at what looked like a newly made clearing accommodating a makeshift campsite. Ranjit could vaguely make out in the darkness a dozen or so hastily constructed shacks made from bamboo and thatch, just enough to provide some shelter from the elements, spread around the clearing. Some were lit dimly with lanterns. Into one of these, Ranjit was thrust. An armed guard was placed at the entrance, and this man was his constant watch. When he had to go to the bushes to relieve himself, the guard was around as well.

'Don't try to run as I have orders to shoot,' said the man.

Ranjit spent a very uncomfortable night on the floor of the hut, with mosquitoes and insects as his constant unwanted companions. He drifted in and out of sleep. He managed to doze off for a while, but very soon after, he awoke on hearing some new voices outside, speaking quite loudly. He realised that he was in the hands of leftist insurgents. It appeared that other cadres from their group had come in from the jungle. From the tone of address his captors used for these newcomers, Ranjit assumed that someone important in their hierarchy was in the group that had arrived.

Day broke soon as most of the night had been spent in his forced march through the jungle. However, despite the passing hours, there was only a half-light at the campsite as little sunshine could filter in. Someone came in towards midday and gave him a few dry slices of bread and water. Ranjit drank the water as he was very thirsty and managed to eat one slice of bread but kept most of the other slices aside for later as he didn't feel in the least like eating but realised that these morsels could be useful some other time.

'Call your leader. I'd like to speak to him,' Ranjit called out to the guard after he had finished his 'breakfast'.

'Shut up!' said the guard. 'Don't give us any orders. Your writ doesn't run here. Don't worry—you will soon learn your fate.'

It became apparent shortly to Ranjit that arrangements were being made to set up some sort of revolutionary court to try him for perceived offences. Although there were no windows in his holding shack, the door couldn't shut fully, and he could see through the crack that a crudely made bamboo table and stool had been placed in the centre. He realised that he would soon learn his fate as the guard had predicted. He was quite terrified at what might follow, but he tried not to show it.

A little later, one of his captors came in. He had taken off the piece of cloth that he had used to cover his face earlier, but Ranjit recognised him from his voice.

'Get up!' he ordered. 'Your trial will begin now.'

Outside, a man—a severe-looking tribal youth in his early thirties, in spectacles and wearing military-style fatigues—was sitting at the desk. The entire group—all armed men with guns—stood around, waiting. Ranjit was made to stand a few paces away in front of the man at the table, with the armed guard pointing his gun at him all the time.

'Ranjit Gupta, you are facing trial in the court of the Revolutionary Tribal Peasants Party for your crimes against the people,' he began.

'You were warned, several months back, to desist from the illegal acquisition of tribal land. Yet you persisted in the process of acquisition, and this has resulted in eviction notices being served on hundreds of tribal peasant families. You are the instrument of oppression carried out by your government, which has continued to exploit the peasantry of this country. Far from improving their lot, even after more than three decades of so-called independence from colonial rule, your government has done nothing for the tribal community in this country. In every state, they remain the poorest, illiterate and starving. They remain in hovels and eke out a subhuman existence from the barren lands they live in. And now despite warnings, you have given orders to throw out the tribal peasantry from even the miserable livelihoods they can earn.

'Such a situation will not be tolerated any longer. The tribal peasantry has risen in revolutionary anger. We have been joined by all peasants and oppressed people in this country. We are at war. We would like to send a strong message to your government that such acts as you have undertaken will not be tolerated.

'You are charged with the crime of dispossessing hundreds of families of their only livelihood that stood between them and starvation. This is a very serious charge that merits capital punishment.

'Do you desire to say anything in your defence?' he concluded sneeringly.

'Well, it seems you have already made up your mind of what to do to me,' began Ranjit hesitantly in his defence at this farcical trial. 'I don't understand why you had to take so much trouble to kidnap me to face this so-called trial when you have already decided the outcome. Anyhow, let me explain my position as well as that of the government on this issue, although I am not quite sure that I can persuade you to change your mind, which seems already made up.

'Very valuable, high-quality iron ore lies beneath the land that is being acquired. It cannot be extracted unless the people living above such valuable deposits are moved. Similar acquisitions are necessary for other valuable minerals such as coal and petroleum, requiring similar displacement of people. Land needs to be acquired for other purposes too, such as building roads and ports and for setting up industry. Without such acquisition, the engine of growth will come to a standstill. It is growth that creates opportunities to expand incomes and provide employment. The government acts on behalf of the people for the greater good of society. This is, however, where two very dissimilar sets of interests clash.

'I fully agree with you that such acquisition of land will cause misery to many people. The business of the government is to eliminate the hardship they may face. I also agree that the interests of society at large cannot trample over the interests of a few who are too weak and powerless to have their voices heard and acted upon.

'It is with this objective in view that we have taken care to see that first the maximum compensation that can be extended legally is provided to the displaced families. Moreover, the district collector has initiated a process to ensure that all possible help is rendered to the displaced families so that they can be provided means to pursue alternative livelihoods.'

'Those are all idle promises!' interjected the man posing as his judge. 'Haven't the tribal community been promised justice since your so-called independence? Are they not still at the bottom of the pile?

'Where have your promises gone?' he mocked. 'What we see, we believe. And we see nothing but continuing misery and destitution. We will not wait any longer for justice to be delivered to us as your largesse. We will snatch it ourselves.'

'Your path of revolution has never succeeded, nor is it likely to do so in the future,' said Ranjit. 'It can only bring misery to generations. I agree with you that we are still far from the ideal situation of a well-functioning and fully responsive government. But rather than working to improve its functioning, you are trying to overthrow it. You are trying to usher in chaos and disorder. Do you think a revolutionary government will be any better? If that were so, they would not be collapsing one after the other around the world.'

'Where order is injustice, disorder is the beginning of justice,' said the man in reply, quoting Romain Rolland.

'Disorder to change systems need not be violent. More change has been brought in this world by Buddha's precepts than by the massacres of Ashoka. You also don't have to go too far back in our own history to realise the strength of non-violent protest. That vanquished in our relatively recent experience the most powerful colonial empire at the time,' replied Ranjit.

Ranjit saw that the dialogue with the 'court' had turned into an argument between the judge and the accused. Barring the grimness of the present situation, it resembled the frequent debates he used to have with his Naxalite college friends. But he was never able to convince them. 'You cannot understand the views of the proletariat with your bourgeois mindset, Ranjit,' they used to say. He realised that his present arguments too were falling on very prejudiced ears.

'Enough of your bourgeois nonsense!' thundered his judge-interlocutor. 'I have heard your defence and there is no substance in it whatsoever. Therefore, this court finds you guilty as charged.

'Your sentence is death by firing squad. We will choose a date and time for your public execution to be witnessed by the persons you oppressed so as to send a strong message to the government. We will let you know a day in advance so you can prepare yourself.'

47

RETURN JOURNEY

$\mathcal{E}$velyn found Ranjit's parcel of the book he had bought in Kulri in her mailbox when she went to check the evening post. It was lucky that it had arrived before she left the Academy the next day, or it would have taken another two weeks for the administration to redirect it and the post office to finally reach it—if at all—at her state headquarters address.

It didn't take long for her to realise that Ranjit had bought the book with the intention of presenting it to her while he was still in Mussoorie but had been prevented from doing so by something. Could it be her disclosure of Vijay's proposal to him? It must be so, she concluded, now recalling that evening and the way Ranjit had turned silent after she told him. In her confusion after reading Vijay's letter, she wasn't quite attentive to Ranjit and didn't quite catch the reason behind his sudden change of mood. She now realised what had happened.

Her confusion at this point was total. Now she had not one but two senior colleagues to contend with, both good friends with each other, and she didn't know what to do. The matter was of the utmost delicacy, and she didn't want to offend either of them or give any hint to rumour-mongers in the state about what was happening. She had put off replying to Vijay till she was back and had a more appropriate personal tête-à-tête with him. And now this book was in her hands.

She decided that she would sleep over the whole matter and hoped that like many problems she had faced before, this too would resolve itself. She had many things to attend to before leaving early the next morning for Dehradun to catch her train for the long journey back to the state, and the Ranjit-Vijay issue had to wait. She had tied up with two other batchmates who were catching the same train, and they were leaving by taxi together the next morning.

A formal dinner had been arranged in the officers' mess for the last night. The men were all dressed up in their black *galabandhs* and black trousers, and the women in formal silk *sarees*. The director gave a short speech reminding them that it was the formal end to their probation and that they were now full-fledged serving officers of the Republic. He asked them to remember the solemn oaths they had taken to defend the Constitution and to uphold the high standards and traditions of the service. Then he proposed a toast.

'To the President,' he said, raising his glass.

'The President!' was the thunderous response from the one hundred and thirty-three newly appointed officers as they raised their glasses together.

A simple formal dinner of spinach soup, roast mutton with sautéed vegetables accompanied with buns, and finally, custard pudding as dessert was served one course after the other by the caparisoned and turbaned waiters. The wine glasses were replenished a few times. This being the last dinner, the mess committee did not economise on the wine, and the most expensive red wine from the military cantonment at Dehradun had been arranged.

The dinner ended with the director's departure from the high table. Thereafter, the officers repaired to the lounge for a final round of goodbyes, promises to stay in touch, and exchange of mail addresses. Most of them were going to states to pursue normal administrative work: routine revenue administration and supporting development. On the other hand, in her case and that of a few others assigned to difficult states, their work would consist mainly with merely maintaining peace and managing basic services through strife and turmoil. Being thus occupied, she would be unable to meet most of her colleagues during her career, except during very infrequent conferences or common retraining programs. Many strong friendships forged during the training at Mussoorie would rekindle only then as preoccupation with their new jobs and demands of family life slowly took priority.

It was therefore with a tinge of sadness that Evelyn finally bid goodbye to the Academy as she crossed its front gates for the last time, in her taxi which turned quickly away towards Library Point and thereafter began its steep descent on winding and twisting roads through forests of conifers to the Dehradun valley. As the valley neared, the pine-scented cool air of the mountains gave way to the humid heat of the plains. Soon her taxi reached the bustling and crowded town and slowly negotiated its way through honking cars, scooters, horse-drawn *tongas*, and pedestrians to the railway station.

By the time her colleagues and Evelyn had paid off the taxi and hired the *coolies* to take their sparse luggage to the platform, their express train had pulled into the station. She was to travel the longest distance among the three and had been billeted in a sleeper coupe with another lady passenger, while her other two colleagues had been allotted seating accommodation in another coach. They were to detrain only a few hours later. However, the three agreed to meet in the dining car for lunch once the train was on its way.

Not too long after Evelyn had settled into her compartment, the steam locomotive at the far end of the train blew its whistle, and with much waving of flags by the station staff, the train slowly pulled out of the station. The rail route from Dehradun to the plains required a gradual descent initially on slightly inclined rails through the Shivalik ranges, and the train therefore progressed downwards slowly, with loud creaking of brakes, till they reached the ageless holy town of Haridwar, with its swiftly flowing Ganga and the hundreds of temples that crowded its banks.

The old town did not appear to have changed much from the ancient days. Was it possible, Evelyn wondered, that many of the ordinary folk she saw hurrying about in the narrow lanes and by-lanes could trace their roots back to those ancient times when kingdoms like Thaneswar thrived? When the train stopped at the station briefly, she saw a *sadhu* in saffron wear and matted hair, sitting on a bench and contemplating the world serenely. Would Aryaduta have resembled such a person after he left the secular world and took refuge in the monastery?

It was a brief halt, and when the train left Haridwar, Evelyn decided to walk over to the dining car, which was a couple of coaches away, connected by flexible gangways, a novelty in those days of the early vestibule trains. When she arrived, the dining car was nearly empty, and her two colleagues were yet to arrive. She took a seat by the window, and the waiter came up with the menu. She ordered a lime juice cordial while waiting for them to join and also requested the waiter to bring her the morning newspaper.

A news item on the front page caught her attention immediately. The news was datelined the day before and it said simply:

> **IAS officer kidnapped.** The newly appointed additional district collector of Nilghat district, Ranjit Gupta, was kidnapped by armed militants near Golmunda while on his way to take charge at district headquarters. Gupta was reported to have been involved in the acquisition of land on behalf of the National Mining Corporation for its mining and export of iron ore. The acquisition was likely to dislodge thousands of mainly tribal villagers. State government sources feel that the kidnapping was the work of the Revolutionary Tribal Peasants Party, which is a Naxalite group active in the area, opposing the acquisition. However, so far no group has claimed responsibility.

Evelyn frantically turned the pages to see if there was any other news of this in the rest of the paper. But there wasn't. It appeared that to the world, Ranjit Gupta and Nilghat were of little consequence. Most of the paper was devoted to what appeared to her irrelevant news of political developments at the centre and big advertisements with smiling scantily dressed models selling various consumer products, all of which appeared to mock at her concern.

When her two colleagues finally appeared, they saw her quite distraught and holding her head in her hands and rereading the same brief news item over and over.

'What's happened, Evelyn?' one of them asked.

'Look at this,' said Evelyn, showing them the news item. 'I've just finished part of my district training in his subdivision when he was SDO! And he was in Mussoorie only last week! How could this be possible? He tried hard to see that the tribals got a fair deal, much more than is normally provided. There must have been a terrible mistake!'

The three of them were silent for some time as the reality of modern-day administrative work in the country sank in. They had been lulled into a belief over the last two years of training that they were to act as bold change agents playing various leadership roles to modernise the country and bring credit to the country, their state cadres, and themselves. Events such as yesterday's formal dinner, which they had joined in proudly, helped instil such feelings. That their work could also end in tragic outcomes was largely ignored, notwithstanding the roll of honour of former colleagues fallen in their line of duty, displayed prominently at the entrance to the officers' mess.

Evelyn's colleagues tried to provide some consolation. She wanted now to be back at work as soon as possible to find out whether she could do anything useful for Ranjit, however little. She felt frustrated that the train would not reach her destination till early the next morning. She willed the train to speed faster, and as though in response, the express train picked up speed as it reached the flat countryside and rushed onwards, while the afternoon changed to evening and evening to a dark and troubled night.

48

THE CAPTIVE

*R*anjit held on to the thin ray of hope that his captors did not really want to kill him—they would have done so, he reasoned, then and there on the road to Nilghat rather than kidnap him, if their only intention was retribution for his perceived wrongs to the tribals. But as he couldn't be sure of this, knowing that the extremists seldom acted logically, he was living constantly with the terrifying thought that at any time, he would be dragged out and shot.

He lost count of the hours and days, and the poor state of his lodgings and diet, aggravated by a spell of heavy rains for several days, which his hastily built shack could hardly withstand, finally affected his health. He contracted a high fever and, for some days, was in a state of delirium.

In his delirious state, he saw many images and visions. These were often of Suneeta, at various times of their short life together as fellow lecturers. The moment that returned most frequently was of the day he had confessed his love to her and learnt that she equally reciprocated his feelings. While initially they met along with a friend or two in tow, he had chanced that day to find her alone in the common room and suggested they go out to their favourite cafe. Suneeta had agreed, without much hesitation. The cafe had a balcony upstairs, which was more private than where they usually sat.

After whiling away time on irrelevant talk, Ranjit picked up courage and said, 'Neeta, you know that I am madly in love with you, don't you?'

Suneeta's face coloured on hearing this. And it wasn't the setting sun that had brought the tinge to her face. But she remained quiet, examining the nail polish on her fingernails, and didn't answer for a while, while Ranjit's world stood still.

Then looking at Ranjit's doleful expression, she reached out and held his hands in both of hers and said, 'Don't be silly, Rana. You know the answer. And of course, I love you too, perhaps more than you can ever know!'

But once in a while, in his delirium, visions of Evelyn took Suneeta's place, and what he considered her rejection amplified his dejection.

After several days, Ranjit's fever appeared to subside, and he began gradually to think clearly again. While he was delirious, his mind had wandered and had not dwelt on his current predicament. Now it came back ever more forcefully to him. That his sentence had not yet been carried out, he felt, was perhaps because he was more useful to his captors alive than dead. They must be trying to negotiate something by putting his life on the line. What would the government do? Was he valuable enough to them to make an effort to try and release him? And what if they failed or were not willing to make the concessions they demanded?

Other thoughts also troubled Ranjit. What value was there of his short existence, he frequently wondered, it were to end soon, as was most likely? To those nearest him, he had tried to be kind. As to his contribution to society, he had been able to do little. He reckoned that in his three years in the service, he had helped preserve the peace at least, and that could turn out to be his most important contribution. Would he be remembered for this? Very unlikely. But so also forgotten, he felt, are the millions of people who live, work, and die.

Like the trees growing silently around him were helping preserve the forest, thought Ranjit. It didn't matter if occasionally one fell, if the forest lived on and thrived.

49

TACKLING THE CRISIS

'*M*ay I come in, sir?' Evelyn enquired, knocking tentatively on the chief secretary's door. His personal assistant had asked her to go right in, but she hesitated to barge in unannounced. One could never predict the mood he was in.

'Come in,' said the stern voice from within.

Evelyn entered the very spacious room and found the CS behind a huge table, looking carefully at the contents of a file in front of him. He was a thin and dignified-looking man with sharp eyes partly obscured by his reading glasses. His thick shock of hair was greying at the temples. He was known to be a highly intelligent man but somewhat unpredictable in his manners and with a quirky sense of humour—such as the Mr Gunia story Evelyn had heard from Vijay. He asked her to sit, and she took a seat directly facing him.

'Well, you've come to join us at a very opportune time, Miss Syiem,' said the CS, addressing her formally. 'We are in a crisis, and you may be of help. Although you should have gone straight to a subdivision from the Academy, there has been a small hiccup and so you have to spend a few weeks here, working with me. Perhaps it's all for the better as we need all available hands we can muster. I have asked the Home Secretary that you will be the desk officer on the Gupta kidnapping case and will report directly to me on this matter. Take this file, read it carefully, and join the meeting starting at 3 p.m. here.' Evelyn looked at her watch and noted that it was just about three hours or so later.

'Sorry I couldn't provide you a more relaxed orientation to your job as Undersecretary Political,' the CS continued. 'The Political Department usually handles crises such as these—of which there seems to be no end nowadays. And your welcome unfortunately will have to be limited to this,' he said, indicating the two cups of tea which an orderly brought in, one of which he placed in front of Evelyn.

Evelyn didn't realise that Ranjit's kidnapping case would now be her direct responsibility. But she was glad that she would be involved in the process.

'No problem, sir,' she said, 'I've had a good break in the Academy and I'm quite ready to start my work.'

'Ah, the Academy!' sighed the CS. 'Hope Dutta the director is OK? I am told he has quite taken to the training business and doesn't want to come back to work in the real world.'

Evelyn smiled politely at this. She knew that the director of the Academy was a batchmate of the CS and so such light-hearted references among themselves were acceptable. Soon, the telephone rang, and the CS got busy in the conversation. Evelyn rose to leave, and the CS nodded, dismissing her.

On arriving at the secretariat earlier that morning, she discovered that she had been allotted a small cubicle in the Political Department, with an ample desk and a tolerably comfortable chair. Apparently, the cubicle had been fashioned by partitioning a part of the department's records and library section and placed temporarily at her disposal. The Home Secretary was also the Secretary Political Affairs and her nominal boss, whom she had reported to first.

Returning to her cubicle, she opened the file which the CS had handed her. It had a red URGENT tab on it. It contained a large number of wireless messages from DC Nilghat and finally a report dated that very day itself, from the inspector general of police, addressed to the CS, summarising the latest information on Ranjit's case. The last part of the report had been underlined in red by the CS with a thick-nibbed fountain pen. The report read as follows:

ADC designate Ranjit Gupta IAS was proceeding to Nilghat in his official car after handing over charge when four armed militants riding on two motorcycles overtook his car at a point about two miles from the Golmunda PS and shot at his car, injuring and incapacitating his PSO, who could not return fire, and thereafter drove away with him in his car after forcing the PSO and the driver to get off. From the deposition of the PSO in hospital and the driver, who was uninjured, the kidnappers were young men of average build and had accents which indicated they were tribals, but as they had their faces covered, nothing more about their identity is known. The driver indicated that they drove off in the direction of Nilghat.

OC Golmunda recovered the vehicle, which was abandoned 10 miles away on the highway near the kutcha road which leads to the Gourimuri Reserve Forest. Track marks at that point indicate that ADC designate Gupta may have been transferred by the kidnappers to another vehicle. Traces of these track marks have been found by the OC till about 12 km inside the forest. Thereafter, it appears that the kidnappers proceeded on foot through the scrub, and further traces of the party could not be found.

A thorough search of about 20 square km of the reserve forest, with the help of 3rd battalion of State Armed Police did not reveal any further traces. Other sections of the reserve forest are also being systematically combed to find more clues as to ADC designate Gupta's whereabouts.

Meanwhile, two days after the incident, an unidentified call was received at Nilghat PS, purportedly from a representative of the Revolutionary Tribal Peasants Party (RTPP) claiming responsibility for the kidnap and setting out the following three conditions for the release of ADC designate Gupta: (i) immediate halt to the National Mining Corporation's land acquisition; (ii) release of the general secretary and the two other office bearers of the RTPP now being held in Nilghat district jail; (iii) halting all punitive action against the RTPP. The caller gave one week's time to the government to meet these demands after which their captive would be executed.

The call was traced to a PCO near Nilghat Road Station, and investigations are ongoing as to the identity of the caller, which, however, has been made difficult, owing to the heavy use of the PCO as several persons made calls from there at the time the call was received.

Evelyn was somewhat relieved reading the report as it indicated that Ranjit was still alive. She looked at her watch and saw there was still about an hour to the meeting. She realised she hadn't had any lunch after her very hurried and meagre breakfast and, seeing a tea boy dart past, called him to give her a plate of samosas and tea.

The tea was terrible—too strong and syrupy. But the samosas were great—hot, crispy, and spicy. She pulled out a notepad from a drawer in her desk and started scrawling out some thoughts as they came randomly to her, in preparation for the meeting.

There were two main issues, she felt. First, should any concessions be made to the kidnappers? Given that the CS was a hard nut and that he would be facing pressures from the governor and the Central Government, he was unlikely to concede anything, perhaps thinking falsely that the kidnappers wouldn't dare harm a service officer. It would be better if the negotiations were conducted by someone in the field—perhaps someone closer to Ranjit, Evelyn felt. She decided that she would offer this suggestion at the meeting.

The second issue was Ranjit's whereabouts. She was puzzled that there was still no clue. She got up and started looking at the shelves which crowded the walls of her cubicle. On one, there was a set of Survey of India maps. She pulled out a Nilghat district map and began looking at it carefully. It had details of the topography, forests, rivers, habitations—everything. She circled in pencil the Gourimuri Reserve Forest area which fell in Ranjit's previous subdivision. Then she drew a line from the Nilghat Road Station, from where the call had been made by his captors. Where in this vast area were they hiding Ranjit, she wondered. Perhaps there would be more information available at the meeting, she thought. Gulping down her samosa with the syrupy tea, she picked up the map and her notepad and rushed to the CS's room.

50

THE STRATEGY

*W*hen Evelyn entered the CS's office, he was still engrossed with his files. She was the first to enter. Seeing her come in, he motioned her towards a long meeting table which was at one side of the spacious room. The room had, apart from the large desk behind which the CS directed the state administration, this long table for meetings and a double sofa set in front, facing large French windows overlooking the well-tended lawns of the state secretariat. Each of these three segments of the room were covered with richly designed although, as Evelyn couldn't fail to notice, somewhat faded Kashmiri carpets which deserved better treatment.

The CS noticed Evelyn hesitating about where to sit and said, 'Miss Syiem, you are the desk officer in this case and so you must sit at my immediate right,' indicating the chair next to the one at the head.

Thereafter the invitees started trooping in one by one. The first to arrive was the Home Secretary with a set of files in his hands, and then a tall gentleman in full police uniform whom Evelyn mistook to be the inspector general of police, but when the Home Secretary made the introductions, turned out to be the IGP (Special Branch), who headed the police intelligence apparatus. The person who came in next was the state IGP—the actual police chief—but Evelyn would not have known this as he was in mufti and looked like any other civil officer, except that he had a distinct bearing of a senior service man, as would befit the head of police forces in the state. He was followed by a slightly harried-looking official who turned out to be the secretary to the governor. Next to come, entering together, were two deputy secretary colleagues of hers in the Political Department whom she hadn't yet met.

And then to her immense surprise, the last person to arrive, dressed now in full military uniform, was none other than Colonel Raghav! The Home Secretary, unaware that the two had met before, began to introduce him, saying, 'And this is Lt. Colonel Raghav from corps headquarters, who is the army liaison officer,' but stopped, puzzled when he realised that they knew each other.

'I've met Colonel Raghav before in an entirely different situation,' she clarified to the Home Secretary. But his sudden appearance set Evelyn's mind on a whirl, and some pieces of the jigsaw puzzle that had been floating about there seemed suddenly to come together.

'Small world, isn't it?' said Colonel Raghav, taking the empty chair next to her. But before they could begin a conversation, the CS looked up from his papers and, noting that all invitees had arrived, left his desk, carrying the case file and ensconced himself in the chair at the head of the table.

'I assume that everyone has read the latest police report,' he began, coming straight to the matter and then, turning to the IGP, continued, 'So to save time, let me begin by asking whether there are any further updates on this.'

There obviously wasn't much as the IGP looked at his intelligence colleague and, not finding much response there, cleared his throat and said, 'Well, further search in the Gourimuri Reserve Forest has been conducted by OC Golmunda and the 2nd Armed Police Battalion, but no further clues about ADC Gupta or his captors have been discovered.'

'Special Branch has contacted all relevant informants in this case and is actively seeking further information,' added the IGP (Special Branch). 'We are also trying to identify all callers still who could have placed the call to OC Nilghat from the public call office at Nilghat Road railway station. But so far have unfortunately no leads.'

'So, am I to understand that Gupta has simply vanished into thin air?' asked the CS, not hiding his exasperation or his sarcasm. Then, looking at the IGP, he added, quite irked at the progress of the investigation, 'This is not acceptable, Prashant. You have to put more resources into this case. I have the whole officer cadre in the state up in arms and have a meeting with their association right after this. We need results now. The Home Ministry in Delhi and the governor too are very concerned and want immediate answers.'

Reference to the governor's concern by the CS was unnecessary as this was very obvious to all those around the table—underscored by the presence of the secretary to the governor, who was sitting silently taking notes.

'And this brings us to Colonel Raghav,' said the CS, turning to him, 'whom I have invited to this meeting specifically to alert the army in case we need help for search operations.'

'Corps Command has received instructions about this already from army headquarters, sir,' began Colonel Raghav. 'We are ready to assist civil authorities in conducting cordon and search operations. Ten companies of the 21st Infantry Division have been already put in readiness for this purpose. More support can be offered if necessary. But we will do this strictly on the understanding that the Indian Army will not engage with any terrorist groups, who have to be handled by the local police as it is their responsibility,' he continued quoting the army rules.

'Moreover, I have been authorised to inform you that two helicopters from the air force's local area air command are also being made available for conducting aerial search and reconnaissance operations. I will be coordinating all support operations from the armed forces, including the air force, and I will leave my hotline contacts with your desk officer on this case,' he added.

Well done, Your Excellency, Evelyn wanted to say to the governor. She realised that all this almost instantaneous offer of support from the usually hesitant armed forces probably resulted more from the many rounds of golf His Excellency played with big shots in the military than the hundreds of telegrams sent by the Home Secretary to Delhi. The Golmunda incident must have really shaken the governor too, she thought.

'Well, that's settled then,' said the CS. 'Now let's move on to the question of what I consider the preposterous but nevertheless quite dangerous demands being made by Gupta's kidnappers. What do you know about this group and how seriously should we take their demands and their threats?' he asked the IGP.

'This seems to be a new extremist breakaway group of the Tribal Students' Union,' said the IGP. 'We estimate that they number at present no more than thirty or forty armed combatants. But they seem to be supported by external agencies from whom they are getting resources and arms. They are aiming to stage spectacular terrorist acts such as the attempt they already made on the governor's life near Golmunda and now this kidnapping. If they are seen to succeed, their numbers may grow.'

'But what about this threat of Gupta's execution in now six days?' said the CS, drawing him back from his rambling thesis. 'Do you think they will carry it out?'

There was total silence around the room as the reality of this diabolical threat was thrust on everyone, with this harsh reminder from the CS. However, there was no response from the participants, who waited for the CS to answer this difficult question himself.

'My own feeling is that we are up against a totally unknown and unpredictable entity. However, we cannot be cowed down by them. The Home Ministry has indicated that we take stern measures against this group and neutralise them while they are still of a manageable size, hence the need to urgently locate where Gupta is being held and to capture or destroy the terrorists.

'Therefore, Abhinav,' the CS said, turning to the Home Secretary, 'issue a press release immediately in all local papers and to All India

Radio that the state government is willing to discuss the demands of the group holding Gupta, provided he is released forthwith unharmed. And that they will face very serious consequences should they harm him in any way.'

Evelyn began feeling that the CS—under pressure from the Home Ministry and the governor—had adopted a line of action which could lead to disastrous consequences for Ranjit. It looked most likely to her that the terrorists wouldn't tamely give up Ranjit, merely being warned by the government to do so.

It also looked as though the CS was about to close the meeting without any serious discussion, as he closed his file and, when there still wasn't any comment from anyone, said, 'I take it then that we are agreed on this course of action—if so, let me close the meeting here.'

At risk of seeming impertinent, Evelyn raised her hand tentatively. She was the most junior and inexperienced official present and that too on her first day of work. Yet she had to take the risk of being snubbed, she felt.

'May I say something, sir?' she asked hesitatingly.

'Yes, of course, Miss Syiem, you are the desk officer on the case— tell us if we've missed something,' said the CS in a tone which Evelyn felt could be bordering on his trademark sarcasm. But she plodded on.

'There are a couple of issues I would like touch on,' she said. 'First about the press release. I suggest that instead of the Home Secretary, it should be issued by DC Nilghat. This is because the telephone call was made to OC Nilghat. If the state government responds directly to the militants, it will be giving the group far more importance than it deserves. Also, there may be need of some sort of negotiations in the future. If so, they will be better conducted at the level of the DC than by the state government.'

'Avinash?' asked the CS of the Home Secretary, seeking his response.

'I think Evelyn is right, sir,' he said. 'We can draft out a press release and get DC Nilghat to issue it. As to future negotiations, they should be delegated to the DC too. It is far better that this whole matter still be treated as a field issue rather than seeming to agitate the state government and far less the Central Government. Besides, DC Nilghat is a very senior secretary-level officer. I am sure he would handle the negotiations most ably and probably better as he would have more and faster access to information.'

'Well, that is decided, then,' said the CS. 'Now to your next issue, Miss Syiem, as you indicated you have more than one,' he added with less sarcasm and appearing now genuinely interested to hear what she might have to offer.

'My second point is that I have a hunch as to where Ranjit Gupta is being held,' said Evelyn calmly. She saw surprise on the faces all round on this. She pulled out the Survey of India map of Nilghat District that she had been studying in her room and placed it in front of the CS and the IGP. The CS took out his reading glasses and began looking closely at the map and Evelyn's pencil marks on it.

'I sensed I may have stumbled upon it as soon as I saw Colonel Raghav today. We happened to be on the train on which there was an attempted sabotage some months back and had a most lucky escape when it failed. It happened here,' she pointed out on the map the location of the bridge over the river where the fishplates on the train track had been removed.

'It was also around this area that Colonel Raghav and I chanced upon some boys whom we later realised were militants. It's very likely that the new militant group has set up a temporary camp somewhere in this forest rather than at the Gourimuri Reserve. There are two reasons why this is likely. First, the call the militants made was from the Nilghat Road Railway PCO, which is also not very far from this area. Second, the two reserve forest areas, although far from each other, are connected by a set of narrow but navigable streams. See this tiny stream in the Gourimuri Reserve,' she said, pointing to a minor stream snaking through the reserve. 'It connects to the Bansiri River and then through this to the Nainpuri Reserve Forest. It's possible that Ranjit Gupta's captors may have taken this riverine route to elude the police who were out on all the roads and set up roadblocks looking for them. This must have been a very well-planned operation.'

The CS seemed to nod his head in agreement. 'Well, conjecture or not, Prashant, our desk officer Miss Syiem has given you a good lead,' said he. 'Let's investigate it. And as to her, I am quite sure you must be getting the feeling that she has landed in the wrong service. So am I, but don't hope even faintly that I will recommend her for the Indian Police Service!'

51

VIJAY'S CALL

Ever since her return to the state from Mussoorie at the end of her training, Evelyn had not reached out to anyone, being fully occupied with her mission to free ADC Gupta. Vijay too had been silent, no doubt busy with his new assignment, and although she often thought of reaching out to him to discuss their common friend Ranjit, she hesitated, not knowing what she would tell him about his letter of proposal to her.

However, one evening after she returned to the circuit house from work, she finally heard from him. She had to go to the reception to receive it as there was no telephone in her room yet. Later, two hotlines were set up for her—one military, directly to Colonel Raghav, and another, civil, to the Home Secretary. But when Vijay's call came, these were yet to be installed, and she had to conduct a not-so-private call, sitting in front of the circuit house manager, who took a walk, pretending to be looking out at the garden. She had hardly had time to think carefully over the Vijay-Ranjit issue, being caught up entirely with Ranjit's kidnapping and therefore didn't know how to react to Vijay when his call came eventually.

The trunk line was not working too well, and there was static on the wires. Vijay was obviously very upset with developments regarding Ranjit and was happy to hear that the chief secretary had assigned her the case. He recounted the events of the day when Ranjit was kidnapped and how he could hardly believe it when Sudarshan Rao, the SDPO, called him up frantically at night, reporting the kidnapping.

He then turned to his letter to Evelyn. She confirmed that she had received it at Mussoorie and was surprised at its contents. Conscious that she was within earshot of the manager, she merely said, 'Vijay, these important things have to be discussed face to face, and you should plan to come over soon to state headquarters. You can't treat everything like one big joke, you know!'

Vijay had a good laugh over this and promised to visit her at the state capital as soon as he could get away. The line being too noisy and noting Evelyn's preoccupation with Ranjit's kidnapping, he said before hanging up that he would call her again in a couple of days when this blew over.

'Let me know if I can help in any way. We can't let anything happen to Ranjit, and I am sure he'll be back soon,' were his closing words.

52

DC NILGHAT'S
PREDICAMENT

*T*he instructions that DC Nilghat had received late at night from the chief secretary were curt and unambiguous. No concessions were to be made: the acquisition process on behalf of the National Mining Corporation must not be halted and must proceed forthwith, and no militants released from Nilghat jail. As to the third demand of the militants, i.e. halting of punitive action against them, there was some leeway if they released Ranjit.

The press release DC Nilghat had issued, drafted by the Home Department, asked for immediate release of ADC Gupta prior to any negotiations, warning the militants with severe action if they harmed him in any way. It had been aired in the twelve o'clock noon news and repeated throughout the day and was printed promptly in the front pages of both the major local papers. Now only four days remained before the deadline set by the militants expired.

The instructions also delegated full responsibility to him as negotiator for all parleys with the militants. DC Nilghat wondered how he could fruitfully negotiate under the severe conditions placed by the government. Of course, he realised that he retained the prerogative of all negotiators of making some concessions if absolutely necessary. He wondered whether someone in the Home Department had come up with this idea—to make him a scapegoat if the negotiations failed and take the credit if they succeeded. Whatever the reason, he realised that he was to be solely responsible for whatever happened.

And that responsibility was grave—Ranjit's life hung in the balance, depending on his decision. Over the three years he had known him, DC Nilghat had grown quite fond of his junior colleague—as though he were a younger brother, or even the son he never had, given the vast difference in their ages, and not a colleague. He was generally given to treating all young people, including his professional colleagues, as part of his large universal family. But in Ranjit's case, it was slightly different—the two had drawn quite close over the many crises and problems which Ranjit had faced and he, DC Nilghat, had helped him handle. He had come to increasingly value Ranjit's advice also and had therefore decided to appoint him as ADC in his office as Satish's replacement.

As he drove out to his office, DC Nilghat felt that it would be a decisive day. The final hearing on the land acquisition case was listed later in the afternoon. There had been no response from the militants after the press release yet. He was under no illusions as to their sinister intent and what they were capable of. All recent intelligence received indicated that they were gearing up for a violent opposition to the state. As they had been audacious enough to attempt assassinating the governor, they were unlikely to care at all about a junior officer's life. It was quite ironical that far from acting against them, Ranjit had worked hard in their favour—if only they were aware of this, DC Nilghat mused.

Entering his court chambers, he rang for his personal assistant and asked him to reschedule all his engagements for the day, apart from the hearing on the land acquisition case later in the afternoon and asked that he not be disturbed. Then he gave himself up to carefully considering his options.

He found himself forced to view the crisis from two angles—on the one hand, as a public servant of the country he was by oath bound to serve, he had to take an objective view of the alternatives and uphold the public interest; while on the other, as a private persona, he felt it essential to honour his personal relationship with Ranjit which far transcended the mere professional bonds between them.

As to his public commitments, there were both good arguments as to why he had to complete the acquisition process immediately as well as clear directions to do so from the government he was bound by his loyalties to obey. He had tried to slow the acquisition process, merely to allow time for the many new initiatives his administration had designed to help the poor families losing homes and livelihoods to yield results. But he could no longer delay the process, he realised. He had to take a final call on the matter this very afternoon. Should he reserve his order on the case to a later date? That would, however, amount to insubordination and did not seem to be a feasible alternative.

However, ordering the acquisition to proceed would directly jeopardise chances to save Ranjit. Only four more days remained till the deadline to meet the demands of the militants would run out and Ranjit would be murdered. Of the likelihood of the latter outcome, he harboured no doubts, should no tangible measures be taken to meet their demands. Merely issuing counter-threats to them would not do.

DC Nilghat was in a quandary. He felt that he should take another good look at the latest report on the acquisition case, so he got up to open his safe where his important files, notes, and confidential documents were stored. When he opened it, his eye fell on a carefully wrapped package. He tried to remember what it was and, failing to do so, opened it to see that it was the ancient Thaneswar necklace which Satish, his previous ADC, had left in his custody on handing over charge. It was to be sent to a suitable museum that the ASI had yet to decide.

DC Nilghat picked up the necklace and began inspecting it closely. Although determined by the ASI to be about two millennia old, the stones still retained their lustre and gleamed in the late morning sunlight streaming into the room. Did its owner too face the same predicament he was facing, wondered DC Nilghat. Were humans condemned to face such predicaments over the ages?

Unfortunately, such dilemmas, problems, and struggles would remain part of the human condition, mused DC Nilghat, and there was nothing that could be done to shake them off. What could possibly change in a more enlightened future was a more humane and fair way to resolve such issues. That could only emerge when the darkness spread by wants and scarcities and the anguish caused by vast differences in living conditions among people had finally ended, as well as when the light of better understanding and goodwill permeated all humanity. Would the world ever see such a future?

Regrettably, he had to act meanwhile within the confines of his present harsh environment. His immediate task was to do everything possible to save Ranjit. He went back to his desk and asked his PA to connect him to SP Nilghat.

'Sharma, you mentioned to me yesterday that the bail application of one of the detainees we are holding in Nilghat jail was coming up before the chief judicial magistrate this afternoon,' began the DC when the SP came on the line. 'Can you give me his details?'

'He is the least important of the three we are holding, nominally a politburo member but really not a fellow of any consequence,' replied the SP.

'Then don't oppose bail,' said the DC. 'I want him freed immediately.'

The SP appeared to be hesitant. 'But the government said not to release any militant,' he said, sounding a bit incredulous.

'I ordered his detention as district magistrate, and now I am ordering his release. Please carry out orders forthwith,' said DC Nilghat, a little irritated, putting down the telephone.

That would go some distance to demonstrate to the militants that the government was willing to negotiate and not totally rejecting their demands, a small way to create some hope for Ranjit's release. Now it was for the militants to take the next step. It was a relatively minor action well within his authority to take, although even this would require a lot of telephone calls and explanations to mollify the CS, thought DC Nilghat.

The PA buzzed his phone and informed DC Nilghat that SDO Vijay Gautam had arrived for the hearing, and would he like to meet him?

'Of course, ask him to come in,' said DC Nilghat.

Vijay, usually a picture of optimism, came in looking gloomy. But DC Nilghat's calm demeanour cheered him a little. Likewise, the DC felt much better seeing Vijay. So long as there were young people like Vijay and Ranjit, he felt there was hope despite the gloom.

He felt better prepared for his afternoon's hearing. Picking up his case file, he left with Vijay, walking briskly to his courtroom down the corridor.

53

JUDGEMENT AND ITS CONSEQUENCE

$\mathcal{T}$he courtroom was full when they entered, fuller than at the time of the first hearing. There was a loud and excited hubbub of conversation as litigants, representatives of the NGO groups and the press, officers and clerks of the district handling the case, and plenty more who were merely interested in what had turned out to be a case of considerable importance waited anxiously to hear its final outcome. The din ceased immediately, and all rose at the DC's entrance.

The DC motioned them to sit and then asked Advocate Susheela Gautam whether she had anything further to say.

'Sir, we have submitted the detailed additional information about the anomalies in the learned subdivisional officer's assessments as directed. These will prove that the process has been faulty, and I request that it be overturned. I also repeat that in view of the extraordinary scale of the acquisition and the immiseration that it will cause, the process should be halted immediately.'

DC Nilghat heard her patiently. Then turning to Vijay, he said, 'SDO Vijay Gautam, would you like to clarify?'

'We have rechecked all the supposed anomalies in the assessments submitted by the petitioners, sir, very carefully,' replied Vijay. 'These were conducted in the presence of the petitioners themselves. A representative from DC's *sadar* office was also present. All previous assessments have been found to be accurate, hence there is no infirmity in the process on this account. I have reviewed all the files of this case and found that there have been no errors as to process either.

'If I may be permitted to also reply to Advocate Gautam's contention about likely immiseration of the large number of tribal households affected, let me state quite unequivocally that no effort has been spared by this district administration to see that the situation of the affected families would be no worse and possibly better than their pre-acquisition status should time be given to us to complete the measures that we have geared up to perform. In fact, if ADC Gupta, who is right now a captive of the militants who are opposing this acquisition violently, were free today, his primary remit would have been to complete these very measures which this administration has introduced and of which Your Honour is well aware.'

Vijay stopped, and the DC noticed that he had gotten quite agitated as he completed his statement.

'Thank you, Mr Gautam,' he said. 'You have clarified the issues well, and there is little for me to add. Let me, for the record, note that given the importance of this appeal under Section 15A of the Land Acquisition Act, I have personally reviewed the documents of this case. I also confirm that I find no errors in the process.

'As to the larger question of the nature of the Act itself, which some may reasonably argue places the interest of the many over the miseries of the few, this is neither the place nor time to consider such matters. Let our legal luminaries and policymakers take note of the emotions it has generated and deliberate over them and possibly arrive at a fairer arrangement in the future.

'But let me also take the liberty to digress a little, knowing that a wider audience is agitated over this case. As our newly established democracy develops, it must grapple from time to time with many issues such as these or even weightier. However imperfect it may be today, our relatively young democracy contains the possibilities of bringing about understanding and reconciliation of opposing philosophies. On the other hand, taking up arms to force one's opinions is an antiquated approach in my view which would not stand up to critical examination in this modern day and age. History has demonstrated that violence begets more violence and solves no issues.

'I apologise for this somewhat lengthy argument to support my decision. However, I have thought long and carefully over it and have no hesitation in now declaring that there is no merit in the Appeal No. 231 on the LA Case 1128, and accordingly, I uphold the award declared by the learned subdivisional officer and direct him to proceed with handing over possession of the acquired land to the State Mining Corporation forthwith.'

A loud commotion erupted among a section of the audience when DC Nilghat pronounced his order. Some tribal youths started shouting slogans daring the administration to force them out of their land. The DC looked unperturbed, however, and Vijay went up to him to retrieve a number of documents he had given him just prior to entering the room. The two were engrossed in conversation at the high bench while a sub-inspector who the SP had deputed to prevent the situation from getting out of hand, along with a number of constables, started to shepherd the agitating youth gradually out of the room.

However, despite the presence of policemen, no one seemed to have noticed the person who came in and threw the grenade. The courtroom had by then emptied, and DC Nilghat, along with Vijay, was about to get up and leave. A deafening blast ensued, engulfing the room in dense black smoke. The sub-inspector who had just left had a miraculous escape. Not so fortunate were the two policemen who were still in the room. Nor were DC Nilghat and Subdivisional Officer Vijay Gautam, whose charred and unrecognisable bodies were found, when the smoke cleared, lying on either side of the high bench.

54

NEWS REACHES HEADQUARTERS

*T*his was the morning of the third day since the ultimatum issued by the militants, and Evelyn realised that only four more days remained before it expired. She felt that time was running out fast, with not much happening.

There was one significant development, however: the IGP (Special Branch) had reported that on close interrogation of a person suspected of having links with the militants, SP Nilghat had confirmed Evelyn's original hunch that the forest hideout where Ranjit was being held was likely to be in the Nainpuri Reserve Forest and not in the Gourimuri Reserve. So, the search of the latter had closed and the 2nd Armed Police Battalion was moving to the former and had begun liaising with the army to place a wide cordon around the point where Evelyn and Colonel Raghav had found the canoe and the youths who ran away on being surprised. But everything appeared to be proceeding at a snail's pace, thought Evelyn, and not as though a state official's life was in peril.

The last three days had passed in a whirl, and Evelyn had not a moment to spare from her preoccupations with Ranjit's case. She pored over intelligence reports earlier sent on the activities of the Revolutionary Tribal Peasants Party to decipher any leads, however slim, that she could lay her hands on and was constantly in touch with SP Nilghat to find out where he might have reached in his investigations.

This afternoon in office, trying to figure out what else the government could do, she recalled Vijay's words about trying to do everything for Ranjit. Feeling she needed to do something, she picked up her hotline to Colonel Raghav to find out what actions were being taken from his side.

He picked up the phone on the first ring. 'Hello, Evelyn!' he said. 'I was about to call you so you could brief the government. The ten companies of the 21st Infantry Div. are ready to move to Nilghat District today for the cordon and search ops. An air force chopper will make a recce first thing tomorrow morning of the area to see if they can find any traces of an extremist hideout. They asked me to be on the chopper as I have an approximate idea of where they may be but was wondering whether you would be able to come as well. We plan to leave tomorrow at daybreak, which is at 0540 hours.'

'I'd like to come, certainly, but I need to check with the CS first,' she replied. 'I'll call you back this evening and let you know.'

Hanging up, she felt a bit better. Some concrete action was under way. If they could locate the militant hideout, it would be a major breakthrough. She wondered whether it would be useful for her to be on the chopper. Two sets of eyes familiar with the area would be better than one, she thought. She decided to ask the CS during her final daily briefing, which the Home Secretary together with her conducted at about 8 p.m. each evening.

She was making a note of points to highlight for the briefing when her phone rang.

It was the Home Secretary sounding distraught. 'Evelyn, please come quickly,' he said, hanging up.

She rushed into his office, notepad in hand. 'Some terrible news has come in from Nilghat just now,' he said. 'There was a grenade attack on DC Nilghat in his court a few minutes back. He's been killed and so also SDO Vijay Gautam, who was also attending court, as well as a police constable. I haven't got the full details as yet, but SP Nilghat was just on the line, calling from the district hospital. We'll know more soon when he sends a full report. I am going to the CS to brief him and you should come with me too.'

Evelyn's first reaction was of shock and disbelief. Surely the Home Secretary was talking about other people . . . it just couldn't be Vijay and DC Nilghat . . . there must have been a mistake in communication. And then when the truth hit her, she was overcome with sorrow, more than she had ever felt in her life.

She sat down at the Home Secretary's desk and put her head in her hands. She just couldn't reconcile the images that she imagined of Vijay's charred and broken body lying in hospital with that of the Vijay whom she knew as ever joking and smiling—the Vijay who had made a preposterous proposal to her by letter and was just the other night speaking to her on the phone.

'Evelyn, are you OK?' asked the Home Secretary, seeing her quite overcome with the news.

'I will be, sir,' said Evelyn, looking up bleary-eyed. 'I'll just go to my room for a minute to collect myself and join you soon at the briefing,' she added, getting up.

55

COPING WITH LOSS

Back in her room, Evelyn gave in fully to the flood of emotion that engulfed her. The usually strong Evelyn felt totally broken. Not only had Vijay, her near-contemporary colleague perished through a cruel act of the militants but also fallen was the towering figure of DC Nilghat, who had provided guidance with wisdom and understanding to all around him, including Evelyn, his trainee for nearly a year. Memories of the crowded past year in Nilghat district flashed through her mind. She remembered the countless parties at the DC's bungalow and the after-dinner debates between the two SDOs with him as the arbiter. She couldn't bear to think of what Nivedita, his wife, was going through.

She realised that of the three principal personalities she had come to know well during her year at Nilghat district, two had now gone forever, murdered by the militants, and another was in their hands. She was convinced after these cold-blooded assassinations that this particular group of militants were not likely to listen to any reason, and unless something drastic was done immediately, Ranjit too was likely to be their next target.

This last thought stirred her to compose herself. Vijay had reposed faith in her that Ranjit would return soon with her help since his case was in her hands. She determined to do all she could to ensure that her remaining Nilghat colleague and friend was saved from the clutches of the diabolical criminals who had taken the lives of Vijay and the DC.

She gathered herself and picked up her notes. When she entered the CS's room, the Home Secretary was already with him. The latter might have mentioned to the CS her brief display of emotion on hearing the news from Nilghat, for the CS turned to her and said, 'Miss Syiem, we understand that this must be very difficult for you, given that you had come to know both of them quite well, I assume, over the last year. It is difficult for me as well as I have known Tushar Narayan, ex-DC Nilghat, now for nearly twenty years. As to Vijay Gautam, he was one of our finest young officers and held much promise. But we seem to be now confronted with an open insurrection, and we have little time to mourn.'

The CS informed them that he had just learnt that DC Nilghat, just before he was killed, had freed one of the three militants in Nilghat jail. 'Although this was contrary to my instructions, it may turn out to be a good move,' he said, 'as it would convey the impression to the militants that the government was serious in negotiating with them and delay Gupta's execution, which now seems inevitable. This would give us a little time to plan a strike to release Gupta.'

'Sir, Colonel Raghav has just informed me that the air force will conduct a recce early tomorrow over the Nainpuri Reserve,' said Evelyn, 'and he wanted me to come along as I have some idea of the probable location. I'd like your permission to go.'

The CS was a little hesitant, but he saw the look of determination on her face. 'OK, Miss Syiem, I agree provided it's only a recce you participate in. I don't want you to take any risks.'

56

RESCUE ATTEMPT

$\mathcal{T}$he first streaks of sunlight appeared on the horizon when the small air-force helicopter lifted off from the airfield in the gradually dissipating darkness. It was today or never, thought Evelyn. The ground fell away quickly, and they flew towards the eastern glow. That faint light spreading slowly above the dark slumbering city had a similar effect on her gloom-riveted mind—appearing to bring a flicker of hope of seeing Ranjit alive.

But she couldn't just hope; she needed to act. While the CS had asked her to take no risks, she had determined to take whatever risks required to help secure Ranjit's release. She, like ex-DC Nilghat, would take all measures necessary to that end, whatever be the consequences.

Colonel Raghav had informed her as soon as they had met early that morning in the dimly lit air-force hangar that the 21st Infantry had been deployed during the night at Nilghat and had begun helping the 2nd Armed Police Battalion set up a cordon. The whole operation was being coordinated by SP Nilghat, but the assault itself would be the responsibility of the commandant of the 2nd AP Battalion. The suspect interrogated earlier by OC Nilghat had provided the police a pretty good idea of where the militants' camp was likely to be, and the cordon had been set up around that area.

It was essential that the bid to free Ranjit be conducted with the utmost stealth and surprise, felt Colonel Raghav. Evelyn felt that the freeing of one of the militants was likely to help by creating a false sense among his captors of the government's willingness to discuss. And this might cause them to slacken their guard. This must have been the ex-DC's intent, she thought, and that advantage had to be exploited fully.

It was with this in mind that Colonel Raghav decided to make only one run high over what they felt the most likely area where the militants' hideout was located. If they were lucky, they would be able to pinpoint its location to the armed policemen, who would be able to rush the site and take the militants by surprise. Too long a recce would give the game away as the noise made by the helicopter could alert the militants of an impending operation against them.

Evelyn realised that the entire plan was relying on lot of luck to succeed. But it was a chance that had to be taken if Ranjit was to come out of this alive. If all went as planned, Colonel Raghav decided after talking to the pilot, they would land at the nearest clearing and join the policemen undertaking the assault. Evelyn could wait with the pilot till the operation was over.

'No, Colonel Raghav,' she replied firmly, 'I'm going too!' She wasn't sure how they would find Ranjit after the assault was over and wanted to be at the scene.

It took over an hour for the helicopter to reach the Nilghat district border. The sun had risen well above the horizon by then, and the undulating ground rushing below them could be seen quite clearly. The pilot was able to make contact immediately with the commandant of the 2nd AP Battalion. In a few minutes, the final assault was to begin, as soon as the coordinates of the militants' position were communicated to him.

Evelyn felt growing tension. The next few minutes would be crucial. The helicopter began flying speedily now over the hilly forested area of the Nainpuri Reserve thick with vegetation, and Colonel Raghav and Evelyn trained their binoculars on the ground and between the gaps in the trees, trying to detect any little sign that would indicate the militants' hideout.

Luck was definitely on their side. There appeared to be no clearing, but it was Evelyn who first detected a wisp of smoke rising steadily upwards in the still morning air from a part of the forest in the centre of a small valley. The militants had done a good job in camouflaging their camp, but the dire necessity of sustenance had betrayed them. She pointed the location out to Colonel Raghav, who also looked carefully through his binoculars and confirmed her sighting. He was quickly on his radio, communicating the coordinates to the commandant of the 2nd AP Battalion.

When the first shots rang out, they had already found a place to land. It took them a few more minutes to locate a group of policemen rushing towards the scene of action. Colonel Raghav ran into the jungle with his pistol in hand, and Evelyn ran after him, her only thought being whether she would see Ranjit alive.

57

ACTION AT DAWN

⌘

*I*t had been another dreadful night in the forest. When he woke up though, the fever seemed to have left him completely, but Ranjit still felt a little weak. His mind was clear, however, and he could hear his captors talking excitedly about something. There surely had been some new development. Ranjit figured that although he was under a sentence of death, the fact that it was not carried out meant only that his captors were trying to negotiate a deal with the threat of his execution as their bargaining chip. Obviously, some event favourable to their ends had occurred. This was confirmed when he saw through the crack in the door that they had lit a small fire and were busy cooking something and appeared to be in a celebratory mood. The strong aroma of fish being barbecued soon filled the air. Ranjit's captors were thrilled enough to share some of their victuals with him.

'Take this,' said the guard, barging into his shack. 'You and your government will soon be on your knees.'

Ranjit asked him what was going on. 'They have released one of our comrades! And soon the others will be freed too,' the guard sneered in response.

It was clear that contact had been established between the kidnappers and the government and the latter had made some concessions. But Ranjit was more than certain that this group that had tried to assassinate the governor would not stop at anything and the threat to his life was real. Should the government fail to meet all their demands, the hot-headed terrorists wouldn't hesitate to shoot him. But those demands were impossible to meet. Would that mean that the government would adopt the only other recourse available, that of an armed assault if they could find where they were holding him?

That was the first problem—they had to locate where he was, and Ranjit wasn't sure whether the police would succeed in finding him. He wasn't certain himself where he was. It was quite probable even that he was not in the Gourimuri Reserve Forest, where the police were most likely to search, given that his captors had used several modes of transport, including taking a river journey in order to conceal their tracks.

Even if the police were to find him and they did try to release him by force, it could be hazardous for him. He could be used as a hostage for the militants to get away, or if totally surprised, they might kill him as a reprisal before trying to escape.

That was unless Ranjit thought ahead of them and used the opportunity of a surprise attack on the camp to plan his own flight to freedom. This he was determined to do.

The release of one out of the three militants being held in Nilghat jail must have been part of a carefully thought-out strategy by DC Nilghat, he felt. This must have been both to buy time to determine where the militants were hiding him as well as to lull them into lowering their guard. The latter appeared to be happening already.

Therefore, the assault was imminent, Ranjit surmised. He was ready. He knew where his guard usually sat with his gun slung over his shoulder. Although the door to his shack was kept locked, it was easy to break open as it was made only of bamboo. The gun was the only problem, and Ranjit had to get his hand on to it before the guard realised what was happening.

Ranjit sat in his hut, waiting and alert. It was the distant hum of the helicopter that provided him with the signal that the assault had begun. He had to take his chance now.

Before the first police shots were fired, he smashed open the door and was able to surprise the guard who was peacefully smoking a *biri*. Although the man was pretty muscular, he had been caught unprepared. Ranjit grabbed his gun and ran towards the forest. At the same time, gunshots rang out from every direction. The comrades now alerted began returning the fire.

Ranjit saw the forms of the first policemen emerging from the forest. But before he could get into the cover of the forest himself, a shot hit him at the back, and he found himself collapsing and then darkness fully enveloped him.

58

ANOTHER JOURNEY

$\mathcal{T}$he police assault on the militants' camp was over in a few minutes. Most of the militants were killed. A few were injured and captured. Prominent among those killed was their leader, a bespectacled youth in military uniform. Evelyn, coming upon the camp immediately after all the firing had stopped, found his inert body and instantly recognised him as the intense youth who had interrupted her meeting with the villagers when she had gone on a field visit to the site of the land acquisition.

It was also Evelyn who found Ranjit's bleeding body lying at the camp's periphery, also still but holding signs of life. Colonel Raghav arranged his immediate evacuation by calling up the medical unit attached to the army column. It was very fortunate that they had decided to use the helicopter for locating the camp as Ranjit could be moved immediately to the nearest army hospital. He had lost a lot of blood but survived narrowly, although he remained comatose for many days.

When Ranjit regained consciousness, he found that he was in hospital. There was a small bouquet of flowers of various hues, with a get-well note from Evelyn at the bedside table. She had apparently been to visit him a couple of times while he was still unconscious.

Learning that Ranjit had regained consciousness, Colonel Raghav came in that same evening and informed him of the details of the big operation to free him and Evelyn's prominent role in it.

'Your daring breakout was what finally saved you,' said Colonel Raghav. 'The policemen ultimately got the militant who fired at you, but if you were closer, his aim wouldn't have faltered.'

He also informed him about the grenade attack that killed DC Nilghat and Vijay Gautam. This news was a severe blow for Ranjit which added to the physical trauma he had suffered. Weak in body and mind, he couldn't help breaking down. Much of the world he had known and found comfort in was vanishing.

'How is Evelyn?' Ranjit asked after some time, concerned that she too would have taken their deaths badly.

'She has gone on leave,' said Colonel Raghav. 'We were not sure how long you would take to come out of your coma, and she asked me to inform her as soon as you did.'

Ranjit thanked him profusely for his help in saving him, and after a while, Colonel Raghav left, wishing him a complete recovery.

Ranjit's body healed quickly enough, and a week or so later, he was ready to be discharged. What hadn't healed yet was the mental state he was in. He felt he needed to get away from it all. He felt he needed to take another journey to the hills.

But the hills he decided to visit now were different—gentler, undulating with canopies of conifers interspersed with meadows and a small town around a pretty lake. That was where Evelyn lived.

When he got off the bus, evening was setting in. As he began the long climb up the hill where her house was, he felt calm after a long time. It stood at the far end of a winding path that rose steeply up the hillside and was partly hidden behind trees.

But Evelyn had seen him coming and came down part of the way to greet him. She held his hand as together they crossed her threshold and stepped into her cheerful hearth.

Kolkata Megalopolis
MID TWENTY-
FIRST CENTURY

1

TRAIN TO LHASA

'Wake up, Akio, you mustn't miss this,' Mikio was saying as she gently shook her friend, trying to arouse her from her deep slumber.

Akio rubbed her eyes and looked out of her train window at a truly magnificent early morning panorama passing swiftly by: an unblemished immense azure firmament above and a similarly vast and blue placid lake below, bordered by high snow-capped mountains touched with golden hue from the early morning sun. Not a soul was in sight—human or animal—anywhere she looked. That is if you excluded the patches of shrubs. Did they too have souls, wondered Akio, now fully awake. They also struggled to live, felt sensations, and breathed.

Akio turned on her communications cube, and the holographic nymph yawned, did a twirl, and informed her that they were passing by the shores of the Nam-tso, the holy Tibetan lake at an elevation exceeding fourteen thousand feet, and that they would be arriving shortly in Lhasa.

She felt grateful for that, as now the railway would descend to gentler altitudes towards Kolkata in India, their final destination. She had passed a fitful night initially as despite their pressurised train cabin, she felt restless and unable to sleep because of the high altitude. But the stunning views of the Tibetan plateau that she now began seeing and had seen the previous day had amply compensated her for the slight physical discomfort she had experienced and made her choice of journey by the newly extended Beijing to Kolkata (via Lhasa) maglev railway line well worth it. She eagerly looked forward to her stopover at Lhasa and the journey beyond to India.

She started getting ready to disembark for her brief sojourn at Lhasa. In the opposite bunk, Mikio, her co-tenant in the Tokyo apartment they shared and fellow participant in the Asian Congress for Peace, had already packed her bag and was ready. The altitude apparently made no difference to her, and she was her usual cheerful self. But Akio got up and wearily made her way, toothbrush in hand, to the restroom at the end of the carriage.

The Asian Congress for Peace had been convened by a large number of pan-Asian civil society groups—too large to remember even all the prominent ones, thought Akio, and with new sponsors and participants growing by the minute. It was a magnificent outpouring of public sentiment all over Asia towards securing peace in the continent—a region that had seen far too much conflict and strife that continued still, and now, in the middle of the twenty-first century, hungered for an end to all discord and violence and to reach reconciliation and peace. On her part, Akio had played a prominent role in her own country among the youth and had been chosen by its apex youth organisation to represent it at the congress.

The venue of the congress was the city of Kolkata, long known as the City of Joy, an appropriate location for the congress to meet ahead of the near-simultaneous Indian and Chinese people's referendums on the issue of total nuclear disarmament. But apart from that singular tag given to it by the French author Dominique Lapierre[30] which had stuck to it perhaps for good reason, the city of Kolkata had become remarkable the world over for the transformation it had seen from a city of dirt, slums, poverty, and pollution to their antithesis in every sense now. It was no longer a city only of the joyful poor—there were very few of those now in any case. It had distinguished itself lately as a model for the whole of Asia to remark upon, and Akio wanted to see this near miracle for herself, as did the large number of foreign delegates converging on it from all corners of Asia.

The congress hoped to influence the outcome of the public referendums taking place in India and China, the mammoth Asian neighbours, and force total denuclearisation all over Asia. For her Japanese colleagues, of course, this was a topic very dear to their hearts. Japan was the only country to have suffered an actual nuclear holocaust—although India and Pakistan had come very near to inflicting nuclear destruction on themselves too. Mikio, for example, was from Nagasaki and had grown up with stories of the last great war of the twentieth century and the total devastation it had wrought on the city and its inhabitants. It was difficult for anyone in Japan to comprehend why the world would continue to harbour this diabolical weaponry—or any weaponry of mass destruction, for that matter.

Akio had included a pilgrimage to Lhasa—that centre of spiritual inquiry and tranquillity—therefore as an essential part of her mission of peace. She hoped to get a glimpse of the Dalai Lama and hear a few comforting words that would bring her better direction and also some inner calm. Yes, the latter especially she needed before beginning another important task—a very personal one which even her college friend and roommate Mikio was unaware of. And that too was centred in Kolkata.

'Hurry up, we're almost there!' said Mikio when Akio returned to their cabin.

Akio looked out and saw that signs of pasturelands were now evident in the countryside with flocks of sheep and goat grazing peacefully. Some greenhouses also began dotting the moving pastoral scene, indicating that an urban habitation was near. A little later when Akio had changed and finished packing her small suitcase, human settlements came into view. And then very quickly, the city was upon them with hundreds of dwellings spreading quickly on either side of the railway line which looked all new, but each had traditional Tibetan facades, and finally all of a sudden when the tracks turned, there was a stunning view of the Potala Palace high on the hillside.

The train began slowing down as it approached the city of Lhasa. There would be plenty of time to disembark, and there was no hurry, this being the terminus of the Beijing-to-Lhasa section. The Indian-operated maglev train to Kolkata which they would take a couple of days later would begin its long journey through the Himalayas and the Gangetic plains from another platform.

The Lhasa station looked quite international in character, being crowded with tourists from various countries as well as Tibetan lamas in their maroon robes and shirts. Akio felt a little heavy in her legs, walking out on the platform as she guessed she hadn't yet acclimatised fully to the altitude, although Mikio seemed fine. They found a taxi quite easily outside and hopped in.

Their modest hotel was in the older part of the city which had retained more of its original ancient character. Ever since the return from India of the fifteenth Dalai Lama and rapprochement with the Chinese authorities following agreement on a large measure of autonomy for Tibet, the Dalai Lamas and their successors, who had a purely spiritual role now, had made many changes to the city, trying to restore most of it to its original character, and the changes were now quite evident. The taxi dropped them at a narrow street in front of a two-storied tenement with a colourful Tibetan facade, and they were greeted by a young receptionist in traditional wear.

Akio saw that they still had a couple of hours before their meeting with the Dalai Lama at the Potala Palace. It had taken some doing to secure this meeting with His Holiness, although it would be with a large group of other visitors in the palace auditorium, and there would be little chance of a personal interaction. Her delegate status at the Asian Congress for Peace had probably played a role; she couldn't be sure. But she had hurriedly planned the trip on receiving a cryptic confirmation from the Dalai Lama's secretary to a fifteen-minute audience scheduled for twelve noon that day.

'Let's try the Sha-Baklap, sounds interesting,' said Mikio when they settled into a tiny restaurant across the hotel.

Akio realised that she was almost starving, not having had much to eat since last night. But her returning appetite signalled that she was gradually getting acclimatised. The po-cha, or butter tea, also helped. It had been served to them as a welcome drink at the hotel and also came with the menu as soon as they sat down at the restaurant. The hot, steaming brew with yak butter seemed an ideal remedy for her altitude sickness.

The Sha-Baklap, consisting of crispy mutton patties in exotic spices, served with fresh green salads, did not disappoint either. The two vigorously set upon their meal, which was quickly finished with not a morsel left behind. The waiter kept filling their tea bowl with po-cha and looked at them with a hint of amusement.

'Would you like something else, or a dessert perhaps?' he asked.

They declined as they didn't want to risk getting in late at the palace. But he helped them with directions that would be a shortcut to the palace gates as the two decided to walk there rather than take an electric minibus or pedicab.

The shortcut took them slowly uphill through street markets selling gaily coloured local handicrafts, clothes, and trinkets. It was thronged with tourists attempting—mostly unsuccessfully—to strike bargains, and their progress was slowed down trying to negotiate their way through them. But eventually they reached the reception centre at the foot of the palace. The monks at the reception were expecting them and issued their visitor cards and directed them to the Great West Hall in the Red Palace.

The long climb of stairs—nearly a hundred metres—was still quite exhausting for Akio, but they finally made it. Several other invitees were also proceeding with them to the same audience, including a large number of Buddhist monks from various countries, each wearing a different colour of robe—yellow, saffron, and red among others. The grounds were also teeming with lamas from the palace establishment itself, in their distinctive maroon outfits.

One such lama who was looking out for them near the entrance to the White Palace approached them and, after glancing at their visitor cards, asked them to follow him. They were glad of his help as it would have been difficult otherwise for them to negotiate the inner courtyards, hallways, and steep staircases to the Great West

Hall. When they arrived at the hall, it was almost full already. But the lama who ushered them in took them to seats near the podium. Akio was glad that they would get a good view of His Holiness, even if a private audience was not possible.

The hall filled up quickly after they were seated. Soon, a loud gong was heard, and a little later, while his audience waited in quiet anticipation, His Holiness the sixteenth Dalai Lama came into the hall and bowed deeply, with folded hands, at the assembly.

2

MEETING HIS HOLINESS

$\mathcal{A}$kio was somewhat surprised to see that His Holiness looked remarkably young, perhaps as a result of his inner radiance and ability to withstand the stresses of life with calm and equanimity. He wore black-rimmed glasses and gave the appearance of a man of wisdom and deep scholarship.

'My most beloved brothers and sisters,' he began, 'all of you have come long distances to see me, a person your love and faith has endowed with more goodness, spiritual understanding, and compassion than I deserve. Thank you all for coming to meet me. But I am no more than a reflection of the same godly attributes in yourself that you see in me, and that is present in every soul in this world of ours.

'I think more and more people in this world are beginning to recognise this essential spark of godliness that is present in all of us, and the need to embrace this inner divine spark rather than dwell on differences that we bring upon artificially between us.

'I feel convinced that we are moving forward, towards universal understanding, compassion, and goodwill between peoples and nations. How else can you explain that you see me standing here in this very palace from where the fourteenth Dalai Lama had to leave nearly a century ago in exile to India with the believers of *dhamma*? The gradual improvement in the understanding between the two great peoples of China and India, which our Tibetan region straddles, allowed the return of the fifteenth Dalai Lama and Tibetans from exile, as you all are well aware.

'We must continue this process of finding our common grounds and understandings and spreading peace on this planet. Consider Asia's commonality rather than its differences. Wherever you travel in this vast continent, you find the echoes of a common spiritual understanding. The light of goodwill and dhamma that Sakyamuni and his followers help spread across the continent emerged from India and touched its extremities—from its southernmost tip in the island of Sri Lanka to its northernmost end in the Korean peninsula. All the other great religions of the world also rose from Asia, and the common teachings of love, goodwill, and compassion have influenced all corners of this vast continent.

'Today, our continent faces a great choice that may further the cause of peace or postpone its progress indefinitely. The two simultaneous referendums that the governments of India and China have called to end nuclear weapons for all time will place this choice in the hands of over a third of the adult population of the world.

'I hope that when each person chooses, she or he will consider this inner spark of goodness within their souls and that present in the hearts of others everywhere and not be affected by thoughts of anger or ill will. Such choices have been faced by humanity in every place and in every period of time and history from the ancients to now and will be so faced by those who follow us in the future.

'There are some among you who are taking part in the Asian Congress for Peace in Kolkata. I am confident that you will succeed in your role of peacemakers and turn the growing tide in favour of peace in this continent and in the world. You have a major task before you, and I am with you in your endeavour. Echoing the words of Christ, I say to you: blessed are you as you are the true children of God.'

The Dalai Lama ended his short remarks to a rousing ovation from the audience, many of whom had become quite emotional hearing him and could not keep back their tears. He bowed deeply, with folded hands, and sat down. His secretary then informed the audience that His Holiness would accept a few questions.

'There are still many in this world who use violence to gain ascendancy over others, and only force can restrain them,' asked what looked to Akio as a young Indian scholar. 'How should society handle such threats, in your view?'

'Sadly, you are right that such people and forces inimical to society still remain and may also remain in the foreseeable future. It may be impractical to dream as yet of a world where universal understanding and goodwill will be reached. But on the other hand, as almost all nations now are run by the will of the ordinary folk of their countries, the majority of whom want peace, not a single nation now remains that advocates violence as a solution to the world's problems.

'Fortunately, the votaries of violence as a means to achieve ends are now mostly limited to non-state groups or individuals. What should our view be to them? This is a problem debated in many scriptures. It was the dilemma faced by Arjuna, for instance, in the Mahabharata. There has been a revival of this debate following the discovery of the Thaneswar relics in the latter part of the twentieth century, as many of you may be aware.

'As one who sincerely believes in the power of good over evil, my answer would be to explore all possible avenues, travel every road possible, implement all measures of persuasion to kindle the spark of goodwill in those who believe in violence. Such a view has led, for instance, to universal moratoriums on capital punishment all over the world.'

'And if these still fail?' persisted the questioner.

'In that case, forceful restraint of the violent person or group to prevent them from hurting others may be construed by a humane society as an act of self-defence. If I were compelled to save peaceful people from a violent opposition through use of force, I would perhaps do so, but would always consider the good in the attacker and ways still of kindling that spark of God in him or her. However, there are no universal rules in this matter, and unfortunately, the right path would have to be chosen by the individual or society based on the context and with the good of all in mind.'

A round of loud applause greeted the reply. A number of other questions followed. After some time, the secretary came over to the podium and announced that regretfully the audience had to end and wished everyone a pleasant stay in Tibet. Getting up and preparing to leave, Akio was quite satisfied with the meeting and particularly happy to note that the Dalai Lama had mentioned the Asian Congress for Peace and glad to learn that others apart from Mikio and her were going there.

But what she was not prepared for was the request by the secretary, who came over hurriedly to her immediately after his brief message of goodbye, to say that His Holiness would be very happy if Akio and Mikio would agree to meet him briefly in private right then.

3

INNER TURMOIL

*T*hey were ushered into a small antechamber next to the Great West Hall, where the Dalai Lama was sitting at an ornately decorated desk, busy signing some papers. On seeing the two ladies, he got up. The secretary introduced the two of them to the Dalai Lama, and each bowed low in the traditional Japanese style when they were introduced. The Dalai Lama bowed, with folded hands, in response. Then he came over, and motioning them to sit on the sofa, took his seat in an armchair facing them.

'The organisers of the Asian Congress for Peace also invited me to attend,' he informed them, 'but although I would have liked very much to go, that is sadly not possible.'

Then looking at Akio, he said, 'When I learnt that the two of you are on your way to the congress, I took the liberty of informing them that I will send my message to the congress through you. Will you, Nishimoto-san, do me the favour of reading out my message at the congress? As the representative of the youth of Japan, a country which is at the forefront of denuclearisation efforts globally, you are the most appropriate person to represent me. It is written in English, which I know you are proficient in. I hope I am not imposing on you?'

'Far from it, Your Holiness,' said Akio, quite surprised and overwhelmed at the request. 'It will be a great honour.'

The secretary handed a scroll which contained a brief message and had been signed by His Holiness and carried his official seal.

'I thought it would be most apt that a true votary of peace carry my message to the congress. It was fortunate that your request to meet me came through at the same time. But I don't think it was really a coincidence. The wheel of dhamma works silently but resolutely to make these things happen.'

The Dalai Lama was a little silent for a while, as though in meditation. Then he turned to Akio, concern showing on his face, and said, 'Tell me, Akio-san, is there something else you wanted to discuss that is troubling you? I can see from your face that you are deeply concerned over something important that is eluding you, which is causing a lot of inner turmoil.'

Akio was astonished that His Holiness had been so perceptive and nodded silently at him. Mikio turned to her in surprise also as Akio had never said anything to her about this inner torment.

'I didn't want to trouble you with my personal matter, Your Holiness,' said Akio, 'but I am looking for someone I have lost and have been trying to find since a child.'

'A parent, perhaps?' asked the Dalai Lama. 'They are the clearest manifestation of the divine in our world according to our thinking, and a loss of a parent can be the most troubling and tragic occurrence in a child's life. You have suffered much, Akio, but I can see you have the strength to keep seeking until your quest is successful. I am confident that your search for peace both for the world and in your own self will succeed.'

Akio noticed that His Holiness had dropped formalities and addressed her by her first name. It was as though he was an elder brother trying to comfort her and not the exalted and distant His Holiness the sixteenth Dalai Lama. She was overwhelmed by this and couldn't control the tears that welled up in her eyes. The severe external wall that she had built over the years to deal with her loss seemed to have been broken by his words. She wondered whether His Holiness really realised how much he had helped her.

'Thank you very much, Your Holiness, for meeting both of us,' she said, getting up. 'And I, Akio Nishimoto, will remain ever grateful to you personally for your kindness.'

4

ACROSS THE HIMALAYAS

$\mathcal{T}$he sleek red-and-black coaches of the Indian Railways Intercity Maglev Express from Lhasa to Kolkata stood on the opposite platform from where Akio and Mikio had alighted a couple of days back after their long journey from Beijing. At the entrance to each coach stood a turbaned and liveried attendant who helped the passengers find their coaches and helped with their luggage. The duo was escorted to a private smartly appointed coupe for two with a lower and upper bunk. This was a new rail service—with state-of-the-art pressurised cabins, and running the entire distance on magnetic levitation—and the Indians were eager to show off their modernised railway system, one of the oldest in the world, to all and particularly their giant northern neighbour.

They had arrived just in time, and a little after they had settled in, the train gently glided out of the station and soon picked up speed on leaving the station and headed out towards the countryside. Akio had become a little quiet after the meeting with the Dalai Lama, and Mikio let her be, not wanting to prod, and allowing her friend the space she needed to gather her thoughts and speak up when ready to do so. So when Akio took her place next to the window and silently began looking out, Mikio pulled out her reading tablet and started to read by herself.

Parting the curtains of their large window, Akio saw the town of Lhasa with its tenements, crowded markets, and streets filled with its miscellaneous traffic of buses, cars, and pedicabs speeding past. Soon the last signs of habitation were lost behind the tall hills through which the distant dazzling snow line of the Himalayas occasionally made its appearance. In a little while, the sun disappeared behind the mountains, and darkness descended on the wilderness across which the speeding train rushed towards its next stop, the town of Shigatse, the second largest town in Tibet, the town where the renowned Buddhist scholar and revered Panchen Lama lived within the cloisters of the Tashilhunpo monastery.

Like the Dalai Lama, the Panchen Lama too had been restored to his traditional role as the most important religious leader after the Dalai Lama in Tibet. Akio had hoped that she would get a glimpse of his famous monastery from the train but was disappointed that the sun had set too quickly and dusk had settled in faster than she had anticipated. Meanwhile, Mikio seemed to be holding a conversation with someone in the coupe, so she turned away from the window to see what was up.

It was the elegantly turned-out attendant assigned to their coach who had entered their coupe and was enquiring about their dinner preferences. It had been a long day, and the two suddenly realised that they were hungry. There was a choice of Tibetan, continental, and Indian cuisines, and both didn't lose much time in settling on the last. And they weren't disappointed as they found out a little while later after the town of Shigatse had come and gone and the train veered sharply southwards, towards the India border.

Dinner finally came in a silver covered serving dish and accompanying porcelain dinnerware on a serving trolley which converted into a dinner table for two, complete with white table cover and napkins. A tiny vase with a single rose completed the table décor. Both the girls were surprised at the elegance of the service, which contrasted sharply with their experience with the previous Chinese no-frills leg of their journey and credited it, perhaps correctly, to the effort being made by the Indian Railways to popularise their service to Kolkata which faced stiff competition from the traditional air services, which had been the only alternative left to travellers earlier.

The menu was simple but satisfying. Beginning with a mouth-watering *chat masala*-based salad, it consisted of *tandoori roti* with *dum aloo* as starters and an entrée of saffron-tinged mutton *biryani* with succulent pieces of tender goat meat cooked in the most delightful of herbs and spices accompanied with *raita*, and finally ended with the traditional desert of *phirnee*.

'Sorry I didn't tell you earlier about this, but I know you will understand, Mikio,' began Akio. 'I have been troubled about this right from childhood. My mother, as you know, raised me alone and had not told me the truth about my father. This I found out only recently.

'In my mother's heart, I think, my father was dead already when they parted, so she wasn't really lying to me when my questions about my missing father—right from the time as a small child, I became conscious of such things and began to feel a big void in my heart—were answered by her with the simple explanation that he was dead. That finality conveniently cut off all discussion and became in fact the truth when the years passed and there was no word from my father and not even the faintest sign that he was alive or cared to find out about us. She had also erased all traces of my father, and there was not even a photograph of him in our house.

'My mother kept the bitter truth in her heart, away from me, her entire life till she died. She didn't want me to learn about him. What great hurt he had inflicted on her I don't know, but it must have been severe enough that she wanted my father never to have any influence whatsoever on me.

'Losing my mother on top of being fatherless left me completely distraught and miserable, to say the least. I began looking recklessly for relationships, which were sometimes fulfilling but mostly empty and frustrating, and was lucky to eventually find you, Mikio, and you have offered me great solace, but the emptiness in my heart has remained.

'Imagine my surprise, therefore, when having gone to meet my grandmother one day recently, I found a photograph of my mother with a strange-looking gentleman against the backdrop of the Fujiyama in one of her dressers. I knew at once that this was my father. I could now trace the darkish tone in my complexion, which you and others more than once have remarked upon, to his.

'With tremendous excitement, I showed the photograph to my grandmother, and she and I wept together at the ending of this family secret, which my mother had also extracted a promise from her to keep undisclosed from me at her deathbed. It was a relief to her to have me discover it myself rather than her divulging a secret she had promised to keep.

'But she knew little more than that. My father was from India and had come to Tokyo as a student to conduct research towards a doctorate in the area of genetics in the same department to which my mother was attached and where the two had met. Their parting was as much a mystery to her as it has remained now for me. My grandmother hardly ventured out from her home in Nagoya, and it so happened that the relationship ended far too quickly for my grandmother to learn much. My mother's silence on the matter ensured that whatever information was available was forever lost with her. The only thing she remembered was that my father was from the city of Kolkata and he had to return hurriedly without finishing his studies. That, and a thirty-year-old photo of him is all I have. And I am going now to Kolkata to find him.'

Mikio considered the odds that this could happen quietly to herself—she didn't want to disappoint her friend. A thirty-year-old photo of a man who might not even be living in the vast city of Kolkata, with its more than twenty-five million inhabitants, was all Akio had, and not even a name. It was clear that Akio's mother wanted to remove all traces of the relationship and didn't want Akio to go looking for him. And why should Akio when her father had shown no desire to meet Akio and her mother?

They were both silent, lost in their own thoughts but on the same subject of the mystery behind Akio's abandonment. The matter had come as some surprise for Mikio, who didn't realise what Akio was going through, although they had known each other nearly two years. She could now connect the occasional spells of the blues that Akio experienced—quite uncharacteristic for this otherwise extroverted personality—to her tragic personal conundrum.

A knock on the door broke the silence. A Tibetan customs and immigration official came in to examine their documents, which he noted from their respective com-cubes. As the train would be crossing the border into India late in the night, he didn't want to wake them up at that time, finishing the formalities now. After he had registered the information, he informed Akio that a message had been sent from the Potala Palace to Akio and that she might like to see it now.

Akio noted that her com-cube had begun flashing in red, indicating that a message of the highest priority had been received. Turning to her device, she saw the secretary to the Dalai Lama had sent her a note, which read as follows:

OM MANI PADME HUM

Dear Ms Nishimoto:

On behalf of His Holiness the Dalai Lama, I would like to present his compliments to you and Ms Mikio Matsumoto.

His Holiness would like to inform you that he has requested Dr Saurav Bandopadhyay, who met His Holiness soon after your audience with him today, to offer his assistance to you on your personal quest while in Kolkata, and Dr Bandopadhyay has kindly consented to provide all necessary help in this matter. Dr Bandopadhyay will contact you soon regarding this.

His Holiness believes that you will succeed in both of your missions to the city of Kolkata.

Wishing you peace and happiness and conveying His Holiness's highest regards,

Jigme Dorji
Secretary to His Holiness

5

AN IMPROBABLE QUEST

$\mathcal{A}$kio and Mikio arrived at the train's dining car early, just as the breakfast service had begun at 6.30 a.m. The train had crossed into India in the night and was traversing the thickly forested foothills of the Himalayas in the state of Sikkim. They were among the first diners, and all the tables were empty save one at the far end, where a lone occupant sat reading a book and drinking coffee.

The train appeared to be on the outskirts of Gangtok, the state capital of Sikkim, Mikio observed, as advised by her shrill-voiced personal assistant in her com-cube. Looking out from the large observation windows, they saw that the city was perched on hilltops and ridges, with occasional Tibetan monasteries with their colourful flags looking out through the thick forests of tall conifers and deciduous trees. Before the train came to a stop at a Tibetan-style ornately designed station, they were able to see the dazzling Kanchenjunga, one of the tallest peaks of the Himalayas, towering over the surrounding hills.

An Indian immigration official in a blue-and-white uniform with brass buttons and peaked cap boarded the train at the short halt, along with a large number of passengers, mainly tourists. The official proceeded to check the identities of the international passengers with the travel information he had received already, beginning with those in the dining car. After confirming their identities, he thanked them and said, 'Welcome to India and a very happy birthday to you, Ms Nishimoto!'

It was indeed Akio's birthday. Mikio had already greeted her the first thing when she woke up, but Akio was pleasantly surprised to be greeted by a complete stranger. She thanked him profusely, and the official folded his hands in a brief namaste and proceeded on his way. Akio hoped that her birthday would bring with it some other pleasant surprises too.

She didn't have to wait too long. The passenger at the far end of the dining car got up and came over to their table. As he came near, she recognised him as the persistent questioner at the Dalai Lama's audience.

'Sorry to intrude, but which one of you is Ms Akio Nishimoto?' he said, addressing the duo. 'I have a request from His Holiness, the Dalai Lama, to contact her.'

'Hello,' said Akio, rising and extending her hand. 'You must be Dr Bandopadhyay. What a pleasant surprise! Why don't you join us?' she said.

Dr Bandopadhyay was a dark complexioned young man with a mass of untidy hair. He wore spectacles that highlighted his scholarly look and had obviously got his doctorate very early. 'I was contacted by His Holiness's office,' said he, taking a seat at their table. 'They found out somehow that we were both on the same train and suggested that it may be easier for me to find you here than in Kolkata. The immigration official made it easy for me by pointing you out.

'But tell me, how may I be of service?' he asked.

Mikio requested the waiter to serve breakfast for all of them at the table. She chose the continental option, but all three, being fully engrossed in the discussion, couldn't do much justice to the menu. Over breakfast, Akio, after some hesitation and encouraged by her friend, related her story and her personal mission in search of her lost parent. She spared no detail, and it took two more rounds of coffee after the breakfast was over to complete her narration. Meanwhile, the train had snaked its way through the gorges and river valleys of the Terai foothills and finally reached the plains. The farmlands flashing by indicated that it had picked up a terrific speed on its last stretch to its destination.

'Well, the task is not easy,' said Saurav when Akio had finished. They had gotten down to addressing each other by their first names by the time Akio's long story was over.

'Kolkata is a city of more than twenty-five million people, and if your father is indeed there, it will still be a very hard task to locate him, going only by this old photograph,' he said, looking closely at the fading photo Akio had given him. He got Akio's permission to scan it on his device before handing it back to her.

'The first thing, of course, is to put out a search on the digital cloud, providing all known particulars of him, including this photo. But you may have done that already?' he asked Akio.

Akio had, indeed. She had searched all sources in the Japanese universities with departments of genetics in Tokyo around the time her parents were there and come up with a few clues. The search had been hard, with universities reluctant to divulge any details without the consent of parties involved, and it was only after making personal trips and persuading the senior authorities with the help of contacts that she was able to make some headway. The student records went back pretty accurately for about a decade or so, but beyond that, they began getting scantier and less informative. While most universities maintained records of names of students enrolled and their home addresses, including foreign students, even going back to the period Akio's parents were attending university, photographs were rare and mainly available only for the more recent years. Akio thus had names and around thirty-year-old addresses of a hundred and thirty-seven possible candidates from Kolkata, any one of whom could have been her father. But that was a start.

'You have done quite a bit of investigative work already, and it does make our task much easier,' said Saurav. 'We will have to try and contact these persons individually and see if we can locate him. But how much time are you planning to spend on this search?'

'We have plans to stay in Kolkata for the Peace Congress for a week, but I can try and stay on longer if necessary. Mikio will, however, have to go back,' replied Akio.

'Well, a week may not be sufficient. We are all involved in the Peace Congress too and will have to work on this simultaneously. I'll have to put some close friends on the job too,' said Saurav.

Mention of the Peace Congress turned the discussion on to the main purpose of their mission to Kolkata.

'I saw a very impassioned plea by Manuel del Rosario, the Philippines' president, this morning just after I woke up,' said Mikio. 'He was speaking in Parliament and referred to the Kolkata Peace Congress. I saw a delayed telecast on my com-cube,' she said.

'He was urging the people of both China and India to vote positively in their respective referendums to—in his words—usher in an Asian peace, and he called for Asia to show the world that peace and amity are possible in our troubled planet.'

The simultaneous referendums on Saturday were now imminent. The Peace Congress was on Thursday, just two days away. The Dalai Lama had played a key role in advancing the rapprochement between these two nuclear giants, home to a third of humanity between them, and in helping organise the Peace Congress. But now he was keeping to the background himself, letting the international community build pressure on the two nations.

'I saw the latest agenda of the Peace Congress, and it suggests that Akio will represent the Dalai Lama . . . Was this why you came to Lhasa?' asked Saurav of the two.

'No, I had no knowledge of it at all—it was a complete surprise,' said Akio. 'His Holiness may have been considering it, however, after we sought an audience with him on our way to the congress.'

'Well, it makes a lot of sense,' said Saurav. 'Requesting you to read out his message is most apt as you would be representing the only nation which had suffered a nuclear holocaust. No one could make a bigger impact.'

'It is a very big responsibility, and I hope I will be able to live up to it,' Akio said with some trepidation.

'Now that we have spoken about ourselves, it's now your turn. Tell us something about yourself,' said Mikio, addressing Saurav. 'To begin with, what made you come to Lhasa?'

'Have either of you heard of the Institute of Humanity?' asked Saurav.

'Isn't the institute one of the chief organisers of the Peace Congress?' asked Mikio in return.

'It is indeed,' replied Saurav. 'I happen to be associated with it. In fact, I am its current director. It was founded by my grandfather at the site of an ancient Indian city called Thaneswar, which was rediscovered in the last century. Over the years, the institute has done some good work. One of its major achievements was helping bring about reconciliation between communities on the Ayodhya issue, which had been a source of acrimony between the Hindus and Muslims in India for decades.'

Seeing the look of puzzlement on the faces of the two Japanese women, he hastened to explain himself. 'Ayodhya is one of most revered and holy towns of the Hindus. It is considered to be the birthplace of Lord Rama. The Hindus believe that there was once a great Hindu temple marking the spot in Ayodhya where Rama was born. Like they did to several temples in India, the Rama temple in Ayodhya is supposed to have been also torn down by one of the Muslim conquerors of India—Babar—and a mosque built in its place which had been in existence for several centuries. However, the Hindu community had always contested its construction. The matter had remained in dispute during the entire period of British rule and even after India gained independence in 1947. In 1992, a large number of impatient Hindu hotheads tore down the mosque with their bare hands, and this incident led to years of riots, deaths, and turmoil in India and was a major irritant between the two communities.

'The institute was successful in steering a peace process and reaching a final understanding between the communities. Rather than forging divisiveness, Ayodhya has become a symbol of religious harmony in the country and may have contributed to the promotion of communal peace that we now enjoy in India.

'The present Dalai Lama has been taking a keen interest in the work of the institute, particularly after the Ayodhya rapprochement. He has employed the institute in many of his peace initiatives, including in the organising of the Peace Congress. That is how I came to be in Lhasa.'

'Very impressive work!' remarked Mikio, now regarding Saurav with unabashed reverence.

'Unfortunately, we will have to pause for the moment,' she said, looking at her watch and rising. 'Let's continue our discussion in Kolkata as we are reaching our destination within the hour and must hurry back to our coupes to get ready.'

6

ARRIVING AT A MEGALOPOLIS

*A*s the train neared the Kolkata megalopolis, the lush green paddy fields which stretched all the way to the horizon, interspersed occasionally with clumps of coconut palms around ponds sheltering small habitations, slowly gave way to roads, bridges, culverts, transmission lines, and concrete structures. The nearer it came to its destination, the more speed the train seemed to be gathering, impatient to reach the terminus. Soon the city enveloped them within its fold but looking out from their coupé window, Akio and Miko noticed that its mass of brick and concrete structures was tempered much by thick foliaged tropical trees along roads and by open spaces consisting of small and large water bodies around which carefully maintained parks and gardens had been built. They got a quick view of a tall bridge on the horizon before the train entered a pitch-dark tunnel, which shut out the view.

'We've arrived,' said Mikio on advice from her com-cube personal assistant. 'We are now travelling below the river Hooghly, and our stop is just ahead.'

The train began slowing down and, soon after, emerged from the tunnel into a platform surrounded by a glittering underground arcade of stores and shops. It gradually came to a stop. 'Kolkata – Esplanade' read the signboards. They had finally arrived at the City of Joy. Picking up their bags and ascending two flights of escalator stairs later, they emerged into bright sunshine outside.

Saurav was waiting for them just outside near the taxi stand. 'Since you have a free day today, why don't the two of you go to your hotel and take some rest and then come out for an early dinner with me?' he said.

'No, no,' said Akio, 'you have taken a lot of trouble already on my behalf, and besides, you need to rest yourself.'

'It's no trouble, believe me,' Saurav replied. 'It'd give us time to discuss your matter further, and besides, as I'll be busy from tomorrow with the congress, I may have no time afterwards. We have to work out a strategy to get to the bottom of this quickly. So finding some time this evening is important. If you prefer, we could meet at the hotel, but I thought you might like to come out and see a bit of our city as well.'

Akio looked at Mikio, and the latter nodded. 'OK, thanks very much. You are being most kind,' she said to Saurav.

'Come, let me show you the way to your hotel, meanwhile,' said Saurav, and the three set off.

The two women were billeted at the Great Eastern Hotel, which was a short walk away. Esplanade was a large square in the city centre, bordered with massive ornately sculpted colonial-style buildings. The entire square was resplendent with gardens where tropical flowers of many hues—cannas, hibiscuses, bougainvillea, marigolds, among others—were blooming. Tall golmohur trees alternating with canopies of red and yellow flowers completed the scene. The two women had left Tokyo when the pink-and-white cherry blossoms were in full bloom. But this was a different experience altogether, and the vibrant tropical flora was a feast for their eyes.

The hotel was a mere two blocks from the station at an adjoining equally large square surrounding a lake over which loomed the impressive eighteenth-century edifice of the Writers Building which Saurav explained was the state government's headquarters. He left them at their hotel lobby and promised to pick them up there again for their dinner date later in the afternoon.

The Great Eastern itself had been a Kolkata icon since it was set up in the early nineteenth century and the first luxury hotel of its kind in the East. After freshening up, the two women went to the Bakery, a restaurant in the basement where the original bakery from which the hotel originated was located—with the same dough-making machinery and baking chambers still intact after over two centuries.

The waiter suggested they try the mutton patties and walnut brownies. Apparently, these were still being made according to the original recipes. Both turned out to be excellent—the patties soft and crisp with a delightful filling, the brownies not too sweet and with the right proportion of walnuts and chocolate. This was traditionally downed by the memsahibs during the colonial times, according to the waiter, with the subtly flavoured light-coloured Darjeeling tea. Accordingly, they also partook of the tea at his recommendation, and turned temporarily into modern-day memsahibs. Mikio explained to Akio that the tea was from the very hills they had just traversed on their train journey to India and still handpicked, which made it the rarest—and most expensive—tea in the world.

Luckily, the hotel being one of the sponsors of the Peace Congress they were entitled to a generous discount for accommodation and all other expenses and their tea break didn't pauperise them. Almost all the rooms in the hotel were taken up by delegates, and some of those curious to savour the bakery's products had similarly wandered into the restaurant. Eager to meet the other delegates, Akio and Mikio introduced themselves to those nearby. There was an elderly gentleman also from Japan, several Indonesians, and a Filipino at the adjoining tables. Apart from Asians, who seemed to be the dominant group, there were delegates from quite a few other places too. For example, there was a lady NGO activist who had come all the way from Chile, a student from Burkina Faso, and a Canadian professor who were sitting just nearby.

The talk was all about the impending congress and the possibility that it could influence the outcome of the referendums. But it wasn't just the congress; it appeared that efforts all over Asia were rising cumulatively to a grand crescendo: within countries, parliament after parliament was passing resolutions; students and labour unions holding massive rallies; peace marches and runs were being organised.

The Congress for Peace at Kolkata was to be held in the largest sports stadium in the city—the Vivekananda Stadium, named after one of Bengal's and India's greatest religious reformers of the nineteenth century who revealed to the world the philosophies of the Vedanta and Hinduism. It had a capacity of over seventy thousand persons, but the delegates' count had already exceeded that number, and seating outside was being organised. In addition to the formal congress, which was expected to take a unanimous resolution representing the peoples of Asia, a public rally was scheduled next day at the Maidan, the central park of Kolkata which was the traditional political meeting ground in this highly politically charged city. For the event, more than a hundred thousand persons were expected to attend.

Where in this large sea of humanity, engrossed with crossing a major historical milestone by Asia, was she to find her father, wondered Akio. But strange and unusual happenings favouring her personal quest had touched her life lately, and she was optimistic. It still was her birthday and she wished her turn of good fortune would continue.

A message from Saurav flashed soon in Akio's com-cube, informing them that he was in the hotel lobby already. When they arrived, they found Saurav along with another Bengali gentleman waiting for them.

'Meet Arnav,' said Saurav, introducing his friend. 'He is a biochemistry graduate, and I thought he might be the right person to help find your father, who studied biochemistry too, I believe.'

'Let's take the airpods—it'll be faster,' said Saurav when they got ready to leave.

There was an aerial pod taxi stand just outside connected from the hotel's second floor through a short walkway, and they didn't have to wait too long at the elevated station for one to arrive. As soon as they settled down, the pod swung away at rooftop level, negotiating smoothly through the grand buildings of Kolkata, and they arrived quickly at the riverside, where Akio noticed the sun was about to set, its glow converting the Hooghly into a vast shimmering tapestry of grey and gold.

7

A TRANSFORMED
MEGALOPOLIS

*T*he first thing the two women noticed some distance away from their country-boat on the river was a school of dolphins with their calves jumping happily around. Arnav, who was a water conservationist, explained that after many years of effort, the Ganges and its tributaries, India's largest river system, had been cleaned up and was now free from all effluents along its entire stretch. Not only were no untreated wastes being discharged, but only traditional country-boats driven by oars as this one, or river craft powered by electric motors or pollution-free energy were allowed to ply. This had regenerated the river and renewed its marine life and brought back the once nearly extinct Gangetic dolphins back to Kolkata.

For the two Japanese women, the city around them seemed to represent a unique blend of its old colonial heritage, which had been well preserved, and the ultra-modern shoots mushrooming all around. The streets were spotlessly clean, and there were lakes, parks, and an abundance of flowers and gardens everywhere. The river itself was a delight to see, its banks bordered with handsome waterfront promenades on both sides, and several high and graceful bridges linking and merging the twin cities on either side into one. While entering the city by train, they did not notice any slums or shanty towns, which had become synonymous with urban sprawls all over the developing world. What magic had been performed here?

'I think it was the people who finally took things into their hands as they felt enough was enough,' said Arnav when Mikio had put this question to the two gentlemen.

'The citizens of the city had seen the worst of everything. They had suffered one of the worst communal carnages India had seen at the time of partition of the country into India and Pakistan. They saw urban class warfare on an unprecedented scale during the Naxalite outbreak of the 1970s when hundreds were being killed daily. They suffered leftist mal-governance and labour indiscipline for over three decades which led to a full flight of capital, industries, and intelligentsia from the state, leaving its youth without jobs, eking out a living by peddling wares, making street food, driving rickshaws, and so on. The city had no revenues, garbage piled up, there was no public housing, and large armies of people lived on the pavements. Hooligans roamed around, terrorising people, and the demoralised police and civil administration had given up working. The city had pretty much reached its nadir in the early part of this century.

'Finally, a group of citizens got together and decided a poll strategy using social media which was getting increasingly influential at that time. The mobile phone had already demonstrated the ability to mobilise ordinary citizens to rally in millions on a common cause. This was used to greater effect by them.

'This citizens' group set up a party of people concerned genuinely only about the good of the state. The first thing they did after coming to power was to arrive at a social compact with labour groups, industrialists, social scientists, and environmentalists to woo back industry, particularly green industry as that was the main problem. The issue of land for industry was solved by ensuring that no one who lost land was penalised—in fact, there was a well-publicised and understood reward system set up for them and soon there was more than sufficient land available and the spectre of the industry demon gobbling up fertile land became a distant memory.

'With industry returning to its natural base—eastern India was indeed the Ruhr of the East with abundance of minerals, energy, water, skilled labour, and now a peaceful industrial environment— the state's growth rapidly accelerated. This was aided by the rapid development of neighbouring countries such as Bangladesh with which a common market had been established. The pavement dwellers quickly disappeared, and the slums transformed into decent public housing for the poor.'

'Why didn't all this happen earlier?' asked Akio.

'For a long time, the politicians called the shots, largely ignoring and misleading the people they derived power from,' said Saurav. 'Social media had a major impact in empowering the people. It was possible very quickly for a million people to espouse a cause or turn down an unwise measure. It began when people started taking interest in social issues that directly affected them. The period of genuine democracy was born.

'People realised how silly unwise policies framed by ignorant or doctrinaire politicians, often against the advice of the experts, for short-term political gains could ruin generations. Banning the learning of English in schools, for example, put generations of locals at a disadvantage in acquiring higher education and getting jobs. Opposing all land acquisition even for building roads let alone setting up factories stymied all growth. Failing to rein in labour which would strike at the drop of a hat stopped all machines from running and turned once-humming factories into haunted edifices.'

'What you are essentially suggesting,' said Akio, 'is that every generation has to take active responsibility for its own welfare. There is risk often in doing so, but that risk has to be taken. Every citizen has to speak up and not sit quietly.'

'Exactly,' said Saurav. 'Just as the time for all citizens of India and China has come to speak up and let their governments and militaries heed the voice of their peoples. Which other place to send out such a call to the citizens of both countries than here, a city whose citizens have shown the world how proactive citizenry can bring about a transformation such as this.'

A pair of dolphins jumped near their sailboat, arcing in unison. Other country-boats were also out, their occupants enjoying the evening out on the river. Their boat took them beside some famous bathing *ghats* attached to temples and the tinkle of bells could be heard, signalling that the evening *aarati* was on. In the evening, the *ghats* turned into rendezvous points for young women and men, many pairs of whom could be sitting together with different degrees of intimacy. The lilting call of a muezzin could be heard from the other bank, calling the faithful to prayer. It was altogether a very peaceful scene.

'This seems to be a very religious-minded city,' remarked Mikio.

'Very perceptive of you indeed!' remarked Saurav. 'There's some religious ceremony or other going on all the time, and the people around here are truly quite devout. There are large numbers of people of different faiths here, living in perfect harmony for over a hundred years—another very special feature of this city of joy!'

When the boat turned around, rowed vigorously by their two oarsmen, to return to the jetty, night had fallen. Saurav suggested that they dine at Park Street, which was the dazzling entertainment centre of the metropolis—a smaller version of Ginza, as Mikio remarked, when they reached the area, another aerial pod taxi having deposited them there after their sunset cruise on the river.

Arnav had made reservations for them at a rooftop Chinese restaurant called Shanghai Terrace. He had also invited his wife Mita to join the group and she was already waiting when they arrived.

After the introductions had been made, the ever-curious Mikio turned to Saurav. 'What about your wife, Saurav? When do we see her?' asked she.

'Not till I have one, I'm afraid,' said Saurav, chuckling.

The evening was getting livelier. They ordered wine and *hakka* Chinese dishes. The restaurant perched at the top of a skyscraper had a view of a glittering metro scape of tall buildings spread out all the way to the horizon. But on one side, the shimmering landscape paused, giving way to the vast darkness of the tree-canopied *maidan*, over which stood only the grand marble dome of the Victoria Memorial, lit up in slowly changing colours. Further still, diminished considerably by distance, stood the Howrah Bridge, its lights a necklace of pearls straddling the Hooghly.

The restaurant was full, and there was considerable chatter and laughter all around. Mikio announced that since it was Akio's birthday, she would pay for the dinner and asked for a birthday cake to be brought to the table before the dinner was laid out. The day had been going wonderfully well for Akio, and she hoped this spell would last. And when she blew out the candles, it was easy to guess what her birthday wish would be.

After the dishes had arrived, Arnav turned the conversation somewhat reluctantly to Akio's search for her father.

'This may be totally premature and entirely off the mark, but I have been getting messages on my com-cube ever since Saurav asked me to spread the word around through my biochemistry network, and one response looked to be particularly promising. A person called Siddhartha Roy who roughly matches the photograph attended a Tokyo university around the time Akio's father was there.'

'That's wonderful!' Akio said excitedly. 'Can't we contact him?'

'One of my colleagues already has,' said Arnav. 'The problem is that Siddhartha Roy denies vehemently that he ever had a daughter. Worse still, he has refused flatly to meet you, Akio.'

8

THE PEACE CONGRESS

'Citizens of our great continent of Asia, and of India and China, the two largest countries of the world who face a crucial choice this week that will set the course of the world's history, and delegates who have come from all corners of the world to attend this historic event—my greetings and good wishes to you!' read Akio from the speech of the sixteenth Dalai Lama.

She was a bit nervous, standing on the podium before this packed audience of almost a hundred thousand people from across the globe. Beginning a little hesitantly, she gained in confidence slowly, however, as the speech progressed, feeling the words finding resonance with the listeners.

'I am deeply grateful to the organisers of this momentous event for your invitation to me—a humble Tibetan monk with no powerful armies behind me but with just lots of wise words to offer,' continued Akio, pausing at the laughter to die down. 'I send you this brief message through the kindness of a friend as I am unable to be present in person. She came to meet me just when I needed such a person to convey my message. I feel this is divine providence. Belonging to the only country which has witnessed the mass slaughter and unthinkable tragedy that a nuclear holocaust can wreak, she would give greater eloquence to my few words to you.

'That event was not only a disaster of colossal magnitude for Japan but it was a catastrophe of even greater proportion for humanity, a blight on its soul. No sane person can ever consider a repeat of the events of 1945. But insanity still lingers. We have therefore come a few times since to the brink of such a precipice, but have been saved through luck according to some but more likely through good sense, in my view. The innate goodness that is present in all humans has protected us.

'The peoples of the two great nations of China and India now face a great test, and the world is hoping that this innate goodness, this divine spark that resides in every person who makes a decision this week will prevail. These two giant neighbours, though dissimilar in many respects, have been tied by strong bonds of culture and religion through the ages and more lately through the links of industry and commerce. Yet lingering discord, distrust, and hostility have often weakened those bonds.

'The world has seen, however, how logic and reason tempered with patience and goodwill can help solve many seemingly intractable problems between nations such as India and China. They have settled their boundaries finally, which was a festering sore in their relations for a century. Similar differences, should they arise in the future, can be resolved again peaceably without rancour, violence, or conflict.

'There can be no place for weapons of mass destruction in a civilised world. The last century was one of wars—this must be one of peace. The beat of the war drum must be replaced with the melody of harmony, trust, and amity.

'There are those that caution against total destruction of nuclear weapons, saying that the world will remain defenceless against rise of tyrants and satanic forces or nations that heed no logic and reason and keep defying the world time and again. They term peacemakers as foolish idealists who will weaken governments and their deterrents against such forces. But it is idealists and humanists who have brought the world forward, not warmongers. As the first half of this century has witnessed, the destroyers of world peace and order have been contained and vanquished without the terrible use of nuclear weapons. New knowledge and technology have given righteous defenders of peace the means to combat and confound such demons without causing hurt to innocents.

'I firmly believe that we are progressing towards a far more rational, civil, and non-violent world order than before. This is the vision that all delegates to the congress share. They bring messages from all corners of the world, from ordinary citizens to entire parliaments of their countries seeking to realise such a dream.

'The twin referendums place the responsibility for creating such a civilised world order on every adult citizen of China and India. The time for making a decision has come. Each person who presses the voting button must choose between allowing their nations to continue holding on to weapons that can kill and maim millions of innocent people—or ensuring such nightmarish possibilities which the world has witnessed once never occur again.

'I am confident that all of you who hold the destiny of the planet in your hands will make the right decision.

'I thank you all.'

Akio bowed deeply, and the entire house erupted in deafening applause. One by one, the delegates stood up, clapping and cheering till the entire audience was on its feet. The ovation did not end till Akio left the podium and went back to her seat, bowing, smiling, and when Mikio hugged her, she realised, crying too, all at the same time.

9

THE PEACE RALLY

'*I* have nothing more to do. I have done my bit, and I am returning to Tokyo,' announced Akio at breakfast. 'It was too fanciful of me to expect that a man who had forsaken all contact with us will relent.'

Akio had indeed played her part in the congress, as had Mikio, who as part of the drafting committee prepared and released a resolution to the world media from the Peace Congress urging the people of India and China to vote for peace, and calling on the two governments to destroy their nuclear stockpiles. The drafting had gone through many versions long into the night. There were no other assigned roles for them to play, and they were free to return, except that later that afternoon there was to be a public rally at the *maidan* in support of the resolution, with speakers from home and abroad, political parties, and the citizens of the metropolis long known for their liberal views who were expected to show their support through a massive turnout—police expecting over half a million people to gather there. It wasn't an event they would have wanted to miss.

'Don't give up this easily, Akio,' Mikio advised. 'We must find out more about Siddhartha Roy and the reason why he has avoided all contact with your mother. We must at least clear up the mystery surrounding all of this. Why your mother, for instance, also on her part, kept it a secret from everybody and denied his existence to both her daughter and her mother.'

The Bakery, where they were breakfasting, had become quite crowded, and they were lucky to have arrived early and found places. People were still looking around for vacant chairs at tables. The old Japanese gentleman they had seen at the Bakery their first day at the hotel came up to them and bowed. Both women got up and bowed deeply in return.

'That was a great speech you read out yesterday,' said he to Akio. 'Rendered with feeling. Congratulations!'

He was also obviously looking for a place to sit, so they asked him to join them at their table. He left to get his breakfast. As soon as he had settled in, he wanted to know how Akio had come to be selected by the Dalai Lama for the rare honour of reading his message to the congress. Mikio filled him in with the details, and he was suitably impressed. They made polite conversation, and as the ladies had finished their breakfast, they got up to leave, pausing to exchange cards.

It was Mikio who noted that the gentleman—Shoji Akimura— was a retired professor of biochemistry from the Technological University of Tokyo and so she immediately sat down again. Akio followed. Mikio was hoping that this chance encounter might lead to something.

'Prof. Akimura, universities with biochemistry departments in Tokyo have been part of our constant conversation for the last few days,' she explained. 'Were you teaching in the Technological University of Tokyo by any chance around 2020 or so?'

'I joined the biochemistry faculty in 2022. But why do you ask?' said Prof. Akimura.

Mikio explained very briefly about Akio's missing father and his connection with Tokyo, where he had gone from Kolkata to pursue a Ph.D. in genetics but left suddenly and how Akio's enquiries had provided only vague clues so far. 'Does the name Siddhartha Roy ring a bell, by any chance?' she asked.

'Unfortunately not . . . besides, it is quite long ago,' the professor said, trying to recall names and events from decades past. 'But let me do something to help. I'll get in touch right away with some of my colleagues who were involved with research work on genetics. We all took particular interest in all our foreign students, and someone may remember the case of an Indian student around that time who didn't complete studies. That would be a rare occurrence, considering that the foreign students from India were generally all very bright as they were usually admitted on scholarships. I am returning to Tokyo this morning, and I'll call you if I hear something,' he concluded, not seeming to hold out much hope.

Back in their room, Mikio suggested they try and get in touch with Arnav's friend who had contacted Siddhartha Roy, to learn more about him. They had some time to spare in the morning with the rally at the maidan only beginning in the afternoon. The remaining time they had in Kolkata was rapidly depleting, and they had to make the most of it. Saurav too was leaving soon after the rally and returning to his institute and so their main resource in Kolkata for the search would be unavailable thereafter.

Fortunately, Arnav, who was at work, responded as soon as contacted by Akio. 'Come to the coffee house near College Square after the rally,' he said, 'and I'll meet you there around seven. Take the moving walkways—they should get you to College Square in a jiffy. I assume Saurav will be with you, so you won't have any trouble locating me. If we are lucky, we may find some answers today.'

Arnav rang off, being in a hurry to go somewhere, but his concluding words seemed to indicate that he was hoping to unravel some of the mystery behind the enigmatic Mr Roy. Akio's state of expectation was heightened many degrees on hearing him. But Akio's thoughts were drawn soon to the rally, and she was momentarily distracted from her personal concern.

The rally went beyond all expectations. It seemed to have generated a spontaneous outburst of feeling, fuelled by the months of hype by the media of the upsurge of Asian opinion that all conflict must finally end. People came out in hundreds of thousands from their homes to join the processions organised by citizens' organisations, trade unions, NGOs, women's groups, and hundreds of other people's organisations. The multitude converged onto the Brigade Parade Ground, a part of the *maidan* that is the traditional rally venue of Kolkata. The ocean of humanity soon occupied every part of the vast open space, and both the Japanese women felt thrilled to be part of this great movement, indeed a quiet revolution that the ordinary folk had wrought. And although a far vaster gathering of people voicing their support had occurred in cyberspace that numbered in the tens of millions, humans still needed the reassurance of physical demonstrations such as this to provide them the comfort that their common intent was shared by all.

The crowd erupted in a roar of applause when the first speaker's words came over the loudspeakers. He was an American ex-president from Chicago, a prominent peacemaker, and the recipient of a Nobel Peace Prize, working tirelessly around the world for disarmament, despite his very advanced age.

'Sisters and brothers of India,' he began, echoing the words of Swami Vivekananda, the Indian monk at the Chicago Congress of Religions a century and a half previously. 'A famous son of India hailing from Kolkata brought the message of friendship, peace, and the wisdom of the ancient Hindu religion to the Western world at the beginning of the twentieth century. I have made an opposite journey to this great city of intellectuals, writers, poets, filmmakers, saints, and spiritualists. Unlike Vivekananda, however, who brought the ancient wisdom of the East to the West, I have merely come seeking to rekindle in this land its own knowledge and traditions that for millennia after millennia have taught the world tolerance, acceptance, and understanding.' Then, pausing and spreading his arms wide, embracing the entire audience stretching limitless before him, he added, 'But I see that you have already—in this great city and nation—set yourselves on the course of peace.'

The mammoth crowd cheered loudly in appreciation; its reverberation must have been heard miles around, and continued in similar vein as other speakers, each a well-known local or international personality, rose and addressed them. The entire Indian and Chinese media as well as reporters from almost every important media house around the world were ranged around the raised podium, and they instantly relayed the messages emanating from the rally that afternoon. In almost every home in the country, people were watching the rally electronically. In several cities in India, processions and rallies were also being held in support. Only a few hours separated this moment from the referendum which was to take place the next day.

The rally ended a few minutes past sunset. The glow from the sunken sun still lit up the sky in many wondrous hues and reflected on the glass panes of the skyscrapers on Chowringhee. The two companions along with Saurav decided to sit for a while on a bench at a park adjoining the maidan, allowing the crowd to disperse and the moving pavements to become less crowded.

Suddenly, Akio's com-cube started flashing, indicating that there was a message for her. Converting it to a reading tablet, she saw that Prof. Akimura had sent her a message.

'Akio-san, I found this after making some enquiries among my colleagues in Tokyo, but it wasn't easy,' it stated. 'It is an internal memo forwarded to me by a former professor. Therefore, please use the utmost discretion regarding its contents. But as it would be wrong to keep it from you as you are directly concerned with the matter, I thought I must share it with you. It is from a former professor who was requested to make an independent enquiry on the case of an Indian research scholar by a university in Tokyo. It may answer some of your questions.' There was a longish attachment with it which Akio started reading with growing excitement. The mystery of her father was beginning to unravel at last.

10

SOME ANSWERS

$\mathcal{T}$he attached memo contained a summary of the findings of an enquiry committee set up in 2015 by the university in Tokyo that Siddhartha Roy had attended. It was in Japanese and the first part read as follows:

> This one-member enquiry committee has been set up on a special request by the Board of Governors of the university to examine the circumstances under which Mr Siddhartha Roy, Indian graduate student at the Department of Genetics, left his research work uncompleted and returned to India. The Board of Governors is particularly concerned that Mr Roy was known to be a student of exceptional ability and some faculty members felt that it may have been the result of an academic disagreement that was not properly handled. As the university has been encouraging the education of international students, this matter has been taken seriously, and the enquiry committee has been requested to examine all issues that led to this unfortunate result, with a view to remedying them, particularly improving the learning and living environment for foreign students to make their association with our university rewarding and pleasant, a reputation it has always enjoyed.

This enquiry committee went into all aspects of the matter. The fellowship Mr Roy earned was supported by a Government of Japan grant and amply covered all expenses. A number of graduate students who were Mr Roy's contemporaries were also interviewed, and Mr Roy was reported to have had a friendly relationship with all, although he appeared to stay aloof more than socialise. They did not indicate that they were aware of any personal crisis of any nature which would have caused Mr Roy to abandon his studies. Whether the requirement of acquiring proficiency in Japanese had caused additional stress to Mr Roy and interfered with his research was also enquired into but was dismissed as a possible factor as Mr Roy appeared to have mastered Japanese and conversed quite fluently in Japanese with his friends and colleagues within a year of his arrival. Therefore, no additional stress was caused to him on the language requirement as it usually does to all foreign students (a factor that is being remedied by the university now).

The focus of the enquiry was therefore mainly confined to the academic matter about which the Board of Governors had been informed. The first unnatural factor was that Mr Roy has been pursuing his research much longer than the average at the department, which is usually three to four years. Mr Roy had completed six years and eight months when he left his research work and returned home. Most of his contemporaries had completed their theses well within the period Mr Roy was in the department and were either in employment in Japan or abroad.

This enquiry committee discussed Mr Roy's academic work with his thesis adviser Prof. Tadao Hori at length. Prof. Hori was extremely complimentary about Mr Roy's academic abilities and described him as 'one of the best brains' that he had encountered. After lengthy discussions with Prof. Hori and the senior faculty of the department, this enquiry committee has come to the following conclusions:

(i)   Mr Roy had chosen an exceptionally difficult topic which, although it could have advanced knowledge in his field quite significantly, was fraught with risk. Normally such topics which question existing knowledge are rarely taken up by doctoral students, owing to their risk of rejection and are usually assigned to post-doctoral students. Prof. Hori had apparently advised Mr Roy not to pursue this line of research, but Mr Roy appeared to be passionate about his choice and could not be persuaded. In retrospect, Prof. Hori felt that he should have been more assertive.

(ii)   Mr Roy's research tended to directly contradict the work of Nobel Prize recipient Prof. Rudolf Scalia, who is a Distinguished Visitor to this department and university and an external examiner. Early results from Mr Roy's work that the department shared with Prof. Scalia were rejected by Prof. Scalia, and Mr Roy was therefore requested time and again to come up with more convincing and confirmatory evidence to support his findings.

(iii)   The department's dissertation committee seemed to have been hesitant to accept Mr Roy's work in the light of Prof. Scalia's strong objections, although Prof. Hori personally tried to convince them. Prof. Hori, naturally, did not divulge the efforts he was making with the dissertation committee to Mr Roy as he did not want Mr Roy to know about the internal discussions and differences within the dissertation committee, all decisions of which are made unanimously. Prof. Hori feels that this may have alienated Mr Roy with him personally, although Prof. Hori remained convinced of the quality of Mr Roy's research work and tried to continue to encourage him.

(iv)   This enquiry committee thereafter perused in considerable detail the research notes Mr Roy has left behind. Several samples from his experiments do vindicate Mr Roy's stand. However, whether this sample set is adequate or not and whether more work over a longer period is needed to provide convincing evidence is a matter of judgement and different positions can be taken. The view of this enquiry committee, however, is that the department should

have taken a more independent stance and rewarded
Mr Roy for his initial results rather than create an
impression to him based on Prof. Scalia's objections
that the quality of his work was inadequate when in
fact quite the opposite was true.

The remaining part of the report suggested norms the university
should follow in future to assess the quality of its research etc., etc.,
which did not interest Akio.

But the information in the report provided sufficient clues as
to why a research student such as Siddhartha Roy might have left
Japan, intensely disappointed with his studies at the university.
Throughout the journey to College Square, Akio kept thinking about
the matter, and the others left her alone to ruminate. Any highly
involved scholar, particularly an introvert with few friends, living in a
vastly different cultural environment compared to his own, pursuing
single-mindedly a sole objective over seven long years, producing
brilliant work in the end without appreciation or reward would have
left in disgust, she felt, and justifiably so. It was also conceivable that
the disappointment he felt could have clouded his vision of the entire
world around him and everything Japanese—of his thesis adviser,
his department, and even (Akio had to accept this fact) his Japanese
girlfriend.

11

COFFEE HOUSE

When Akio and her companions arrived through the now less crowded moving pavements at the College Square, it was already dark, but the square and the stately buildings surrounding it were brightly lit.

'This is the intellectual heart of the city,' explained Saurav as they got off the travelator and walked the short remaining distance to their destination. 'The major universities and colleges that are located around here date back to the early nineteenth century. And now it is a tourist hub too, as you can see.'

The area belonged to an older part of the city with Victorian-era houses restored to their former looks and narrow lanes which had been pedestrianised and were lined with bookstores, cafes, antique dealers, and flower shops. The city had retained its tramway, mostly for tourism purposes, and an electric tram—its looks virtually unchanged over a hundred years—came clanging down the street. It stopped near them, and a whole lot of tourists got off. The square had a large lake in the middle, bordered with gardens and a walkway. The streets and the entire area around the square were lit with gas lamps which had been reintroduced, explained Saurav, as part of the restoration work in the area.

'I am told that fifty years back, the old city was entirely run-down, its houses crumbling, its streets taken over by hawkers and squatters,' said Saurav. 'The view of the lake in this square was totally blocked by slums. The students in the institutions around, however, took the initiative to clean up the area and then the colleges and universities pitched in.'

'Something like this happened in Kyoto too,' said Mikio. 'From an old and decaying town, it's now the top tourist destination in Japan.'

'And finally we have arrived at Kolkata's renowned College Street Coffee House, the mecca of all artists, writers, and intellectuals in this city,' said Saurav. They had reached the entrance of what looked like an old theatre house or community hall with several elegant bookstores on its ground floor. The Albert Hall, as it was originally called, was later converted to a cafe about two hundred years back.

The cafe comprised a very large hall, its tables crowded with customers on the first floor, and a somewhat less crowded balcony area overlooking the hall on the second floor, where Arnav was waiting for them. A turbaned and liveried waiter came to take their orders, and they asked for mutton coverage cutlets and cups of cold coffee with cream, which were the most popular fares of the place.

Arnav, aware that Akio was impatiently waiting to hear more about her parent, paused for the waiter to bring the orders before disclosing the new information he had acquired about Siddhartha Roy. Again, the source was one of Siddhartha Roy's college friends who had somehow kept in touch with him. Apparently, Mr Roy had deliberately avoided his former contacts after returning from Japan, and this was one among the very few persons whom he occasionally turned to for some professional advice on matters he was working on.

This was the same friend who had mentioned to Siddhartha Roy about Akio and been rebuffed. Siddhartha Roy had apparently totally ridiculed the idea that he could have any grown-up daughter and was convinced that it was a case of mistaken identity.

'But where is he now and what is he doing?' a very impatient Akio wanted to know.

'I hope we will have some answers soon,' said Arnav, getting up and leaving the table to meet a person who was standing at the doorway, looking around at the tables, trying to guess who Arnav could be. The gentleman was in his late fifties with a shock of white hair and dark glasses. He carried a cloth bag on his shoulder, the hallmark still of an avant-garde Bengali intellectual.

Arnav brought the gentleman to the table and introduced him. 'This is Shekhar Dutta, the person I was talking about. You can hear the rest of Siddhartha Roy's story directly from him.'

12

MYSTERY UNRAVELLING

$\mathcal{A}$fter the introductions had been made, Shekhar Dutta requested that he be left alone with Akio, and when the others had discreetly moved away to another table, he ordered a cappuccino and began recounting the story of Siddhartha Roy.

'I realised how nerve-wracking this must have been for you,' he told Akio, 'to feel that you are so near to discovering who your father is, yet Siddhartha not wanting to meet you. So I felt I had to come and see you, however difficult it may be. You see, I live quite far out in the suburbs—I had to change trains twice to come—and wasn't sure I could make it and so I didn't want Arnav to tell you that I would be here.

'I told Siddhartha that you had a copy of his photograph from his university days in Tokyo. And now seeing you, Akio, I am sure that you are Siddhartha's daughter—the family resemblance is striking. And I think after I let him know about this, he may also relent. Apparently, your mother never disclosed to Siddhartha that she had conceived you at the time he decided to leave, and he had not kept in touch with her or, for that matter, anyone connected with academics in Japan or in India. It is really hard to understand him being and living always as an enigma.

'Siddhartha hasn't told me the full story of what happened in Tokyo. But all I know is that he suddenly seemed to take a total dislike to research and academic pursuits. Perhaps you know more about that side of the story than me. It was several years after he had returned that he contacted me. He was doing some work on drought-resistant crops and wanted my advice as I had been working on genetic engineering of crops myself.

'He called me out of the blue one day and told me that he was living and working with tribal folk in the Chhotanagpur hills, and his work with them was much more rewarding than research and academics and directly benefiting people. He seemed to be quite happy. He appeared to be getting good results with his drought-resistant varieties of wheat and millet particularly. Those were the years when global warming was at its peak, and many parts of India were facing heat waves and long spells of drought.

'It wasn't just farming practices that he was helping the tribal peasants with, but also use of new technology to access education and health and build low-cost homes. He once asked me to help him get in touch with doctors in Kolkata as he was setting up a telemedicine platform to enable the villagers obtain access to top-notch doctors and specialists.

'These were infrequent contacts, and many years have passed since he began this type of work. He rarely visited Kolkata, so it's been years—five or six—since I last met him.'

Akio had been listening with rapt attention to this sudden flood of information about her father and did not want to interrupt the flow. However, on learning that Siddhartha Roy wasn't in Kolkata, where she held out hopes, even though slim, of meeting him, she broke in.

'So he's not living in Kolkata?' she asked, quite disappointed that the door she thought had opened on Siddhartha Roy appeared to shutting once again.

'No, he doesn't seem to have a settled place of residence. He's been doing a lot of work with different groups of villagers, mainly tribes. As a result of his good work, several state governments in India have been hiring him frequently of late as an expert on tribal development. I'll try and get in touch with him, although it's always difficult to track him, and let you know. I think right now he may be in Varanasi.'

'The ancient holy city?' asked Akio.

'Exactly. But it's not too far from Kolkata—just about an hour's journey by air but also connected very well with our new high-speed maglev trains. You could consider a visit actually. How much longer were you planning to stay in India?'

Akio hadn't considered the possibility of travelling anywhere beyond Kolkata. But now that it arose, she said, 'I have a flight out to Tokyo tomorrow, which makes that quite impossible. Besides, he's not keen to meet me and may continue to refuse seeing me,' she said.

'With Siddhartha Roy, this is distinctly possible, and I shouldn't give you any false hopes. But I think you should take the risk of trying to meet him. Couldn't you defer your return by a couple of days? After all, having come this far, why hesitate taking the final step?'

'But what of his family?' Akio asked. 'How would they react? I am a little anxious on that score too.'

'Oh, I should have told you about this. I don't think Siddhartha is married—at least in all his infrequent communications with me over the years, he never mentioned about any marriage. He seems to be a modern-day *sanyasin*.'

'*Sanyasin*?' queried Akio. She hadn't heard of the term.

'It refers to a person who renounces his worldly life and family and lives like a hermit preoccupied with holy work or helping others. It is a tradition with some religions that arose from the Indian subcontinent such as Hinduism, Jainism, and Buddhism.'

'Such as Buddha?' she ventured, 'who left his kingdom, wife, and infant son to pursue the life of an ascetic?'

'Yes. Like Siddhartha Gautama, after whom your father is named,' said Shekhar Dutta.

13

GIANT LEAPS
TOWARDS PEACE

*R*ushing in her superfast maglev express through the vast Gangetic plains towards Varanasi, Akio realised that the outcomes of two immensely important enterprises that she had undertaken would be revealed that day: the global peace mission, of which she was a miniscule part, and her effort to locate her father.

As her train traversed villages and towns rapidly on the way to her destination, she wondered which way the people in those humble dwellings, tiny apartments, or affluent homes speeding by were deciding on their own fate and that of their country and the world. Gone were the days when people were required to queue up in long lines at polling stations. Now, most were voting from the comfort of their homes by transmitting their unique identification codes through cyber links and making their choices. The very few who did not possess access to the array of electronic alternatives available to vote had to trudge still to the nearest community hall or school where polling continued in the old-fashioned way.

Across the Himalayas, in China too, their mammoth populace was engaged in a similar exercise. By the close of the day, the results of both the referendums would be known.

But while the world would collectively celebrate or suffer on hearing those outcomes, the result of her personal quest would be hers to deal with alone. Mikio, her close and constant companion so far on this journey, couldn't stay on, and Saurav too had to return to look after the affairs of the Institute of Humanity. Akio couldn't really be sure whether their unavoidable preoccupations were genuine or made to appear so as to allow her the private space she needed at this time.

Mikio, of course, she would meet soon on return to Tokyo and the apartment they shared. Saurav had also gone, leaving his calling card behind and a surprise offer.

'We are looking for a research fellow at the institute,' he had said when they were alone together having a late-night coffee at the Bakery in the hotel a couple of nights previously. 'Perhaps you could consider the position if you are interested?'

Mikio had retired for the night as she had to catch the flight back early in the morning. Akio had decided to stay on a week longer. She had heeded Shekhar Dutta's advice and stayed on to take that final step, whatever its outcome. He was yet to get back to her with Siddhartha Roy's whereabouts, but she decided to stay put at the hotel a couple of days or so more and await further advice from him.

Before saying his final goodbyes, Saurav suggested that they stroll over to the Bakery for a chat.

'But I may not be qualified,' replied Akio, quite surprised at his offer.

'Oh yes, you are Dr Akio Nishimoto,' said Saurav. 'In this day and age, it's quite difficult to hide one's accomplishments. I have done a little research of your qualifications, and I find you are eminently suited. We are also trying to get more international faculty interested in our programs. This is not an idle offer.'

'Well, thanks for the offer, but . . . I have to decline,' said Akio. 'I am already exploring returning to Nagoya to be with my grandmother, who needs my care. Besides, I have too many things to consider right now to give any serious thought to this.'

'Of course, I understand perfectly,' said Saurav. 'Here is my card, and if you ever consider doing some work in our institute's areas of expertise in the future, please get in touch.'

'Thank you so much for all your help!' said Akio. 'I would never have been able to find my father's whereabouts without you.'

Akio initially considered a formal bow but then switched to a handshake instead. Saurav grasped her hand warmly and then left, looking back momentarily at the exit to wave briefly to her before disappearing into the night.

Was that the last she had seen of Dr Saurav Bandopadhyay, wondered Akio while her train raced speedily towards the holy city of Varanasi. What had caused him to take a special interest in her, she thought to herself, enough to want her in his Institute? Was he trying to be generally helpful—she was aware that he felt obligated to help her, given the Dalai Lama's request, but was it merely that? Was he really interested in her only as a potentially valuable academic researcher for his institute? Or was it more than that?

Life seemed to be a set of riddles to Akio at that point. When you try to solve one, another crops up. But the one concerning her father would soon be resolved, she felt, if she was lucky. And so far, her luck had held up. Throughout her life, she had wanted to find out about her father and then when she had learnt that he was possibly alive, she wanted to resolve the mystery behind his disappearance, and—she did not allow herself to hope but should there be even an iota of that possibility—to be accepted and loved by him. This had become her primary need—almost an obsession.

Now, one by one, the facts about her father's strange abandonment of his girlfriend with whom he had shared the closest of intimacies, and his life in Japan were becoming clear. Having come very close to major discoveries in knowledge after working tirelessly many years, and not to have these findings accepted would have devastated many a scholar. This could have caused him to renounce the world around him and seek solace in other places. But why abandon his girlfriend?

It was clear that Siddhartha Roy wasn't aware that his girlfriend had conceived and quite possible she had refrained from telling him when it became clear that he had made up his mind to leave everything and work with the tribals of India. This might have been particularly so in order not to deter him from the life that he now wanted and she couldn't share. Or seeing the strange animosity Siddhartha Roy had developed to everything she held dear, she might have wanted to end their relationship of her own accord. Either was possible.

But there was no need to speculate, Akio felt, as hopefully she would have some of the answers soon.

While she waited impatiently for the train to reach its destination, and these riddles in her personal life to be answered by her previously lost parent, should he agree to meet her, the answers to the large public question of the outcome of the twin referendums kept pouring in bit by bit in her com-cube. With each message that flashed on her device, more results were being announced.

By the time the train had reached the bridge on the River Ganga and began slowing down before entering the Varanasi station, the trend was quite clear. The result for India was as she had anticipated after seeing the public mood in Kolkata. With nearly two thirds of votes compiled, 61 per cent had voted yes to the proposition whether India should destroy its entire nuclear arsenal.

What she had not anticipated was the Chinese result. There nearly 80 per cent of the votes had come in, and the yes vote for destroying its nuclear stockpile was a resounding 89 per cent!

As the train pulled into the station, the celebrations had begun. She could hear the sounds of firecrackers bursting around the city. As she slung on her backpack and stepped on the platform, an impromptu bhangra dance was on, the dancers cheered on by an appreciative crowd.

Witnessing these spontaneous public celebrations signalling a major success on the road to world peace, Akio wondered, as she made her way to the crowded concourse outside, whether there was even a slim possibility that her personal quest too would meet with similar success.

14

AN ANCIENT CITY

*T*he electric taxi meandered through the crowded streets and lanes of the old city, which seemed to have remained in a time warp, unchanged through the centuries. The taxi itself was an anachronism, as many metropolises such as Kolkata had dispensed altogether with cars. The ancient buildings in various shapes and sizes, some majestic and some modest, many with ornate facades and verandas, clung close to each other. Twisting narrow lanes, weaving in between them, busy with all manner of tiny shops, disappeared into a confusing labyrinth of narrow passages that made up much of the ancient part of the city.

Because of the heavy traffic, the taxi made very slow progress. Akio had only the address passed on by Shekhar Dutta, who had informed the manager of the dharmashala, a boarding house for pilgrims where Siddhartha Roy lived when in Varanasi, about Akio's arrival. The manager had confirmed that he was still there. But there was no word from Siddhartha Roy himself. She was therefore still uncertain whether she would be able to meet him, but had decided to take the chance.

The taxi entered a narrow street filled with pilgrims making their way to the many temples and ghats—the broad flights of steps leading to the river. But the houses, tenements, and temples that bordered the riverbank blocked her view of the Ganga still. The taxi stopped in front of an old three-story building, the dharmashala where Siddhartha Roy lived.

She had arrived finally, a pilgrim like millions of others before her, following in their footsteps, doing as they had done through the ages, equally in search of peace and fulfilment.

But she was beset with anxiety. After searching for nearly two decades, she was at the doorstep of her father's home. Would he accept her, or turn her away? She dared not think of the disappointment and anguish that would overwhelm her should the worst happen. She only dreamt of the unspeakable joy that she would feel if he accepted her. With beating heart, she climbed the steps to the manager's room.

The manager received her kindly, seeing that she had come a long way. Siddhartha Roy was still a resident, he confirmed, and had received her message. But he was out, having left soon after receiving information of her coming. But this was not unusual as he kept leaving and returning during the day as his preoccupations necessitated. The manager informed her, however, that he never missed the Ganga Aarti—the evening worship conducted on the riverbank daily in praise of the Ganga and that she should therefore wait a while.

A wide terrace overlooking the broad expanse of the ever-flowing Ganga was where he asked her to sit. From the terrace, a very large ghat could be seen, its numerous steps leading to the river on which a large variety of boats and river craft were moored. Multicoloured bamboo umbrellas under which pilgrims performed their prayers were arrayed across the steps. The manager explained, bringing a cup of tea for her, that this was the famous Dasashwamedha Ghat built according to legend by Lord Brahma himself, the creator of the universe, to receive Lord Shiva the destroyer, from whose matted locks sprung the mighty River Ganga.

The twilight afterglow tinged everything she could see—the sky, the assortment of buildings, the many temples with their fluttering pennants—with a soft auroral hue. The auspicious hour was nigh, Akio realised.

Her thought appeared to set off the blowing of the first conch shell, its long lone note echoing all around. This was followed by several others. The temple bells began to ring, and the cymbals began their rhythmic clash. A row of priests wearing white dhotis and chadars took their positions on the upper steps of the ghat, lit their brazen lamps, and began the aarti, circling their brightly lit lamps facing the river. Melodious chanting of *shlokas* in Sanskrit by other priests accompanied their ritual, witnessed now by thousands of pilgrims sitting on the steps and a great number also looking on from the boats.

'What are they chanting?' enquired Akio of the manager.

'It is a prayer to the Ganga,' he said. While the chanting rolled out, he translated the words for her.

> O Goddess Ganga! Divine river from heaven,
> Saviour of all the Three Worlds,
> Pure and restless
> You flow impatiently towards the vast ocean
> Like a lover anxious to meet her beloved.
>
> Giver of happiness, the Vedas sing praises of your sacred streams
> You destroy all sins; you are full of compassion.
> You purify your devotees with your holy waters.
> You save them from perdition.
> Your feet are adorned with the gems of Indra's crown.
> Those who seek refuge in you are blessed with happiness.
>
> O Mother! May my mind always rest at your feet.
> Take away my illnesses, O Bhagirati,
> Remove my sins, sorrows, troubles, and morbidities.
> O Devi full of mercy, protect me.
> You alone are my refuge in this world
> With its never-ending cycle of births and deaths.

O Ganga! O Jahnavi! O Bhagirati! O Mother!
Praise to Thee![31]

Would this river which had provided solace to millions of souls over the aeons, also bring comfort to her, thought Akio. There was something in the permanence of this ancient city and the wide flowing river which seemed to reflect the indestructability of humanity and its quest for immortality. The realisation that she was a part of this infinite continuum appeared to bring her some calm.

It had become quite dark. After reaching a crescendo, the Ganga Aarti ended, and suddenly, all was quiet. A few stars appeared in the sky. Far away in the distance along the riverbank, the glow from several funeral pyres became visible—a reminder to the devout of their belief in the never-ending cycle of life.

'Extremely sorry to keep you waiting,' said a voice behind her.

On turning around, Akio saw Siddhartha Roy walking towards her across the long terrace.

15

A PARENT FOUND

*T*hey stepped towards each other tentatively, each not knowing how to break the gulf of time and silence that had stood between them and their relationship. That there was a relationship was not in doubt the instant they saw each other. Akio looked remarkably like Siddhartha Roy, a fact that the latter noted immediately.

He took her hand in his gently and held her close to him. Akio couldn't hold back the tears that flooded her eyes. Before she knew it, she was sobbing uncontrollably, a thing that had never happened to her in her adult life. Siddhartha Roy made her sit down. His own eyes were moistening too, seeing Akio. How his daughter must have suffered all these years, he thought to himself. They were silent for a long time, as Akio struggled to regain her composure.

'When I learnt that someone calling herself my daughter was looking for me, I was in utter disbelief. No word from anyone all these twenty years and then suddenly this information . . . I hope you understand why I dismissed the idea and suggested that there must have been a mistake,' said Siddhartha Roy after Akio had taken hold of herself.

'But as more information started coming in since your arrival, filling in the numerous blanks in our lives, many things have become clear to me,' he continued. And then after a long pause, he added, sighing, 'I didn't even know about your mother . . . that she has passed away. Nobody informed me.'

On the peacefully flowing river, a floating earthen lamp released by a devotee flickered in the water, joined later by several others, partly dispelling the darkness. In Akio's mind too, the shadows were lifting as they talked about Siddhartha Roy's past, but some unanswered questions remained, nevertheless.

'There are several mysteries in our lives that still need answers,' said Akio, the hurt that had built up within her all these years apparent in her voice. 'Why was your disappointment with your research so traumatic that it made you leave everything and come away? Why didn't you keep in touch with each other? What made my mother keep her conceiving me a secret from you? Why did she never disclose to me that I had a father living?'

Siddhartha Roy was silent for a long time, carefully considering the questions that Akio had put to him. 'Your mother was an extremely independent-minded person, as you know,' said he, breaking his silence. 'We were colleagues in the research lab, and the long hours together in the workplace threw us together. And finally, we were drawn to each other romantically and physically. Our growing relationship was interrupted, however, by a set of events at the lab.

'You correctly term my disappointment at not receiving the recognition I felt I deserved as a trauma. It made me feel utter disgust at the superficiality of the honour and fame that I was pursuing— stemming from nothing but intellectual arrogance. What was I actually achieving, I questioned myself, and couldn't I do much, much more for the world with the effort I had invested in all those years, resulting in just a few more paltry strands of scientific knowledge?

'I decided that I had to leave and start a new and more meaningful life. Your mother fully understood my views and supported my decision. She had her own life to lead and would not have felt fulfilled with the type of life I pursued subsequently here. We therefore agreed to part, never having established any formal bond, fully understanding each other.

'I now realise why she kept her pregnancy a secret from me. Disclosing it would have caused me to hesitate in the path I was taking and might have changed my decision. She didn't want me to look back.

'She therefore must have kept the knowledge of you, Akio, away from me and didn't also keep in touch with me for the same reason. Any contact between us could have led sometime or other to the unravelling of her secret. She wanted perhaps to raise you by herself. She must have felt fully capable of it, and so never disclosed to you either about my existence.'

'But why did my mother not tell me the real truth about you? I feel most terribly hurt about that,' said Akio.

'I think you are judging her too harshly, Akio,' said Siddhartha Roy. 'There are many things a child would not understand which an adult would. Had she lived till you were older, I am sure she would have told you all about us.'

Akio considered all these revelations quietly. They had cleared up much of the mysteries of her past life. But while she had finally found her father, the yearning to be loved by him—a vital need of her existence, missing throughout her life but now made possible at last by finding him—was acute. She needed to discover more about him and what he felt about her.

'Are you happy leading this lonely existence?' she therefore asked.

'I am content,' he replied. 'And I am not lonely. I live and work with those who can benefit most from my knowledge and skills— the much-neglected tribal community. I don't know whether I have achieved much, but I know I have won their love and affection and they have slowly become my family.'

Night had stolen upon them as they talked mostly now about Akio and her mission of peace. After a long while, Siddhartha Roy stood up. 'You must be quite tired and hungry, and I haven't even offered you anything to eat,' he said. 'Let me find you a room here and then we can continue our conversation over dinner.'

The restaurant was in the floor below, and there were only a few diners. Siddhartha Roy was a regular guest and had a table reserved for him next to a window looking out over the river.

'I'm afraid I can't offer you anything but vegetarian fare,' he said when the waiter turned up for the order. 'The old part of the city has continued the tradition of vegetarianism over thousands of years, and that's all that the restaurants serve here.'

'That's no problem,' said Akio. 'I'm almost a vegetarian myself and beginning to like the local spices.'

Dinner was a vegetarian *thali* or platter containing *puris* accompanied with spicy lentil and fried okra, *pilau* with *mutter paneer* and *raita*. For dessert, there was a choice between *gulab jamuns* and *pista kulfi*, and Akio chose the latter. Siddhartha Roy avoided the dessert and asked for some coffee instead.

'Perhaps you understand, Akio,' said Siddhartha Roy, sipping his coffee, 'discovering that I have a full-grown daughter has been quite an emotional shock for me—as much of a moving experience for me as it must have been for you, finding your biological parent at last.

'All these years, I have lived without familial ties in the traditional sense. I was the only son of my parents, who had both died even before I left for Japan. When I broke ties with your mother, I felt initially as though I had lost my boat and was floundering in the open sea. But gradually, I became accustomed to swimming, the distant shoreline became visible, and the inhabitants of that unfamiliar land welcomed me and became my family. I lost sight of my boat and the memories of the refuge it had once provided me.

'Perhaps I was never meant to be on the boat, and this is my true domain. This is my true inheritance and my succour, my realm and my calling.

'But, Akio, you have evoked in me a resurgence of that lost and forgotten melody I once possessed. I see Shigoku, your mother, in front of me again.'

Siddhartha Roy took Akio's had in his and wept, and his daughter's tears also fell silently.

Outside on the river, a fishing boat glided silently past their window, its solitary lamp shining brightly as it floated by and then disappearing slowly into the still night.

16

PARTING

*W*hen she awoke next morning, daylight was streaming in from her window. Akio found that her com-cube was flashing with a red tint indicating that an urgent message had arrived. On opening the device, she found a letter from Siddhartha Roy, written in the old style, which read as follows:

Dear Akio,

When you read this letter, I will be quite some distance from Varanasi and with it you as well, as I had to depart hurriedly all of a sudden before sunrise.

It is a matter of extreme urgency—there has been a major earthquake, and several villages I had been working at have been badly affected, I am told. You will learn of this from the news reports when you wake up. The village folk will need my help at this time, and I must be there at their side.

Seeing how tired you were and needing a good night's rest, I thought I would not wake you up, and this would be the best way to part. As you may have surmised, I have freed myself from personal family ties forever and merged with the immortal ocean of humankind. Our time on this planet is very short, and I have still much to do. I feel that devoting my time to the welfare of others is like immersing myself with the ever-flowing, never-ceasing Ganga.

Our immortality lies in participating in the progress of humanity and fostering an ever-brightening future for the inhabitants of this earth. While clouds gather around us, I am certain that the sun will shine through in the future more brightly than it has ever done before. Of this, I have little doubt, seeing how the forces of good are beginning to prevail in the middle of the twenty-first century.

I am immensely proud to see that you are among the peacemakers who are already helping shape a better future for all citizens of the world. I am sure your mother too, were she alive, would have been equally proud of you. I wish I was around during your difficult growing-up years and do feel responsible for the pain you have endured. Allow me at least to be of a little assistance to you as a small token of my love and appreciation.

I have left instructions with my family lawyers (Stuart and Deb Advocates of 31 Old Court House Street, Kolkata) to transfer titles of all my possessions to you immediately. These include our ancestral house at College Square, Kolkata, and what remains of our family estate at Birbhum district near Santiniketan. I cannot think of a better owner of these possessions than my own daughter, and not but wonder how fortuitous it was that you arrived in time to take them over!

With this, I hope to make some amends, however little, of the wrongs you have suffered in life so far and my inability to be a true parent to you. I do hope, however, that henceforth you will regain inner peace, and happiness will be your constant companion.

With love and blessings
Siddhartha Roy

17

SPARKLING IN
THE SHADOW

*A*kio, whose personal life had become an eternity of emptiness, and who longed for filial affection with all her heart, realised that she had lost her father again soon after finding him. Although she felt some comfort through his acknowledgement of paternity, she had become lonesome once again with his sudden departure, albeit on a matter which could not be put off, but it left a future meeting, given his life of constant public service, uncertain and perhaps unlikely too.

Mikio too had left, and there was no one with whom she could discuss and share her thoughts. She had to get a hold of her life, she felt, and move on. Nothing helps more to distract one from one's personal afflictions and to heal them than tending to the routine chores of life. With that in mind, she decided to pack her clothes and make preparations for leaving.

But go where? She had still a few days left before her flight back to Tokyo, and there was nothing more to do here in Varanasi or in Kolkata. She didn't want to contact the lawyers yet about the properties that had come into her possession, leaving that to a later time when she had had more leisure to reflect about what to do with them.

Going through the contents of her purse to see how much money she had left and to confirm the exact time of her flight, she found Saurav's calling card among its contents. It contained the telephone number of his office. He had given it to her when offering a position in his institute before wishing her goodbye at the hotel, and it presented her an idea of what she would do.

A chat with the manager of the boarding house confirmed that the Institute of Humanity was in a town which was quite far—about half a day's journey from Varanasi. It required taking another fast train to a destination further westward from the city and then a road journey up the hills. However, it was possible to reach the institute, spend a day or two there, and still have sufficient time before taking her return flight home. But she wanted to be sure that Saurav, with his many engagements, was actually there at the institute when she arrived after the long journey.

However, when her call was finally answered, it was the director's personal assistant on the line, and not Saurav. To her great disappointment, she learnt that Saurav was not at the institute this week and was out on an assignment.

Akio concluded that the stars were all misaligned and not in her favour. She decided to move her flight forward and leave as soon as possible for Japan. She was successful in doing so, but her fast train back to Kolkata wasn't due to arrive until the following morning, and she had the whole day to kill, with apparently little to do in Varanasi.

'Why don't you visit Sarnath and see the Buddhist stupas and the museum?' suggested the manager. 'That's the place where Buddha began his teachings after attaining enlightenment. It's an important pilgrimage site for Buddhists. There's a beautiful Japanese temple there too. You shouldn't leave Varanasi without visiting the place.'

Akio thought that would be a good idea. The very helpful manager arranged a taxi, with its chauffeur also acting as a guide who would show her around Sarnath. She set off soon, therefore, her taxi winding through the crowded streets of the old town before reaching the quieter suburb of Sarnath.

She took a lot of photographs, mainly to show her grandmother, who would be delighted seeing them. She prayed at the bodhi tree where Buddha preached to his first five disciples and visited the Japanese temple, where she met several Japanese tourists, drank green coconut water with them outside its gates, and exchanged stories of travels in India.

Her last visit was to the famous museum of the Archaeological Survey of India. On entering, she was confronted with the impressive Lion Capital of Ashoka, with its four lion heads looking out to the four corners of the world. A large crowd of tourists was admiring it while a guide analysed for them in detail the meaning of the various Buddhist symbols associated with it. This massive finely polished sculpture carved from a single rock of sandstone was obviously the main item of interest for tourists. The rest of the corridors were less crowded, of interest to only a few history students and researchers.

She moved from room to room, studying systematically each item on display and hearing carefully the recorded explanations from the earphones of her electronic guide. In one corner of a long, almost empty corridor, a particular item caught her attention.

In a glass case stood a shining gold necklace whose centrepiece was a large blue sapphire. Several other gems ringed the centrepiece. Rays from the afternoon sun were at that time streaming in from one of the skylights above and fell directly on the necklace, the gold chain of which glittered brightly and might have been the reason that drew her to that item.

A display board below the artefact simply read, 'Royal Necklace of Thaneswar, circa 280 BCE'. Akio was concentrating on the recorded voice—which seemed to suggest that there was some mystery associated with the necklace that was still evoking debate among scholars—and so did not notice the other person who was also peering at it.

'It so happens that it was my grandfather who arranged to bring this necklace to this museum,' said Dr Saurav Bandopadhyay, addressing Akio. 'And isn't it strange that all these years I had never seen it although it's been an integral part of our family lore, and the very day I decide finally to take a look, I find you here too?'

Akio turned to him, startled and smiling. The stars which were misaligned earlier had reached an optimal configuration now, she decided. Saurav explained to a still very surprised Akio that he was in the city for the day on a conference and had decided to seize the opportunity to see the relic.

Sitting at the museum's cafe afterwards, he recounted the remarkable story of the necklace, how his grandfather had been involved in its rediscovery and that there were still major mysteries around it that needed unravelling. As the institute was involved intensively in comparative studies of religions, the philosophical controversies evoked by the discovery of the necklace comprised a core area of its research.

'I hope you understand now why we need someone like you at the Institute,' he said, repeating his offer. And then placing his hand gently over hers, he asked, 'You will accept, won't you?'

Akio looked into his smiling and imploring eyes and nodded, blushing.

The End

ENDNOTES

1. A Brahmatman is 'one whose atman has become one with Brahman, one who has found his identity with the self everywhere. He is called Brahmavid, the knower of Brahman'
(Swami Chinmayananda). See https://www.facebook.com/SwamiChinma yananda/posts/a-brahmatman-is-one-who-atman-has-become-one-with-brahman-one-who-has-found-his-/155763601140783/

2. One who has progressed far on the path of enlightenment, according to Buddhists.

3. The basic doctrines of Buddhism have been lucidly presented, among others, by His Holiness the Dalai Lama. See for example his 'Lectures on the Buddhist Path to Peace', the Dalai Lama at Harvard, August 1981 Snow Lion, Boston, 1981.

4. A Pali word whose Sanskrit equivalent is *dharma*, it connotes religious law to Buddhists and is set out in a series of edicts of Ashoka.

5. Ajatashatru was a king of Magadha during the time of Gautama Buddha and imprisoned and killed his father Bimbisara to ascend the throne. See Romilla Thapar, *A History of India*, Penguin Books.

6. Asuras in Hinduism are powerful beings who constantly fight the devas or gods.

7. *Havan*, also known as *homa* or *homam*, is Sanskrit, meaning any ritual where offerings are made into a consecrated fire in order to propitiate the ancestors and gods.

8. Main or principal

9. A cook or steward in households or government guest houses in British India

10. An Urdu word meaning arrangement, used commonly by British Indian officials

11. Administrative area within a subdivision also often referred to as 'circle' with a *tehsildar* or sub-deputy collector in charge.

12. *Nazir* is the Head of the Accounts and General Administration branch called

405

Nezarath in district offices in some states of India.

13   *Dak* originally referred to mail carried by relays of horsemen or runners in British India. Later, this term was used for all general mail received by a district office.

14   Morrum or reddish gravel used often in driveways in India to give an attractive look

15   *Pukka*, taken from Hindi, was an Anglo-Indian term used to mean 'true' or 'solid'.

16   Khana, drawn from Hindi, meant meal.

17   Tehsildar is the administrative head of the tehsil or circle, several of which comprise a civil subdivision.

18   Short form for British Raj or British rule

19   Dharma means 'duty' in this context.

20   Dhaba is an informal roadside eating place mainly for truckers.

21   Chitrangada, a fabled Manipuri princess who married Arjuna, was popularised in Rabindranath Tagore's dance drama of the same name.

22   A friendly form of addressing a friend in Indian English

23   Dust storm in North India

24   *Murdabad* means 'down with' or 'death to'.

25   *Gherao* was a form of protest action initiated mainly during the left movement in Bengal where groups of protestors surrounded and held captive persons they were protesting against.

26   Bad guys or crooks

27   The Maharaja of Patiala, after whom the Patiala peg is named, was known to offer especially large pegs of liquor to his guests.

28   Angulimala was a bandit living in the forest and had spread terror across the land. He was rumoured to have murdered 999 persons and cut up their little fingers which he strung around his neck in a garland, hence his name: anguli (finger), mala (garland). He was waiting for his 1,000[th] victim when Buddha came along near where he was hiding. Legend has it he had approached Buddha with a thunderous roar determined to kill him, but when he saw the latter's peaceful visage, he turned totally pliant, all anger and savagery left him and he fell penitent at Buddha's feet. He became one of Buddha's most ardent followers, and he is supposed to have attained enlightenment.

29   Betel leaf

30   City of Joy (*La cité de la joie*), a French novel by Dominique Lapierre (1985) based on Calcutta (now Kolkata).

31   Adapted by the author from Sri Ganga Stotram by Bhagavatpada Jagadguru Adi Shankaracharya, early eighth-century Indian philosopher who unified the main thoughts in Hinduism current at that time.

Lightning Source UK Ltd.
Milton Keynes UK
UKHW011855040220
358169UK00001B/44